D0866419

JUST OFF FIFTH

JUST OFF FIFTH

by *Edith P. Begner*

RINEHART & COMPANY, INC.   NEW YORK   TORONTO

For my parents

Published simultaneously in Canada by
Clarke, Irwin & Company, Ltd., Toronto

PART ONE

In the East Seventies there is a cream-colored brick apartment house of unusually beautiful design that pierces upwards from the bed of low brownstone mansions at its base. It is known as Number Ten and it stands less than a hundred feet from the corner of Fifth Avenue. Lawrence Rider built it there on purpose sixteen years ago, because he believed in the elegant understatement of a side-street address.

While Number Ten was still nothing more than a hole in the ground, Rider acquired his first tenant. He was Hunt Parrish, a man of theatrical appearance with a luxurious thatch of pure white hair, a neat white mustache and finicky-moving hands. Mr. Parrish was not an easy man to do business with. His shiny, hairless fingers darted at the blueprints, condemning them foot by foot, and only because Hunt Parrish was such a wealthy and important man did Rider finally consent to build (for a large additional consideration, of course, and a safe, long-term lease), a special apartment for the Parrishes that would occupy one half the eleventh floor with adjoining terraces.

From then on, the renting went very well. Hunt Parrish's name drew many a hesitant signature to a lease. The five-room penthouse was taken by Walter Marsh, president of the Atlantic Paper Company, with the proviso that practically the entire roof be allotted to him so he could engage a landscape architect to construct a living garden up there for his wife, Flossie, who rarely went out because she was too fat to walk.

That same morning, Rider rented a three-room apartment on the seventh floor to a short, sweet-faced widow by the name of Mrs. Lesser, and her sister, a Miss Forsythe. They were twins and had the same small features, but they didn't look at all alike, for Mrs. Lesser was stout and, despite her widowhood, wore a contented expression; and Miss Forsythe was skinny as a bean pole and, even when she smiled, she looked as if she were about to burst into tears over the days of her considerable years, all wasted in virginity.

Applications came in steadily and Rider selected from them people he knew personally or by reputation, keeping the social level of his building high, and by the time Number Ten was ready for occupancy, there were only three apartments left vacant, two of them on the ninth floor, and a five-room on the twelfth. For no apparent reason, Lawrence Rider was unable to find the right tenants for these three remaining units. But profit had to be realized, so against his own judgment, he finally rented the three-room apartment on the ninth floor to Mrs. Kerakis, a wiry, sad

Scotswoman, who was said to be the widow of a notorious Greek gangster; and with similar sentiment, he rented the four-room apartment on the same floor to a youngish couple who did not impress him favorably, but whose credit was undeniably good. The five-room apartment on the twelfth floor inexplicably remained vacant for almost six months, but then John d'Auriac, a young French nobleman who disdained the use of his title, came over from Paris with his beautiful, barren wife, Suzanne, and he made grand, large gestures of delight over this apartment and it became his.

Mrs. Kerakis, in spite of Rider's doubts, remained quiet and soft-spoken and gave no trouble to anyone; but the dubious young couple turned out to be violent alcoholics who threw things at each other, broke windows and wandered in the lobby in their night clothes, and it took Rider nearly two years to dispossess them because they had so much political pull. But he succeeded finally, and that is the only reason why there was a vacancy for Tyler Fay when he came looking for an apartment for his eighteen-year-old bride, Julie. On the day that he brought her to New York from Indiana, he carried her over the threshold and set her down into rooms empty of furnishings except for one magnificent, oversized bed and multitudinous baskets of flowers banked against the walls.

So much for those "charter-tenants," as Mr. Rider referred to them. In addition, there had been many young couples living there then, and each year there had come more and more infants who filled the halls with the sweet odor of baby talcum. However, since the apartments were mostly small, one by one the young families had moved away to larger quarters until there was, by some strange chance, only one boy left, by the name of Robin Fay, the son of Tyler and Julie Fay, and he was already thirteen years old.

1 :   *Monday, April Sixth*

It was one of those sudden balmy days that teases one into believing that spring has really come to stay. More likely than not, there will be snow tomorrow, but who wants to think of that now when, after shivering with the wind on chapped cheeks only yesterday, one can feel the warmth of the sun on one's skin, pouring through heavy clothing, melting frozen bones and forcing one's mind to slip ahead to summer to be filled with images of sea and sand, or perhaps cool mountains. One can even smell the pine and moss, or the salt and fish and clams, and for the day at least, why not pretend?

The whole neighborhood was out today. The park benches were packed solid. There wasn't a free seat anywhere, not even in the shade where, truthfully, it was too cool to sit for any length of time. Grey-haired nurses abandoned their winter dignity and sat on blankets on the coarse brown stubble that would soon be grass, while their small charges were permitted to play coatless in the sun. Bare of encumbering snow-suits, scarfs and gloves, the children staggered about like drunkards, spiked with the warmth and their new freedom.

Fifth Avenue, which borders the park, is the street for quiet walk-ing, where many elderly people like to stroll. Some prefer the more crowded park side, shaded in summer by great leafy trees, but others seek the sunny eastern side with its beautiful mansions and apartment buildings.

At right angles to Fifth Avenue run the quiet side streets that lead to Madison Avenue. Here one sees mostly four- and five-story private dwellings, interspersed only occasionally with a tall apartment building similar to Number Ten. These side streets are residential thoroughfares, each block a means to an end rather than a place one would select for a walk, and movement is more purposeful here, the object being to reach one of the avenues. However, there are always small groups of lady resi-dents who stop to chat, and a policeman will often pause to exchange a joke with a doorman, and the delivery boys brake their bicycles and whoop at each other as they pass.

East of Fifth Avenue and parallel to it runs Madison Avenue, an exciting street for a walk. It is lined on both sides by attractive small stores and many art galleries, and one may spend a pleasant day peering into shop windows, pricing paintings and treasures from all over the world, gossiping with store clerks and stopping every block or two to chat with a neighbor. It is here that one may observe the celebrities, walking with eager smiles, anxious to be recognized and hailed, espe-cially on a day like this when the soft air caresses delivery boy and matinee idol alike.

But perhaps the only man in New York City who did not care for the first springlike day was Klaus Gruppmann, the superintendent of Number Ten. Klaus was a big, muscular Bavarian with a red face, a wide snub nose dotted with enlarged pores, and a hearty, booming voice. Although he had come to this country when he was only ten, thirty-eight years of speaking English had not modified his strong German accent. He spoke fluent and colloquial American, but he said "Gottem," for God damn, and "bestar-r-rt" for bastard and "Cheesis Gr-r-rist." He looked fat, but he was solid muscle, except for the backs of his hands which were pudgy and soft and always chafed. Klaus was proud of his strength and he liked to demonstrate it whenever he could. Above all things he loathed a weak body, and he exercised morning and night before his open window, and often attended the German *Turnverein* on Eighty-sixth Street.

For this reason, Klaus was not impressed by spring. Any weakling could enjoy its gentle warmth, but only a rugged hunk of man could walk around outside in the freezing snow weather, wearing nothing more than a business suit with a woolen scarf around his neck. During the cold winter, Klaus could stand outside the entrance of Number Ten with Phil, the delicate, wheezing doorman, next to him, all wrapped up to his ears, and Klaus, by contrast, would draw admiring comments from the tenants as they came and went. "Why Mr. Gruppmann, how can you stand here like this? Won't you catch your death of cold without a coat?"

"Who, ME?" Klaus could then boom. "Not *me!*" Here he could pound his chest, grinning all the while with his lower lip protruding, his expression one great brag. "*I* don't need to be all wr-r-rapped up like him!" Here he would slap poor asthmatic Phil on the back.

Winter, too, gave Klaus the additional advantage of being able to take a nip or three or four because of the chill. "Cold as hell down there in the basement," he could say to Mr. Rider if questioned concerning the smell of alcohol on his breath. In the hot summer, he could equally as well need some delicious, cold beer. "Hot as hell down there in the basement." But spring, what challenge did spring offer? What recompense? What excuse?

He stood now outside the entrance next to Phil, watching old Mrs. Lesser make her unsteady way towards the park leaning on Miss Forsythe's arm, her pink face flushed crimson with effort, but laughing at her infirmity nevertheless. She had aged so much in the past year that Miss Forsythe looked to be her younger sister by a good ten years. Klaus watched her tottering steps, counted them as he counted along with the referee when his favorite fighter hit the canvas—one, two, three, four, five—and then she had to stop to rest. He could see the wizened sable's head that eternally chewed its own tail moving up and down between Mrs. Lesser's shoulder blades with her heavy breathing.

"She's real bad today," Phil said in his high voice.

"Stubborn old woman, she should be in a wheel chair!" Klaus cried from his heart. His voice carried farther than he had intended, its sound conveying anger rather than the fondness he felt. Miss Forsythe, standing patiently by her twin sister's side, looked back at Klaus with reproach.

"She heard you," Phil whispered.

"Don't care if she did. Killing herself, trying to walk when the doctor says she shouldn't. Don't care if she did."

But Klaus did care. Damn that cursed voice of his that resounded from his great chest, that voice that seemed to have a will of its own and refused to reflect what was in his heart, that voice that frightened everyone, each little child, each tender woman he had ever met, each little dog—even Tanzy, his own. He turned about and strode into the lobby.

Phil followed him. "That party coming to see 8B today?"

"Ja, Rider's sending them over this afternoon."

"Young couple, you think?"

"You kidding? There ain't been a young couple come looking in Number Ten since—Gottem, I don't remember since when! No, she's a bookwriter, Rider said, supposed to be very famous though I never heard of her myself. Probably older than God. This here's getting to be a regular old folks' home." Klaus pressed the back elevator bell. "Funerals every month." He pressed the bell again almost angrily. "And then more funerals," he whispered, thinking of old Mrs. Lesser who was going to be next; any fool could tell that.

Tanzy whined and scratched at the door of his apartment even before he reached it. "Old girl!" He picked her up and she licked his face. He laughed and kissed the soft ruff of her yellow neck. "My girl." He threw his hat onto the chair and, still carrying her, though she was no small dog, went into the kitchen and poured himself a shot of Scotch, which he tossed down neat. Then he blew into Tanzy's face and watched her recoil and struggle in his arms, his laughter booming. He put her down. "You no dog for a hearty-drinking man." Timidly, she shrank under the kitchen table and peered out at him from there. "Come on, Tanzy, I was only joking. Come on, girl."

The house phone rang. "Gottem, just as I was gonna lay down!" He glanced at his watch and saw that it was only two thirty. He wasn't supposed to be off duty until four. Nevertheless he cursed, "Cheesis Gr-r-rist!" He lifted the receiver and screamed into it, "What now?"

"That couple to see the apartment, Mr. Gruppmann. Mr. and Mrs. Harewood."

"Harewood? That's them. Be right up." Klaus put on his hat again, a brown snap brim that distinguished him from the house staff. "No, you got to stay here," he told Tanzy, who shrank down as if punished, her belly to the ground. "I take you out later."

Mr. and Mrs. Harewood were sitting in the lobby in a corner where there were two comfortable leather chairs separated by a lamp table. Like many couples who have lived together a long time, they resembled each other. Though their features were quite different, their expressions were alike; they were growing old alike. The pattern of their wrinkles was the same, the same furrows above the nose that made them seem to frown always, the same dewlaps forming below the corners of their mouths, the same strange absence of crow's feet at the corners of their eyes that betrayed an absence of smiles. Albert Harewood was a small, slender man of fifty-five, almost natty in a charcoal business suit with a dark red tie. His white hair was combed squarely across the top of his head to cover his bald spot and he wore rimless glasses that magnified his sad blue eyes.

His wife, Maud, was small, too. She had great, moist eyes and a well-shaped nose and mouth. Her figure was good. Her legs were almost beautiful. She should have been attractive, but she wasn't. Her brown hair, fuzzed at the ends with an uncared-for permanent, was pushed back under an ugly black hat that was too bulky for her little face, whose expression held more than sadness: petulance lay in the corners of her mouth and distrust in the constant tightening of her eyelids. Though she was under fifty, her hands were old hands already, the skin rough, the nails clean but unmanicured. She disdained all make-up, all grooming, any attempt at ornament. It was as if she deliberately chose to unsex herself, to make herself as undesirable as possible, encasing her beautiful legs in heavy-gauge stockings and her feet in thick black Arch Preserver shoes. She was just what Klaus had expected. But for the absence of spectacles, she was the prototype of all lady writers; dowdy, high and mighty, with a sour face.

He introduced himself and shook hands with Mr. Harewood, bowing deeply from the hips. He waved them to the elevator and watched Mr. Harewood help his wife from the chair. Sickly, he thought, eying her with distaste, for he hated delicate women. He only sympathized with them when they exhibited fight, like Mrs. Lesser who shook her fist at sickness and death. "You folks are lucky," he said. "There ain't been a four-room apartment vacant here in years. But you might not even want it." He rang for the elevator. "Four beautiful large rooms and a small dining room—a five, really. View of the park. Very airy and cool. You might not even like it, though." He shrugged, watching her pale face with the look of inner suffering that made the eyes appear luminous, as if filled with tears.

"Is it quiet?" Mrs. Harewood spoke for the first time, and as Klaus anticipated, her voice was high, like a whine.

Why the hell you so sorry for yourself? Klaus wondered, looking at her worn, half-pretty face in profile. Lady, you're famous, you got a nice husband and plenty of money, what more you want? Aloud, he said, "Of course it's very quiet." His voice was aggrieved. "This is a quiet street and a fine, quiet house. It ain't easy to get apartments here. We don't take just anybody who's got the price, you know. Eighth floor, Terence."

Old Terence mumbled a respectful something and pressed the button that closed the elevator door. Like Klaus, he had been working here since the building went up. He stood in the corner as the car rose, one hand behind his back, so tiny, so frail, so white-skinned and white-haired a man that one wondered what kept him going, why he didn't simply give up and flutter to the floor; like a dried leaf, he wouldn't make a sound.

Klaus unlocked the door of 8B and allowed the Harewoods to enter before him. He snapped on the lights in the foyer and showed them around the stale-smelling, empty apartment, whose bare walls outlined in grime the furniture that had once stood against them, now appearing like sad diagrams in every room, attesting to the fact that this naked place was once a man's home, but was now only a ghost of it, since a few weeks ago old Mr. Collins had died here in his sleep. Klaus flung open some windows. The place still smelled of death.

But the Harewoods hadn't known of Mr. Collins. Somebody had moved out. That was all. They followed Klaus from room to room and admired the apartment. Klaus showed Mrs. Harewood the closets and the kitchen, details always interesting to a woman, but all she did was glance where he directed her and nod with a detached, tired expression. Housekeeping evidently didn't interest her.

Her husband called her to the living-room window to show her the view. "You can see the whole park, darling."

"I believe you." She remained in the foyer.

"Come and see it. Come on, Maud."

"Oh, all right." Wearily she descended the two steps into the living room and glanced out of the window to please him. "Very nice."

"See the lake over there?"

"Yes." She turned away.

"You should be very happy here."

[13]

She gave a little mocking laugh.

"Mrs. Harewood hasn't been too well," Mr. Harewood confided in Klaus. "She needs rest and quiet and our present apartment is too large, much too much of a chore for her to run. This would be perfect—so easy on her."

Klaus nodded politely.

"Yes . . ." Mr. Harewood murmured, staring absently at Klaus's hat. Then he forced a bright smile and turned back to his wife. "And there's three exposures, Maud; did you notice? It would be cool in the summer."

"Coolest apartment in the city," Klaus said.

"You're sure now it's quiet? I can't write unless it's quiet."

Quiet as the grave is quiet, Klaus thought. "Very quiet, only the best people."

"And what exactly does that mean?" Her luminous eyes fastened themselves upon him.

"What I said, nice, quiet people."

She continued to stare at him and Klaus shifted his glance to the floor. Such a strange expression smoldered in her eyes now that the ridicule had died away, as if she contemplated violence.

"You like it, darling?"

"I guess so," she sighed.

"Good! That's all I wanted to hear." Mr. Harewood's hand disappeared into his pants pocket. "We're taking it, Mr. Gruppmann." He withdrew his hand and held it out, fingers curled under. "I hope you'll help us along as much as possible."

They shook hands. What was left in Klaus's palm afterwards was crisp, brand-new, and it felt big. Klaus grinned. "Be glad to. When do you think you'll move in, sir?"

"As soon as possible. Right, Maud?"

"Anything you wish."

"I can get the painters for you anytime," Klaus said, eager to please. "And we'll have the floors scraped and varnished, new Venetian blinds, stove, refrigerator."

"Get them tomorrow, then, if you can. The sooner the better. That all right with you, Maud?"

"Anything's all right," she said, "just as long as I don't have to be here. Let them paint it all cream color, Mr. Gruppmann. No fuss, just cream color everywhere, and as soon as the paint is dry, we'll move in. I hate fuss." She drew in a deep, sobbing breath as if the energy required in talking so much had sapped all her remaining strength.

"You sure you don't want wallpaper or some pretty colors, Maud? Make it cheerful; some yellow, maybe?" Mr. Harewood appealed.

"Just cream color, Albert. For God's sake, what difference does the color of a wall make?"

He nodded meekly. "You can take care of it for us, then, Mr. Gruppmann?"

Klaus had peeked at a corner of one of the two bills in his hand while the Harewoods were discussing the paint color. His heart was racing with excitement. "Anything, anything at all. Glad to, sir!"

They went downstairs to the lobby again and Mr. Harewood gave Klaus his business card. "In case there are any questions, you can reach me there. I'd rather you didn't bother Mrs. Harewood." He cast her a look of such respect that Klaus was forced to follow suit.

"You can count on me to attend to everything personally," he assured them. He accompanied them out into the street. "You want me to call a cab?"

"No thanks, it's such a beautiful day," Mr. Harewood said.

She made an annoyed sound.

"You must walk, Maud, you know." He took her arm. They walked a few feet towards Madison Avenue. Mrs. Harewood stopped suddenly and turned back. "Oh, Mr. Gruppmann!" she called. She ran to him, surprisingly supple and light on her feet for a weary, sick woman. "I almost forgot the most important thing. Children."

"Children?" Klaus frowned down at her.

"Are there any children in the building?"

"She asks this only because of the noise," her husband said quickly. "Her work, you know."

"Children. Why, there used to be many children in the building," Klaus said slowly, "but now there's only one left—that's right, now I think of it, only one child left, and he's almost a man. I don't know how it happened, but there's only this one boy."

"You're sure?"

"Of course I'm sure, though I never thought of it before. Only one child and he's a man already," Klaus said wonderingly.

"Well that's fine, then." She gave him a queer stare that was probably meant to be as much of a smile as a woman in her poor condition could manage, took her husband's arm and walked away, leaning heavily upon him.

"So that's the famous bookwriter," Phil said. "Looks like a schoolteacher. Ever read anything she wrote?"

"No."

[15]

"They ain't so old. At least they ain't ready for the grave yet."

Klaus watched Harewood help his wife into a cab at the corner of Madison Avenue. So much for the walk she needed. "He's rich as Rockefeller. A member of the stock exchange."

"Fine. We'll get good tips," Phil chuckled.

Klaus remained silent.

"I said, we'll get good——"

"Ja, ja, very funny." Klaus walked towards the door. "I'm gonna lie down now. Don't disturb me for nobody but Mr. Rider."

It was only three thirty; nevertheless, Klaus knocked off and went down to his basement apartment. He sat in his comfortable chair with Tanzy on his lap and, stroking her long yellow coat, he wondered if it mattered. Now he felt somewhat guilty about the whole thing, but Cheesis Gr-r-rist, two hundred dollars! He held the two one-hundred-dollar bills in his hand and admired their unfamiliar engraving.

After all, no one could object to Robin Fay. He might be only thirteen, but he stood five foot ten or more already, and looked sixteen if he looked a day. And no one could say that Robin Fay wasn't a fine, well-mannered youngster, who was always courteous and kind. Lively, happy boy, full of natural good spirits, of course, but respectful, ja! Even people who hated kids liked him. Take me, for instance, Klaus assured himself. I never liked American boys much, always noisy, fresh, answer you back. But Robin was different.

No, now that he had examined it from every angle, he was satisfied that there was no reason in the world for him to have told the Harewoods that the one child left in the building happened to live in 9B, the apartment directly above theirs.

It was too late to deposit his money in the bank today. Two hundred dollars! He kissed Tanzy's icy nose. "I'll take you out when I'm off duty, after four, you beautiful girl." He shooed her off his lap and got up to pour himself a celebration drink.

2 : *Thursday, April Sixteenth*

For ten days it was cold again and half the time a penetrating rain fell, but today the sun came out at last and even though it wasn't as warm as that one tantalizing day earlier in the month, the weather was pleasant nevertheless.

A boy wheeled his bicycle slowly down Madison Avenue. He was only thirteen and a half, but he was already five foot ten. He was slender but strongly built and moved with unusual grace, lightly, as if he didn't have this tall body to carry along with him. The watery five-o'clock sun glistened on his tow head and it was hard to tell which was hair and which were sunrays, so alike were they in color. The boy's skin was fair with an ivory cast. He was an aggregate of pale gold except for his eyes which were large, round and almost black. In spite of their sudden darkness, however, they were not hard or sharp; rather were they peaceful, their glance candid. There was no curtain over Robin Fay's eyes, for he had nothing to hide and nothing to fear.

He could have gone directly home from the park without going near Madison Avenue, but he never did. Instead, he invariably took this short walk along the four or five blocks that formed his immediate neighborhood. He had to greet his friends in the various stores and keep up with what was going on. He had to be a part of everything around him, for he felt that the neighborhood belonged in some special way to him. For instance, he had just now heard from the florist that the Dennis cat had three kittens the day before. It was important that he check on this information. There was a reason.

He leaned his bike against the wall of the building and went into Dennis's Delicacy Store. He stopped for a moment at the round counter near the door where the candies were displayed and inspected the mints, the hopjes and the little baskets of lifelike marzipan fruits that looked so much better than they tasted.

"Don't drool on the merchandise, Robin." Mr. Dennis, wearing his grey linen store coat, slapped Robin's shoulder as he came back into the store from one of his many coffee breaks at the soda fountain on the next block. Mr. Dennis drank between twenty and thirty cups of coffee every day and bragged that he had never known a sleepless night in his life.

"I really came to see the kittens," Robin said.

Mr. Dennis crooked his finger over his shoulder as he walked past Robin to the back of the store. His thin face was expressionless but for a certain sparkle in his eyes, which Robin knew to be his smile. "Back in there."

Mr. Dennis's brother, Frank, was in the back room slicing a fat Nova Scotia salmon. "Hey there, Robin."

"Hi, Frank." Robin's eyes rested on Frank for a moment as he considered how strangely the two brothers resembled each other. When they were together, they didn't seem to look alike at all, but whenever Robin met them separately in the street, he would have to think hard before he was sure which one it was.

"They're over there in that crate," Frank said. "Born sometime during the night."

Robin approached the crate cautiously and held out his fingers to the black cat, Cleo, so she would smell a friend. Then he came closer and inspected the three tiny kittens. "Think the black one is pure?"

"Don't know. Didn't turn it over. Too young."

"If it's a pure black, don't forget Mrs. Kerakis gets it."

"You know Cleo don't give off pure blacks like herself. They always got a white streak down their chests. Why won't your friend take a cat with a white streak? What's wrong with that?"

"Her old cat that died was a pure black."

"So what? What's a few white hairs?"

"Search me. You know how old women are. Think I can turn him over tomorrow?"

"Gotta give him a chance to get some strength. He's weak as a kitten."

Robin smiled. "I know how to handle animals." He approached and watched Frank use the long sharp knife expertly. "How much do you want to bet that kitten is pure black?"

Frank held up a slice. "Here."

"Thanks." Robin ate the salmon, then wiped his fingers on his khakis. "Great stuff."

"You can say that again, at two seventy-five a pound." Frank tasted a sliver himself. "Best Nova in New York."

"Best store in New York."

"Why don't you tell that to the new folks in your building? Just a gentle hint. I hear she's a famous writer or something."

"She is? They're going to be right under us in old Mr. Collins's apartment. I saw the moving van on my way to school this morning. I guess they're moving in today." Robin walked over to the crate again. "Couldn't I just turn him carefully?"

"Don't know how Cleo'd feel about that."

"Oh, Cleo wouldn't mind, would you, Cleo? Nice Cleo . . ." Robin murmured to the big, watchful cat and very gently reached his hand towards the black kitten. Cleo's ears stood straight up and she touched Robin's hand with her nose as he carefully turned the kitten for a moment. "I knew it! Pure black! How do you like that, Frank! Not a white hair! What did I tell you?"

"No kidding," Frank put down the knife and came over to see for

[18]

himself. "Well, what do you know? It's the first time." He rewarded the worried mother with a bite of salmon.

"Mrs. Kerakis will be tickled to death when I tell her."

"Well now, I don't know, Robin. She don't buy as much as an apple from us and a pure black is a valuable cat."

"But you promised long ago!"

"I never spoke a word to that woman in my life."

"You promised *me!*"

"I did?"

"You know you did. When you told me Cleo was expecting . . ."

Frank grinned. "Simmer down, boy."

"You and your deadpan! For a moment I thought you meant it."

"Don't you know with me a promise is a promise?"

"For a moment you scared the bejesus out of me."

"Using mighty foul language lately, aren't you, kid?"

"Bejesus? That's mild."

"That's nice," Frank said. "Fine thing to brag about."

Robin gave him an unsure smirk and moved towards the door.

"Come again soon, bejesus," Frank said.

Robin's quick grin radiated the good fellowship of lusty-mouthed men. "I'll see you tomorrow, bejesus."

In the front of the store, Mr. Dennis was waiting on a customer. From his expressionless face, one eyelid flickered at Robin as he stuffed five pecans into the boy's pocket as he passed. Robin grinned and whispered, "Thanks," and held his hand over the bulge to conceal it from the customer as he went out.

He wheeled his bike very slowly, wishing he didn't have to go indoors. Though it was a crisp day, the sun was still warm on his face. A middle-aged woman with Ace Bandages on her legs limped slowly towards him. Her face was screwed tight with pain, but she paused to smile at him as he passed. "Have a nice ride?" she asked.

"Great, thanks," he said, wondering if he knew her. He turned and watched her torturous progress with pity for a moment and then forgot her. Whistling, he wheeled his bike across the street and down towards Fifth Avenue to the entrance of Number Ten.

Phil was on his dinner hour and the front door was unattended for the moment. The lobby was deserted. He wheeled the bike over to the back elevator and parked it there. He rang for Joe, the back-elevator man, using his own special signal, two longs, two shorts and a long. He could hear Joe whoop down in the basement as he got the message. "I'm gonna get that Robin today!" Joe shouted and closed the elevator door with a bang.

Robin muffled a laugh and moved up very close to the door so that when Joe opened it and stepped out, he crashed into Robin. "Ow!" he shouted. "My nose! Oh, my nose!"

Robin slapped his knee and took great catlike steps away. "Got you that time. Oh man, did I get you!"

"You broke it," Joe said quietly, holding his large nose between two dirty palms. "Hear it click? Listen. Broke clean through, I'm not kidding."

"How corny can you get?" Robin scoffed and made the same noise, catching his concealed thumbnail across his front tooth.

"You're getting just too smart for me, Casanova," Joe said. "Casanova, the demon lover of Number Ten."

"Yah, demon lover yourself."

"The regular Don Juan of the khaki pants bunch. Did I tell you your girl friend come by?" Joe's little close-together eyes became red-rimmed slits when he smiled and all his front teeth glittered because each one was edged in pure gold.

"What girl friend? Who's got a girl friend?" Robin was pleased.

"Oh, I know all about you and Sally. She's sweet on you, all right. Every day she comes by and asks, 'Has Robin Fay come home yet?' in a squeaky little voice, and then she giggles and giggles and runs out. Yah, yah, Sally's sweet on Robin, Sally's sweet on Robin!"

"Want to make something out of it?"

"Oh, no, you don't!" Joe dodged Robin's cuff and ran to the center of the lobby with Robin after him.

The front elevator opened and frail old Terence came out. "Quit it," he said testily. "Quit it. What do you think this is?"

They horsed around and paid no attention to him.

"Quit it, I said!" Terence bellowed.

Robin stopped.

"You know you're not to leave your bike in the lobby."

"I didn't. Joe's going to——"

"Your bike belongs in the basement and you know it."

"Oh, shut up, Terence. Don't pay any attention to him, Robin. On your guard, here I come!"

"Goddammed Joe get in hot water," Terence muttered, sitting down on the small bench near the elevator. "Get in plenty goddam trouble someday."

Joe stopped with one fist in the air. "I'll take the bike down when

[20]

I'm good and ready. Now shut up, you old sourpuss," he said amiably. Then he started after Robin again.

Klaus Gruppmann came in with Tanzy on the leash, carrying a big bag of groceries, mostly beer. He paused, smiling, near the door and watched the two sparring harmlessly, appreciating their speed and agility, noting that although Joe was a rock, muscles hard as stone, the kid moved like lightning and Joe would never catch him. "You get him now, Robin; paste him one in his yeller belly! In the belly, Robin!" Klaus encouraged. "Go on, you get after Joe now. On the jaw—on the big nose—squash him in his big nose, Robin!"

"Tcha!" Terence turned his head away in disgust.

Robin made a light pass at Joe's jaw, then darted behind Klaus and dared Joe to get at him from that ample cache. "I'm behind old Boulder Dam!" he taunted. He stuck his tongue out at Joe, then bobbed to the other side, his hands grasping Klaus's waist from the back while Joe tried to get at him around Klaus's generously proportioned front, and Klaus laughed and roared directions and banged Joe's head with his elbow to help Robin, and juggled to keep hold of his marketing bag and Tanzy barked and jumped, not knowing whom to help or attack and Terence sat on his bench and cursed them all under his breath as Hunt Parrish walked in.

Everything stopped.

Hunt Parrish stood tall and elegant in the center of the lobby like an aging matinee idol and his head moved slowly from face to face, his eyes under startling black brows darting silent looks.

"'Scuse me, Mr. Parrish . . ." Joe ducked into the back elevator forgetting Robin's bike. Klaus gave Mr. Parrish a hasty smile, a quick tip of his hat, which choked Tanzy on the leash, and hurried after Joe, dragging the coughing dog.

Robin was left there smiling awkwardly, his face red and perspiring and two moist streaks of grime on his cheek. "Hello, Mr. Parrish." He stood aside for Parrish to precede him into the elevator.

"Good evening." Mr. Parrish made no move to pass him, but instead, his cold eyes stared down at Robin from under heavy lids. "I don't suppose it makes any difference to you, but there happen to be many people living in this house besides you, young man. When I first came in here, I thought I had walked into the menagerie by mistake."

"Hah!" Robin guffawed at Mr. Parrish's sarcasm hoping to mollify him, but there was no softening of the chilly eyes.

"And I see that you've left your bicycle in the lobby again. . . . No, don't interrupt." Mr. Parrish held up one hand, covered with shiny, hairless skin. "I've complained to Mr. Rider about this several times. Are you ever going to learn to be a considerate human being or is that too much to ask?"

Robin appeared to be listening with courteous interest now, but actually he wasn't hearing a thing. He had decided to close his ears. It was the only way to handle Mr. Parrish.

"I told him about the bike, sir," Terence said with relish, "but he wouldn't listen to me."

"Well, you'd better start listening, Robin, because I will not tolerate such goings on. I will not tolerate them any longer, do you hear?" Mr. Parrish stepped into the elevator and Robin got in after him. He stood straight with his hands in his pockets and his expression withdrawn.

"Disgraceful!" Mr. Parrish said.

The elevator stopped and Robin stepped forward quickly, but Terence barred the door with his arm. "Eleventh floor, Mr. Parrish."

"You forgot me," Robin said. "Nine."

"Elders first."

"Thank you, Terence." Mr. Parrish stepped out.

"Welcome, sir."

Robin shrugged his shoulders. He dug at the linoleum with the toe of his sneaker, then decided to make one more stab at good fellowship now that Mr. Parrish had left the car. "Could I run the elevator down to my floor, Terence?"

"No, no; now you move away," Terence pressed the button that closed the door. "I might have let you do it," he continued testily as they rode down, "if you woulda said please. But you didn't. You never do."

Robin started to object, then shrugged his shoulders again and was silent. He didn't want to run the old thing anyway. He had only asked because it was the first thing that had come to his mind. He'd been running it ever since he was tall enough to reach the buttons and he didn't get a bang out of that kind of kid stuff any more. The elevator stopped at the ninth floor and Robin got out. He said, "Thank you," very loud and with angry emphasis, but probably Terence didn't hear that either because the door was closing noisily at the same time. Robin whispered, "Old sourpuss!" under his breath, took out his key and opened the door to apartment 9B.

Thursday, April Sixteenth

Although Hunt Parrish invariably carried a key to his apartment, he could rarely find it when the time came to open the door. It was never in the right-hand pants pocket where it belonged, along with his change. Every morning he would put it there automatically when he dressed, but later, when he paid the cab driver or tipped a delivery boy, he would pull out the key as part of the change and then, with a grunt of annoyance, transfer it somewhere else. It could be in any pocket. So that each evening he would hike his portfolio under his left arm, search for a few seconds and then give up and ring the doorbell, impatient with himself, first, for repeating this act of absent-mindedness so constantly, and second, for the continuous feeling of guilt that overwhelmed him as he pressed the little white pearl button. After all, why shouldn't he ring? For what reason did he employ three domestics if not to open the door willingly for him? God only knew, each of them had little enough to do. Besides, once over his momentary attack of guilt, he had to admit that to see the quiet, respectful Hilda, uniformed in black silk and fine lace, smiling her evening greeting at the door, always kindled in him a little thrill, a momentary intoxication over his material success that often spread goose flesh down his back.

But tonight he experienced nothing but irritation. He entered his apartment still shaking his head over the disgraceful attitude and behavior of Robin Fay and handed his hat and topcoat to Hilda with an absent nod. From the living room he could hear the strains of his favorite Prokofieff symphony, but even these pleasant harmonies did not soothe him. "Utterly impossible," he muttered.

"Pardon, sir?"

"Nothing, Hilda. Is Mrs. Parrish home?"

"Yes, she's in the living room, sir."

Hunt took a few steps down the hall, but Irene had heard his voice and was already coming towards him, tall and graceful in her black silk dress, her pearls hardly whiter than her white skin, her black hair lustrous and gleaming from a hundred strokes of the brush, her eyes an utterly impossible royal blue. Irene was still, at fifty, one of the most beautiful women in the world. At her worst, she looked no more than forty-five, but when she smiled, showing large, flawless white teeth, her whole face sparkled and she dropped another five years in the flash of a second. She was smiling at Hunt now, moving towards him, her arms outstretched.

As always, when she came at him like that, Hunt's body tightened, his calf and thigh muscles, his buttocks, his arms, even his neck, and he held himself there by sheer will power; he commanded himself to stand his ground, even to smile and let those soft white arms enfold him. And as usual, the dread was worse than the actuality and Hunt was able to give nervous little chuckles that sounded like grunts of comfort as he allowed himself to be overwhelmed by her softness; soft white arms, soft black silk and the soft fragrance of her favorite scent, all of which she wore for his sake, eternally trying to please, pleading with him through her beauty.

"How are you, my darling?" she wanted to know. Her dark blue eyes surveyed him tenderly and she continued to smile, but there was a heavy slowness in all her movements which incited him to pity and he strained to be gentle with her.

"Fine, dear, fine. And you? You look completely rested, as if you hadn't done a thing all day. Absolutely exquisite, as always. I don't know how you manage it." She was so physical, any compliment intoxicated her. She would remember it, treasure it and tuck it away with her collection to bring forth on all sorts of future occasions.

"But you don't look well, Hunt. No, you look tired." She passed her finger tips under his eyes. "My poor darling."

He submitted to her attentions, his rapid chuckle turned on again like the purring of a cat. "I'll wash my hands," he said after she had kissed his cheek again and rubbed the lipstick away.

"Yes, do that, darling, and join me in the living room."

"Be right with you." As he moved away from her, his stomach tightened, but it was only one small spasm that left him with a pang, like hunger. He felt angry, not at one special circumstance, but generally angry, put upon. He found that he was complaining silently to himself that it was too much, everything was too much, and even as his mind whispered these words, the burden of hopelessness enveloped him as it invariably did when his working day was through. He panicked a little every evening when he closed the office or laboratory door behind him, but that was nothing compared to the panic he felt as he walked away from the taxi and into the lobby of Number Ten. Suddenly his thoughts came back to the boy, Robin, his irritation gathered, fused and centered about the vision of Robin's expressionless face in the elevator, pressed there into the corner, withdrawn—and superior, too, that haughty child, keeping his stubborn silence, as if he were being martyred. A thoroughly unpleasant child, impossible to reach, impossible to touch, impossible to impress in any way.

Except for one time, years ago, before Robin had built up those cool defenses of his. Yes, there was that one time when Hunt had reached him, touched him, taught him a lesson he would never forget, a lesson his own flighty parents should have given him themselves.

As Hunt washed and washed his hands under the steaming water, relathering them countless times and rubbing the skin to a fine-honed shine, he clucked his disapprobation. Why, the child hadn't been more than four or five years old that snowy Sunday morning, the week of the blizzard it was, and the snowdrifts piled higher than the cars at the edge of the street. Hunt had emerged, shod in his galoshes, to inspect New York under the heaviest coating of snow anyone could remember. In the street in front of the house, many of the tenants had gathered. A few children were running about, screaming and throwing the snow. Hunt frowned at the animal sounds they made.

Suddenly a snowball hit him square on his mocha-gloved hand, breaking there and spraying over the front of his black cashmere coat. Hunt was startled, so startled that he let out a cry. Before him he saw a small, laughing face with cheeks bright red from the cold and pale yellow curls spilling out from under a snow-cap. The child's lips were pink and moist.

"Ha, I got you, Mr. Parrish!" the small Robin cried. "Scared you too, din't I?"

Hunt glanced around and saw the tenants grinning at him. Robin's mother, standing over to the side, was frankly laughing. He brushed away the snow deliberately, careful not to show a trace of the indignation that exploded within him. His glove was wet through, ruined probably for all time. The child still stood before him, impudently grinning. There was a feeling of waiting in the air and Hunt could sense it through the smiling silence. He was being tested. That small piece of flesh, untouched by suffering, by learning, by confusion, loneliness, responsibility, untouched as yet by life at all, stood before him and challenged him.

There was a way that men behave in situations such as this. There were approved responses for all things, Hunt knew, and he wondered about them as he continued to mark time by carefully dusting and re-dusting his coat. He glanced at the child again and saw that he was no longer smiling, and a great sadness came over Hunt, a terrible loneliness. "So you threw a snowball at me, did you?" he asked, and was astounded to hear how menacing it sounded. Therefore he smiled and

[25]

was gratified to see how quickly the child responded by breaking into his former teasing grin.

"You bet I did!" the child giggled.

For some reason, the child's mother was convulsed. She remained off to the side, laughing so hard that the tears sprang to her eyes. Hunt could see nothing amusing in the situation, but he wished he could. So he chuckled along with her and then turned back to the child. "Well then, young man!" he cried and swooped down suddenly. He picked Robin up and held him high. The child screamed with tentative laughter. "I'll show you, young man. I'll teach you to throw snowballs at me!" he bellowed and bore him, squirming and squealing, to the curb. "I'll give you some snow!" And Hunt threw him into the great, soft snowdrift.

The child screamed and everyone ran to help, but Walter Marsh reached him first and pulled him, weeping, out of the snow. The boy's mother comforted him as she brushed snow from his eyes, mouth and hair, while Marsh struck it angrily from the child's clothing. "You ought to be ashamed of yourself, Parrish," he said, "picking on a little kid."

Mrs. Fay said nothing, but her young face was as hurt as the child's as she took Robin in her arms and carried him into the house, still trying to quiet him.

There was a murmur among the tenants and Hunt found himself the center of a unified, hostile group. He was confused. "But I was only playing," he said, looking about him, "I was only trying——" He stopped for there was no use. There was utterly no use trying to appeal to a pack of insensitive, bourgeois idiots for understanding. They understood nothing, comprehended nothing, pondered over nothing other than the conventionalities and how they might still further adhere to them. Oh, the unified emotion about him! The sameness of their reactions, the similarity in their expressions! Fit in, fit in, belong, belong, be alike, be alike. He was nauseated because for one short moment, he himself had aspired to conform to their puny rules of behavior. Picture the absurdity of the situation, that he now had to defend himself against their inadequate judgments, as if they were a group of his peers.

"That boy committed an act of deliberate disrespect towards me, and since his own mother didn't have the good sense to reprimand him, I took it upon myself. Since when is it considered proper to encourage children to throw objects at their elders? Since when?" Hunt glared about him.

"It wasn't disrespect, Parrish," Walter Marsh said. "It was only fun.

He was full of high spirits. He wanted you to throw a snowball back at him. Don't you realize, man, the child was showing you favor?"

So that was this particular convention: he should have thrown a snowball back at the child, Hunt thought bitterly. That is what these idiots would have done. "Favor! Mr. Marsh, where I come from, children are taught to respect their elders and I will never, under any circumstances, condone the raising of a new generation of savages to take over a world that has already retrogressed to the level of the Cave Man." With that, he turned his back upon them all and strode away.

Hunt turned off the water and reached for a towel. Shocking, the unfitness of parents, he thought, wiping his hands to a dry shine and remembering how Julie Fay had laughed when the snowball struck him. And the unfit *will* propagate. It is because they are unfit that they dare.

Well, at any rate, he had managed to give Robin one good lesson in his life, probably the only lesson he'd ever had. Robin had never thrown a snowball at him again, nor ever would. That was your answer. Teach them swiftly and teach them young; a good lesson it had been, too, snow for snow, the punishment fitting the crime.

He took his brush from the medicine chest and smoothed the sides of his shining white hair, inspecting himself with admiration at the same time. Then he put the brush back and stepped away so more of himself might appear in the mirror. Not only was he an uncommonly handsome man—he smoothed his well-tailored coat and tightened the knot of his tie—he was also quite distinguished. He gave himself a smile. Patrician, too. He looked back at himself once more before he left the bathroom, as if reluctant to leave his image.

Yes, it was sickening to consider the popularity that mediocrity enjoyed all over the world, Hunt thought, returning to his irritation as he made his way into the living room. It was all around, stifling as a thick fog; ignorance, thoughtlessness, carelessness that smothered those few men of real sensitivity that had somehow managed to exist. We reach through this thickness choking on it, trying blindly to peer through it to find only one, just one other kindred soul, one other thinking man to talk to. . . .

Irene was seated on the pale blue couch with the cream wall behind her. Everything here was a setting for her black, pink and white beauty. Anywhere else she selected to sit would have been equally becoming. She smiled up at him and patted the seat of his chair, straight with wooden arms, that stood to her right. Hunt abhorred overstuffed chairs. They made one slouch. Their softness pulled one in. He sat down and sighed a little as he faced another cocktail and dinner at home. Irene put ice into the cocktail pitcher and stirred it just enough. She poured the amber liquid into chilled glasses and handed him one, still smiling her brilliant, youthful smile. Hilda came in with a tray of small hors d'oeuvres. She passed them, bending over humbly, her fine Swedish face wearing the respectful expression which this time pained Hunt, for he liked to be well served, but without humility. The only true human classification should be that of the intellect, and he wouldn't have cared if he knew Hilda looked humble because she knew she was stupid. But that wasn't the case. She was humble because she was poor. Quietly, Hilda placed the platter on the coffee table and slipped out of the room.

"Well, here's cheer." Irene raised her glass.

Hunt said, "Cheer," and sipped. "Excellent, dear." He relished the tang of Irene's sidecar made from the velvety old brandy he liked so well. He began to feel more cheerful.

"I finished the Faulkner book you gave me," she said, and made a deprecatory face.

He looked at her with pity. "Yes?"

"I'm sorry, darling, I just didn't understand it, all those idiots and things. I loved it," she added quickly, "but I didn't understand what he was trying to say."

"Yes, well," he sighed, "I'll try to explain it to you another time."

"Something's troubling you." She put down her glass and wiped her finger tips on an embroidered linen napkin edged with lace.

"Oh, it's not important really. Just a small annoyance, but there have been so many of them over the years, so damned many of them, Irene, that I've reached a point of saturation. Yes, a point of saturation!" His voice grew more irate, and suddenly he exploded into an indignant recital of Robin's countless delinquencies and the delinquencies of the parents who had brought him into the world. His smooth pink skin flushed with vexation and his slender, hairless hands writhing, Hunt went on to condemn the world and all the people in it. "The deterioration of standards!" he cried. "And a child like Robin is the living symbol of it. No manners, no courtesy, no respect. There is no such thing as *quality* left in the world. Look at industry today. Where are our skilled craftsmen, our fine workmen who used to take pride in a job well done? What has happened to the art of handwork? Vanished, Irene, disappeared and disposed of for all time. And instead, what have we? Quantity. Cheap, flimsy, machine-made quantity. And along with it, rudeness instead of courtesy, vulgarity instead of refinement, thoughtlessness instead of kindliness. And mark my words, all a result of the deterioration of the human being into savagery, accomplished paradoxically by the advancement of science. We don't need to fear the hydrogen bomb we have invented. We're destroying our civilization without it!"

Irene listened and slowly her smile faded and even as he continued to speak, he felt her withdraw as she always did whenever he criticized the existing order of things. Or especially if he criticized one of the Fays, whom she admired. She spoke reverently of their tall, blond beauty, of their constant smiles, of their life of pure pleasure. She envied them their ability to laugh in the face of a world in turmoil and decay. Yes, well, each to his own, and Irene was, after all, one of them, another member of their complacent bourgeoisie. She was one of the takers of this world and that was why it was useless for him to keep trying to provoke her into serious thought. She had neither the desire for it nor the capacity. And yet he kept on trying, perhaps because he had to get these things off his chest whether she understood him or not; and perhaps, too, because he hoped that a little something of what he had to say might rub off onto her, if only to provide her with a catchword or two that sounded bright in intellectual company. Although they rarely attended parties, still there were occasions when they were forced to, and on these occasions, she repeated dutifully phrases he drummed into her, as she would one day interpret by rote the meaning of the Faulkner book she had just read and failed to comprehend.

So, although she looked angry and bored and impatient, Hunt continued to tell her exactly what he thought. He, himself, was very nearly repeating words by rote, for he was watching her analytically as he spoke and noting her changing expressions. As he mentioned Robin Fay's name again, he saw her face go smooth and soft and he wagered she was remembering the first time Julie Fay had let her hold the infant in her arms. Irene had come home in raptures and had to describe the baby's smell and softness to him and cradled her arms unconsciously as she did it, nauseating him with her fleshy, physical gestures.

At last Hunt tired of speaking, as it were, to the air, and became silent. He drained his sidecar and delicately poked at his moist, red lips with the edge of his napkin. "Disgraceful!" he whispered as a final, suitable ending to his tirade, and reached for another canapé.

Irene filled his glass again. "I'm sorry, Hunt," she said in a low voice, "but I can't see that Robin did anything wrong at all. He's a young——"

"Nothing wrong? Why his attitude was positively brazen." Hunt spoke tiredly. He could never voice an opinion and be done with it. There always had to follow this foolish, reasonless arguing.

"What was brazen? What did he——"

"His superior silence, that look of being put upon, instead of begging my pardon."

"But what should he beg——"

"My God, the noise, the screaming, the ever-present bicycle in a beautiful lobby. Sometimes I don't understand you at all, Irene, defending an insolent boy like Robin against me."

Irene shifted in her chair and poured herself another half a drink. As if to gain courage, she took a long gulp, then put her glass down on its coaster and spoke without looking up at her husband. "The only brazen thing about Robin is that he dared to be born, Hunt; that he dared to be born and to continue to grow up strong, healthy, polite and happy in spite of your great logical theories. Robin is the living denial of them, and this you cannot stand." Her voice remained low and terribly bitter.

Hunt listened. His eyes passed over her, noting every small movement of each feature. With experienced accuracy, he evaluated her mood. This was one of her I'm-not-as-dumb-as-you-think days, wherein, if given the chance, she would dig at him, try to depreciate him all evening. His own attitude melted abruptly from tired irritation to condescension. "Every once in a while you go off on a tangent of illogic, Irene, and it becomes my duty to put you straight again."

"Don't bother, please."

"I'll admit it has gotten to be a bother, very much of a bother, but it's also a duty. One thing I can't bear is illogical thinking. Your glib statement that Robin is the living denial of all my theories happens to be a masterpiece among your many misconceptions. Robin means nothing more to me than an ever-present, unpleasant, spoiled child who annoys."

Hilda came to the door and announced dinner. Irene rose and moved so swiftly into the dining room that Hunt knew she was hoping the change of scene might cause him to forego his lecture-for-the-day. However, it took them only a moment to get seated and the soup was already before them, steaming, and she should know well by now that his attention span was not this short.

He eyed her with malice, as a lesson formed in his mind. "You're so immature, Irene," he said. "Even at your age, you can't see any further than simple cause and effect. Your reactions themselves are so simple that, were I to place before you right now the mixings for a cake, you would proceed at once to bake it."

"You can spare me the insults and the funny jokes," she said sourly, but she clenched her spoon tight, for she knew what she was in for.

"No, no, Irene." He held up his hand for silence. "I'm making an important point. Hear me out. You think that was a ridiculous statement I just made. Well, of course it was. We're at dinner. Were I to put before you the makings of a cake, you would more likely put them aside and continue with your meal. Right?"

She went on drinking her soup, thinking: Why do I have to bear this—really, why?

"Answer me, Irene. Right?"

"Right."

"Good. Now let us merely change the setup a little. God presented you with a uterus, as I laid before you the mixings for a cake. You admit that it would be ridiculous for you to get up and bake the cake simply because I placed it before you. So is there any more reason for you to go and bear a child simply because you have within you the makings?"

She glared at him across the table, baffled, knowing only too well that one had nothing to do with the other, but not able to pin-point the fallacy on the spur of the moment.

"People do not have to follow biological laws simply because they have been provided with the apparatus," Hunt continued, with a superior smile. "It is far wiser to *think* first, to think not about whether you are *able* to bear a child, but whether you are *fit*."

He always did that, switching the point slightly with each speech so that she could never have time enough to think about one answer before he required another. "I'm fit," she said quickly.

He swooped down upon her words like a falcon grasping its prize. "You're fit, are you? Let's see about that. Tell me, Irene, do you know right from wrong?"

"Oh, God, that again!"

"It's a simple question. Answer it."

"Yes, I do know right from wrong. I can't tell you how I know it, but when the time comes——"

"All right, the time has come. Let's assume——"

"No. Let's not assume. I'm not going to play, Hunt."

"I beg your pardon?"

"I'm not going to play. I'm not going to let you make a fool of me."

"I'm surprised at you, Irene, to retreat like this. You made a statement. You said you did know right from wrong. Far from trying to make a fool of you, I am merely anxious to have a discussion with you. This is known as the art of conversation, now practically extinct. Am I to assume that you take back what you said, that you have changed your mind and that you do not know right from wrong?"

"Damn it."

[31]

"Well?"

"I guess so. Oh, I don't know, anything to keep peace!"

"And admitting that you don't know right from wrong yourself, how do you dare, how do you *dare* to presume that you can bring another human being into this world and try to teach it what you yourself do not know?" His final point made, he smiled his victory at her across the table.

She put her fork on her plate, unable to eat any more. Her mouth was drawn down into bitter lines. "When I was just an innocent girl blindly in love with you, I thought this the most brilliant argument in the world, but I don't any more, Hunt."

"That's because you're not as receptive to learning now as you were then. You were truly shocked at my refusal to bring children into this world, but when I'd finished explaining it to you, you not only understood, but you fully agreed. Since then, however, you have retrogressed mentally, Irene. Your mind is not pliable as it used to be."

"Thanks."

"It's pure stupidity for a woman who doesn't know right from wrong to bring a child into this world and pass on her own ignorance! Ignorance piled upon ignorance! She can follow her natural instinct for creativity elsewhere. You yourself have found completion as a human being in the charitable work you're doing, which is far more important work than that of bringing boys like Robin Fay into this world."

"I have found completion? I?"

"Of course you have. But you childishly persist in sulking over the one piece of candy you couldn't have."

"I could have had it, Hunt. There's nothing wrong with my apparatus."

"Nor mine," he said blandly. Then he shook his head and gave her a sad smile. "Such a child. Your day is crammed with important and interesting work——"

"Let's just say it's crammed. Boredom and loneliness and bitter disappointment expressing itself in hysterical activity. That's what my day is crammed with. Hysterical activity."

"Hysterical activity, you say. The United Hospital Fund, for instance——"

"Oh please, Hunt, let's not——"

Once again he held up his hand for silence, and she bent her head and sat there, reduced to impotency under the onslaught of his logic as step by step he proved to her that (1), she could not have felt "bitter disappointment" since she had known and agreed before their marriage that there were to be no children, and (2), that rather than pass her day in "hysterical activity," she spent it in important, valuable productivity, that (3), far from being bored or lonely, she was the most fortunate of women, leading an active, interesting life of luxury and sophistication, and (4), that she was, compared to any other woman in this world, supremely fortunate and happy.

Having reduced her thus to silence, and having won his points all the way around, Hunt now proceeded to mollify her. From a stern inquisitor, he changed suddenly into a charming child. He smiled winningly at her across the table and when she refused to look over at him, he tossed a ball of bread at her. "Oh, stop it," she muttered, so he tossed another and another until she could no longer refrain from laughter, and then it was kisses he threw at her until she melted. Having won this round, too, he was able to put his entire attention to the enjoyment of the rest of the meal. After strong coffee with lemon peel, he excused himself as he always did and retired to his room. He closed his door. He scrubbed his hands with a brush, using deodorant soap. Then he sat down at his desk in his straight-backed chair and began to compose an essay on James Joyce. He was a prolific writer and had toiled countless hours every evening for twenty years at it, but he had only sold one piece in his life, a critical essay on the works of Maud Harewood, which had appeared many years ago in *The American Scholar*. Nevertheless, the publishing of this one article he accepted as proof of his professionalism and of his right to call himself an essayist and critic. His failure to publish anything since then he attributed to the stupidity of the editors and continued to write for posterity.

Irene wandered about the apartment looking for something to do. Although Hilda would have done it eventually, she put the records away and straightened the bric-a-brac in the living room. She looked into the kitchen, but everything was under control. They never needed her in there. So she went into her own room. She lay down on her bed and only then realized how exhausted she was from the mad rush of her monotonous day, addressing envelopes at the Republican Club, attending a luncheon meeting of the East Midtown League, shaking a coin box for the Crippled Children and barely making a board meeting of the Cancer Society. She hated it all, but she did it to occupy her time. There was absolutely nothing else for her to do. One could spend just so much time shopping and going to museums and concerts. Somehow, a woman had to produce something. "Lady Bountiful," she thought wryly. That was what Hunt called her, and with such pride!

In confusion, she wondered about her husband, about what manner of man he really was, obsessed with contempt for everyone and everything, full to the brim with hate, even for a delightful young family that shouldn't mean anything to him at all. Yes, it was true. The Fays shouldn't mean a thing to Hunt Parrish. They shouldn't inspire hate or love, but rather a complete indifference. By all rights, Hunt shouldn't know if the Fays were dead or alive. Or care. How to explain his preoccupation with this family? Certainly not only because years ago she had ventured to tell him what a beautiful baby Robin was?

And why his insistence on repeating and repeating the so-called logic of his theory, falsely spiraled so that it proved the human race should cease to reproduce?

It was here that her anger against him broke as it always did, here that she put her hand to her forehead in a gesture of complete confusion. For if beneath all of his deliberately formed fallacies lay the tormenting secret that Hunt knew he was sterile and could never have a child—oh, then, how she would love him, how she would comfort him, how she would help him, if he would only tell her the truth!

But no. The explanation was not as heartbreaking as that. Hunt was not a liar. That much credit she had to give him. And he had always assured her that he was perfectly capable of having children, dozens and dozens of them if he chose. Therefore, she could not bring herself to forgive or condone any part of his point of view, and even though she knew it was now too late for her to have children, she still longed for them, she still dreamed about them, and she still felt that Hunt had cheated her, taken advantage of her youth and simplicity, and of the depth of her love.

How was it possible for a woman to live with a man for so many years and know so little about him? Nothing at all, really; nothing about what kind of a boy he was, or what his mother was like, or his father, or his brothers and sisters—nothing. Bitterly she decided that he couldn't ever have been a child at all, just as now he wasn't a man, but either a great, cold brain on legs or else a charmingly vain, thoroughly delightful goon when it served his purposes, and she began to weep, for a woman who was married to someone who was not a man, was not a woman.

Although Tyler and Julie Fay were interested in art and devoted most of their spare time to the collection of the fine paintings that hung on the walls of every room in their apartment, the heart of their home remained the small, yellow and white kitchen where Julie exercised the art of cookery. At one time she had curtains at the window, but she replaced them with a Venetian blind. It was more workmanlike. There should be no ruffles in a laboratory, she said, and after all, wherever experiments were in progress, a laboratory was there.

When Julie cooked, she tied her ash-blonde hair into a pony tail to keep it out of her face. To tell the truth, this was only one of her numerous excuses for wearing her hair that way since she admitted that pony tails were too kittenish for women of thirty-three. Today she had pulled it back so tight that it lifted the corners of her eyes and made her feel like someone else, someone slant-eyed and sexy, and such an impression could not be ignored for long, especially since it persisted through onion-peeling, mushroom-paring and the washing of two heads of lettuce. She wiped her hands on a yellow and white kitchen towel and went into her bedroom. Rover, Robin's oversized Chihuahua, looked up at her from the boudoir chair. She wagged her tail twice, blinked her great dark eyes and went back to sleep with a small grunt.

Standing before the mirror, Julie was disappointed to find that she didn't look slant-eyed at all. Nor especially sexy in her blue shirt and sweater with a demure white collar poking out. "Just a typical, healthy, athletic American girl, damn it," she muttered. She leaned forward to look closer at her eyes which she loathed. No matter how she tried to elongate them with mascara and a pencil, still two grey-green baby eyes stared out at people with such a falsely innocent look that she was called "sweetie" and "honey" and "darling" even when she wore her new black satin cocktail dress cut practically to the waist. Hadn't John d'Auriac called her "cutie" only last Saturday night, and that coming from a Frenchman was pretty conclusive, wasn't it?

She left the mirror, disappointed, but the moment she stopped looking at herself, she felt slant-eyed again. Back in the kitchen, humming in a throaty voice, she continued with the preparation of the meal, defiantly thinking of herself as slant-eyed because it pleased her to feel that way.

But Julie would have been shocked to know that to others she appeared neither slant-eyed nor healthy and athletic, but rather ethereal and fragile, as if, when held up to the light, she would be transparent. Even though she stood five-feet-ten in her heels and was as strong as a work horse, people felt they had to protect and watch over her, including her own husband who lived with her and should have known better. She had never given Ty any reason to believe in her frailty and yet secretly, and quite unreasonably, too, he did. Perhaps Julie was not wrong in blaming it all on her eyes, for they were so piteously wide and childlike that people were prone to look no further for proof of her condition.

It was fortunate that Julie did not know how Ty worried about her fragility, for she would have been highly insulted. But she thought all husbands removed the bedspread at night because it was too heavy for a woman to fold and she thought all husbands changed the electric bulbs because a woman might get dizzy and fall off the ladder. She also thought all men scolded their wives for moving furniture or lifting something heavy and that every gentleman slept lightly enough at night so that should his wife move suddenly or make some sound in a dream, he would awaken and reach over, "Is anything wrong, darling? Everything okay? . . . Good, go back to sleep, dear." Julie also believed that every husband insisted that the house cleaning be done by a maid, and she took it (rightfully, in this case) as a tribute to her ability as a cook that Ty had not demanded full-time help in the home but compromised with her on a cleaning girl three mornings a week. Julie had such a great personal attachment to everything in her home that she disliked having strange hands care for it.

She added a jigger of brandy to the Boeuf Bourguignon she was preparing and replaced the lid of the casserole dish, smiling. "It's that little touch, *ce petit je ne sais quoi,*" she whispered and sniffed the fragrant steam that filled the kitchen.

She heard the gu-ruck gu-ruck of Rover's tiny paws as she ran over the carpet towards the front door and a second later she heard the elevator door open out in the hall.

Robin came in quietly tonight. Usually he banged the door behind him, yelled "Hi, Ma!" and dropped to his knees in the foyer to greet his little dog. Or sometimes he would come in with a dreamy look in his eyes, as if pleasantly tipsy, and then she would know he wanted to be alone with his thoughts of Sally and of love, but tonight he mumbled

"'Lo" through tight lips and made for his room at once, wriggling his fingers absently at the dog who scampered at his side demanding more of a welcome. By the time Julie wiped her hands and came out of the kitchen, Robin was in his room with the door shut.

Julie went back and lowered the flame under the casserole, for she knew these things always took time. Then she followed Robin to his room. She knocked at his door and heard his reluctant "Come in." He had thrown his jacket over the back of a chair and was lying on his day bed with one leg outstretched and the other bent, a torn khaki-covered knee towering in the air.

"Nice affectionate greeting you gave your old lady," she said.

"I'm sorry." He pulled himself up and pecked at her cheek.

"What's new? What's the dirt?"

"No dirt." He lay down again.

"Tired?"

"Yep, a little."

"Have a nice bike ride?"

"Okay."

"Mmm." She sat down on the ottoman across the room from him and waited. Whenever Robin came home like this with a problem, she worried that she would not be able to handle it properly. Had she been born a generation sooner, this would not have been the case, but a new science had appeared in the last few decades, a frightening new science that hung like a ton weight on a string over the head of every parent, the science of psychiatry that demanded inhuman wisdom and insight, and more than that, an impossible amount of patience and control. How many psychological mistakes had she and Ty already made with Robin, she wondered, and how many more would they make before he grew up? Would this be the day she would pull the big boner, the psychiatric boo-boo that would send the ton weight crashing down on her head? Would this be the time about which Robin would someday complain in bitterness on some psychiatrist's couch, "My mother didn't understand me at all. She—"?

"Why is Terence so nasty to me, Ma?" Robin sat up and looked across at her with aggrieved eyes.

"What happened?" She smiled quietly at him, concealing her anxiety. From what he had already said, she knew he was placing her in the position of a judge. She was going to have to tell him whether he had been right or wrong about something, and would she know?

"Well, I came in with my bike and rang for Joe——" Robin left the bed and paced up and down, gesticulating with his long, thin arms as he told her the story. "Everyone yells at me about my bike and it isn't fair," he concluded. "If I bring it upstairs, you scold me because there isn't room in the apartment. If I leave it out in the hall, the Emmerichs complain it doesn't look nice. If I ring for Joe and leave it in the lobby until he comes, Terence and Mr. Parrish yell at me. And Joe won't let me take it down to the basement myself. What do they want me to do with it, eat it? I don't know. . . . And it isn't just about the bike, either. They don't *like* me!" The fact acknowledged, disbelief clouded his eyes.

His mother made an objecting sound, but he interrupted her. "It's true. Terence is bad enough, but Mr. Parrish is stinking mean. He hates me and I've never done anything to him. I haven't done anything to Terence either. Maybe I make a little noise, but any kid does. Old sourpuss and old fisheyes." His own eyes burned with resentment and the whites veiled over suddenly with a hurt moisture as little pink capillaries appeared.

"Well, I must agree that they treated you very unfairly, Robin, if you told me the whole story correctly."

"You can ask Joe! You can ask Mr. Gruppmann!"

"I don't have to. I believe you. There was no reason in the world for either of them to speak to you the way they did. But I'm glad you held your temper and were respectful anyway. I'm proud of you for that." Julie relaxed and stretched her legs out in front of her.

"Why are you proud of me for that?"

"Because you kept your dignity."

He thought about it for a moment. "What good was that, Ma? Look how mad I am. I should have told old fisheyes off."

"That's a matter of opinion. Personally, I believe in telling people off only when they mean something to you. And even then, it should never be done in anger."

"But why do they act like that to me only when I'm alone? Why don't they ever do it in front of you?"

Julie looked at her son reflectively, then decided to be as candid with him as she expected him to be with her. "Because I'd knock their teeth out, that's why," she said. "They think you're defenseless and they know you're well brought up and won't take a sock at them. They take advantage of you because you're a child."

"Why?"

"Lots of people don't like children, Robin. They're annoyed at the noise they make and at their selfishness."

He frowned. "I'm not selfish."

"You're not exactly a child any more, either. When you were

younger, though, you were selfish. Every normal child is. You made tremendous demands on people; you insisted upon their incessant attention. And many people prefer not to have to put up with this, even though they know it's normal."

"Do you think that's how Terence and Mr. Parrish feel about me?"

"Terence, maybe. But Mr. Parrish is more complex. He must be a miserably unhappy man. Did it ever occur to you that of all the tenants, like Mrs. Lesser, the d'Auriacs, the Marshes and ourselves, who've lived here for years and years, he's the only one who hasn't made a single friend in the building?"

"That's true."

"And have you noticed how stiffly he holds himself, how he hardly ever smiles? To me, these are dead giveaways for insecurity in a man. And when he's nasty to you, it doesn't necessarily mean that he dislikes you personally. He may dislike—even be jealous of—what you stand for, you and your bike."

"Jealous of *me*? Mr. Parrish?"

"Why not? I have a theory about men like him, who are always picking on children. They've missed something themselves, and when they see a child who is luckier than they were, they're jealous of him."

Robin considered this. "Just children, Mother?" he asked at last. "Why just children?"

He was back to that again. She thrust her hands under her knees and reflected further. "Well, in Mr. Parrish's case, I guess you're right; it's not just children. From the little I know of him, he seems to hate everybody. He probably hates Dad and me, too."

"Why?"

"Gosh, Robin, I don't know him well enough to tell you why! But what happened to you today—I have a theory about that, too, if you'd like to hear it. Mr. Parrish came into the building and you were having a fine time. You were running and laughing, making sounds of happiness. If Mr. Parrish had any memory of making those sounds himself, he would have *had* to smile. Instead, he got angry. So perhaps they were sounds he had never made but wished he could have made. And your bike stood there, a symbol of fun, a toy he perhaps never had. No, you really shouldn't be angry at Mr. Parrish, Robin. You should be sorry for him. Whatever's wrong with him, boy, it ain't simple and it ain't small."

"It's hard for me to be sorry for him, Ma, but I *am* sorry for her."

"Mrs. Parrish?"

[39]

"Yes, the way she smiles at me and says how I've grown. And when I was a kid, she always used to touch my head and look sad."

"You're quite an understanding boy." Julie got up and came over to kiss him.

He giggled and pulled away. "Hey, quit it, Ma!"

"I've got to kiss you, I simply have to kiss you."

"Hey, Ma!" he tussled gently with her, deferring like all men to her appearance of fragility.

"For goodness' sake, can't I even kiss my own child any more?"

"Who's a child?" He held her gently by the wrists, laughing, but she broke the hold and leaned forward quickly, landing a peck on his temple.

"There. And for your information, young stinker, when you're fast asleep and helpless, I steal in and kiss you as much as I like, without any trouble at all."

"You do?" He smiled and looked down at the floor, embarrassed because he was pleased to hear it. "No fooling? From now on, I'll have to stay awake."

Even Rover knew the discussion was at an end, for she jumped onto his bed and nudged his hand with her nose, her ears flat back, her tail wagging seductively.

"Play with her, poor thing. She waits all day for you to come home. I have to finish dinner."

"What's for dinner?"

"Fried nails."

"No, really."

"I told you."

"And monkey's ass?" He looked at her uncertainly.

"Robin!"

"Sorry." He flicked his hand at Rover and she went for it.

"It's all right to talk like that with your friends and with your father, if he doesn't mind, but never in mixed company, honey."

"Sorry."

Julie averted her face so he wouldn't notice her amusement, for one of her favorite diversions (in Robin's absence, of course) was to startle people by innocently dropping a single four-letter word into the midst of a serious conversation. "And wash up for dinner," she said, "and hang up your jacket."

"Okay, okay."

She went back into the kitchen smiling. It was such fun to watch a boy grow up and send out feelers for new privileges. It was so exciting to observe how every day his depth of understanding grew. This was the best age of all, she concluded, but then had to admit that she repeated this same sentiment every year. It was inconceivable that some people disliked children. Punishing themselves, depriving themselves, that's what they were doing. Didn't they realize they would never have a second chance? Didn't they know that this was it, this was the paradise they were promised? "The waste," she whispered, "the downright waste!"

At about a quarter to six, Rover's mysterious Inca instinct told her Ty was coming home even before he entered the elevator downstairs. Perhaps she'd heard his footsteps on the sidewalk outside, or perhaps he'd cleared his throat or greeted someone in the street. At any rate, she was waiting for him at the door, whining, crouching, slightly incontinent from the ecstasy of her love. She gave Ty no choice but to greet her first. She hardly gave him a chance to put his hat and coat in the closet. "All right, Shortie, all right, okay." He picked her up and she covered his face with kisses. Over her butterfly-shaped ears, he saw Julie waiting beside the table, smiling, her face rosy from the heat of the stove.

"Hello, beautiful."

"Hey, Dad!" Robin shot out of his room.

"Well, how's the man? How's old guffle-head today?"

"Did you see what the Yanks did to Boston? Eight to two. Boy, what a slaughter! You owe me ten cents."

"Is that so?" Ty put Rover down. "But you owe me a dime from last night."

"I do not."

"You do. On the Jamison fight."

"I had Jamison."

"You did not."

"I did! Ma, didn't I have Jamison?"

"Leave me out of this."

"Fine gyp you are!"

"Who? Me?" Ty looked innocent and sauntered towards Robin. Suddenly he ruffled Robin's hair.

"Yah, you shouldn't have reminded me of it. You owe me *twenty* cents." Robin reached up to muss his father's hair in return, but Ty caught his arm and held it. Robin poked him in the ribs and they were off.

"Not in the living room! Look out for that chair! Watch the lamp! Not in here, I say. Stop it! Oh, look out!" Julie was after them. "Who's boss around here?"

"Listen to her." Ty flicked his hand at Robin's cheek.

"Can't hear a word." Robin, grinning, made a dive for Ty's knees.

"I'll show you who's boss around here." Julie socked Ty's shoulder. "I said stop it."

"Ouch! See what your mother did to me?"

"And that goes for you, too." Julie socked Robin's shoulder, then crossed with her left.

"Hey, Ma," Robin laughed. "Hey, I warn you." He raised his fist.

"Can't hit a lady," she said and socked him again.

"Hey, Dad, this isn't fair. Dirty pocket-pool."

"Yes, Julie, it's dirty pocket-pool."

"It is?" She turned on Ty suddenly with fists flaying and he backed away protecting his chest with his arms, helpless with laughter.

"Now for you," she said, and went for Robin again.

"Hey, Dad! Hey, Ma!" He was laughing so hard he could barely talk as she pranced before him shadow-boxing, landing occasional punches in his ribs, his shoulders and arms. "Hey!"

"Remember, can't hit a lady."

"Isn't fair——" he gasped. All of a sudden he dropped his guard. He stood up straight, his face bright with a new idea.

"Can't hit a lady!" Julie warned again. She gave him four quick punches.

"Oh, oh," he said. Suddenly, he blew hard in her face.

She stopped.

He blew again, this time with such force that little droplets of saliva shot through the air.

She bent double, laughing so hard that she sank to the floor. Ty strode around holding his sides, pointing at Robin and then at Julie, his face bright red, unable to talk. Robin danced about her, delighted, blowing whenever he could manage it between laughs.

"Oh!" Julie gasped. "I never saw anything so funny in all my life! The poor kid, so impotent, all he could think of was to *blow* at me!"

"Oh!" Ty collapsed on the sofa. "Oh, my sides!"

Just then the telephone rang. . . .

5 : *Thursday, April Sixteenth*

Maud Harewood was not well enough to help with the moving. Even two Seconals and four fingers of whisky hadn't put her to sleep the night before and she had tossed in furious wakefulness until three o'clock in the morning, so that, although Albert waited until the last possible moment to awaken her, she could hardly open her eyes and had to take a Benzedrine in order to function at all. While Albert supervised the moving men, she sat apathetically in the park, then made the first show at the Trans-Lux where she had a little nap, and then took a bite at a nearby coffee shop. After this late snack, she felt well enough to walk down to her new apartment.

Albert had just left for the office and Emma had sent her two hired assistants away and was working alone on the linen closet. It was just after three o'clock, but the place was tidy and very nearly in shape.

"That was quick, Emma darling," Maud said listlessly. Then she added, observing the maid's tired face, "It looks fine. I don't know what I'd do without you, you're so kind to me."

Emma was moved. Her leathery face broke into a thousand creases. "Oh, those movin' men were wonderful, Mrs. Harewood. They even hung the pictures for us. I gave them each a bourbon and they were that pleased. Real nice boys."

"That's fine," Maud sighed. "Now how about getting *me* a bourbon, honey? I feel just awful." She was soaked in weariness and the new place depressed her. She felt like some heavy toad tossed on an unfamiliar rock. "Did you order dinner?"

"A quick one, lamb chops. I've got a mess of work in the kitchen still."

"Lamb chops are all right, Emma. Food is food. I think I'll lie down." She plodded towards the north bedroom.

"The bedroom's there, Mrs. Harewood." Emma pointed to the south room.

Maud shook her head and a little frown raised one eyebrow.

"But Mr. Harewood picked it because it has such a lovely view of the park."

Still Maud shook her head. She peered into the north room where Albert had arranged a quiet-looking, comfortable den where she could work. She sat down on the big wing chair where she used to do her thinking and rested her head back, her eyes closed. "They'll have to change it around, Emma honey."

"But this is a dark room. It never gets the sun. It's just the kind of room you like to work in."

Maud gave a bitter laugh. "Subtle as a hammer blow, aren't you, Emma? Get the porters, darling."

"Right now? This late?"

[43]

"Yes."

"All right." Emma made a tight mouth. "But Mr. Harewood——"

"Mr. Harewood, Mr. Harewood—I'm the one that's home all day. Besides, you forgot my drink, Emma."

Emma gave her mistress an annoyed look and went to call the superintendent. Then she brought Maud a stiff bourbon and water.

Maud sat in the grey room until Mr. Gruppmann came up with Joe and Carney, the colored porter. Klaus stood at the doorway sliding the brim of his hat in his fingers, finding himself ill at ease in the presence of her despondency. "Welcome to Number Ten, Mrs. Harewood." His greeting sounded as mournful as she appeared, though his red face glowed, the consequence of two off-duty schnappses which he had downed in anticipation of his evening freedom an hour or so before it was due.

Her voice came from the abyss of the wing chair, so papery that it crackled. "Thank you." He heard the clink of ice against a glass.

"Hmm." Klaus deepened the crease in the crown of his hat with a fat red finger. "The maid said you wanted all the furniture moved around?"

"Just the bedrooms."

"Ach, Mrs. Harewood, what a job! And why you want this dark room to sleep in? The other room is more cheerful."

"Please," she said, "don't argue. I ought to know where I can work best."

"All right, all right, we do it, but you won't get no sun at all when you wake up. This room here faces north. This is the better room for work."

"*You're* trying to tell *me*?" she whispered and closed her eyes. "Everybody knows, everybody knows."

"Okay. Anything you say. 'Course we all off duty at four o'clock, you know, and this job gonna take time."

"Mr. Harewood will take care of you."

"'Bout me, I don't care, he's been more than generous already. But it's my men here——"

"Mr. Harewood will take care of them."

"Okay, we go ahead. You better sit in the living room, Missus, out of the way."

She sighed and got out of the chair with effort. She dragged herself into the living room and sank down onto the sofa where she made febrile attempts at falling asleep, disturbed constantly by the noise of the moving and the nerve-wracking sound of Mr. Gruppmann's bellowed commands. It was five thirty before they left and she was trembling with strain. But she calmed somewhat when she re-entered the north room and saw that her chaise longue was there where she wanted it, before the window, with her table and lamp beside it. She could lie here and look out into the square courtyard at the brick walls.

She didn't bother to look into the other room to see where her desk was. She closed the bedroom door behind her and lay down in the chaise without removing her oxfords. Her hands lay limp, palms upward, at her sides. No, she thought, it was going to be the same, the same here as anywhere else. She wasn't going to be able to write, so why put the desk in the dark, quiet room? Better to put the bed in here and the chaise longue, for nothing could change her situation, nothing could help her— Florida, Europe, California, no change of scene could alter inalterable circumstances. Albert was a fool, such a doggedly pathetic fool, it made her sad to think of him. She would just go on here as she had left off elsewhere, suffering in the chaise before the window, pulled in, folded up and clenched within her misery, longing for the release that writing could give her, but totally unable to work. And she didn't even care any more, to tell the truth, just as long as she could remain quiet and alone. She wasn't going to suffer before that typewriter ever again, facing the blank wall with the blank white paper trembling there in the roller and no words, no words at all, not even a thought. No. She was through, purged dry, wasted. There was nothing left. She'd said it all. A certain amount of suffering made a good writer, but too much of it, like anything else, was lethal. So she had better admit, give in, lie on her chaise longue and slowly die.

But there was no peace even here. From the open windows, a thousand sounds disturbed her; the clatter of pots and pans, the call of voices, ring of telephones and doorbells, all sounds that carried so clearly that the population of the building might just as well have been right in this room with her. She opened her eyes and glanced out at the courtyard, noting that the house was built around it in a square, forming an echo-chamber. And that superintendent had assured her it would be so quiet. There you are. She sighed. It was just as she had said to Albert: no move could ever be an improvement. It wasn't her surroundings that inhibited her. It was her soul, her ambition, her creativity that was deteriorating and rotting for want of . . .

Suddenly she sat up. Her heart began to pound.

"*You owe me ten cents!*" She heard it as clearly as if it came from her side.

"*Who? Me?*" This was a man's voice now, teasing, bordering on laughter.

Some indistinguishable words and then, "*Leave me out of it.*" A woman's voice, amused.

Maud started from the chaise longue, her mouth fallen open, her lower lip trembling. She looked out of the window.

Once again she heard it, that first sound—the laughter of a boy. "*You owe me twenty cents!*" And more laughter, more of that special laughter, the deep-and-high breaking ring of the laughter of a boy.

But there were to be no children. Maud stood at the window rubbing her hands. *There were to have been no children!*

It was from up there, just above her, where she could barely see at right angles part of a yellow and white kitchen. The sounds were coming from up there, from the apartment directly above her.

There was only one child left in the building, the superintendent had said, and he was almost a man.

But he wasn't. He was a boy.

And he lived directly above her.

A cry that was half sob, half sound of anger, came from her. To stifle it, she bit the side of her hand. She bit it hard, hard.

A boy above her.

She heard muffled sounds from the ceiling. She followed them into the living room. Panic-stricken, she stood at the living-room window and heard laughter, laughter. The laughter of a boy, the laughter of his father and mother. Laughter, laughter, cries of joy.

Who were they? What was their name? Quick, quick. She ran into the kitchen and picked up the house phone. No one answered. She jiggled the hook. "Hello, hello! . . . Oh, this is Mrs. Harewood. Who lives above me?"

"Anything wrong?"

"Wrong? Wrong? What's their name, the people who live above me?"

"That's Mr. Tyler Fay——"

"F—A—Y?"

"Yes. Is there——"

Maud hung up and ran back into the foyer. "Telephone book, Emma. Where's the telephone book?"

Emma stared at her.

"Hurry!"

"You all right?"

"Yes. Get me the phone book, I said!"

[46]

Emma pulled it out of the linen closet and slammed it on the table before her.

"Hear that noise up there? Do you hear it?"

"Noise?"

"My God, from upstairs!" Maud tore a page in her anxiety. F's. F—A. . . . Fay. Arthur, Herbert—here it was. Tyler Fay.

She heard a new burst of laughter drift in from the living-room windows, joined laughter, all three voices at once.

"Oh, God!" Maud sobbed, and dialed their number. She rapped her knuckles excitedly on the table as the telephone rang and rang up there. "Hello? Oh. . . . Mrs. Fay? . . . This is Mrs. Harewood in apartment eight—in the apartment just under you. . . . Yes. . . . Oh, thank you. . . . Yes, thanks. Mrs. Fay, I wonder—I wish"—her strained voice broke suddenly into tears—"Mrs. Fay, I'm not very well and we just moved in here today. I wonder if you could *please* try to keep your—boy—a little quiet? I have such a headache and all that noise and banging, it sounds as if it were right here in my apartment——"

"Oh?" Mrs. Fay's voice sounded incredibly young and bewildered as she said, "I had no idea. I'm awfully sorry. It never occurred to us. Of course we'll be more careful."

"Oh, thank you. I know how a—boy—likes to—run and play, but I'll never be able to work if it continues——"

"Please don't try to explain, Mrs. Harewood. It must be an exhausting experience to move, especially these days with so little help around. You just take some aspirin and lie down and rest. We'll be quiet, I promise."

"Thank you," Maud whimpered. "You're so kind; you're a dear."

She went back into her bedroom and lay down on the chaise longue again. She held herself tight, her fists clenched and her teeth clenched. She hardly breathed. She pressed her lids together and listened. She concentrated on listening. There was complete silence now from upstairs. Maud listened and listened to the silence with gathering satisfaction, for that was the way it always was in her home—silent, silent like right now. Slowly she relaxed until her hands lay limp again at her sides. She could hear other voices and sounds from other apartments, but they no longer bothered her. She rather liked the noise of life going on, somehow going on. It was only the voice of a happy child, only his laughter and that of his parents that made her heart race, her head throb and her insides grind.

As she lay there, she felt the dizziness come on. Even when she opened her eyes, the room swayed. Her body heated; she felt she would suffocate. Her head throbbed. Perspiration sprang in drops and glistened on her scarlet cheeks.

Maud suffered the flush in gasping silence. Concurrent with it, she suffered the presence of incipient old age, of a restless, purposeless day, of a thwarted career.

6 :   *Thursday, April Sixteenth*

Tyler Fay was considered something of a freak along Madison Avenue. His blue eyes moved with lazy good nature and he had a languid, kindly smile. Even the movements of his body seemed slow, but this was an illusion caused by his great size. (He stood six-four in stocking feet.) Actually, he moved like a panther, so fluidly that there was no apparent effort. He was an exceptional athlete, had played football and basketball at college and in his youth had gone on mountain-climbing trips with his father.

His father was a man whose religion was self-control. He himself had never raised his voice in anger, despair, sorrow or pure joy. He had an impassive face and an impassive will. On the rare occasions when Ty's mother wept or lost her temper, her husband simply left the room. But any similar outburst on Ty's part was more severely dealt with:

"Come here."

Ty would move towards him fearfully, holding his breath as his father's powerful arm made the expected arc and his large hand crashed across Ty's face.

"I never want to hear you raise your voice again, son."

If Ty cried after the blow, he received another. If he controlled himself, he was rewarded with his father's approval which often took the form of a mountain-climbing expedition, and if there was one thing Ty hated, it was to climb a mountain.

From this stern upbringing, Ty learned how to panic with a smile on his face, but he was much troubled with heartburn and always carried a package of bicarbonate-of-soda tablets with him. The doctor warned him that too much self-control was bad for the body and that eventually he would come down with ulcers, but it was a habit pattern that Ty found hard to break. One thing he could do about it, though, was to resist imparting this type of Spartan control to his family. If something had to explode—and often it did—let it be laughter, he decided;

let it take the form of horseplay, a free and easy good-fellowship; let it be lusty affection and lusty language, too, if need be, devoid of any dishonest morality. It was not at all necessary to climb mountains.

Although he felt uneasy as Julie spoke on the telephone, noting the frown that formed a vertical crease on her forehead, he smiled and put his arm casually on Robin's shoulder.

"Well!" Julie said, hanging up. "This is definitely not our day!"

Ty's smile interrogated her calmly.

"That was the new tenant downstairs, complaining about our noise. It seems the Fays are getting hell from all sides today."

"More hell? What other hell?"

"Robin got it from Mr. Parrish in the elevator a while back."

"Old fisheyes."

"That's some disrespectful name for a multimillionaire," Ty said and gently cuffed his son's shoulder. "I didn't raise you to be a brat."

"No more horsing around," Julie said, pointing to the floor.

"I didn't think we were making so much noise. All we did was laugh. Mr. Collins never complained. A family's got a right to laugh," Robin objected.

"And a boy's got a right to speak up, not to whine. Face it, Rob, we were hacking it up and she must have heard our footsteps."

"So what? We hear the people upstairs, too. We've got a right, Dad. What if we could never laugh or kid around in our own home?"

"Why make a big deal of this, Rob? That poor woman downstairs is probably lying on the living-room couch with a miserable headache, exhausted from moving. She's no ordinary nag. Know who she is? Maud Harewood, the writer. You've read her books, Julie."

"No kidding. She's Maud Harewood? Are you sure, Ty?"

"It's all over the building."

"I can't believe it." Julie pursed her lips and gave her head a little, disappointed shake. "She seemed so—whiney."

"Maybe we make more noise than we realize," Ty suggested.

"So what? For a few minutes once in a while? Who cares who she is?" Robin was completely unimpressed by Maud Harewood's reputation. It might have been different had she been a basketball player.

"Oh, for a few minutes in the evening, I'm sure——"

"But that's all it ever amounts to," Julie said.

"She'll realize that in time. Give her a break. This is her first day. Now, what's for dinner?"

Ty, too, was told it was fried nails, and Robin was ordered to wash his hands. He was back in a moment with white hands and grey wrists. He sat down at the table and banged for service.

"Shh!" Julie said. "Mind our temperamental artist downstairs." She brought out the casserole and the salad.

Ty shut the window. "Just so there won't be more complaints."

Julie spooned a generous portion of beef for him and passed the plate to Rob. "For Dad, dear. She hasn't written anything lately, has she, Ty?"

"Only that weird book that came out a year or two ago—the one about the crazy child. What was it called?"

"*Child's Face Behind Bars*. I thought it was beautiful."

"It stank. It was degenerate."

"How could you say that? It was full of love. It broke my heart. That child wasn't crazy at all."

"No? Symbolic, I suppose; a variation of the Dostoyevsky touch, all crumpled up. She didn't prove her point to me. Oh, she wrote about love, I'll grant you; love was on every page. Only thing, it wasn't love at all she wrote about."

"I didn't know you hated the book that much."

"So did the critics. Every one of them."

"I don't care. I still think Maud Harewood's a genius. I'd love to get to know her."

"Easiest thing in the world. Just make a little more noise."

Robin gave a sudden laugh. "I was just thinking, wouldn't it be funny if Mrs. Harewood turned out to be another Mr. Emmerich? Remember when he moved in next door?"

Ty remembered it well. He remembered meeting Mr. Emmerich in the hall as he and Julie were on their way to an opening. The man stood with a perpetually bent head and averted eyes and spoke in a mournful voice that sounded as if he had a mouthful of food. He wanted to be sure it was going to be *quiet* around here, and the inference was as subtle as a pie in the face. He told them he was a hard-working man who went to bed at eight o'clock every night and had to have *quiet*. Mentally, Ty dispensed with the flowers and drinks they had planned for their new neighbors. However, he nodded and smiled. But Julie's cheeks burned and though he pressed her arm to signal her, she would not be still. "Oh dear, Mr. Emmerich, I'm afraid you've rented the wrong apartment and it's too late now to change. What a shame!"

"Why? Isn't it *quiet*?" Mr. Emmerich asked, gloomily inspecting his shoes.

"Lord, no! Your bedroom and our living room adjoin and the wall

[50]

between them is like paper. Mr. Fay is in advertising, you know, and we have some mighty rough drinking parties that last until two or three in the morning. Eventually, after a few hours of tossing in your bed, you'll either have to call the police or come to the conclusion that if you can't lick 'em you'd better join 'em, but in either case, quiet is the last thing you'll have around here, Mr. Emmerich!" And with that, Julie had flounced to the elevator and rung the bell. Mr. Emmerich, with his chin now tucked into his vest, gave forth with a mournful, braying laugh.

"Quiet, quiet, all he wanted was quiet!" Robin cried. "And then they turned out"—and he leaned back in his chair, laughing—"and then they turned——"

"You'll choke," Julie said.

"And they—oh, they——"

Ty pointed to Robin and gave a high, forced cackle that invariably made him laugh harder.

"Stop it, Ty, he's got a mouthful."

"And they turned out to be the noisiest——" Robin still couldn't finish.

"Honestly," Julie said.

"—the noisiest people in the whole building!" Robin got it out.

"Sounds like the monkey house," Ty said, "with the dog barking, the grandchildren howling and all the Emmerichs, big and small, shouting to each other from room to room. Poor old guy, all he wants is quiet. Quiet in *that* menagerie!"

"That's what old fisheyes said when I was kidding around downstairs with Joe."

"Oh, the hell with fisheyes. You have your fun. Soon you'll be in the advertising business."

"No, Ty." Julie made a special face at him. "Mr. Parrish is to be pitied. He can't help himself."

"Oh yes, of course. He can't help himself," Ty said, and then added seriously, "that's probably true, Rob."

"I'll bet fisheyes turns out to be old Mrs. Haretits' best friend," Robin dared. He glanced at his mother, then looked down at his plate, a smile pulling at the corners of his mouth.

"Your son is using terrible language lately. You must talk to him about it. It isn't nice, not in mixed company, and he knows it." Julie tried to look prim. She didn't dare meet Ty's eyes across the table, but the thought of his expression was enough to break her down and she began to laugh. "Oh, Robin, I don't know what I'm going to do with you! You're growing up to be a juvenile delinquent."

Robin was delighted.

"Get your mother a Kleenex," Ty said. "Why can't you ever laugh without crying?"

Robin brought it to her and she wiped her eyes. "Thanks, you little monster. Hey, come on, the beef is getting cold. No more nonsense, now."

"Yes, Rob. No more nonsense. I mean that," Ty said quietly.

"Shut mah big mouf?"

"That's right."

"Okay, Dad," Robin said. "You're right. I'm sorry."

7 :   *Thursday, April Twenty-third*

Hunt Parrish learned about Maud's arrival the day after she moved in. A good share of the gossip in Number Ten was transmitted to the tenants by Terence, who was at the controls of the front elevator most of the day and who took advantage of the short moment he held folks captive within the confines of the mahogany car. Usually Terence's news bulletins held very little interest for Hunt, but this particular bit of information affected him greatly. Although nothing had changed in his life, he had been particularly restless and dissatisfied for a long time now, and to blame Irene for this, he realized was not entirely fair. Admittedly, she took up very little of his time, less and less as the years passed.

At nine o'clock sharp, he was always downtown at his desk. Although three floors of the office building were occupied by Parrish Paints, Inc., Hunt never ventured beyond his own private suite which was separated from the general offices of the company by a locked door in his secretary's room. No one, not even his executive vice-president, ever spoke directly to him without first announcing his business to Mrs. Lawrence, and Hunt knew personally only a handful of his many employees, who respected and disliked him to a man. He attended to the business and financial problems of his many enterprises until one o'clock every day when Mrs. Lawrence would bring in his luncheon tray consisting of a bowl of soup, a salad, toast and coffee, after which he would remove his jacket and tie, roll up his sleeves, don a heavy white duck coat and lock himself in the private laboratory which adjoined the office. There he would conduct experiments with paints, dyes, waterproofing finishes, cleaning fluids, paint removers, varnishes and lacquers; and regularly new patents would emerge from these experiments to be manufactured and sold exclusively by Parrish Paints, Inc., and its numerous subsidiaries. Although he had a full staff of research technicians out in the New Jersey and Long Island experimental plants, their combined efforts had never equaled his own solo accomplishments. There seemed to be no end to the new ideas that sprouted in his head, nor was there any letup in his frantic quest for increased technical knowledge and each day it was a struggle to decide whether to study or experiment that afternoon.

Hunt Parrish was known to be one of the outstanding chemists in his field and many a time the Government of the United States had requested projects from him. As a matter of fact, during World War II Hunt had been happy to put aside all personal experimentation and devote himself to the service of his country, producing many compounds necessary to the national defense and the fighting forces at no personal gain whatsoever. True, his plants were sometimes awarded the production rights to these compounds, but in all fairness to him, at no time had Hunt ever taken advantage of his situation to press for such a contract. His new formulae, once completed, were always handed over to the proper department with no strings attached. After that, if Uncle Sam felt that the Parrish plants could handle the manufacture of any particular compound better than another company, they could come to him with their proposition.

At five o'clock each evening, Hunt would emerge from his laboratory, scour his hands, comb and brush his beautiful white hair, replace his jacket and tie and tend to any calls or mail that had come in during the afternoon. By five thirty, he was ready to leave. His special taxi was waiting for him downstairs to drive him home. The cocktail and dinner hours were awarded to Irene, after which he retired to his room to work on the literary essays for which he was certain he would one day be acclaimed. On the dot of midnight, he would put aside his work and help himself to a piece of fruit and a glass of milk, usually consuming them in Irene's room to keep her company for a few minutes before bed. At twelve thirty sharp, he retired, knowing the time without ever consulting his watch.

On Saturdays he took a short walk (sometimes with Irene), and spent the rest of the day on his literary work. On Sundays, he took a long walk (usually alone), read the papers, indulged in the only afternoon nap of the week, and took Irene out to dinner. For years, his routine never varied except when he had to visit his out-of-town plants or fly to

Washington, or when he couldn't avoid a certain dinner party, or when a play was good enough to merit his viewing. He never took a vacation or a weekend away.

And this past year had been no different from those that preceded it, so that Hunt could not explain why he was increasingly restless and discontented and why, all of a sudden he, who had always preferred his solitude, had begun to feel lonely.

More and more, he longed for conversation; not small talk, but serious philosophizing. At the dinner parties he attended, the standard of conversation was invariably commonplace, always the same, and tryingly boring, centering about the political situation, with every second guest claiming to be a particular authority who had "inside information"; or else it would concern the state of the stock market with "tips" flowing about the table *sotto voce*; or perhaps a median-level commentary on the latest movie or play. Once in a while, they might discuss the best-selling novel. But real talk, the kind of beautiful conversation that was an art form in itself? No, Hunt had found none of that. He had met so-called intellectual men here and there, mostly in connection with his literary efforts, but it was always in the nature of a business conference, a well-meaning editor attempting to justify his criticism of Hunt's work. Years ago, he had attended a few literary gatherings, but the crowded, smoky rooms and flowing whisky had not induced serious talk, nor did he believe the guests to be serious thinkers to begin with.

So that, when Terence told him about the new tenant in Number Ten, Hunt could not believe in his good fortune. Although he had never met Maud Harewood personally, he had been in touch with her several years ago when his critical essay on her works was published in *The American Scholar*. She had been most appreciative and had telephoned and written him several times to thank him for his high opinion. They had mentioned getting together, but somehow the meeting had never taken place.

Now it could, though. Their proximity made it not only possible, but imperative. Without rearranging his heavy work schedule, he still could find time to converse with Maud Harewood by occasionally taking his cocktail with her instead of Irene.

So one week after Maud had moved into Number Ten, Hunt Parrish came out of his laboratory an hour earlier than usual (this once, he would steal time from his schedule), and he telephoned her. She was more than cordial. She remembered his name well and was thrilled when he told her where he lived. At once she implored him to have a cocktail with her. She said she was lonesome and ached for understanding company.

Hunt threw his topcoat over his arm, grabbed his brief case and hat and hurried out of the office, calling to ask Mrs. Lawrence to inform Irene he might be late. Mrs. Lawrence watched him leave with a bitter nod, assured that at last this god who was her employer had stepped down from his pedestal to enter into a common "affair," and, of course, with someone other than herself.

Maud Harewood was waiting for him. She had dabbed some lipstick unevenly on her mouth and had made some attempt to brush her dull, frizzy-ended hair. She wore soiled black velveteen slacks and a black wool cardigan jacket covered with peasant embroidery. She was lying on the couch in the living room and, although she did not get up when Hunt walked into the room, she stretched out her hands to him in a gesture that was designedly theatrical, "Hunt Parrish, at last!"

He hurried across the room, his face flushed with pleasure at the enthusiasm of her welcome, and on impulse, kissed both the hands she extended. They might have been old, old friends, so immediate was the *rapport* between them. He, looking into her large, piteous eyes, saw there a totality of suffering that shocked him; never before had he seen it revealed so nakedly and so he did not let go of her hands at once, but held them and pressed them, a small gesture that almost made her want to weep because she, noting the shy smile and the blinking of his lids, knew that his gentle pressure on her hands was as much of a supplication as it was a sign of his own understanding and sympathy for her.

They had too much to talk about from the start. They had to express their delight in the good fortune that had brought them together, veritably beneath the same roof. Then Maud had to tell him how much she admired him, how she kept looking for more of his critical essays in the magazines, how graceful was his prose, how unbelievably sensitive he was to the gentlest nuances of a writer's work, and he glowed as she spoke and interjected, "How extraordinary that you should have sensed all this!" Then he spoke about her work, kindly avoiding any mention of her disastrous last novel, but emphasizing instead her steady literary growth which reached its pinnacle with her masterpiece, *The Gesture*, undoubtedly a modern American classic. He had covered most of this in his article on her, but nevertheless she accepted it all as if spanking new. While he spoke, she slowly came to a sitting position on the couch as if revivified, listening to him with a great, childlike grin as she stirred the contents of a silver pitcher before her and then poured crimson Bloody Marys into old-fashioned glasses.

Hunt spoke automatically. Beneath the surface of his words, he was still trying to recover from the shock of discovering how sick a woman she was. In his interpretation of *The Gesture*, he had come to the conclusion that Anna, the heroine, demonstrated Maud's erroneous self-judgment, but now, watching her with concern, he was forced to admit that this judgment had been painfully accurate; his analysis, therefore, had been off a shade, but he could not admit this to her, for that would be tantamount to accusing her of mental instability. So that he held, verbally, to his former course. "I was certain when I read *The Gesture*, that I was seeing you painted with your eyes closed and looking inward, so to speak, revealed not as the world sees you, but as you see yourself," he said, moving on safe ground. Her moist, tortured eyes stared unblinking at him, almost blankly, as if she could not hear a word he said. He shook his head and sipped the Bloody Mary.

"Why do you shake your head?"

"Why? My dear Maud, have you any idea how I argued about that book when it came out! How I was criticized for my opinion! It shocked me to realize how few people had any comprehension whatsoever of what you were doing there. There never was a question in my mind but that this was an intense, symbolic autobiography—a heroic task to tackle and admirably successful, too. I don't have to ask you now to verify my opinion, to look at you is verification enough. Your Anna in *Gesture* is what you think of yourself."

"And was I right?"

"That's a low blow," he hedged. "After all, how long have I known you?"

"As long as you've been reading my books," she said. Suddenly she leaned forward, her face close to his. Her breath smelled of tomato juice. "Dear Hunt, I feel such a togetherness with you. You're right. How long has it been? A half hour? And yet you are my brother. I know it." She put her hand on his and her sad eyes trusted him.

Her touch was not a touch to make him shudder, for there was nothing physical about Maud Harewood. She represented only one thing—The Writer, greatly talented, perhaps even possessed of genius, but a Writer only. She had nothing else to give or be. She was her books. Read them and there was Maud Harewood, all of her, no more, no less. Hunt covered her hand with his and for a few seconds was silent, reflecting on the sadness of what she was, nothing more than an instrument to deliver a series of written words.

She smiled and slowly withdrew her hand to pour herself another drink from the pitcher. "Tell me what else you saw in *Gesture*." She curled her legs under her and leaned back with the drink in her hand, like a child about to hear a fairy tale.

"I saw loneliness."

"Yes," she whispered. "*You* would recognize that, wouldn't you, Hunt?"

His only response was a twitching smile, for though he longed for understanding as much as she did, her quick knowledge of him came like a stab and he was suddenly rendered uncomfortable. He had much the same unpleasant feeling as when he sat in too soft a chair.

"And what else? Tell me."

He struggled back to the subject of her book. "Then there was Edwin, your rejection."

"Yes, the rejection of my love!" she murmured. "Love is the whole book, Hunt; it's all of my books." Her eyes glowed and her lips parted; she breathed heavily the effect of what she said.

He smiled at her, wanted to pat the disarray of her brown hair to comfort her for the fact that she was lying to him and knew it, knew that deep down inside the secret core of Maud Harewood's soul was no love at all, any more than there was love within himself. "Love?" he queried gently. "But this is not a book about love, Maud. It's about suffering; about loneliness and rejection, yes, but never love."

She looked displeased and sat forward. "If you didn't see love in it, then you didn't understand it," she said, and her eyes took on a brooding, sulky look.

He said quickly, "I saw beauty in the book."

"Well then?"

"We're quibbling about the meaning of a word."

"I'm not so sure of that."

"What is love, Maud?"

"Love? Oh, love is something sad and wonderful that fills you like an expanding gas until you can't contain it any more, until you must sing and shout and——" She paused, for he was shaking his head. "Well, then, you tell me what it is."

"It's a selfless emotion, isn't it? When one loves, it is understood that there must be an object of this love—who was it said 'The verb *to love* takes an object'?—and the object becomes uppermost in importance. In *Gesture*, you speak of physical love, but this is not what we are discussing. Pure love has to be——"

She sipped at her drink and stared straight ahead as he spoke. When she interrupted him, her gaze remained where it had been, somewhere off towards the foyer, and her voice was hard and held a tinge of scorn.

"One can love oneself, truly love oneself," she stated, and then slowly turned to give him a queer stare.

"But 'self-love' is another word, the 'self' modifying the 'love.' A synonym for that would be the word 'selfish' and this is not——"

Maud gulped her Bloody Mary and then quite suddenly turned to him as he was speaking and flashed him a brilliant smile, a smile that was completely ingenuous. "We mustn't quarrel, Hunt. I couldn't stand it if we quarreled."

Once more he was forced to abandon his reflections. She had a nervous mind that could not rest with one subject long. Her condition was too disturbed at present for the kind of conversation he enjoyed. It was inconceivable that she could write anything under these circumstances, he told himself, and this would account then for that calamitous last novel of hers. His concern grew. Something had to be done about this. She was in urgent need of help. He would have to be pliable and allow her to lead the conversation wherever she needed it to go. Gently he assured her, "We couldn't quarrel if we tried. As different as we are, we are paradoxically that alike. You couldn't pore over chemical formulae in a laboratory or work out a careful, analytic essay any more than I could sit down and write a book like *Gesture*, and yet we share so much —a mutual loneliness, for instance."

"Yes," she said, and the hardness came back to her voice. "And what you left unsaid, I'll say, for I'm not afraid. A mutual superiority." Even the moist surface of her eyes seemed hardened, shining bright as lacquer. "That's got to be voiced."

"Another reason why we can't quarrel. By loneliness, I suppose I meant that, in a sense."

She filled her glass still another time without offering any to Hunt, but he was not offended. It was understood that the pitcher was there for his consumption as well as hers, so he reached forward and poured himself half a drink. She tried to light a cigarette, but her hand shook so violently that he had to help her. "Too much booze, too many cigarettes, too many Nembutals, Benzedrines and tranquillizers," she muttered. Her gaze was miserable over the cigarette, lit by the orange flame he held. "You know I can't write any more," she blurted suddenly.

He shook the match and placed it in the ash tray with a deliberate motion to demonstrate that he was not shocked by her statement, for he knew that any indication of perturbation on his part might very well send her into a panic. "What happened?"

"It started when I was working on *Child's Face*. Suddenly all of the —the *outside* things that I had been able to push aside—you know how one has to do that in order to work at all. Suddenly, though"—her voice cracked—"they came up. Like vomit. I couldn't shove them back to where I usually hid them. I couldn't cover them again. There they were. I couldn't think of anything else."

"Writer's block."

"Oh, they have names for everything, don't they?"

He smiled a little but remained silent, encouraging her to speak.

"I thought if I moved, things might change. Rather, it wasn't my idea, but Albert's, and I went along." She belched, delicately holding her shaking fingers before her mouth. "But what's a change of rooms? It's the kind of simple solution that would occur to him."

"But it sometimes works. Have you honestly given it a fair try?"

"What good would it do me?" she said bitterly. "There's so much noise around here, I couldn't work if I wanted to."

"In *this* house?"

She pointed to the ceiling. "The people upstairs. I can't *think*. Some noises I have learned to ignore, like voices in the street or the sounds of traffic, but not this."

"Upstairs?" he repeated, trying to remember who lived there.

"The Fays. Know them?"

"Oh, Fay!" He couldn't repress a smile and he pressed his palms together, matching finger tip for finger tip. "You have Robin, *dear* Robin!"

"You know him then."

"Ever since he was born. He is quite a boy and they are quite a family, all right."

"Tell me about them." Once again she curled up and leaned back, eager for a story, suddenly oblivious of the fact that these were her tormentors. "First tell about the father. What's he like?"

"Very tall, six four or five, I'd say, and handsome, too; a big, blond giant, right out of *True Confessions*."

"Blue eyes?"

"They'd have to be blue. He's it, you know, the real thing. He's a wise, pseudo-intellectual Madison Avenue Boy. Precocious, too. In his late thirties, I'd say, and already top vice-president of Clarkson's. Must have been a fabulous athlete, one of those big, physical fellows who has eternally just emerged from a shower bath."

Maud laughed delightedly. "Oh, you tell it so well! I can just see him. Go on."

"I've never visited their apartment, but I'll bet they have a million-dollar hi-fi set that plays faultlessly their valuable collection of Frank

Sinatra and Elvis Presley first editions." Her enjoyment spurred him on. He himself was blissful. They *were* spiritual siblings. He couldn't remember when he'd had a better time. "They must have an art collection, too, of course. Toulouse-Lautrec posters, at least one; Picasso and Matisse drawings of dubious authenticity and very little value to give the collection class, and dozens of non-objective bowel movements which they call oils, to which they point with smug authority—'This one is a Milquetoaste; that's a Schultz over there'—until you find yourself wondering at your own ignorance and lack of progress to be still believing in such outdated abstractionists as Klee, Kandinsky and Miro. This is the Fays."

"Oh, tell me more!"

"He's one of those fellows who makes a fetish of appearing gay. 'Let's all have a helluva time, goddammit!'"

"Tremendous, Hunt. And his wife? Tell me about her."

"Well, she's pretty. She's tall with a good figure, wears lots of cashmere sweaters to prove it. She has big, soft eyes and silky blonde hair which she wears long and well brushed and which she keeps tossing to make it shimmer. She just loves to cook, I understand, crazy about it. This gives her a very distinct personality, you see, because everyone knows she could afford a dozen cooks to do it for her, if she wanted them."

"Makes a regular celebrity out of her, doesn't it?"

"Certainly. She's enough like him to be his sister; brittle, sweet-as-you-please. They're professional optimists, both of them, professional fools who extract so-called joy from the very air, from a cesspool, if you will, who laugh gaily in the face of Korea, Indochina, Suez, communism, fascism, our foreign policy, the witch hunts in Congress—what you please. They just have to laugh, Maud, because it's all so gay!"

Maud squinted at the scarlet fluid in her glass. "That, of course, is where it ceases to be funny. I seem to have drawn the worst card from the deck. I know the Fays from way back, from when I was a child. *They* were the ones. . . . No, it isn't funny any more."

"Taken all in all, I would not call them an amusing couple."

"Nor so charming, either."

"*Hardly.*"

"And the boy?"

"What would you expect from such a union?"

Maud turned the glass between her shaking fingers. "What am I going to do?"

"Be ruthless. You've been ruthless before, I'm sure. You know as well as I do that this is your only defense against such people. A huge joke it is, because the Fays of the world, who harass and disrespect us, are the very individuals who derive the most pleasure from what we create. I say 'we,' but that's an error, for I doubt very much that the Fays have read my essay. It's a certainty, though, that they've read your books."

"Without much understanding."

"Granted. But like Toulouse-Lautrec, Picasso and Matisse, you are chic. It's the duty of all sophisticates to admire your work."

"Then you'd think they'd help me instead of hindering me. They stamp, jump, blare jazz records——"

"As bad as that?"

She nodded. "So what chance have I to write?"

"You must insist on the chance."

"I'll try. I have been complaining. But I don't know. . . ." She drained her glass and put it down. She clasped her hands and rubbed the fingers together, knuckle to knuckle. "Will you help me, Hunt? Will you help me to start to write again?" Her eyes were pitiful, though no tears covered their gelid surface.

Hunt was deeply moved. "I would want to, you know that."

"Then talk to me, Hunt. Stimulate me with ideas, *make* me think straight again!"

Her cheek was hot and papery dry under his finger tips. "I promise I'll try. But I can't do it unless you unwind. If you'd only relax and stop thinking about yourself, I could promise you we'd lick this together."

"I will. I'll rest. I'll relax right now. Bless you, Hunt Parrish." She threw herself back on the couch and closed her eyes tight to prove it to him. "See, I'll relax right now. . . ." she whispered. He stroked her hair and in a moment, the Bloody Marys had put her to sleep.

He whispered good-bye and tiptoed out, closing the front door soundlessly. He stood in the hall a few minutes before ringing for the elevator, stealing a moment of solitude before returning to his apartment. True, his first visit with Maud Harewood had resulted in little of the conversation he so earnestly desired, but everything couldn't come at once. First of all, one had to tie the bonds of understanding and friendship, and this had certainly been accomplished today. Beyond this, she herself had beseeched him to make her think again, so that from now on, they could plunge into a veritable waterfall of worded thoughts. The next time he saw her, he would come armed with a thousand ideas to stimulate her. She could have her choice. Little by little, she would begin to curb her preoccupation with Self. A good place to begin these conversations might be with that very question of self-love which she had interrupted today.

He shrugged his shoulders to set them neatly into his jacket and rang the bell. From Maud Harewood to Irene Parrish in a single moment was like diving into icy water; one had to take a deep, deep breath first. He took it. From the sublime to the ridiculous, he told himself. The fingers of his right hand dug at the seam in his coat pocket as he faced the monotony sub-layered with a thousand silent tensions that awaited him upstairs.

8 :   *Tuesday, April Twenty-eighth*

All afternoon the breeze brought whiffs of earth, new grass and forsythia from the park and with them, a summer nostalgia that had taken Julie back to Cape Cod, but then suddenly it grew so cold in the kitchen that she had to close the window and turn on the steam heat. She poured herself a cup of coffee and sat down. It was much too soon to start longing for the Cape. She had a good two months to wait before she would see the harbor again, before she could run from her house down the small strip of lawn to the sun deck and swim out to the "Heartburn II," their sixteen-foot sea skiff. A good two months before she could start the motor and speed up and down the bay with the wind in her hair, shrieking hello to all her friends, while Ty slumbered in the pink and white bedroom, his long limbs flung helter-skelter across the bed, making up for hundreds of hours of sleep lost to the Advertising Industry throughout the winter.

Julie's sigh had a catch in it, like a little girl recovering from a crying spell, and its sound was so pathetic that she had to laugh at herself. For she was merely suffering the first spring symptoms of the disease from which all Cape Codders suffer, and it would have to run its course. She would battle it for another week, perhaps, and then one day out would come the pictures, the black and whites, color slides and movie reels. Then she would start calling the Lower Cape crowd, their summer friends from Wellfleet, Truro and Provincetown, and there would be gay parties and an exchange of pictures and negatives. By May fifteenth, she'd be telephoning Ginny and Foster Sutro long distance to find out how her garden was coming along and when Mike would finish painting the house yellow with white trim and black shutters, and by Decoration Day she would have overcome Ty's objections to the long drive for such a short time, and they would race down for the weekend with Robin, Rover, and like as not, one or two of Robin's friends.

"I wish I hated the damn Cape," she whispered, but her eyes were shining because before her, instead of seeing the near-naked pin-up girl on the calendar Robin had given her on Christmas day, she could see the sweep of water, the silhouetted lighthouse in the distance, the flats and rock jetties at low tide, dotted with hopping sandpipers and grave sea gulls. . . .

The front door banged and Julie came out of her dream with a start.

"Hi, Ma. Door slipped," Robin said. His khakis were rolled up, his sneakers black with mud, and his hair clung in wet spears to his flushed face. "Terrific game. Hit two homers." He was swinging his bat back and forth and she eyed it with growing nervousness, thinking that he had already made noise banging the door.

"Stop that, Robin."

He didn't know what she meant.

"Stop swinging that bat I said!"

His face stiffened and there was a remote, resentful look in his eyes as he stilled the bat's motion.

She didn't blame him. "I'm sorry, Robin. Honestly, I'm sorry. I'm so scared of that genius downstairs that I——"

But he wasn't holding it against her. He gave her that masculine smile that allowed for a woman's shattered nerves. "That's okay, Ma." He started for his room, careful not to swing his bat. At the entrance to the bedroom hallway, he paused. "I'm going to my room. If you don't mind, I'll close the door."

"Of course, honey."

This, then, would be one of those times when Robin had a deep need to be alone in his room. Although she and Ty respected this need, neither of them were above peeking at him through the kitchen window for, being at right angles to Robin's room in the courtyard, it offered an excellent view. Sometimes he would be playing Canfield at his desk, cheating in solitude without a shade of guilt; sometimes he would only be reading in peace. When he was younger, he used to drape himself in Julie's old black silk summer coat, surround himself with the screen and preach sermons to his congregation with arms outstretched. But most of the time he meditated, lying on his bed. And that was what he was doing with his aloneness today. Julie saw him through the kitchen window, lying on his back, his hands behind his head, staring straight up at the ceiling. So he hadn't been playing baseball *all* afternoon since school.

No, it was obvious that before the game, or maybe even afterwards, with grimy face and muddy sneakers, Robin had been to Sally's house.

Julie wondered what Robin saw in that girl. She evaluated Sally's stubby figure and heavy features while she set the table and could find nothing in the girl's favor beyond an abnormally large chest development which Julie considered disproportionate and downright ugly. She was wondering if the possession of this great, ungainly pair of breasts was enough to so completely charm Robin that he never raised his eyes to Sally's face, when Ty came home.

He looked tired, but Julie knew better than to tell him so because then he would exert himself to prove to her how chipper he was. In this respect, he was dishonest with her; his masculinity allowed for no lapse; weariness was for women. She knew he was having trouble with new accounts and Ty was not the sort who could relieve his mind by talking it out at home. That would be "passing the buck," unsportsman-like, and a real man was like a rock standing hard against the tide. That its base was being subtly worn away was something she would like to point out to him someday (all those rolls of Tums in his pockets) . . . someday, but not yet, not just now.

Ty missed the vital greeting of his son. "Isn't Robin in yet?"

"Sure, but he's closed his door."

"Oh, Sally again. Well, I've got to let Shortie out or she'll have a heart attack." Ty tiptoed to Robin's door behind which Rover whined and scratched. He opened it a crack to let her out.

"Hi, Dad," Robin said dreamily.

"Hi, Robin. It's okay, stay where you are." Ty closed the door and came back into the dining room carrying Rover under his arm. "I could use a good strong bourbon today. How about you?"

"What's the matter?"

"Spring fever, honey; couldn't get that harbor out of my mind."

"You, too?" Julie flung a kitchen towel back on the rack.

"I'll admit I did have a look at a new motor——"

"Ty, we're painting the house this year, and you know it!"

"We are?" He smiled. "Come on, let's have a drink in the living room together. We're never alone, and since Robin's deep in sex revery, how about stealing a sophisticated tête-à-tête, just you and me?"

"It won't do you any good. We're painting the house this year."

The telephone rang. It was Bobby Linkholm for Robin. Ty hesitated to disturb him, but Julie reminded him that they had long ago proved that Robin shut the door on adults only, and this was verified again by the fact that Robin was delighted to speak to Bobby and chose to take the call in the privacy of his parents' bedroom rather than out in the foyer where he could be overheard.

"Top secret, I'm sure." Julie laughed, for why in heaven Robin insisted upon telephone privacy she would never understand, since his conversation could invariably be heard throughout the apartment. He always left the door slightly ajar so as not to offend them.

"That you, Bob-tail? Brrrh! Blah-h-h!" He gave forth with a shriek of laughter followed by a particularly long and moist "razzberries" while Julie made a mental note to remember to wipe off the receiver with a damp cloth. "Hey, quit it, Bob!" More laughter. "Hey, you're busting my eardrum! Hey! Blah-h-h! Brrrh-h-h!"

Julie put a slice of her own homemade pâté on a plate with Melba rounds while Ty prepared the drinks and carried the tray into the living room. Just as they sat down, Robin and Bobby Linkholm finished with initial greetings and got down to the business of the telephone call. "Oh, *her!* Yeah. You know what Jimmy Parker calls her, don't you? . . . Yeah. Ah-ha! Yeah, Bob-tail, okay, okay, ouch! That's enough, I mean it. Perfect name, isn't it?"

"I wish I'd gotten it," Ty said.

"I thought we were going to have a tête-à-tête."

"It'll have to wait. This conversation might prove enlightening."

"Oh, *him!*" Robin screamed. "He's not a suede, he's a goddam fairy! Came to the dance in a tux and slippers with bows. Honestly, bows. What a fairy. His mother's always tagging after him. . . . Yeah. . . . No, Sally hates him, I tell you."

"See how you learn? Don't you go tagging after Robin now." Ty helped himself to some pâté.

"Listen, Bob, your complexion's gonna go just like the rest of us. No one gets away without the hebes. Me and Jimmy went over to Eighty-sixth yesterday to that cut-rate place. I got a new complexion brush and some pimp-cream—Acnetol. That's the best stuff. Write that down, Bob. You'll be needing it soon."

"Poor Bobby Linkholm, no acne," Julie mourned. "It's killing him not to be a member of the club. I think Robin is sweet to reassure him."

"Listen, Bobby, I don't advise you to go over to Sally's. I'm warning you, she's sort of my girl, we decided definitely today. Ah-ha! Yah! Ah-ha! Brrh-h-h! Blah-h-h!" Abruptly the conversation was at an end. They heard Robin move through the bedroom hallway and they heard his door close. Then silence.

"I've got to peek," Ty said.

"He'll only be dreaming about Sally again." Julie knocked off her shoes and curled her legs under her on the couch. She lit a cigarette and let the smoke out in a slow stream.

Ty came tiptoeing back from the kitchen window, grinning. "He's done with Sally for the day. Now he's changed into his basketball uniform, red satin trunks and all. He's in his stocking feet and he's tossing his clean, rolled-up socks into the wastepaper basket which is standing on the bed. He can't possibly make any noise and yet he can play a fairly respectable game. He's taken care of everything. You ought to see him practicing hook shots. Clever kid. Chip off the old block."

"He's not practicing," Julie said. "He's playing a real game. The team is losing to Bancroft and the score is sixty to nothing. At the last moment the coach says, 'I know it's impossible, Fay, no one can score sixty-two points in five minutes, especially with a bum knee, but WE NEED YOU, FAY. Get in there, think you can make it?' Fay hobbles onto the court. From a spot under the opponent's basket, he makes a shot that flips in without touching the rim. He intercepts their out-of-bounds pass and scores again. Again and again he intercepts and scores, limping painfully. Nothing like it has ever been seen before. The crowd goes wild. The coach blacks out. Fay saves the day for the team. He is carried out on a stretcher amid the cheers and hurrahs. . . ."

The telephone rang again. "Bobby again, asking how to spell Acnetol." Ty crossed to the foyer. "Hello. Who? Oh. . . . Yes, Mrs. Harewood."

Julie put down her drink. "Now no one's made a sound, not a sound."

"Oh? That surprises me because he's practicing basketball. . . . Yes, basketball shots, but in his stocking feet, Mrs. ——"

Julie marched to the telephone and stood beside him. "Tell her to go to hell," she whispered. "I'm serious."

"(Shh!) I'm very sorry, Mrs. Harewood. He doesn't mean to disturb you. You seem to feel this alleged noise is directed against you personally. As a matter of fact, you'd get a kick out of this if you could see it. He's taken great care not to make a sound. The wastebasket is on the bed and he's using rolled-up socks instead of a ball. Chip off the old—— But he's wearing socks. . . . I realize that, of course. . . . Yes. . . . No, it's perfectly all right. . . . Yes, well, that's true. I'll speak to him. All right, I'll do it now. . . . Yes, Mrs. Harewood, you're welcome."

"Why were you so nice to her?" Julie exploded. "That's the trouble, we're much too decent about all this, Ty. She's going too far."

"It's possible that Rob's footsteps *do* make noise. If she's down there trying to write, I can see her point."

"Why is she writing at this hour? I don't even believe she is."

"Why would she lie to us? What purpose would it serve?"

"That's just it. Something's fishy, Ty. She seems to smell it when Robin comes home. He can't do anything any more. She calls every time he has a friend over and they play records, every time he plays with the dog——"

"I can still see her point, though, if she's down there trying to concentrate."

"At five thirty, six o'clock?"

"You can't tell a writer when to work. We've just drawn a bad deal, Julie, and we're going to have to make the best of it. After all, it's no great tragedy for Robin to confine his athletic efforts to the great outdoors."

"All right then, you tell him to stop. I won't."

"And if I don't make it snappy, she'll call again. Cheer up, sourpuss."

"Spoil his game—innocent fun!" Julie whispered. "Just because she's Maud Harewood. . . ."

Ty knocked at Robin's door. "I'm sorry to disturb you, kid, but——"

Robin squinted at him.

"Mrs. Harewood again. I'm afraid you'll have to stop."

"Oh, great!" Robin slammed the socks to the floor and threw himself on the bed. "I wasn't making noise. She's just a mean old bitch."

"Watch your language, boy."

"Mother's not here."

"Yes. Well. . . . Say, Rob, that's the cleverest method of practicing hook shots quietly that I've ever come across. I never would have thought of it myself."

"Lot of good it does me."

"She claims she can hear your footsteps. She says the whole ceiling sounds as if it's coming down on her head. You're no lightweight, you know."

Robin sucked in his lips.

"Look, it isn't the end of the world. You can play in the park." Ty ruffled his hair. "Come on, quit sulking. Dinner's almost ready and you stink."

"I took a shower today in school."

"Yep, I remember those showers we used to take in school."

Robin giggled. "But I did."

"Into the tub!"

"I had a bath last night."

"Last night we ate at the d'Auriacs'."

[67]

"Oh."

"And the night before was Sunday and we ate out."

"Okay, okay, you win."

"And the night before was Saturday——"

"And I took a bath because that was the night of the dance!"

"So you took a bath Saturday. This is Tuesday."

"Okay, okay, you win awright!" Robin swung his legs around and pulled off his socks.

"And a clean bath, kid. Dig those filthy toenails! I mean use soap. S—O—P—E!"

Julie had brought out the bourbon bottle. "I'm going to get drunk," she said bitterly. "In memory of poor old Mr. Collins whom I never properly appreciated when alive. . . . Here's to you, Mr. Collins. We miss you!"

"Amen." Ty poured himself another drink.

"I don't know what you're drinking for. You don't care. You don't even realize Maud Harewood is beginning to spoil our life together as a family."

"Now, Julie, it isn't as bad as that."

"Oh, you don't think so? Well, you know what I did today when Robin came home? Instead of giving him a big welcome like I always do, I screamed at him because he was swinging his bat—really screamed at him, I was so afraid he'd drop it and make noise. Can't you see what's happening? Can't you see what she's doing?"

"Believe me, Julie, it would take a helluva lot more than some cranky writer's complaints to spoil our fun. I'm sick and tired of hearing her name. Change of subject?"

"All right, you change it."

He leaned forward. "About that motor—I saw the most beautiful twenty-five horsepower Johnson electric——"

"Our boat isn't heavy enough for twenty-five horse——"

"Well, about our boat, honey, I was thinking——"

"Uh-uh."

"I saw the prettiest little eighteen-foot——"

"I knew it!"

"——Barracuda, white with mahogany——"

"Enter 'Heartburn Third,' exit the much-needed, oft-postponed paint job on the house."

"What do you need a pink house for anyway?"

"Yellow."

"Last year you said pink."

"I know. And instead you got the 'Heartburn Second.'"

"That was two years ago."

She was silent, running the tip of her finger around the rim of her glass. "Ty, I try to keep reminding myself who she is, how talented she is, how important silence is for her work. All that. But it doesn't help. I'm beginning to hate her. I really am."

"I thought we were going to——"

"I know, but she's got me so upset, I just have to talk it out. Things don't *feel* the same as they used to. Everything's less nice, somehow. Like somebody unwelcome who's moved right into our apartment. Do you know what I mean?"

"You're really taking this pretty hard, aren't you?"

"Well, what do you think? You're not around here all day to see what it's like. For example, how did you feel making Robin stop playing just now? Tell me the truth. Did you think it was fair to him? Did you think it was right? Did it make you feel good?"

Ty looked thoughtfully at the bourbon in his glass.

"Don't you sense the difference? We're always under a strain lately. And for no reason, no reason at all! We have a right to live and laugh. A child has a right to run and play in his own home and I don't care who lives below."

He thought more about it. Then he leaned back and crossed his legs decisively. "I'll take care of it next time, Julie. I didn't realize——"

"Tell her enough is enough."

"I'll take care of it," Ty said.

9 :   *Wednesday, April Twenty-ninth*

After a restless night interrupted by nightmares from which she kept awakening in terror, Maud Harewood took a long, hot bath to ease her tension, Anacin to soothe her headache, and dressed herself in a green tweed skirt and an old black sweater. She drank three cups of coffee for breakfast. Her after-breakfast cigarette brought on an attack of dizziness which left her weak and embittered. So even this one last little pleasure is to be denied me, she thought, staring at the broken cigarette she had ground into the ash tray.

She sat at the dining table pressing her fingers to her temples, unable to decide upon a dinner menu, while Emma stood by with her heavy arms crossed over her chest, stubbornly refusing to help. Too many new duties were being thrust upon her lately and she wasn't going to accept the additional chore of planning and ordering the meals, not if they had chicken and string beans every night from now till doomsday. She was on to Mrs. Harewood's tricks. Maybe she was a genius to the rest of the world, but to Emma she was nothing but a selfish, spoiled woman. She was through being sorry for her. She had gone through the change herself and no one had held *her* hand; no, sir! On her knees, scrubbing floors, she was.

When she'd first come to work for the Harewoods, her duties had been clearly outlined: no laundry, no mending, no shopping, no errands. But now, only three years later, here she was doing Mrs. Harewood's undergarments and stockings, all the mending, at least eight out of ten errands and the bartending to boot, for Mrs. Harewood was too sick to get up and mix her own drinks every two minutes. Too sick! Too lazy, that's what she was. She wouldn't mind so much if Mrs. Harewood was at her desk writing all day, like when she'd first come to work for her, but doing nothing like this, nothing at all but lying around drinking and feeling sorry for herself—well, it was disgusting. You couldn't go on pitying a person who didn't even *try*, genius or no genius; it was poor *Mr.* Harewood she pitied, if the truth be known. She didn't blame him for hiding out down at the office until dinnertime every day.

Maud bent over the marketing list. "What kind of meat. . . . Oh, I don't know, Emma; I just can't think. My head is buzzing. And we have to have a first course. What could we have? Why don't you just make—anything." She looked up at Emma with distraught eyes and since Emma stood there stolidly, offering no suggestions, Maud made an excited gesture with her hands and said, "Oh, who cares anyway? Let's get it over with already, for God's sake, so much time wasted on just a dinner. Let's have tomato soup and chicken and string beans and canned fruit. I can't think of fancy menus. I can't think of anything!" Impatiently she scribbled the items on her marketing list, broke the point of the pencil on the k in "chicken" and hurled the pencil across the room. Then she dropped her head into her hands and gave a muted cry through clenched teeth.

Quietly Emma retrieved the pencil, sharpened it and returned it to Maud, who looked up at her with reddened eyes and apologized pathetically, "I'm just so nervous, Emma darling; my head feels like it's going to burst. Look how my fingers tremble! I can't help myself, Emma honey. I don't get any rest or sleep at all. What am I going to do?"

"A walk in the air will do you good," Emma said, handing her the marketing list.

Maud grabbed the slip of paper, picked up her purse and slammed out of the apartment, thinking that Emma was getting too lazy and impertinent lately and she'd better watch out; for what she was being paid, she could be replaced by someone who would take over completely.

She pressed the elevator bell and waited impatiently as it passed her and traveled up to the penthouse. Now here was a new irritation that even superseded her annoyance with Emma. Naturally, whenever she rang, the elevator had to go all the way up there; not just to the fourteenth or fifteenth floor, no, but right up to the penthouse. She counted to forty while it parked. Then she rang again, and counted ten and rang again, this time keeping her finger on the bell until her finger tip ached. "That'll show him." As soon as she stopped ringing, someone else rang, and finally the car began to move. "The whole building waiting," she muttered. The car stopped on the floor above, so Maud pushed the button once more. "Good Lord, how long, how long?"

At last the elevator door opened, revealing Terence's wrinkled face twisted sourly. "I can't be in two places at once, Mrs. Harewood."

Maud felt uneasiness at his reproof. These flash-tempers of hers weren't her fault, but she couldn't begin to explain this to the elevator man. Instead, she provided him with an excuse for his tardiness. "I'm sure some inconsiderate person was keeping you in spite of the fact that the bell was ringing."

She had chanced upon one of Terence's favorite beefs, so now he beamed at her. "Just what happened. Talk, talk, talk, while the bells keep goin' and what am I to do, Missus?"

"It isn't right." Maud sent an accusing look to the skinny old woman who looked incongruous in a mink jacket, standing in the opposite corner of the car. Was she the culprit?

But the old lady innocently mistook Maud's glance for a greeting and broke into a grateful smile as if she were not accustomed to being noticed. "I'm Mrs. Kerakis. Welcome to the building, Mrs. Harewood. We're all so proud to have you here." She rolled her r's softly with the faintest remnant of a Scottish childhood.

"You're very kind," Maud said unsmilingly and turned back to Terence who was inquiring if she was settled now and if there was anything he could do. She awarded him her complete attention to discourage any further neighborly advances on the part of this old woman. From experience, she had learned that only the direct snub proved efficacious and she had to protect herself from being overwhelmed by bores.

"I guess I'm as settled as I'll ever be in this house," Maud answered him, her back to Mrs. Kerakis.

"Something wrong?" He had a pleased expression, as if he really did want to know that something—anything—was wrong.

So Maud raised her eyebrows and looked put upon. She was not pretending. In all honesty, she felt she had been tricked into taking this apartment. Had she known a child lived above her, especially a boy. . . .

Mrs. Kerakis persisted, undiscouraged, eager in her loneliness for a word from anyone, and especially eager to establish contact with the author of *The Gesture* (which she had tried to read, but hadn't been able to understand), for she had great respect for any writer whose work was "too deep" for her. "You moved in 8B, Mrs. Harewood?" she queried, as if there had been any other vacancy in years, but Mrs. Kerakis talked only to be talking, only to hear an answering voice.

Maud gave her a cool nod, then looked away at once, tapping her fingers on the metal frame of her purse.

"Well what *is* wrong, Mrs. Harewood?" Terence insisted. Although they had arrived at the main floor, he kept the door shut to encourage the conversation.

She replied charmingly to him to emphasize the snub to Mrs. Kerakis. Actually, she hated having to do this, but it was a matter of self-protection. Everyone wanted to be the friend of a celebrated writer. "It's just a question of renting the wrong apartment, that's all. Mr. Gruppmann assured us that it was quiet. You can imagine how important quiet is to my work. He had no right to lie to us about it."

"But it should be quiet," Mrs. Kerakis said to the back of Maud's head. "Mine is."

"Yes," Terence said, not necessarily to agree with Mrs. Kerakis but more to prod Mrs. Harewood for further information.

"The traffic bother you?" Mrs. Kerakis wanted to know, "because you could put in air conditioners. That's what the Emmerichs did. He's very nervous, too."

This Maud couldn't ignore. It was an uncalled-for familiarity from a stranger who considered Maud her property simply because she had read her books. "It happens," she said coldly, "I'm a native New Yorker and traffic has never bothered me, Mrs. —— Mrs. ——"

"Kerakis. K—E—R——"

"Yes. You seem to think you know a great deal about me, but for your information, although I hardly know why it should concern you, I happen to be an easygoing, placid individual. But even the nerves of a saint would be shattered by those people upstairs."

"The Fays?" Terence asked.

"I guess that's their name."

"Oh, well, Robin!"

"That's the boy. He plays basketball in his room."

"No!"

"All you have to do is ask him to stop," Mrs. Kerakis volunteered. "I'm sure he will."

"No, he won't. I've asked this favor of him many times."

Mrs. Kerakis frowned hard.

Maud closed her eyes for a moment of painful recollection. "But it doesn't let up. Bouncing balls, jumping, pounding, all day, all night." She saw the boy in her mind, tall, fair, laughing. . . .

"Tsk, tsk," Terence said.

Mrs. Kerakis clamped her lips tight. "I can't believe it."

Maud gave her a cold stare. "It couldn't matter to me less, Mrs. —— Believe me." But suddenly she realized it did. She turned back to her friend, Terence, ostensibly to talk to him, but actually with a feeling of growing panic, to think how she could now win this dull little woman to her side. She hadn't meant to make an enemy, only to keep her in her place. A few years ago, she would have been able to carry off this little exchange with dignity and even with charm, but lately she had collapsed into a bundle of nerves and unpredictable emotions. "Look at me, Terence. I'm almost ready for a breakdown." Feeling that this might have touched the old woman, she turned back to her. "How long do you think a person can go without sleep? And in my case, I particularly need rest. I have to be fresh in order to work. Writing is a tremendous effort; you haven't any idea how hard it is." She noted to her satisfaction that Mrs. Kerakis was nodding, responding to her appeal. "Now wouldn't you think his parents would control that child, knowing I'm right below them, trying to accomplish something worth while? But they're as bad as he is. They have so much company—almost every night I have to call them and plead with them to close their windows, to lower their voices, to stop dancing, to turn the radio down, but they only laugh at me." Maud was carried away by her story, but even while reciting it, she felt a single twinge of guilt, which she was able to erase by assuring herself that only last night she remembered hearing the sounds of music and laughter from above.

"You talking about the Fays?" Mrs. Kerakis asked. "The Tyler Fays in 9B?"

Maud suppressed a sharp retort, recalling that for some reason she had changed her mind and wanted this old woman to like her. "I think so," she said. "Didn't you say that was the name?"

"Well!" Mrs. Kerakis snorted, her nostrils stretched so tight they turned dead white, "I happen to be one of their next-door neighbors and I've known Mr. and Mrs. Fay for fourteen years. I promise you, if they made the sort of noise you say they do, I would hear it and I would be the first to complain. And as for Robin, he's one of the dearest boys in the world and I will not listen to any vile words about any of them, especially from a rank stranger not three weeks in the building! And I don't care if you write books or pick potatoes!" With this, Mrs. Kerakis stalked out of the car.

"Listen to her!" Terence marveled.

Maud was speechless. She was shocked and afraid. She couldn't understand why this woman, who had seemed so eager to know her, should doubt her word and take the part of people like the Fays. She could have been her friend, the friend of Maud Harewood, and yet she had taken the part of the Fays.

Terence still chuckled. "Don't pay her no mind, Mrs. Harewood; she's bound to have a big mouth, though this is the first time I've heard her shoot it off. She don't belong in this house. She's not your kind. They say she's the widow of a gangster who got shot up years ago and she's livin' off his stolen money. She don't even know what she's sayin' half the time. Batty." He pointed to his head. "Nuts. Whenever there's anyone in the hall outside her apartment, she scares the livin' daylights outa them by peekin' out with one eye through a crack in the door. She's so crazy that she thinks they don't see her. But she's harmless."

"Are you sure? She seems like a dangerous person to me. If I weren't telling the truth, it would be different, but he does play basketball. Why only last night I had to call them. . . ." Maud's heart was pounding. She had done something wrong, but she didn't remember what it was. Everything was wrong for she had made an enemy instead of a friend.

"Listen, Mrs. Harewood, you don't have to tell me, because I know Robin Fay. Mrs. Kerakis likes him ever since he told her he was giving her a kitten, that's all. But I know him, a noisy, bad-mannered brat, who never says please or thank you or good day. But I fix his wagon." Terence nodded his satisfaction. "I don't let him run the elevator. The other men do, but not me. And what's more, he'll never run it while I'm on duty, and he knows it. He knows!"

"Oh, I—I really don't see how I'm going to be able to stay on in this house," Maud worried. "I really don't."

"Now don't be sayin' that, Missus."

"You have no idea——" Maud was still thinking fearfully of Mrs. Kerakis's reaction, although the cause of it had grown confused in her mind.

"I'll send Mr. Gruppmann up and you tell him; you tell all about Robin."

"Oh—Robin—yes. Well, I wouldn't want to do that. I wouldn't want to get them in trouble."

"Look, if they won't listen to you, they'll listen to him. There won't be no trouble. He'll just tell them, that's all. You're a famous bookwriter, Mrs. Harewood. Who is Robin? Nothin' but a fresh kid."

"That's true. He's being very disrespectful towards me."

"I'm sendin' Mr. Gruppmann to you this afternoon," Terence said firmly. "He'll take care of Robin for you. That boy will keep dead quiet after Mr. Gruppmann gets through with him."

"Do you really think it will make a difference?"

"I know it will. Now you stop worryin', Mrs. Harewood."

"You're so kind, Terence."

"Well, I'm here to tell you, no famous writer's gonna move out of here because of Robin Fay."

"You're very kind," Maud repeated.

The fresh air was cool on her face. The street scene delivered new impressions and another wave of irritation passed over her. She crumpled the marketing list into a ball in her hand but didn't dare to throw it away. If it wasn't one thing, it was another. Here nearly half the day was gone, and how had she spent it? Ordering a meal, wasting all this time on an aged gangster's moll and an old elevator man, attempting to bring about sufficient peace and quiet so she could work; and now, instead of being given the opportunity to sit at her desk, she would have to stand on line at the butcher's, the baker's, the candlestick-maker's. . . .

Things had gotten out of hand; that was the size of it; that was why she couldn't work. Hunt Parrish was right; she wasn't ruthless enough. Somehow she had let go of the reins with which she used to guide her life and hold it under control. Now everyone was walking all over her—Emma, the Fays, even Albert, pressing her into the role of a housewife. How did they dare? Was she wrong in claiming to have contributed enough to the world of letters to deserve better than this? Was she wrong to believe the products of her talent more important than the mending of a stocking, the buying of a pound of meat? Was she wrong in demanding the respect that was due her ability? But, of course, the treatment she was receiving was an old story. Ask any person of accomplishment and they would agree with her that little people always try to pull you down to their level, eternally try to compare themselves with you, like that old woman reducing the monstrous upheaval that had occurred in her life by attempting to pass it off as ordinary nervousness!

Their level. She had always avoided their level. But unfortunately, illness was a great leveler, the greatest, second only to death. She made a sound like a gasp, thinking that this was her cross, that they all knew she was too ill to write, and that this dragged her down, made her an object of pity rather than adulation. But her illness wasn't permanent and she would have her day again. Chemical changes were taking place in her body and these changes temporarily affected her emotional patterns, she told herself, repeating what the gynecologist had said to her. It would pass soon, very soon.

But the doctor didn't know about the horrors that spun around in her mind at night, or the explosions of fury that shook her over the least little setback, or the fear that strangled her, creeping up on her at any odd moment of the night or day, just as she had been so terribly afraid in the elevator before, and she couldn't think why. No, he didn't know of these things because she hadn't told him, wouldn't dare to tell him. . . .

Even the thought of the fear brought it on and she had to pause and lean against the wall of the building on the corner, choking and trying to swallow a lump that rose in her throat.

See what happened when they tried to force a sick woman to prowl the streets, stand on line and carry heavy bundles? Pitying tears stood in her eyes as she gathered herself together again, and, martyred, dragged herself around the corner to the butcher shop.

Meanwhile, Terence brought the elevator to the basement and shouted for Joe to relieve him for lunch. Joe slid into a uniform coat that was too small for him and pinned a black bow tie to his shirt. "Anything innarestin' goin' on? Anyone sick or dyin', Terence?"

Terence snorted. "You can joke, but let me tell you I never saw anyone look so miserable and sick as that poor Mrs. Harewood that moved into 8B."

"Change of life, Terence, just change of life."

"What do you know? You a doctor or somethin'? I'll tell you she's goin' through hell, that's what, plain hell with that noisy brat Robin livin' over her. Do you know what he does? Plays basketball in his room and won't stop even though he knows she's tryin' to write. That's no way to treat a famous bookwriter like her. I asked at the public library on my way home the other day, and she's really famous. That kid has a nerve."

"Cool off, Terence. He don't play all day because he's in school," Joe reasoned, "and he don't play all night because he's asleep. The truth is, if he plays basketball at home at all, he probly plays ten fifteen minutes before dinner, and what the hell's she workin' for at that hour anyways? This ain't no goddam office building!" He stepped into the car. "And what's more, I got it from the horse's mouth who happens to be her own maid, that she ain't written a line in over a year. Put that in yer pipe and smoke it!"

Terence muttered vilifications at the elevator door as it closed. Then he shuffled down the basement hallway jerking his right shoulder angrily. "We'll see about all this, we'll see." Joe was always contradicting him, always taking the other side, making a fight out of anything he said. This time he'd started to argue even before he'd had a chance to tell him about how Mrs. Kerakis had hollered at poor Mrs. Harewood. Well, it was no hair offa his chin; it was Joe's loss, him and his big mouth. Terence stopped before Klaus's door and knocked.

10 :   *Wednesday, April Twenty-ninth*

At four o'clock that afternoon, Klaus slammed into his apartment, threw his hat on the chair and strode into the kitchen where he tossed off two Scotches, one after the other. Then he flung himself into a chair and fumed. Gottemmed woman, she kept him almost an hour and now maybe he'd miss Rider and there'd be hell to pay. He reached for the phone and dialed Rider's number.

"Hallo, Mr. Rider! Lucky I still caught you. Gruppmann here." He made an unconscious little bow, a quick, respectful motion from the waist. "I'm awful sorry to call so late."

"Almost gave you up. What kept you?"

"Harewood, 8B."

"Uh-uh."

"You picked yourself some dilly there, Mr. Rider. She give me a helluva time."

"What about?" Rider's voice sounded weary.

"Noise."

"Oh, that north bedroom."

"No. The Fays."

"The *Fays!*"

[77]

"Ja. It seems they scream and yell and throw things and pound on the floor and jump up and down all day and all night. Robin plays basketball twenty-four hours a day. She says she can't rest or sleep or work and when she calls them to be quiet, they pay no attention."

"Well, I'll allow for a few typical Gruppmann exaggerations."

"Mr. Rider——"

"You serious?"

"Sure I'm serious. Well, Robin—perhaps she don't claim he plays basketball twenty-four hours a day, but almost. What a time I had! I tried to explain you could always hear some little noises from the walls and ceilings of all apartment houses."

"So——"

"So she gets all upset and says this isn't some little noises, it's a regular din and it never, never stops."

"Klaus, stop laying it on."

"So help me God, those are her very words. So to catch her, I told her I couldn't do anything about it unless they made noise before eight in the morning or after eleven at night."

"Very good, Klaus, you're becoming a real statesman."

"So she almost starts to cry, she says she's a sick woman and needs her rest and she's sorry she moved into this house, and if you could haf seen her wringing her hands there, I didn't know to be sorry for her or angry or vot——"

"Nobody's ever complained about the Fays before. Did you tell her that?"

"Sure I did. I spoke to her almost an hour. I told her maybe it was the Emmerichs she was hearing because they was pretty noisy people, but Gott in Himmel, you should haf heard her scream at me that it was Robin, Robin who done it."

"Tell me the truth, Klaus."

"Sure, Boss."

"I know you like the boy, but is there any reason why he should inspire such anger? First Mr. Parrish, now Mrs. Harewood——"

"Ja, there is."

"What?"

"He's the only kid in the building."

"That's right. I could almost be accused of being one of those landlords who refuse children and pets."

"Certainly not pets, Boss."

"No, I suppose that saves me. Well, to get back to our new friend. She screamed at you; so, of course, you screamed right back at her."

"No, no, I kept calm. I tried to quiet her."

"How? By shouting 'Shaddup!'?"

"Mr. Rider, please. I just said, 'Calm yourself, lady,' like that."

"Good for you."

"Then she got what you might call calm—like furious ice, so calm she trembled all over. I never saw such a thing, never. She asked ain't I gonna do anything about it, so I said real nice that Robin was entitled to amuse himself in his own home and what if he plays a little during the daytime? He's only a kid. I tried to joke her into it, you know."

"I know."

"So honest to Gr-r-rist, Mr. Rider, she come for me, I thought she was gonna hit me, but instead she pushed me outa the house and slammed the door in my face."

"A little woman like that? You're slipping, Klaus."

"Ja, I shoulda pasted her one, I suppose?"

"Listen, Klaus, all this is my own fault. I have a waiting list a mile long here in my files, all quiet, conservative, substantial citizens, but along comes a Big Name and I fall for it. I admit I was impressed and I've been bragging all over town that Maud Harewood is my tenant. Just to show you the kind of name-dropper I am, I've been mentioning her name and not her husband's, even though he's one of the most successful stockbrokers in the city. I'm a name-dropper and a snob and now we're——"

"No, no, Mr. Rider——"

"Yes, yes, Klaus. And you might as well know that you're the one to suffer for it because I'm going to be a real bastard and ask you to keep her out of my hair. I should have known better than to rent the apartment to a neurotic writer, but it's too late now. She's going to be a problem—those kind of people always are—and it's all yours. I'm sorry, Klaus."

"You can't help it—it's my chob——"

"I could have made it easier for you."

"Oh, forget it, Boss. I do my best. But just this one thing—what I gonna do next time she complains?"

"See that she doesn't. Take Robin aside sometime soon and speak to him. Ask him, man to man, to help you keep the old girl happy. Robin's a nice kid and he's fond of you. He'll co-operate."

"What am I gonna tell him not to do?"

"Not to bounce his basketball. That can be pretty noisy. They have a linoleum floor in there."

"And that's all? Because after all, a kid has a right to play."

"That's all."

"And if she still complains?"

"Tell her that legally there's nothing more you can do. Tell her to take it up with Tyler Fay."

"That's a lousy thing to do to such a nice fellow."

"Oh, he'll handle her. I'm sure he's had worse nuts to crack. We're going to have to pass the buck around—me to you, you to him."

Now Klaus was silent.

"You there, Klaus?"

"Yes."

"Anything else?"

"Oh, just a little thing—a leak in the bathroom in 17C. I called the plumber and he thought it came from upstairs."

"From where upstairs?"

Klaus answered grudgingly, "From the Marshes' apartment."

"Well, does it?"

". . . looks like——"

"That's the third leak this year."

"It's fixed now, Mr. Rider."

"You sure?"

"Sure I'm sure." Klaus said, looking unhappy.

11 :   *Saturday, May Second*

Although it was only eleven o'clock in the morning, the temperature had already reached seventy-eight in the shade and Flossie Marsh, perspiring on her contour chair out in the sun, had to ring for her maid to bring some Eau de Cologne and a fan. She put her book down and loosened her blue silk wrapper. She lifted her huge breasts out of the nightgown one at a time and sprayed the scented lotion on the hot skin underneath. Then she showered the cologne recklessly under her arms and over her chest and neck until she shivered from the touch of the breeze on the icy alcohol. A fat woman had to be extra careful about herself, and Flossie at all times was clean and fresh from her manicured toenails to her carefully coiffed head. In spite of this cologne bath, however, she was only momentarily cool. She replaced her wrapper and buttoned it modestly, for she expected Robin's regular Saturday visit. Already he was later than usual. She leaned back and fanned herself, whispering, "Whf! Whf!" at the unseasonable heat.

But in spite of it, it was a beautiful day and nowhere was it more beautiful than right here in her penthouse garden. Her lawn was coming up thick and rich and had the delicate color of spring green. The dogwood was in full bloom, spurting great pink and white blossoms and her gardens were a glory of color—masses of deep yellow jonquils, violet iris and multicolored tulips, behind which azalea bushes bloomed in pink, white and coral. Flossie could not remember another spring that had been this kind to her garden, not even that first year when it was photographed by all the magazines.

She looked out over the New York skyline from her chair under a pink dogwood tree. Lord, how good it was to be alive! She picked up her book again, Maud Harewood's *Child's Face Behind Bars*. Ever since Walt had brought her the news of the celebrated new tenant who had moved into Number Ten, she had been rereading Maud Harewood's works, hoping one day to make her acquaintance. It had been a pleasurable assignment, for Maud Harewood's books bore up admirably under a second reading; all but this one, her last. Flossie flipped through the pages thoughtfully. She wasn't at all sure what this book was about. The Child wasn't a child. It wasn't even human. Was it a symbol? And if so, a symbol of what? The fact that she couldn't understand this book disturbed Flossie no end, for she was a professional reader, one who occupied herself with books six to eight hours every day, whose taste and opinion were valued by several publishers of her acquaintance who often made use of her ability by presenting her with difficult manuscripts to evaluate. And for the life of her, she couldn't make head or tail of this weird hodgepodge which never should have been printed in the first place. Frowning, Flossie applied herself to the book once again. She turned back to the beginning. Perhaps she had missed some important clue. Perhaps she had read it too fast.

Beside her on the wrought-iron table were heaped all sorts of delicacies. There was a bowl of fruit and a pitcher of lemonade, a dish of chocolates, assorted licorice candies, lemon balls, pecans, dates and a tin of Turkish figs. Every once in a while, without lifting her eyes from the page, Flossie reached over and popped something into her mouth. She picked up the sweets with her left hand and turned the pages with her right. She had too much respect for books to soil their pages with sticky fingers.

The sound of the doorbell interrupted her reading. She pulled herself up and patted her brown hair into place. Behind her on the brick path sounded the click of Rover's paws, so she wasn't surprised when the little dog leaped onto her lap without permission, kissed her and then settled herself in the curve of Flossie's thighs with a sigh.

Flossie called hello to Robin and Robin smiled and lifted his hand in silent greeting. Slowly he removed his coat and hung it over the back of a chair. He selected some licorice candies and lay down on the new grass at Flossie's feet. Rover jumped down and tried Robin's belly as a bed, but finding it too lean, returned to her place on Flossie's soft lap. Flossie reached for a chocolate, ate most of it and gave the dog what was left.

Robin closed his eyes and Flossie thought he was asleep. She studied his peaceful face, pink from the heat of the sun, and noted with amusement how, in spite of how manly he thought he was, he still had baby eyelids, soft full cheeks and the tender lips of a little boy.

"You know, Flossie . . . ," he said slowly.

"I thought you were asleep."

"No, just thinking. You know what? You have all the good things for kids here—grass, trees, things to eat. You even used to have dogs." He paused.

"Everything but the children, eh?"

"Well, yes. I mean—do you mind? I know it's none of my business." He sat up and wound his arms around his knees, gazing up at her seriously.

"I don't mind at all, Robin. Walt and I wanted children, but somehow they never came. That's one reason why we're so fond of you. You're like a son to us."

"Boy, you picked a real dilly, you did," he said to cover his pleasure.

"Why do you ask, Robin?"

He flushed. "It's none of my business. But I just wanted to know if you ever wanted them. That was all that was important, wanting them, you know."

"Oh, I see," she said, but she was mystified.

"Do you care that you never had kids, Flossie?"

"Of course I care, Robin."

"You act so happy. I mean, you don't act as if it was a tragedy in your life."

"Well, it isn't."

"But I thought you said——"

"People make their own tragedies, Robin, for the most part. There's unhappiness in everybody's life. Take the most fortunate person you know and you'll find that something tragic has happened to him or will

[82]

happen to him before he dies. It's part of being alive to be unhappy at times. You have to put up with it; accept it, if you can't do anything else about it, and make something else do."

"Like you got Pete and Wendy?"

"Yes, in part. We got Pete and Wendy and then there was you, too, Robin."

"Oh, how I miss Pete and Wendy!" Robin sighed.

They were Flossie's two pug dogs who had died within one month of each other the year before.

"I miss them, too, but we shouldn't complain. They lived good long dogs' lives, thirteen years," she said. "Besides, why should you grieve so, you have your own Rover?"

She could see him calculate Rover's remaining years and glance worriedly at her. "What I can't stand is the way things change," he said.

"Like what for instance, Robin?"

"Oh, you know—everything. Like Pete and Wendy dying."

Flossie knew this was evasion and that something quite different lay at the heart of Robin's mood, but she also knew that he might or might not tell her about it, all in his own good time. Meanwhile, the tin of figs was out of her reach and she asked Robin to pass them to her. "I'm so darn fat, I can't even reach over any more."

He handed her the tin, then lay down again on the grass. Once more he was silent for a long time. Then, "You know, Flossie. . . ."

"Yes?"

"I was just thinking. I bet I know why you stay so fat."

"Oh, you do, do you?"

"I think so."

"Well, tell me."

"Sure you won't be mad?"

"Promise."

"It's so you won't have to work in ladies' clubs and sell tickets for charity and go downtown shopping and cook and clean all day, because that's what you'd have to do, isn't it, if you weren't too fat to move? That's woman's work, isn't it?"

"Well!" She was taken by surprise and didn't know what to answer. "Well!" she repeated.

"Isn't it true? I mean, for instance, if you didn't do your own housework, you'd have to be a clubwoman or something. You couldn't just do nothing like you do?"

Flossie looked away for a painful moment, then turned back to meet his serious gaze. "I guess so," she said. She even managed to smile at him.

"So this way you get to do what you love best, and no one can stop you. Mother says you know more about literature than most college professors."

"And is that 'doing nothing,' Robin?"

"Well, no, but I mean, it's what you like to do. You don't have to do what you don't like to do."

"I have to die and pay taxes."

But he didn't smile. He was too intent on working out some private problem of his own. "Some people are so nice, no matter what," he said.

"I hope that includes me."

He nodded and slowly got to his feet. "Of course it does."

"Even though I'm a lazy good-for-nothing?"

He was shocked. "Flossie, you're not!"

She shook her head. "Then I'm afraid I don't know what you're trying to say, Robin."

His eyebrows met and formed the edge of a crevice, shadowing his eyes underneath. "Yes, well . . . I don't know. Things are just—different and I'm trying to figure out why." His voice trembled suspiciously and he was silent.

"What is different, Robin?"

"Oh," he murmured, "nothing."

"I wish you'd let me try to help you."

"I guess I don't feel like talking about it any more, Flossie."

Worried, she searched his face for clues. "There's nothing wrong between you and your parents?"

"Gosh, no."

"Well, then——"

"Really, I don't want to talk about it."

"All right, then," she obliged him. "Say, kid, promise not to tell anyone, now."

"What?"

"About why I stay so fat."

"I won't."

"It's our secret."

But she shouldn't have said that. It sounded patronizing. It was the way one spoke to a child and he gave her a quick glance to see if she was teasing him. "Okay." He pulled Rover's leash from his pocket and attached it to her collar. "I have to go now. Thanks for everything, Flossie."

"So soon?" His visits grew shorter every year. When he was a little fellow, he used to stay all morning and delight her with his chatter. But today he was like an old man with the weight of the world's problems on his shoulders and he was leaving before she had further opportunity to pry into the source of his confusion.

"It's almost time for lunch."

"All right, kid, run along."

"See you next Saturday. Tell Walt I'm sorry I missed him."

"Will do."

As soon as he was gone, Flossie's smile faded. She leaned back and stared at the blue, cloudless sky. The candor of childhood could be charming at times, but it could also cut deeply. For example, what Robin thought of her (in spite of his shocked denial). Nothing better than a lazy, spoiled woman who fled from her natural duties and hid under the protection of extreme obesity. Why had he decided this? Why to her disfavor when he could have thought of other more gentle reasons? She felt scolded, chidden and disapproved of. It was not like Robin to take the negative view.

Undoubtedly, he compared her immobility to his mother's energy and could find no reason for it other than selfish escape, but from what climate had he picked this decayed fruit? Certainly not from the easy, kindly atmosphere of his own home. Certainly not from Julie or from Ty. What was rotten in Denmark?

Oh, well, she told herself, at any rate it was better to have him think this of her than to know the truth and perhaps grieve over it; better to have his disapproval than his pity. She took a deep breath and passed her tongue over her underlip. There was a small element of respect in disapproval, but pity was nothing but degradation, pity was. . . . Suddenly she slapped the arm of her chair, abruptly cutting the thread of her thoughts. "Can't let this get you," she whispered, and looked about her, forcing her eyes to drink in the beauty of her garden until she was revived. Yes, she avowed, her life was charmed and she was blessed to have such beauty to sustain her. How could she have a sad or complaining thought surrounded by all this? Her gaze traveled lovingly from one bright glory to the other, letting them prove to her anew her good fortune. Her garden and Walt and a few close friends to visit. No one could ask for more. Serenity returned and automatically reaching out, she took another fig from the tin.

She heard the terrace door open and her heart gave a little jump as it always did when Walter came home. When he was gone, in spite of the beauty about her, she was aware of an uneasy void out here, but when he was with her, then the garden was complete.

He came from behind and slid his hands over the blue silk that covered her shoulders. "Hi, babe." He bent and kissed her. "Jesus, you smell good!" He cupped his hand under her breast and pressed his face into the curve of her neck.

She shivered pleasantly and put her arms around him. "That's the 'Replique' you gave me," she whispered.

"Mmm, it's——" He pulled away from her as the maid came out with a tray. His normally red face flushed deeper and he lowered his eyes, embarrassed, as he shoved the sweets aside and helped her make room on the table. Walt was far from a prude, but he loathed public displays of affection. To cover his embarrassment, he turned his back to the maid. Flossie grinned at him, enjoying the sight of his discomfiture. It was the little boy in a man that she loved second best. Here was Walt, big, heavy-set (some might even call him beefy, she conceded), with much grey in the red stubble of his crew cut, with folds already forming on his neck, furrows on either side of his snub nose and lines about his small blue eyes—but boyish with it all, evincing a boy's embarrassment at being caught fondling his own wife at the age of forty-nine! She loved the bashful way he smiled under her amused scrutiny, and the way he tried to speak casually, as if undiscovered. "I caught Robin at the elevator. He gets taller every week." He watched the maid walk back into the apartment.

"He was in a miserable mood today," Flossie said.

"What was the matter?" Walt's red face dripped perspiration and he mopped it with his handkerchief. "This is a scorcher. Eighty in the shade already. Mind if I take off my jacket?" He slipped it off before she said yes. He also removed his tie and looped it over the back of the chair and unbuttoned his shirt. Then he spooned ice cubes into the cocktail shaker.

"He wasn't his usual happy self at all."

"He's thirteen, Floss, the age of masturbation and guilt."

"You and your psychology books!"

"If you're so worried about him, why don't you speak to Julie?"

She gave him a grateful look. Already he was handing her the telephone which was extended by an extra-long cord from the living room. "You're sure it isn't meddling?"

"Of course it's meddling. So what?"

She dialed. Julie's greeting sounded cautious. Her voice was breathy with relief when she recognized Flossie. "Never know these days if it's friend or foe."

"Why, you haven't an enemy in the world! What's the matter with the whole bunch of you? Is Robin home yet?"

[86]

"Yes. Anything wrong?"

"Can he hear you?"

"Not at the moment. He's still in his room."

"Well, he was just up here and I didn't like the way he acted, Julie. Not that it was anything serious, but he seemed upset."

"In what way?"

"It's hard to put a finger on it. He was almost impolite."

"Robin?"

"Oh, he said thank you and all that, of course. No, impolite isn't the word. Bitter, that's it. He seemed old and bitter. I couldn't follow the drift of his conversation at all. He seemed disturbed over the question of change, among other——"

"Ah ha!"

"If I didn't know you and Ty so well, I would have called him insecure."

"Well, that does it, Flossie." Julie's voice was sharp as backfire. Then it softened. "I'm glad you told me. You're a real friend."

"Is there anything I can do?"

"No, thanks, but I promise that by next Saturday, Robin will be his old self again."

"There isn't something wrong with you and Ty?"

"Lord, no! . . . Oh, yes. Yes, it certainly is the hottest day I can remember in May." Julie's voice changed again. Robin must have come into the room.

"All right, kid, I know you can't talk now. But let me hear, will you? I'm anxious."

"Don't be. Nothing to it. Thank you for calling."

Flossie replaced the receiver and Walt put the telephone back on a small table. "Feel better now?" He mopped his hairline, drawing the handkerchief over the stiff bristles of his hair which lay flat for a second and then popped straight up again in a damp brush.

"Frankly, no. Julie couldn't talk."

"Oh, you women, worry, worry over nothing. Robin's okay. Let the poor kid live. And let's us live, too. How about you and me having a sociable little drink?" Walt handed her a glass. "Best damn Scotch sour in New York," he boasted, holding his glass up to the light. "What do you say, babe?"

"I've had better somewhere, I'm sure."

"Old bitch."

"Young bitch, please."

"At forty-two a dame ain't no spring chicken, love."

[87]

"Forty-one and don't you forget it. Look who's talking age? Old goat!"

He grinned. "Just cutting my booze teeth, honey." He applied himself to his drink to demonstrate and drained the glass. "I've got a peachy story for you. Clean, too."

"No kidding, clean?" She leaned her head back and waited, a smile ready on her lips.

"Mike was a jumpy guy who'd never kept a job. After a few weeks, he'd always quit, saying the work made him nervous. His friends worried about him until at last he got the calmest, easiest job in the world in a potato-packing plant. All he had to do was sit in a comfortable chair and sort out the potatoes into three piles, small, medium and large. His friends relaxed, positive that at last he had found his niche in the world, but after two weeks, he quit. By now everyone was disgusted with him. 'For crying out loud, Mike, the easiest job in the world!' they objected. 'Easy?' he screamed. 'Easy? My God, I was a nervous wreck. How'd you like it, all day long from nine to five, nothing but decisions, decisions, decisions?' "

Flossie laughed heartily, from deep within her chest. None of your delicate ripples for her. Walt mopped his hot face and rolled up the sleeves of his shirt, exposing powerful forearms covered with bright red hair. "I knew you'd like it."

"I have one for you now."

"Fine. You haven't told me a joke in ages." Walt poured himself a third drink.

"Hey, old man, aren't you hitting it hard?"

"Quit it, Floss, don't be a nag."

"I'm not nagging. I was only going to suggest that you switch to straight Scotch, that's all, touchy."

"Not a bad idea." Walt emptied the Scotch sour back into the shaker and poured straight whisky into his glass with a lump of ice. His eyes were bloodshot and his face a beefy scarlet. Little red capillaries appeared all at once like lace in his cheeks. "How about you?"

Flossie considered a moment. "Okay, pour a little Scotch—just a little—that's fine—hey, I said——"

"I don't like to get potted alone, babe."

"You aren't. I assure you I am peeling no fain."

"Drink up, come on."

She obliged with a good gulp.

"Now tell me that joke."

"Okay, if I can talk straight. Three little French boys, aged seven, nine and eleven, went for a walk in the park in the evening. . . . My God, I'm beginning to feel good! Wow!" She kicked her feet and one slipper went sailing across the lawn and landed in a clump of orange azaleas. Chuckling, he fetched the slipper and tickled her foot as he fitted it back on. She retaliated by threatening him with the contents of her glass. "Sit down and behave yourself now."

"You going to tell that joke or not?"

"If you let me. Three French boys, aged seven, nine and eleven walking in the park in the evening. The seven-year-old stops. 'Oh look,' he says. 'Zere is a couple in zere behind ze bushes. Zey are naked and zey are having a most terrible fight!' The nine-year-old looks. 'It is true zat zere is a naked couple behind zose bushes,' he says, 'but zey are not fighting. Zey are making love.'"

Walt finished it for her: "So the eleven-year-old looks. 'Yes,' he says, 'and badly, too.'"

"Oh, you heard it."

"I told it to you."

"You didn't."

"Sure I did. Last week."

"Damn, I can never tell you anything!"

The maid came out to set the table for lunch.

"I don't want to eat now. I want to preserve my glow," Walt said.

"Well, I'm famished."

So Walt held on to the Scotch bottle and continued to drink while Flossie ate. She knew better than to cross him now by informing him that his "glow" was irretrievably drowned, as indicated by the appearance of the capillaries on his face. He'd find out soon enough. Poor Walt always took a few too many and then bellyached because he couldn't drink.

"You can eat and then put on a new glow later. I can't," he was saying now. "Women get all the breaks."

She continued to eat unconcernedly. "Nevertheless they say it's a man's world."

"What a laugh!" He took a long swig of Scotch because he knew secretly that the glow was slipping away from him and he was beginning to feel mean. He had to bring back the proper balance, and this was a delicate maneuver. "Even in sex you got it all over us. You can go on and on and on——"

"Perhaps, but who's got the energy? We could, but we can't."

"Nothing you women can't do if you make up your mind to it," he said meaningfully. "Now, Flossie . . . Jesus, Flossie, can't you give yourself a break?"

[89]

"I always give myself a break, old man." She helped herself to another portion of chicken salad.

"Will you please let me call that doctor from Baltimore?"

"You know he won't do any more for me than the others."

"He's got this new extract——"

"I know all about it. Diet and injections. How many times have I dieted and taken injections? You know it's hopeless. I'll always be fat. I'll always be a cripple——"

"Baby, you're no cripple." He got up and came around to caress her clumsily. "I only want to go to Europe—just once—and I want you to come with me."

"Fine traveling companion I'd be. Too big even to fit in a wheel chair."

"Yes, you'd be fine. You could try. You could make the effort."

"If I thought for one moment that you would enjoy a trip with me, don't you think I'd go? But I couldn't go sight-seeing with you, I couldn't go night-clubbing with you, I couldn't even take a walk. I'd be a regular whiz in Europe, I would, and how would you feel locked in a hotel room with me, or taking in the sights and leaving me alone?"

He was beginning to get dizzy now and the glow was all gone. He went back to his seat and poured one more. This would be the last. If the glow didn't come back, it would be the last.

"Why don't you fly over for a few weeks alone? I swear I want you to. I went abroad many times with Dad, but you've never been. You could have a wonderful time and get rid of that wanderlust of yours. Fool around with some of those cute little French women—up to a point, I mean—and then come home to Mama."

Walt lapsed into silence. He knew she meant it, she wasn't being falsely noble. It would console her to know she wasn't imprisoning him. But, oh, she was, he thought gloomily, she was. Without knowing it, she had him tied to her so tight he could never escape. He took another sip of his last Scotch and waited vainly for the returning glow.

Of course, he'd had his little flings. Though Floss didn't know it, he'd had them all right, on business trips. There was that pretty gal that time in Tacoma. Kitty. God she had a beautiful face! Figure too skinny for his taste, but good for tight clothes, with fine breasts and a cute fanny. When she danced the rhumba with him they were so tight together you couldn't get a tissue paper in between. She showed him what the hell the rhumba was for. Back at their table in the corner of the night club, like a green kid, he couldn't keep his hands off her, so they didn't bother to finish their dinner. It was her own fault she didn't get fed.

And there was another brunette—he forgot her name—but it had been dancing in a different way with her. It was in Washington, D.C., and Tubby Wagner sent her up to his room as a gift along with a magnum of champagne, and they drank most of it and then she did a certain special dance for him.

But in the end, no matter if it was the girl Kitty from Tacoma or that brunette from Washington or any other girl he'd tried it with anywhere, it was always the same when they finally got down to it; when he held them naked in his arms, there was nothing there but skin and bones, ribs and sharp hips, nothing to grab hold of, no woman to them, just ornaments in pretty dresses and sexless string beans undressed, and he couldn't do it; nothing would happen, nothing at all.

He finished his Scotch and, of course, it hadn't brought back the glow. Some people could drink and drink and get happier, but not he; he couldn't even do that, couldn't drink, couldn't philander, couldn't travel. . . . He put the bottle away. Resentfully he glanced at Flossie eating so peacefully across the table, her brown hair neatly waved, her youthful face rosy and serene, so content, so unaware of how he was tied to her, of how he was her slave and could never get free. He picked up his fork and began to eat in sullen silence.

The food made him feel a little better and a cup of steaming coffee cleared his head and banished some of his alcoholic resentment. Now he looked upon her massive body with compassion. Poor Floss! Perhaps she was right. What good could that doctor from Baltimore do her? She had always been stout. She was a pretty big gal when he married her, but light on her feet and a fine horsewoman, the best in the state of Arizona. But even then, though she exercised and took care, she kept gaining. No, he wouldn't want to see the poor gal go through all that again: the starvation diets and those needles and pills and the periodic weighing-in, and the tears as each week brought no results and the doctor accused her of cheating. And after six months of sleepless nights and taut nerves, maybe a fifteen-pound loss; or once it had been seventeen or eighteen—a drop in the bucket—and she'd ended up with anemia to boot, sick and weak and still not able to get around.

He took a second cup of coffee and felt even better. No, he wouldn't mention that man from Baltimore again. Nor would he mention Europe. If Flossie loved to eat, let her. She would always be crippled by obesity and the arthritis that it caused, and to force her to diet in order to travel with him would be cruel. So the hell with traveling. There was nothing wrong with his life as it was. She was a sweet, game kid and he hoped he hadn't hurt her with all his drunken nonsense.

With his head bent over his plate, he observed her secretly and saw the calm, unlined face of his wife as she crushed a strawberry with her strong white teeth. She was used to him when he drank. She never took his complaints to heart. He smiled at her across the table and she smiled back. "Feeling better," she said. It was a statement. He nodded, more ashamed than before. He was a real bastard to rub it in. As if she didn't know how much of life she was missing! No theaters; she was too fat to fit into the seats; no concerts, no movies, lectures, swimming, tennis, horseback-riding or golf. No night clubs or dancing. Not even a short walk in the sun. She could barely last a block once she was pulled to her feet, and to see her struggle up that one step at the building entrance. . . . Yet she bore it all without complaint and made the most of her solitude by reading and study. Floss was a real Person, an admirable human being.

As well as a Woman—and what a woman! A real hunk of woman. Something to love, was Flossie. None of your skinny clothespins with built-in femininity; no, sir. Sure he was bound to her, but she was a warm and loving mistress, so what was he complaining about? Walt got up and came around the table to her. He sat on the edge of her chair. "This is a woman!" he murmured. He passed his hands over her softness, her soft fullness, her skin smooth and flawless, scented and warm. He laughed. "Remember, honey? 'Acres and acres of it and it's mine, all mine!'" She laughed, too, and turned towards him. He pressed himself against her, felt all of her surround him like warm foam, full soft breasts and belly and the grandeur of her thighs.

It was not easy to interrupt, but they were in the garden after all, in full view of other roofs, and the maid would be back any moment. He pulled himself away and suddenly felt cold and incomplete without her great and wonderful body enfolding him. "Come on, Floss." He stood up and held out his hand. He helped her up from the chair and they went into the bedroom.

12 :   *Saturday, May Second*

Automatically Maud noted, glancing from her window, that it was the kind of day when her doctor would want her out in the fresh air. Ordinarily she paid little attention to his instructions, but today was one of those rare times when she happened to remember them, so immediately after lunch she retired to the bedroom to dress. She was still in her nightgown but had already slipped into her shoes and stockings when Albert came in wearing a new coconut-straw hat with a red and tan silk band, jaunty as a college boy at his twenty-fifth reunion. "I'll be at the club if you want me, dear," he smiled and his eyes rolled huge and indefinite behind his spectacles. All she could do was stand there and stare at him as he straightened the overlap of his double-breasted jacket and touched his pocket to make sure a handkerchief was there. "See you about six, dear." With that, he was gone. He hadn't bothered to notice that she was getting dressed. He hadn't even considered the possibility of spending a Saturday afternoon in the sun with her, even though he knew very well she was supposed to take walks and be out of doors. Did he honestly expect her to go into that park alone to be molested by every bore who recognized who she was? Or worse still, to stay at home by herself, entirely by herself on Emma's day off? Wasn't it bad enough that she had to spend every weekday in solitude, twiddling her thumbs until he came home (not at five or five thirty like other men, but seven, seven thirty—as late as he could)?

Oh, she knew what was up. It had been a different story when she was producing, when she was healthy and able to work herself into exhaustion, only to push the typewriter aside the moment she heard him come through the front door, to rise and greet him with a cheery smile although she was still confused between the world of her own creation and the world of reality and all she was fit for was her bed. It was different then, when *she* was the one to make the effort, to pretend she wasn't tired, to sit and listen to his interminable stories of dull finance, the state of the market, who bought what stock and who made a mint or lost a fortune today, and why. Different when she was still an active celebrity for whom the telephone rang constantly, to whom invitations poured in from all over the world, to whom the elite came on bended knee—*yes, on bended knee!*—to offer banquets and cocktail parties in her honor—and all the favors that went along with her fame, like the Captain's Table on board ship and an invitation from the President of the United States. It was different then. Albert was only too glad to be with her. *Be* with her? Why he stuck to her like a jellyfish. He preened in public when their photographs were taken; he was officious and pompous in restaurants.

But now that she was sick and couldn't write, she was as much of a has-been to him as to the others. It didn't seem to occur to him that all his millions couldn't bring him one iota of the public attention her fame had brought, or that if she was a has-been, then he was something lower still, the husband of a has-been, and if he suffered from public neglect, how did he suppose she felt?

How quickly they had all run away, and how complete was their disappearance! Look how alone she was; even her editor and her agent had stopped calling her. It was over six months since she'd heard from either of them and two or three years since she'd seen any of her so-called friends. Although Albert stubbornly referred to her illness as having started about a year ago, actually it had been much earlier than that—two years before that, while she battled it out at the typewriter, writing words she didn't want to write, words that forced themselves onto the typewritten page with a will of their own, words she couldn't control or organize. "Experimental," she had called the book to cover up, and as such, her publishers had printed it, but not without skepticism which was reflected in the small first printing they produced.

The day it was reviewed in the Sunday *Times* and *Herald Tribune*, the telephone remained ominously silent: no call from her editor and only a short, embarrassed word from her literary agent. To comfort her, clumsy Albert said, "Well, darling, everybody's entitled to one flop. Forget it and begin on another."

That marked the end of the battle for her. She took to her chaise longue and refused to speak to the few who finally did call. It was a rotten world peopled with false friends. She was through with all of them. Write a good book and they come rushing over to celebrate with you—champagne, caviar, the press—oh, those Sundays when the rave reviews came out! But make one mistake, produce one confused novel borne of your heartbreak and illness, and whish! . . . Now they're here, now they've vanished for good.

And Albert was no different from the rest of them. So get back to your chaise longue, old woman, because that's all that's left you.

She stretched out flat and closed her eyes. She tried to imagine herself in death, but the heat of the day prevented her from conjuring up the frozen state that would eventually be her end. Perspiration coursed from her hairline and traveled down behind her ears to the nape of her neck where it soaked into the cushion of the chaise.

Outside the sun was golden on the walls of the courtyard. All the windows in the building were open and voices drifted up clear and magnified by the eternal echo. Musical notes jarred against each other as radios, victrolas and television sets poured forth competitive rhythms. Maud lay and listened. She rarely heard a sound from the apartment upstairs any more. What were they doing, the fools, going about on tiptoe, whispering, as if she were a patient soon to die? Or were they out today?

She slid off the chaise longue and approached the window. She leaned out and listened hard. She concentrated upon the room directly above hers, for that was his room, where he dressed and undressed, slept, read, did his homework and played, every day growing taller, stronger, wiser, forming into a man. She imagined the smell of his room, the clean smell of a youth still beardless, with the smooth skin of a child. She imagined his bathroom: damp towels hung carelessly, some fallen to the floor, the soap floating in jelly in the soap dish, his toothbrush encrusted with leftover, drying toothpaste and his comb and brush not altogether clean. His drawers were filled with chewing-gum wrappers and bits of old, hidden candy bars, the chocolate grown white and dry, and broken objects of every variety that long ago had lost their usefulness for him, but which he could not bring himself to throw away, for who knew when he would need a yellow plastic wheel or an enameled Canadian maple leaf with the pin torn away? Papers in those drawers, too, old calendars and baseball schedules, and spelling tests and history notes, shoved away because his mother told him to clean up his room and ignored even now when he shook a fraying baseball card from inside the undershirt he was going to wear.

All this she saw in her mind, peering upwards at where he lived, straining to hear a single sound, wishing to hear it, but not wanting to: the dichotomy of her feeling for the boy.

And then it came. Above all the other voices, above the cacophony of music, the clash of pots and dishes—Robin laughed.

Pain tore across her eyeballs and soothing tears sprang up as she strained to hear more and caught only small, indefinite sounds that might or might not have been made by him. She closed her eyes to sharpen her hearing and tried to imagine what he could be doing, and at last she heard a small yelp which brought on a new peal of laughter from the boy, so then she knew he must be playing with his dog.

Oh Lord, such happiness! Hear the pure laughter, brought on by the antics of a small animal! Oh God, feel the weight of that great cone of happiness that spread down from those rooms above and sifted in here to send spasms of pain shooting through every part of her body! She covered her face and pressed her fingers against her eyes, trying not to cry. She was going to have to control herself and forget. Of course she had to forget. Remembering was the root of all her trouble. If only she could forget as she used to, then her sickness would leave her, she would be well again, she would write again and everyone would come crawling back to her.

But it wasn't as simple as forgetting alone. One had to understand

and, most important, to believe as well. Even though they had told her there was nothing she could have done, still doctors were like that, they never told the truth once it was too late to make a difference anyway. They kept insisting that neither she nor Albert had made a single mistake, but she couldn't believe them. If she did believe them, then she was lost. No, they were lying to her to protect her, and it was trauma, trauma that had made him that way, trauma inflicted by Albert or herself. It had to be.

For instance, being a writer, hadn't she neglected him often? Needing her, and being so tiny and unable to express his need, while she clicked away at the typewriter in her room?

Or perhaps if they had tried to love him more?

But she had not written much in those days, and never except at night when he was asleep. She was always around, always. And they had loved him—God, they had—with all the power of love within them, and even this had not been enough, for they had never heard such laughter, or any laughter, ever.

So shut up, shut up, up there. What are you trying to do to me!

She pressed her hands to her ears now, but Robin's laughter resounded in her head, bounced from side to side, became so tangible that she could see it as well as hear it, his laughter which was barrel-shaped, dark and twisting, growing larger and louder. . . .

No, this was too much, it was inhuman to torture a person so. It had to stop, it couldn't go on and on like this or she would go. . . . No, she wouldn't—no!

She ran into the foyer and pulled the telephone to her. Her fingers trembled as she dialed and the knuckles of her left hand whitened around the receiver. It was Mrs. Fay who answered. "Please, Mrs. Fay, please, why doesn't the boy go out into the sunshine on such a nice day?" Maud cried. "Must he play so—so noisily with his dog? I know how hard it is to keep a boy quiet, I've had a boy of my own, but really, Mrs. Fay, if you could only hear how it sounds down here, if you could only understand what it's doing to me. . . ." She paused to clear her throat.

Mrs. Fay was silent on the other end. Maud waited, then said weakly, "Mrs. Fay?" She heard the sound of breathing. "Are you there, Mrs. Fay?"

"Yes." Another pause.

"Well, won't you please help me? I'm sure——"

"Now you listen carefully to what I have to say. Are you listening, Mrs. Harewood? Robin hasn't made a sound all day. Nor all week. We've gone out of our way to live as silently as you would have us do, but this time you've gone too far. I don't know what your motives are, and I don't care any more. There is such a thing as invasion of privacy. From now on, I expect you to stop annoying us. You've taken advantage of our respect for you as a writer, and in doing this, you have made us lose all respect for you as a person. I promise you I won't hesitate to make a formal complaint if you ever bother us again. I mean that. Never call this number again, do you hear? Or I swear you'll be sorry. Good-bye."

The receiver fell from Maud's hand and clattered to the floor. She sank into the chair staring at the telephone which menaced her. She shook her head slowly, trying to clear it so she could understand what awful thing had happened. For something terrifying had happened, she knew that. Something dangerous. All she had done was call—make a telephone call, that was all. She had called because—because he was making noise, and she couldn't sleep. And he was making noise. She'd seen him up there in his room with the dog, making noise on the floor to hurt her; all he did was try to hurt her. And now, what would they do? Something fearful. . . .

She tried to dial Albert at his club. Twice she had to hang up and try again. At last she got him. "Come home quickly," she whispered, "Hurry!"

Albert found her slumped over the telephone, her head on her arm. He called her name and ran to her, thinking she had lost consciousness, but she moved, she lifted her head and he saw that her eyes were dark with fear. Perspiration sparkled on her white face and she shivered.

"What happened?"

She opened her mouth several times and tried to speak. She sipped the water he offered her, but she shook her head when he wanted to take her to bed.

"Then what? What, Maud?"

". . . so frightened!" she whispered.

"Of what?"

"The people upstairs . . . going to make a formal complaint against me . . . try to put me away . . . I don't know . . . I only called them . . ."

Something whirred in Albert's head and for a moment he thought he was going to black out. With horror he saw her queer stare and noted her incoherency, the crazy things she whispered, though there was no smell of alcohol on her breath. "Please, Maud," he murmured and drew his hand across his forehead.

"Oh, be good to me, I'm so terribly frightened!" She threw herself against him.

[97]

"It's all right," he said mechanically. "There's nothing to be afraid of. I'm here." He led her into the bedroom and sat with her on the edge of the bed until she stopped crying. "Now tell me," he said, dreading to hear her speak again.

But she told a straight story. She hadn't mentioned the noise from upstairs before because she thought she could handle it herself. It seemed such a simple problem and for a while she was successful in controlling it, but today it had started again. And all she had done about it was to make one little telephone call, a polite request. . . .

As he listened to her, his fear turned to indignation, for the very proof of the truth of her story lay in her face, grey-white and exhausted. It was obvious that she had not been able to rest as the doctor ordered. "You should have told me about this long ago," he said. "Now calm down. They can't do anything to you."

But she wouldn't be convinced. "They can twist things, say things that would sound——"

"Nonsense. You leave that to me. Rest that imagination of yours, and from now on, please stop sparing me, Maud. You're the one who isn't up to snuff. Just look at yourself! And all because of one rowdy, thoughtless family. I'll take care of it right now. I'll pay them a little visit and have it out, once and for all."

"Would you? Oh, Albert, if you only would! Because I really can't take it any more. It's too much. It isn't fair. I've had more than my share, you know that. I've got to get well, Albert."

"You will."

"Because if they don't stop, I'm going to have to move. I mean it. To a hotel, anywhere——"

"That won't be necessary. What's their number?"

". . . but she said never to call——"

"The hell with what she said! I'm taking over now, and I'll deal with him, not her. What's the number?"

Ty glared at the telephone after he shoved it away from him and felt the constraint of anger in his stomach. "Julie!" he bellowed.

"In the bedroom, honey."

He strode in and slammed the door behind him. A man had to be a man in his own home. "What happened between you and Mrs. Harewood today?" The situation had gotten ridiculously out of hand. It was childish, kid stuff already.

Julie smiled as if remembering a delicious secret. "How do you know about it?"

"Never mind. What happened?"

"She called again, that's all."

"Oh she did! And where was I?"

"In the bathroom."

"I was, was I?"

"So I told her a thing or two. Now don't look like that, Robin wasn't making a sound——"

"I know that. But why did you take things into your own hands? I thought it was understood that I was going to take care of it from now on?"

"What's the difference who does it as long——"

"I said I was going to do it! You could have called me!"

"You were reading there for an——"

"All you had to do was call me! Goddammit, Julie——!"

"Tyler Fay, a locked bathroom door may mean nothing to you, but I happen to respect it. And I suppose I can't tell her off just as capably as you?"

"I know you can't. It just so happens that was Mr. Harewood on the telephone and he's coming up to have it out with me right now. What did you say to her?"

"I told her never to call this number again. Anything wrong with that?"

"What else?"

"I told her that if she did, I'd make a complaint. That there was such a thing as invasion of privacy. I spoke very well, if I say so myself. I used my 'terrible' voice."

"Fine, fine. You did a neat job, you did!" Ty pounded his fist against his palm. "A—neat—job!"

"You're shouting at me!"

"I never shout."

"You are shouting and I won't stand for it!"

Robin edged in. "Hey, what's going on here?" His voice sounded frightened.

"Oh, don't mind us. We're yelling at each other, but we don't mean it. Just fed up with those Harewoods, that's all," Julie said.

"What'd I do now?"

"Who knows, but he's coming up."

"He is? Good! You give it to him, Pop!"

"I will, if your mother——"

"Tyler Fay, I didn't——"

"Hey, please, quit it, you two."

Ty controlled himself by taking a deep breath, then smiled at his son. "Sorry, Robin, but you know your mother has always wanted me to lose my temper for the sake of my health."

"Well, I take it back," Julie said. "I didn't know what I was saying."

"All right now. I'm calm. But you've got to let me do the talking, do you hear? And you, Robin, I want you out of here. Take Rover for a long walk."

Robin looked perplexed.

"Dad thinks it would be easier if you were out of the house, that's all. You haven't done anything wrong."

"Hell, no! Sorry if I sounded rough, but these Harewoods have a special effect on me. You're a good kid, Rob, and you've done nothing wrong."

"Darn right I've done nothing wrong! I'm getting sick of feeling like I was a criminal or something, and that damn old bitch better stop this or I'll really give her something to bitch about and I mean that."

"Whoa there, slow down!"

"Sorry, but there comes a time when a guy's got a right to curse, even in front of his mother. Here, Rovie, want to go for a walk? Give him hell, Pop!" Robin yelled from the foyer and slammed the front door with a sound that made them both wince.

13 :   *Saturday, May Second*

Robin was the only member of the Fay family whom Albert recognized on sight. He could only guess, because of his age and obvious resemblance to the boy, that Tyler Fay was the tall fellow with the good-natured smile he'd seen in the elevator once or twice. Julie Fay he supposed to be a certain exquisitely turned-out blonde who never greeted anyone but stood with proud eyes examining the elevator ceiling. He had met her often coming home around six-thirty or seven, suffusing the elevator with French perfume and warming it with soft mink.

Though his intent had been to act with firmness, tinged with enough rage to give it authority, he hesitated a moment outside the apartment before ringing the bell. His desire to run away angered him. He made an impatient sound and pressed the doorbell.

He had identified Tyler Fay correctly. He was, in fact, so pleasant-faced that Albert smiled at him in spite of himself, then quickly composed his lips into grimmer lines. He stepped from the hallway into a white foyer, sparsely furnished with simple chairs and a table of graceful lines. On the walls he spied the vivid colors of impressionistic paintings and had to force himself, for reasons of propriety, to look away from what he suspected to be a fine Soutine, and just beyond it, one that had to be a Braque. Ahead of him the living room glowed in warm tones that pulled him into surroundings of ease and friendliness. The contrast between this apartment and his own, identical in layout, but so different in treatment, was disconcerting. He wanted to stay angry, but the rooms calmed him and he found his determination ebbing away, especially now that he discovered that Mrs. Fay was not the aloof blonde he had supposed. She stood up as he came in, a slender, delicate woman who wore a white sweater with pearls at her throat, and who looked far too young to be the mother of such a grown son. Now that Albert saw the two of them together, he recognized a youthfulness that transcended chronological age and he could not help sighing, for lately youth always made him sigh.

Mrs. Fay gave him a tentative smile, then sobered even as Albert had done at the front door, remembering the severity of the occasion. She tossed her pale hair back with her hand, probably a mannerism she employed when ill at ease, and invited him to sit down. Albert thanked her stiffly and selected a small comfortable chair. Tyler Fay sat on the couch and Julie took the seat across from Albert.

The Fays were waiting for him to start but Albert, who had prepared his speech in advance, was left tongue-tied. These were decidedly not the rowdy upstarts he had visualized. The soft face of the woman opposite him had melted his indignation and the attention of the young man on the couch was turned upon him with the courtesy of a gentleman well trained in the art of handling any social situation. These were his peers; not, as Maud seemed to suggest, the product of an inferior society. In addition, Albert noted that by remaining silent in this not unpleasant manner, Tyler Fay was placing him on the defensive. It was impossible for Albert to utilize the firm superiority he had planned without seeming like a boor himself. For want of any other alternative, therefore, and as a stall, he asked permission to smoke, accepted one of the Fay cigarettes and allowed Tyler Fay to light it for him. Now that he had figuratively broken bread with them, his task became more difficult still. "Don't know where to begin," he admitted. "I believe I've met you once or twice, Mr. Fay, but I don't ever remember seeing Mrs. Fay before."

"No, we've never shared the same elevator." Even her laugh was delicate.

Albert eyed her with pleasure. "I thought you might be that elegant blonde who never greets anyone."

"Oh, poor Suzanne again! That's Mrs. John d'Auriac, and everybody who doesn't know her thinks she's a snob. Actually, she's the shyest person in the world, and painfully modest, Mr. Harewood. She doesn't think she's pretty and she doesn't think she's intelligent. She has the worst kind of inferiority complex."

"Is that a fact? Well, in that case, I'll make a point of saying hello to her next time."

"Please do. She'll be very grateful, you'll see."

"It's a mistake many people make, calling shy people snobs." Albert paused because he could think of nothing further to say, no other stall, and Mr. Fay had begun to smile, turning with comic interest from one to the other as this little conversation took place.

But at last he took pity on Albert. He uncrossed his long legs and sat forward. "About this 'nasty situation' as you called it on the telephone, Mr. Harewood . . ."

"Oh, yes." Albert squirmed in his chair. He had an itch just below his right shoulder blade and couldn't bring himself to the indignity of scratching it. "It seems your boy is quite—athletic." He laughed to temper any possible sarcasm.

Fay lit himself a cigarette and held it in the corner of his mouth, his right eye squinting to screen out the smoke. "You're referring to his basketball activities. He's quite a player."

Albert tried reaching back unobtrusively with his left hand and managed to scratch himself while pretending to straighten a crease in the back of his jacket. "That could be pretty rough on someone in the room below, you know."

"Before you say anything else, I'd like you to inspect his court and equipment."

Albert didn't care for the glitter of amusement in Fay's eyes, but he got up and followed him. Fay switched on the lights in Robin's room. He produced Robin's basketball uniform and the heavy woolen socks he wore when playing. "He doesn't wear shoes because stocking feet make less noise."

"Well, but the ball on this floor——"

"Here it is." Fay opened a drawer and displayed a hodgepodge of rolled-up woolen socks. He selected one, placed the wastebasket on the far bed and demonstrated how Robin played the game. "That's the whole story," he said, retrieving the socks from the basket.

Albert thrust his hands into his pockets and toed a crack between a brown and a beige linoleum square. "I see." He didn't know what else to say and felt a quick resentment towards Maud for having placed him in such a position.

He was glad when Fay continued: "Today, for instance, when Mrs. Harewood called, Robin was lying on his bed playing with his dog. I can't imagine what she could have heard, unless it was Robin laughing. I will admit he was laughing. I will also admit that the windows were open because it's a hot day. But what could Mrs. Harewood have wanted of Robin when she called? She complained of the noise he was making and that noise was only laughter."

Albert turned away. Of course it was the laughter. . . .

"Only laughter, Mr. Harewood. Now, the first time Mrs. Harewood called, I remember we were having a tussle. We were chasing each other up and down the living room and she must have heard our footsteps. I admit it might have been annoying, but this is something one has to expect when one lives in an apartment house. In our defense, I will say that these little tussles didn't last for more than a few minutes, and it seems a shame that because of your wife, we've had to cut them out. A healthy family needs this kind of exercise once in a while, Mr. Harewood. I take it you have no children or you and your wife would understand. It's too bad. We haven't had much fun around here since you moved in. And we were here first, remember."

Albert sank onto Robin's bed. He couldn't believe this; no, he couldn't believe that Maud's complaints were so close to invention. She might be prone to exaggerate, of course, but to deliberately lie, to invent? No, she wouldn't do that. "You're sure Robin doesn't ever bounce a ball?" he asked hopefully.

"We've never allowed that. We can't stand the noise ourselves."

"Maybe when you're not at home?"

"That would only be at night."

"Well?"

"But you're home then, aren't you? *Does* he make noise?"

"Well, not that I've noticed," Albert said miserably.

"Tell me honestly, have *you* ever heard Robin?"

"Maybe, but I didn't pay attention to it. No, I guess not."

"There you have it, Mr. Harewood. Your wife has been very unfair."

"No she hasn't—no, no."

"I don't follow you."

"I mean, she hasn't—it isn't a question of . . ." Albert looked up at Tyler Fay, who leaned his tall body against a chest of drawers. To the right, standing quietly at the doorway, was Mrs. Fay with round, wondering eyes. It was obvious that these were kindly people, people who could share a confidence, and unless he undertook to move Maud to another apartment in these days of scarcity, the only remaining course for him was to let them understand her trouble and hope they might sympathize with her as he was forced to.

"If you could just control her a little," Mrs. Fay ventured.

"But that's just it, I can't. She wasn't always like this, you know. She was a lively, attractive girl with the most beautiful smile you've ever seen." He closed his eyes a moment and saw that smile. "She was a regular young hellion, but full of intelligence and wit. Our home was always overflowing with friends. Even when our boy was born, even in the difficult years that followed, when she took care of him herself, trusting him to no one else, and did her writing far into the night, she was —wonderful." Albert noticed their faces go suddenly watchful, as if they breathed the presence of unpleasantness in the air. "He was a beautiful boy—and still is. At the age of twenty-seven, a beautiful baby."

Julie's face crumpled. Albert gave her a faint smile, in apology for what he was forcing her to hear. "He wasn't mentally deficient, if that's what you're thinking. To bring into the world a Mongolian idiot is a relatively common tragedy much too banal for us. No, the gods had a special form of torture prepared for the Harewoods."

Fay moved uncomfortably. "Say, Harewood, you don't have to go on with this——"

"Thank you, but the way things look to me now, you're going to need plenty of understanding. You see, our boy was a born schizophrenic. He didn't become that way because of any childhood shock or mismanagement, and he didn't inherit it from either side of the family. He was a 'sport,' a 'case,' the one child in I don't know how many million who is born that way, and for whom there is no known treatment or cure. But Mrs. Harewood wouldn't accept what the doctors said. She kept fighting it. She devoted all her time to him, but he just sat and stared at his fingers for six years, withdrawn from the world, knowing nothing and no one. Then one day, right before his sixth birthday, Maud was feeding him lunch. He didn't want to eat and kept turning his face away from the spoon. But she wanted to feed him, he was so thin. Suddenly he picked up his milk glass and broke it in Maud's face. She has the scars to this day. He tore handfuls of hair from her head, clawed at her with his nails and bit pieces out of her hands. It was the only time he ever responded to anyone in any way. Maud wanted to keep him even after that, but I wouldn't allow it. I put him in a private sanitarium where he's well cared for and where doctors come to study him, although they never get anywhere. He doesn't know us. He doesn't know anything. He doesn't even know how to talk. All he likes are chocolate malteds. But he isn't a mentally deficient child. I wish he were. At least we could understand it then."

Tears stood manifestly in Mrs. Fay's eyes. "Oh, what a terrible thing for you and your wife!"

"That's why I decided you'd better know the truth. When someone behaves unreasonably, Mrs. Fay, paradoxically there's always a reason."

Fay gave his head a quick shake. He looked as if he wanted to say much more, but all he produced was, "That's rough, Harewood," and then was silent again, possibly thinking how utterly impoverished his statement was. "Glad you told us though. It makes a difference. I'm sure Robin will feel as we do," he continued after a moment.

Mrs. Fay moved from the doorway to sit beside Albert on the bed. Her action was impulsive, as if sitting near him might bring him some comfort. "No wonder Mrs. Harewood can't get it out of her mind."

"Well, she was never the same lively girl I married, but she tried to live a normal life, Mrs. Fay, and she managed very well, writing her best books and relaxing pleasantly enough in between until last year when she began to have her—time of life, you know. She stopped writing completely, and that's a tragedy to someone with her talent. She's tried often, but she can't work at all, can't get one sentence on paper. The doctor assures me this isn't unusual and that she'll pull out of it soon. That's why I sold our apartment and moved here to smaller quarters to reduce her responsibilities. But it hasn't helped her yet. She still refuses to face the facts. She keeps reviewing everything she ever said or did to the boy, trying to ferret out her possible mistakes. She's sure that either she or I gave him some terrible shock in his infancy that made him withdraw from the world, which is ridiculous, of course. It's a compulsion with her, though, and I can't understand it. And what happened today is most upsetting to me. It's apparent she's gotten so that the mere sound of a happy boy like Robin is intolerable to her—the sound of his laughter, for instance. So what can I do? I want to help you, but what can I do?"

There was no answer, of course. Albert sat there shrinking beneath the blanket of compassion that oppressed him. It was obviously time for him to go, yet he would have liked to initiate some small talk first in an attempt to regain a part of his lost dignity, for he felt that to be pitied was to be rendered inferior. But he could think of nothing more to say, so he stood up silently.

They accompanied him to the door. They told him not to worry. Now they understood, they would do everything in their power to see that Mrs. Harewood got her rest and quiet and would also try to keep Robin's laughter directed away from the echoing courtyard to spare her pain. Their whole concern was for Maud.

Albert returned to his apartment convinced that he had cleared the air and solved the situation wisely, even though he had been forced to reveal a privacy to strangers. In reply to Maud's question, "Did you give it to them on the line?" which was accompanied by a hard glitter of waiting satisfaction in her eyes, he repeated to her the Fays' promise of co-operation and told her how warm and kind they were, how different from Maud's picture of them. She would have no further trouble from them, he assured her.

He expected that their sympathy and consequent capitulation would please her, but instead her fingers moved nervously to her mouth and she tottered away from him. He followed her, asking confused questions but she wouldn't answer.

She felt herself trembling all over and her head whirled. She had a feeling of complete devastation, as if she had been pushed to the wall by everyone, including Albert. She felt repulsed, impeded, full of anger and a reasonless desire for revenge. She would get even with them for doing this to her, for putting her in such a position. They were all against her, Albert, too, all, all . . .

She threw herself upon the chaise longue and wept, uttering cries of temper, beating her fists upon the arms of the chair, writhing like someone in a convulsion, pushing away Albert's timid hands, pushing away the cold washcloth and the water he brought her, drowning out his fearful questions with her cries.

But when at last he gave up his ministrations and left the room, she leaped up and followed him, suddenly wary of his intent, and reached the telephone in time to tear the receiver from his hand. "Who were you calling?" Her new fear calmed her. Although the course of tears still stood in wet lines on her cheeks, she was no longer crying.

"You need a doctor, Maud."

"I've got one."

"I know. I was calling him."

"Dr. Prince? Who are you fooling?"

"He hasn't helped you at all. You need a specialist. You can't go on like this."

"A specialist!" She pushed her head forward, the veins of her neck protruding. "So now you're trying to tell me I'm crazy. How convenient for you. Everything will be my fault. Put me in the nuthouse and absolve yourself of all the blame."

"What blame, Maud? I don't understand you. I only want you to be better. There's no blame——"

"I don't need a psychiatrist. You know very well that if I'm ever analyzed I might never be able to write again."

"That's not true. You'd write better, you'd begin to write again."

"I suppose you know better than Jung! I don't need a crazy-doctor, Albert. I'm going through menopause, which is torture for any woman, but you won't understand that, will you? Any general doctor can treat it. And that's all it is. That's all it is, do you hear?"

"I'm sure of it, Maud, but——"

"But you'd rather think I was crazy; you'd rather get rid of me than live through this with me!"

"That isn't so."

"You do think I'm crazy, don't you?"

"I don't. You need a little help and I don't know how to give it to you."

"Oh, so you admit I need help!"

"Yes."

"Well, why don't you help me then? Why don't you give me a little affection and encouragement? That's all the help I need."

"I try to. My God, I try to."

"How? By going to the club and leaving me alone all afternoon? By staying downtown long after the market's closed?"

He blinked his eyes miserably. He couldn't defend himself. It was true that of late he had been running away from her.

"And you get that specialist idea out of your head. I'll never see him, as long as I live I will never see him or any other man like him again! Impotent fools! Who did they ever help? You ought to know that yourself. If you want to help me, stop trying to shove me off on some fool who calls himself a doctor, and show me some personal consideration and love!" She was weeping again, but differently, normally, like any other unhappy woman.

So Albert took her in his arms. They stood close together, deriving no comfort from each other, each separate heart chilled with the same fear they both denied.

Upstairs in 9B, Robin returned with the dog. "Did you give him hell, Pop?"

"Not exactly, Rob."

"Wouldn't you know it! Boy, wouldn't you know it!"

But as Ty told the Harewoods' story, the spleen drained from Robin's eyes. He winced as he saw the glass shatter in Mrs. Harewood's face, envisioning the mad assault of a six-year-old child. "Cripes!" he whispered. Then he wandered off to his room and seemed to forget. He lay on his bed and read a sports magazine while he listened to hit songs on his radio, tuned unusually low.

But a little later, while they were having a constrained and silent dinner, he brought up the subject again quite suddenly. "You know, Mrs. Harewood should have gotten herself a dog," he said.

It was his solution to all the troubles of the world.

PART TWO

PART TWO

Klaus Gruppmann rang for the back elevator at the seventeenth floor and cursed under his breath. He wouldn't mind it so much if the Leopolds in 17A were old tenants who had a right to growl, but they had only lived here a few years, and who the hell were they anyway, butchers or something like that, and always complaining as if they owned the place, the meat grinders!

Even Joe's usually good-natured face wore a bitter expression as he opened the elevator door. Neither said a word until they reached the basement. "Well?" Joe ventured then, interrupting Gruppmann's fuming silence.

"So it's another leak—whole gottemmed living-room ceiling!"

Joe made a tight line of his mouth and slammed the elevator door.

Klaus went back to his apartment to wait for the plumber's final report. He poured himself three fingers of Scotch and sat down at his desk. Tanzy slowly lowered her rear quarters to the floor next to him and rested her head on his knee. "Better we should haf been gym teachers, Tanzy, all day von two tree, von two tree, up side down." Klaus took a mouthful of Scotch and let it slip down his throat slowly. "Ahh!" He reached for the house phone and asked for Mrs. Lesser's apartment. "This is a bad day, Tanzy. I'll remember it as a bad, bad day." He sighed and took another mouthful. "Hello, Miss Forsythe? Gruppmann here. How is Mrs. Lesser? . . . Ja? No fooling? Fine, fine, I'm glad she's better. Tell her to rest now. To take it easy. Okay, Miss Forsythe, just tell her I called. . . . Thanks. . . . Come in!" he bellowed in response to a knock at his door.

It was the plumber. "Well?" Klaus barked.

"Same as last time. I told you then——"

"Yah, yah, I know."

"You act like it was my fault."

"Nyeh!" Klaus turned his head away.

The plumber waited.

"I'll call you after I speak to the boss," Klaus muttered, rubbing his forehead.

The plumber observed Klaus's glass of whisky and passed his tongue over his underlip.

"I call you after I speak to the boss," Klaus repeated.

"Okay, okay."

Klaus downed the last of the Scotch after the plumber left and wiped his mouth with the back of his chapped hand. He searched through his pockets until he found a stick of chewing gum, which he munched on for a few seconds before dialing Rider's number.

"Gruppmann here, Mr. Rider."

"Yes, Klaus. What's up?"

Klaus lowered the receiver a moment, covered his mouth and belched. Then he raised it to his ear. "It's 17A , Mr. Rider—again."

"Another leak?"

"Ja, in the ceiling of the living room. Wet as hell. The plumber checked again and says there's nothing wrong with the pipes. It's comin' from the Marshes' terrace."

For a moment, Mr. Rider was silent. "Well, I'm sorry," he said finally.

"Could be from outside the building, some loose bricks or plaster?" Klaus suggested hopelessly.

"We know what it is," Rider said. "There's no use beating around the bush any longer. The Leopolds have been most co-operative up to now."

"Not today they ain't. Shoulda heard her just now."

"Can you blame her? She's had that living room replastered three times in five years. And look what it's cost me. No, I'm afraid this is it, Klaus."

Klaus said nothing.

"I won't be able to come by for a few days. Mrs. Rider's in the hospital."

"*Lieber Gott,* what now, what else?"

"Appendicitis. They're operating on her in an hour or two, so I've got to get over there. Look, Klaus, the lease is in Mrs. Marsh's name, so do me a favor and go up there and order her, nicely, of course, to remove everything, plants, trees, earth, everything, and repave the terrace as was originally called for in the blueprints. Then she is welcome to go ahead and plant anything she wants as long as it's all in raised boxes. Stress that part of it, you know, that she can have her garden back, but this time according to more conventional plans."

"*Gott in Himmel,* Mr. Rider!"

"I can't help myself, Klaus. She knows damn well there's a clause in her lease that says she'll rebuild the terrace as originally planned should her setup prove faulty. And it certainly has. So you'd better go right up and see her now, and I'll have an official letter sent to her from here. But I want you to give it the personal touch first, you know."

"Me? Hey, not me, Mr. Rider! How you think that looks, the super telling a lady like Mis' Marsh a thing like that? You gotta tell her, Mr. Rider."

"Haven't I got enough trouble of my own, with Mrs. Rider in the hospital? I should be over there now, Klaus. Look, I appreciate how you feel. I feel just as rotten about it as you do. But you have to admit I've bent over backwards on this thing up to now."

"Mr. Rider, what I gonna say to her?"

"Just what I told you. Only be gentle. Take your time. Give it to her easy."

"I rather quit."

"Oh, come off it, Klaus. Don't make things harder for me."

"Ja, but I mean it. A loud-mouth I am, but a bestar-r-rt, never."

"Put it to her softly."

"Easy for you to say, Mr. Rider."

"I know. But you've got to take the bad with the good. You've got a good job with me, Klaus."

"What a day this is! Old Mrs. Lesser collapses in the street outside and I haf to carry her in. Now this. And your poor wife."

"I'm sorry about Mrs. Lesser. Is she all right now?"

"All right! How all right can she be with that ticker? But you'll see, she'll be out walking again tomorrow. Stubborn old woman!"

"She's a brave old woman, Klaus. She wants to die on her feet, she told me. Look, I may not be in touch with you for a few days. Don't call me unless there's a real emergency. If so, you can get me home about nine or ten. How about the Harewoods? Any more trouble there?"

"No, thanks Gott, everything's been quiet for a while."

"Good. Now you stop taking everyone's troubles to heart and get up to that penthouse."

"Easy to say. Now I got to worry about Mrs. Rider, too."

"I'll do that. You've got enough with Number Ten. Mrs. Rider's operation isn't a real emergency. It's a subacute appendix, not acute. She'll be home in a few days."

"Well thanks Gott for that."

"Now to the penthouse!"

"Ja. And my best to Mrs. Rider."

"Thanks."

Klaus replaced the receiver slowly and pushed the telephone away from him. Suddenly he got to his feet, stormed into the bathroom and spat the chewing gum savagely into the toilet.

2 :   *Monday, May Fourth*

The heat wave had passed during the night and although the sun had been out for an hour or more in the early morning, the sky had clouded over and it looked like rain. Flossie sat in her chair in the garden nevertheless, wearing a sweater under her white woolen dressing gown. She hoped there wouldn't be a frost to kill her flowers, for actually it was the heat that had been unseasonable. May up East here was usually a cool month, about like today, fifty-eight, sixty degrees. The chill she felt came not so much from the temperature reading as from the damp New York breeze, which didn't always indicate frost. As a matter of fact, all it definitely brought were viruses, and her throat was feeling a little dry. She bet she had a cold coming on. Well, no wonder, with such sudden changes of weather! That was New York for you, and personally, you could have it. She'd take Arizona. It would be dry and warm there today. At her father's ranch on a day like this, she would have been out riding, pushing her pony into a gallop, faster, faster, with the wind in her hair.

Walt used to try to ride out after her in the days when he was calling on her, shouting that he'd catch her and throw her to the ground and neck with her until she cried "Uncle," but he never got close to her, not on a horse, at any rate. She loved to tease him that way, and how mad he used to get! He used to blame it on the ranch hands, claiming it was a trap, that they were all in cahoots together, that they gave him rheumatic old mares to ride, but the real answer was he didn't know how to get speed out of her father's sensitive animals. You had to make them feel the essence of speed, love it as much as you did. Then they would fly, loving the feel of the wind in their manes as much as you loved it in your hair.

Yes, her old man knew how to breed and train a fine horse. They didn't come like him nowadays, a man who never asked a hand to do anything he couldn't do better himself. He had raised the finest horses in the West, and the best cattle, too, though Flossie had never cared much for that end of it, which was why she had Walt sell the place after her old man died. They couldn't live out there (although it would have been good for her old bones). There was no point trying to run a cattle ranch in Arizona and lumber camps and paper mills in Washington state, all from a penthouse in New York. Walt had to travel often enough from coast to coast as it was, and besides, he didn't know anything about ranching, being an old lumberman himself.

And very like her old man in his way. He could fell a tree and split a log with the best of them, besides knowing all there was to know about every machine in his mills. Once, early in their marriage, he had taken her on a business trip with him, from lumber camp to mill, and she had proudly observed how he received the same respect from his men as her father had. He had that same air of friendly authority, and it was after that trip that Flossie took to calling him "old man." "I picked you out because you were the only fellow in the U.S.A. who could stand shoulder to shoulder with my old man," she told him, and he retorted, "I married you because you were the only gal in the entire West with enough flesh on her bones so a guy could grab a hold of something."

Oh, weren't those the days! Flossie sighed. It was a shame they had to come East, although she really shouldn't be complaining. After all, when a business grows into an empire, the center of it has to be New York, Walt said. But that wasn't true, either; look at Detroit. . . .

The maid interrupted Flossie to tell her Mr. Gruppmann wanted to see her. "Fine, tell him to come out." Flossie sat up and patted the sides of her immaculately coiffed hair. She liked Klaus and always enjoyed a chat with him.

He ambled out to her, playing with the brim of his brown hat. "How you today, Mis' Marsh?"

"Just fine, Klaus. How about you? Take the weight off your feet."

But he hesitated by the side of the chair. "Cooler today."

"Yes. I was a little worried there might be a frost. The flowers are so special this year."

He stood there feeling miserable.

"Something wrong with you, Klaus? Why don't you sit down and have a drink?"

Reluctantly he sat on the edge of the chair.

"Pour yourself a Scotch. I'll have one, too."

He eyed the decanter longingly, knowing it was twelve-year-old stock or better. "Don't think I should before lunch. . . ." How could he drink her liquor today? Like a regular Judas he felt.

"Oh, come off it, Klaus Gruppmann! Who're you kidding?"

"Well." He shrugged and obeyed her.

"Now what's up?"

[115]

"Well—it's—you know, them Leopolds downstairs again, Mis' Marsh."

He saw her fists fly to her breast and remain there, pressing tight. He felt her fear and despaired. Her whisky glass burned his fingers. Judas! he thought to himself. "Meat grinders!" he grunted aloud.

Her fingers were shaking as they curled around the edges of her housecoat over her breast.

"Butchers, butchers, that's their business, wholesale butchers we got now in Number Ten, troublemakers . . ." Klaus was getting nowhere. She was sitting there holding her breath and offering him no help. He couldn't bear her suffering. He knew she must be whispering little words like prayers to herself. He hated what he had to do and hated himself for agreeing to do it. He needed reinforcement. He downed his drink, feeling the fire of the alcohol burn a soothing course to his belly. It gave him strength enough to forge ahead. His only thought now was to get it over with quickly and be gone from this garden and from Flossie's presence. "Their whole ceiling's comin' down in the livin' room, Mis' Marsh, wet through, and Mr. Rider says it's because of watering your garden, so he says you got to——"

"My *garden!*"

"Mr. Rider says it's a violation——"

"Violation! The best landscape gardeners in the world planned it, specialists in terraces, and the best of everything was used. It has nothing to do with my garden and I won't allow the Leopolds or Mr. Rider or anyone else to say it has! Those Leopolds are impossible people; they're envious because they wanted a terrace apartment and couldn't find one and if they can't have one, they don't want anyone else to have one. What right have they to complain?"

"It's no picnic for them, Mis' Marsh, to have their place replastered and repainted all the time——"

"All the time! Once or twice! And why come to me? It's not my fault. There's a leak from the outside of the building. Anyone will tell you that. Water can't seep through my garden, not the way I had it built with special copper lining and everything. It's impossible and you know it."

"Well, the plumber says——"

"No one's ever examined the outside of this building! That's where it's coming from, I know that's where it's coming from!"

"Please, Mis' Marsh, I only——"

"But this is—this is impossible! You know it's impossible, Klaus. It can't happen, you know that."

"Mis' Marsh, please don't be so excited——"

"I have a right to be excited! No one's going to tamper with my garden. Just look at it. How could anyone even dare to suggest——"

"Well it's not me, Mis' Marsh——"

"I know it isn't. It's the Leopolds, damn them. Now you just go back and tell them I don't want to hear another complaint. I can't help it if their goddam apartment leaks. They're on the top floor and every top floor leaks. Our apartment leaks, too, only I have no one over me to blame. If they don't like it, let them move the hell out."

"It's not up to me——"

"Yes it is. You can handle them, Klaus. Just yell at them. They'll back down. If they don't complain any more, then nothing will happen, will it?"

"I guess not."

"So you tell them to shut their mouths."

"I don't know . . ." Klaus twisted the brim of his hat so hard that he tore it. "Gottem, look what I done."

"You will tell them, Klaus, won't you?"

"'Course I will," he said unhappily.

"Newcomers! All the trouble in this building comes from newcomers."

"That's the truth."

"People take apartments and don't even have sense enough to know that a top floor leaks, and then they try to blame it on others."

"I tell them that," Klaus said miserably.

"Thank you, Klaus. And I don't want to hear another word about this. I mean it. You can tell Mr. Rider I said that."

"I tell him."

She breathed deeply. She wiped her forehead with the back of her hand. "Would you tell the maid to bring me a hand towel when you leave?"

"You all right?"

"Sure, just got a little hot under the collar." She tried to laugh. "You can't blame me."

"No, Mis' Marsh, I sure can't. I tell the girl."

"Thanks."

Klaus escaped.

Flossie's heart wouldn't slow down from its unsteady pitch. She mopped herself with the towel the maid brought and then shivered. The breeze felt chilly on her damp skin and she'd probably get her death of cold sitting out here. But she couldn't leave her garden now. Not after this. She took another drink to calm herself, a stiff one, and felt the benevolent effect of old Scotch. After all, what was there to get so excited about, she told herself, feeling quite drunk. One had to handle situations like this with firm finality. Which she had. The best thing now would be to cast it from her mind altogether, not to think of it at all any more.

Flossie wouldn't leave the garden, even though she sneezed three times in a row, a sure sign of a cold. She sat out there staring at the rich glow of color against the cloudy sky and sniffing the blossom scents and she decided again and again that she had heard the end of this thing at last. Yes, she had heard the end of it. She was certain, now, that this was the end of it. . . .

3 :   *Monday, May Fourth*

Mrs. Marsh's Scotch wasn't setting well in Klaus's stomach. For one thing, he had taken it down too quickly and too soon after his own good-sized drink. For another, it was Mrs. Marsh's Scotch, fine, smooth, twelve-year-old liquor, given in innocent friendliness. Oh, he was a bestar-r-rt to have taken it, a regular Judas. Klaus smothered a belch behind his fingers and stared down at his desk, his eyes moving vaguely over the papers. Now what was it he had to do? Oh, yes. Gottemmit, yes! He brought his fists down hard on the surface before him and relished the pain of the blow against his knuckles and the protesting jingle of both telephones. But it wasn't enough. He suppressed a hankering to lift them and throw them across the room, throw them hard into a great pane of glass so things would shatter about him everywhere. Oh, he was furious, furious with himself for having been such a yellow-belly and made such a mess of the job, furious with Mr. Rider for having put him into this position in the first place, furious with Mrs. Marsh for being so gottemmed unrealistic, and there was no way to vent his anger except to dial Rider's number in such a temper that he made three mistakes before he got the thin-voiced girl at the answering service, who said Mr. Rider was out of touch and was there any message, to which Klaus screamed "No!" and slammed down the receiver. He had forgotten Mrs. Rider's appendix in his fury.

He strode up and down his room until part of his rage was spent. Then he sat down to think. He wouldn't be able to reach Mr. Rider until nine or ten o'clock that night at his home. Mr. Rider would undoubtedly be on edge, worried about his wife and very tired. He would most likely be—well, cranky. He would not be pleased to hear from Klaus, no sir, he wouldn't. Klaus rested his head on the clean white napkin he always pinned over the back of his chair and figured out how the conversation might go:

"Gruppmann here," he would say, as usual.

"Oh-h-h," a descending groan from Rider. "Now don't tell me there's trouble. Haven't I got enough?"

Here Klaus would inquire politely about Mrs. Rider and Rider would tell him how awful she looked coming down from the operating room with that horrible thing stuck in her mouth. Then he would say halfheartedly, "I take it you had a bad time or you wouldn't be calling me."

Here Klaus would have the option of denying this, which would then put him in the ridiculous position of trying to explain why he had bothered to call Mr. Rider in the first place, or he would have to say, "You gottem right I had a bad time!"

"So she refused to co-operate!" Klaus could think of no words to describe Rider's tone as he uttered this.

"What you expect her to do, throw her arms around me? Gottem right, she refused! Won't hear another gottem word about it. And that's that."

Mr. Rider would be in no mood to receive this news calmly. "Well," he would snap, "well, I knew you would have a bad time with her, but I didn't expect this. No, I certainly didn't expect this, not after the way I've treated her, I didn't expect this. So this is what I get for being sorry for her, for spending my own money trying to delay this thing so she could have her garden one more year, one more year. There isn't another landlord in the country who would have done what I did, and now this is what I get for it. Well . . . All right, Klaus, I'll handle it my own way from now on."

"Hey wait, boss, you got this a little wrong——"

"I don't think so, Klaus."

"Yes, Mr. Rider—see—look, I don't really think Mis' Marsh understands. I mean, she closed her mind, wouldn't listen——"

"Are you implying that *you* made a mess of it, Klaus?"

Well, now, what could Klaus say to a question like that? "I didn't make no mess!" He'd have to deny it, of course. "I done just what you told me. This is a mess to begin with. *I* didn't make no mess."

"Then why are you making excuses for her? She refused to co-operate, didn't she?"

"Well, in a way, yes, but——"

"No buts. Either she co-operates or she doesn't. That's all that interests me. And she isn't going to."

"What you expect, Mr. Rider? You send me up on a stinkin' job like this, what you expect? That she screams for joy? 'Oh thanks, Mr. Gruppmann, for taking away my beautiful garden'? That garden is like her life, Mr. Rider."

"And the hell with the rest of the world. She'll keep her damn garden if my whole building falls down. The hell with me, the hell with the Leopolds, the hell with my wife in the hospital, the hell with everyone but Flossie Marsh. Okay, I'll take over from now on. It will give me *great pleasure* to take over. This is the last time any tenant of mine is going to make a fool of me. From now on I go by the books like everyone else. And I'll throw the book at Mrs. Marsh, Klaus, believe me, this time I will!"

Klaus grimaced as another belch rumbled up from his stomach. No, not for anything in the world, not for a million dollars, should he make such a telephone call. If he let the whole thing drop, what difference would it make? What could happen that wouldn't happen anyways? Nothing to him, certainly, he had done his job. And in any case, Mr. Rider would do his. Tomorrow a nice, polite letter would be sent to Mrs. Marsh, making the request official, and what happened after that should be none of Klaus's concern, for he couldn't change things. He certainly couldn't make Mrs. Marsh face the facts, nor, at the same time, could he blame her for avoiding them. On the other hand, he couldn't blame Rider, either, for blowing up if he knew about Mrs. Marsh's reaction to his request. No, even if Klaus were one of those real smart operators, a real clever politician-type fellow, he wouldn't be able to accomplish one thing by reporting the results of his visit with Mrs. Marsh to Mr. Rider. This was a case where things would take their own course, no matter what. After all, he was only the superintendent of this building, and a damn good one at that, and gottem, this was none of his affair! That was right, this was none of his business. When you got right down to the bottom of it, Rider was making him the goat and if he didn't watch out, he'd be getting kicked in the ass from all sides. All right, so he'd go by the books, too. He'd do his job like the union said, no more, no less. He had followed orders, and his conscience was clear. "Don't call me unless there's a real emergency," Mr. Rider had said. Well, this was no *real* emergency. Mrs. Marsh was going to lose her garden and that was that. This was only small trouble, annoying, heartbreaking trouble, not at all the kind of trouble Mr. Rider meant when he had said "real." Ja.

Of course. A real emergency was if the building caved in or something. That was what Mr. Rider meant. So his conscience was clear. He wouldn't think about this thing any more. It was none of his business, anyway, Klaus decided.

4 :   *Tuesday, May Fifth*

Hunt pushed his laboratory notes away from him with such a sudden motion that he almost upset the rack of test tubes before him. What was the matter with him lately? . . . Inattentive, apprehensive, sleepless, querulous, dissatisfied, and worst of all, experiencing more and more often moments of complete mental black-out—as just now when, poring over his notes, he suddenly awoke, as it were, to the realization that for several minutes his mind had simply gone to sleep, and that with sightless eyes open, pen in hand, he had dozed for a while. He wasn't getting enough sleep, that was it. He had succumbed to insomnia only a month or two before and he couldn't lick it no matter what he tried—warm baths, hot milk, hot toddies. If it kept up like this, he would have to resort to the use of sleeping pills.

He tried to return to his work but found it distasteful. This was another alarming new facet of his breakdown; his lifelong, carefully disciplined work habits were being undermined, and lately he entered his laboratory with a sense of regret as if he were leaving something more desirable, even though nothing more desirable existed for him. He had been to see his doctor, who had found him well enough physically, but who had advised (as all doctors did when confronted with various neurotic ailments that had no physical basis) a vacation. Other than his honeymoon, Hunt Parrish had never taken a vacation. He didn't believe in them. He hated them, as a matter of fact. He hated to sun himself, hated to swim, play golf or tennis, or to dance and quip and banter with people he didn't know or like.

Perhaps it would do him good to knock off a bit early today. He might persuade Maud Harewood to meet him for cocktails. He could justify time taken off from work in this manner, for it wouldn't be wasted with Maud. It was possible that he might be able to help her in some way, and perhaps she might be well enough to help him, too. At any rate, it wouldn't hurt to be able to discuss his troubles with an intelligent and perceptive soul.

Maud's maid was doubtful that her mistress would come to the telephone, but even as she expressed her doubts, she was interrupted and Maud spoke to him. Her voice was heavy with depression.

"I thought perhaps you'd join me for cocktails at the Algonquin, Maud. Do you good to get out," Hunt suggested.

She made an annoyed sound. "The Algonquin! Oh, you don't really mean the Algonquin! For God's sakes, Hunt, you're nothing but a baby after all. Shades of the round table, you wide-eyed boy. Anyway, I can't get out. I really couldn't manage it. Why don't you drop over here, instead, darling? I miss you *so*." Her voice, edgy at first and steaming with sarcasm, modified to petulance at the end.

Hunt bore her outburst with good humor. "I'm always drinking your liquor, Maud."

"So what? Albert can afford it. Do come over, Hunt darling, please."

"You're sure you're well enough?"

"I'm miserable, but you always perk me up so."

"All right, then, I'll come."

But this time, feeling guilty at accepting her hospitality without return, Hunt stopped at a liquor store and bought her a bottle of the very best Scotch, even though it was raining heavily, a real spring downpour that didn't look as if it was ever going to stop.

He found her stretched out on the couch in her dressing gown with a blanket over her and a pillow behind her head. Since he had seen her last, she had had her hair cut short in a Dutch bob like a small girl and it improved her appearance to have done away with the burnt, frizzy permanent that had been so untidy and unbecoming. But only her haircut was an improvement. She was paler than he had ever seen her and the dark circles beneath her eyes were almost purple, her skin dry and wrinkled. Her large eyes seemed floating in jelly tears that were too thick for her to shed.

"I've brought you something."

"How bourgeois of you to feel you have to return my liquor!" She undid the parcel and frowned over the label. "But you know I don't drink Scotch. I like bourbon or vodka."

"I was sure you drank it. I thought everybody drank Scotch. I'm sorry."

"It's Albert's favorite," she was gracious enough to say as she put it aside on the floor. "Now, Hunt darling, what have you been doing? Sit down and tell me."

The maid brought the eternal pitcher of Bloody Marys, this time accompanied by some little dry crackers, and Maud gave her the Scotch to take into the kitchen.

"I've had a rotten week," Hunt said.

"Oh, poor Hunt."

"For the first time in my life, I find myself losing interest in my laboratory work. I'm sleepless at night. I don't know what's the matter with me."

"Did you go to the doctor?"

"Yes. He told me to take a vacation."

"Good idea. Why don't you? Hunt, tell me something." She smiled and wrinkled her nose coyly. "You've never really discussed this with me, not to the point, I mean. Do you believe I'm a genius?"

He was taken by surprise. The sudden shift was proof that it was impossible for Maud Harewood to talk about anyone else, utterly impossible. He would get little interest or understanding from her. He sipped his drink and determined not to be led. "Do you think *I'm* a genius?" he parried.

"I asked you first."

"Well, first of all, in order to answer your question, we have to establish just what it is you mean by genius."

"Oh God! Hunt Parrish, why do you insist on constipating every attempt at conversation? You crush all spontaneity and try to turn the cocktail hour into a class on dialectics!"

"I was merely exercising the art of conversation," he said dryly, "under the mistaken belief that you also enjoyed it."

He thought he saw a gleam of dislike in her eyes, just before she dropped her lids. "Now you're being unkind," she brooded, "and you can be pretty mean when you want to."

"I guess we both can."

She surprised him with a sudden, impish grin. "At least tell me whether you think *you're* a genius."

He laughed. "I'm only beginning to get used to your sudden changes of mood. Living with you can't possibly be dull. Difficult, yes, but never, never dull."

She liked what he said and chuckled over it. "Now don't you change the subject. Do you think you're a genius?"

Hunt took a moment to consider his answer. With careful honesty he told her that he had no doubt his mentality was highly superior. He had proved this in school, in college and in his career. But to go so far as to believe he was a genius, no, he couldn't truthfully say that he was. He couldn't truthfully believe that anything he had accomplished thus

[123]

far would live on through the centuries. He did not use the word "genius" lightly, as a measure in an I.Q. test. To him a genius was a man who created something so superior that it could stand the test of centuries. Michelangelo was a genius, Edison and Shakespeare. But certainly nothing that he had created, either in his writing or in his laboratory experiments thus far, would be remembered or perhaps even utilized a hundred years from now. So that . . . no, he did not think he was a genius—yet.

"Well, that shouldn't distress you. You're happier this way," she said.

He regarded her with a quick, suspicious narrowing of his lids.

"A genius pays for his gifts," she continued in a brooding voice, "by having to stand alone. One pays for eternal renown with one's personal happiness. It's no great shakes, this being a genius."

He regarded her with wonder now, faced for the first time with the full impact, the true extent of her egotism. Egotism—it was far stronger than that—narcissism. Why, she placed herself, without a qualm, on the same plane with Shakespeare!

"You be glad you're not a genius, Hunt darling."

He wasn't going to let her get away with this. "I don't have to ask you what you think of yourself. You've already stated your case. One with Shakespeare, eh, Maud?"

She gave him a malignant look. "Thank you. The tone of your question states your own position as far as I'm concerned—quite clearly, too. The essay you wrote on me was nothing but crap."

"I never called you a genius, if you remember. That's for another generation to decide. You just took unfair advantage of me, Maud. I was honest and completely self-detached and you tried to use my self-evaluation as a basis for establishing your own superiority over me. Did you really think I would fall in line?"

Sullenly, she lit herself a cigarette. She took a deep draw and expelled the smoke noisily, throwing her head back on the pillow. She stared up at the ceiling, her mouth alternately tightening and relaxing. She was pouting.

"You're in a bad mood today, Maud."

"You're no delight yourself."

"I guess not."

Suddenly she sat up and stared wildly at him. "Oh, Hunt, please let's not quarrel! I couldn't stand it if we quarrelled! We have to stick together, you and I. If we don't what have we got? Who have we got?" She wasn't play-acting. She meant this.

"It was just a spat. Of course we'll stick together," he said, but his tone was gloomy. He didn't belong with Maud, either. It seemed that no one in the world spoke his language.

"Please don't look so nasty. Smile. Please smile, Hunt. That's better. Now take another drink and let's not be hateful to each other any more. I couldn't stand it. I have enough. You know that." She bit the corner of her underlip and her eyes narrowed miserably.

"Still having all that confusion from upstairs?"

She didn't answer him, but her expression of sick despair served very well. Hunt muttered to himself and shook his head.

"You were going to help me," she said. "You promised to help me and instead you're being cruel."

"I know. I'd like to help, but I'm not sure how."

"I'll tell you how." She curled her legs under her and tucked the blanket securely about her small body. "Tell me a story."

"Again? About what?"

"Tell me about your wife."

He frowned.

"Please tell me about her. What does she look like?"

He sighed. What was the use of forcing this thing? She liked stories, so he'd tell her one. "She's beautiful," he said. "Her beauty is her profession. Not that she spends undue time with herself, mind you, but in her own opinion, she isn't really a wife and a clubwoman. In her opinion, she is a Beauty. So that everything in her home frames her, the furniture, the colors she chooses, her clothes. She's quite tall and has a good figure, a little on the sensual side, but not fat. She has perfect, blue-white skin, black hair and the most fantastic navy blue eyes."

"I still don't see her. I only see colors. You're holding back on me," Maud complained.

"Her eyes are wide apart and long rather than round. She has a slender, short nose and slender cheeks. She's delicate-looking. Her face, not her body."

"And what kind of a person is she?"

"Utterly charming. Warm and full of love. She's completely a woman." Hunt paused. "Yes, completely a woman."

Maud's eyes gleamed with another sudden burst of impish humor. "And tell me, Hunt, if she's so admirable, why is it you don't love her?"

He scrutinized her carefully to determine whether she was conversing with him or baiting him again. But the gleam in her eye was only one of delight for having made an accurate diagnosis. She was proud of what she had deduced, that was all. So he answered her honestly. "I'm afraid I can't love anyone, Maud, not in that way. I believe there is very little love in me."

"That's true. You're cold as a man, Hunt, ice cold."

It was all right coming from himself, but her positive agreement peeved him, and her search to establish superiority over him whether as a genius or as a sensual person hurt him. This was no basis for friendship. Once again he had to flatten her. "No colder than you, Maud," he retorted, "and much more honest."

"That's not true. I'm not cold—I'm just not well now—it isn't fair to judge me as I am now," she insisted.

He was about to press his point when the front door slammed and Albert Harewood came in, wearing tweeds and exuding the clean smell of after-shaving lotion. He looked as if he'd just come from a steam bath, a swim in the pool and a fresh shave. He approached them, smiling through his thick lenses, cheerfully rubbing his hands together.

"Well, Albert! . . . At last you get a chance to meet my husband, Hunt. . . . We've spoken about you so much, Albert, but no matter how late Hunt stays, you never come home and he has to leave without meeting you. . . . That's because Albert is a 'rich millionaire,' Hunt, and stops by his club every evening and all that sort of thing."

Albert flushed. He put on a new smile as he shook hands with Hunt.

"Now I've hurt his feelings," Maud said cheerfully. "Albert's very strictly puritan and middle-class. According to him, certain topics are taboo, you see, and one of them is money. It's awfully bad form to discuss one's money. The fact that everyone in the room knows he's a rich man doesn't excuse one's mentioning it. It's like a social disease."

"All right, Maud," Albert said quietly. "She gets carried away sometimes," he said to Hunt.

"I must say I agree with her, Mr. Harewood. After all, your business is making money. Why should you be ashamed of your success? It's as if Maud wrote a good book and then refused to have it published. I'd hate not to be able to compliment her on it. That wouldn't be fair."

"Oh"—Albert folded his hands nervously—"I don't know." He sat down and poured himself a drink.

"Yes, tell us why it's bad taste, because that's what you were going to say, isn't it, darling?"

"It *is* bad taste," Albert stated quietly. He sipped his drink. He had said all he was going to say.

"Or is it because it's too sacred, darling?"

Albert didn't answer her. He accepted her baiting with resignation. He was evidently used to it.

[126]

Hunt declined to join her, although there were many things he would have liked to say on this subject. That she was being determinedly unkind was evident, but that she also happened to be right in this case was unquestionable. But Albert Harewood wasn't fair game.

She seemed offended that he didn't help her. "Hunt and I have been fighting all afternoon," she said.

Albert raised his eyebrows, then gave Hunt a deprecatory smile.

"No, she's right. We have," Hunt said.

"He doesn't think I have any talent at all."

"That's not what I said, Maud, and you know it." Hunt grinned at her.

"You most certainly did."

"You adore misquoting people, don't you? It causes so much trouble."

Albert looked from one to the other expressionlessly. He was listening to be polite, but he wasn't interested in what either of them had to say. When a silence followed, he filled the gap with a courtesy that was habitual. He turned to Hunt and said the first thing that came to his mind, since any talk was better than no talk at all when entertaining visitors. "You're on the eleventh floor, aren't you, Mr. Parrish?"

Hunt agreed that he was.

"Had a special apartment built, I understand."

Hunt said that he had, when the building was put up.

"Belong to a club, Mr. Parrish?"

Hunt said that he didn't.

"You should. Best thing in the world for you. A dip in the pool, a steam bath, a shave and a rubdown and you come home feeling like a million, no matter how bad a day you've had downtown. Nothing like it."

"I imagine so. But I don't have the time."

"Make it," Albert said with conviction. "Make it. You'll never regret it. Be glad to put your name up any time you decide."

Hunt said it was very kind of him and consulted his watch, exhibiting great surprise at the hour. "Have you any idea how late it is? Much as I'd like to talk with you longer, Mr. Harewood, my wife is waiting for me upstairs."

"Oh, must you go? Just when we were all getting acquainted?" Maud cried, terribly amused. It was all she could do to keep from laughing out loud.

Hunt repressed his own smile and escaped. It wasn't difficult, for Albert made no effort to detain him.

His apartment was dark and quiet and Hilda hastened to light the lamps. Mrs. Parrish wasn't home yet, she told Hunt in a shocked tone. Hunt was surprised himself. For all the years of their marriage, Irene had always been there waiting for him. No, this wouldn't do, he thought as he scrubbed his shiny-skinned hands. He didn't mind if she had a lover, but he did mind when it interfered with his own routine. Somehow he would have to get this across to her. Poor girl, she had always been so careful to conceal her lovers from him, as if it would have made a difference. He simply didn't care. She hadn't the brains to know that he was fully cognizant of both her affairs, the long-term one and that little quickie, over almost before it began, and that far from blaming her for them, he was only amazed that she hadn't had more. He stood away from the mirror and admired himself at a distance. He was a fine-looking man, missed his calling, should have been on the stage. She'd have to go far to match him. Perhaps it wasn't so amazing after all.

He went into the living room and sat down with the evening paper, but he couldn't bother to read it. Irene's tardiness annoyed him and his afternoon with Maud disturbed him. Although they had done nothing but bicker for two hours, still the bickering had some interest, some point. And see what had happened to their conversation when Albert came in. Steam baths, rubdowns. It was always the case when someone like Albert walked in. So what did it all boil down to? That although Maud was not his soul mate either, since they needed to take from each other what neither of them could give, still, if grouped against the others, against the Alberts of this world, they could help to sustain each other; they could then give each other—what? Courage?

Hunt tossed the paper aside and looked at his watch again. Where could Irene be? Lover or no lover, this wasn't like her. Could something have happened to her? But then he heard her key in the door. He hastened to pick up the paper so she would find him busy and unconcerned.

5 :   *Tuesday, May Fifth*

By four o'clock in the afternoon, Julie lost patience sitting around waiting for the rain to stop. Her last kitchen towel had fallen to shreds in her hands and she could no longer put off her visit to the housewares shop. It served her right. She had known weeks ago that she needed kitchen towels, but it was much too simple to cross the street and pick them up the day she thought of it. Why, she must have passed by the housewares store every day since then, walking Rover. It was always the easy tasks she neglected, like buying paper clips around the corner, or picking up the telephone to order a white flower pot from the florist. She still hadn't done that! But just give her something really cumbersome, like going to Brooklyn to pick out beach furniture for the house at the Cape, and she'd knock it off the very day the idea came to mind. Yes, it served her right and she deserved to have to make a special trip now in the pouring rain. Grimly she put on her rubbers and raincoat and struggled through the wet gusts to the housewares store across the street. All day long the store had probably been empty, but right now it was packed with women all demanding to be waited on at once. It was hot in there and smelled of wet clothes. Both salesmen were harried and the waiting customers quibbled about who was first. Julie, rather than get herself into the thick of the haggling, decided to wait until the crowd thinned out. She wandered about in the meantime and inspected the gadgets displayed on the amoeba-shaped shelves that twisted around the walls of the store. She recognized two ladies who were fairly recent tenants of Number Ten and then remembered with amusement that she had been tagging them as "recent" for several years. One of them was being curt with Mr. Barker who owned the store. He wouldn't give her credit for a year-old coffeepot that was dented out of shape. She eventually delivered to him the last of her opinions and flung herself out of the shop in a rage, colliding with Irene Parrish, whom she blamed for the accident and muttered, "Well, some people!"

Irene, splendid in a royal blue velvet raincoat with a slender blue umbrella, looked back at her and brushed away the woman's impact with a gloved hand. She caught Julie's eye and smiled. "Nice woman. Perfectly charming," she said. "Isn't this an awful day?"

"Miserable."

"What a mob in here. You been waiting long? I have to get to a meeting." Irene glanced at her watch. She looked harassed and Julie noticed that her right upper lid was twitching. "We'll never get waited on. Oh, by the way, Mrs. Fay, I should thank you again for your tremendous donation to the Crippled Children's Fund. My eyes nearly popped out when I saw that check."

Julie was embarrassed and changed the subject. "I can't imagine why everybody waits for a rainy day to come here and buy pot holders. I thought I was the only lighthead in the neighborhood."

Irene made a sound that was halfway between a sigh and a gasp. "I've been downtown all day and now back up again to change into dry clothes." Nervously she pushed up her velvet sleeve and glanced again at her watch. "I'll never make it." She held up her hand and waved. "Oh, Mr. Barker, do you think I can get waited on?"

". . . a minute, Mrs. Parrish."

"Oh dear, I guess I'll have to let it go. I have to be at Fifty-fourth Street in three minutes. I can't possibly make it." Irene's hands fumbled with her purse.

"Make what, the meeting?"

"Oh, no, I *have* to go to the meeting." Irene buttoned the collar of her coat. Her eyelid twitched again and she put her finger to it for a second.

"Why must you?"

Irene's lovely navy blue eyes swept back to Julie's face in surprise. "But I'm on the Board."

"So what? It's such a miserable day, I bet half the ladies won't be there."

"But I *have* to be."

"Why? You haven't missed a meeting all year, have you? Why don't you chuck it and come to Schrafft's with me for tea?"

"Schrafft's for tea!"

"Yes, come on."

"I'd love to go to tea with you and you're very sweet to ask me, but some other time."

"Come on, be a devil. Live a little."

Irene had to smile. "It's crazy. Besides, it isn't right. It's what my husband would call an irresponsible action."

"Tell him I made you do it. . . . Mr. Barker, have you forgotten us?"

Julie ordered six kitchen towels, three dishcloths and some plastic freezer containers. Irene ordered two pot holders, an earthenware casserole dish—"Every time my cook uses one of these, she breaks it!"—and some assorted paper doilies. Once again she protested that she had no right to shirk her meeting, but Julie swept her out of the store. They bucked the wind and rain with their umbrellas and struggled up the block to Schrafft's.

"Schrafft's of all places, too," Irene said as they stood behind the brown velvet rope and waited for the hostess to show them to a table.

"What's wrong with it? It's wholesome."

Irene agreed. Her eyes sparkled and laughter bubbled inside her for no reason. She hadn't done anything like this in years. No one dared ask her to.

The hostess showed them to a table against the wall from which they could see the entire dining room and left them each with a small red tea menu. They put their coats and bundles on an extra chair and arranged themselves comfortably.

"Fifteen minutes ago if anyone told me I would be having tea in Schrafft's, I would have told them they were crazy," Irene said. "Do you do this often?"

"Hardly ever. I've had lunch here on occasion but never tea. It suddenly occurred to me."

"I'm glad it did. You did me a favor, Mrs. Fay."

"Julie."

"Julie. I've been rushing around so madly lately that this is just what I need. There's something restful and wholesome about a tearoom."

"Music by Muzak" alternated a classical number with a tender popular song to please all tastes. Just now they were playing "Apple Blossom Time" and Julie hummed it as she studied the small menu. "Of course you're having the tea sandwiches?"

"I am?" Irene looked at the sparse menu. "Yes, I suppose I am."

"And tea?"

"I'm afraid not, my dear. Schrafft's, fine; even tea sandwiches, but that's as far as I'll go. I'm having coffee."

"I hate tea," Julie admitted, "but somehow it's so fitting."

"I was under the impression you were a nonconformist."

"Me?" Julie's grey eyes looked so honestly amazed that Irene had to laugh.

"Well, you certainly don't conform to the mores of Number Ten. For one thing, you have the nerve to have a child, and for another, you have *no maid!*"

"I haven't a child any more."

"I know. He looks like a college boy."

"Almost six feet and only thirteen. It isn't fair to me," Julie said proudly. "People look at him and decide I must be an old bag."

"They probably think you're his sister. You look like a baby yourself. How old are you, or shouldn't I ask?"

"You shouldn't, but I'll tell you. Thirty-three."

Irene sighed. "Oh to be thirty-three again!"

"It goes so fast, doesn't it? In no time at all, I'll be saying what you've just said. Only yesterday, I was eighteen. No more than ten minutes ago, I was twenty-five. It's all over so soon."

"It's frightening." For a moment, Irene's eyes held a spark of terror, which she dispersed with a quick, low laugh and a shake of her head. "And I suppose Robin's saying, 'Oh, to be twenty-one!'"

"Probably. He doesn't know about Time yet."

"He's such a nice boy, Julie. I hear he's quite an athlete, too."

"How did you hear this?"

"I don't know, someone in the building. I understand he plays basketball very well."

Julie groaned.

"It must be tough on him to be the only child in a house full of bitter old people."

"It never was until recently."

"I'm afraid Hunt hasn't been too kind to Robin, but he doesn't mean anything by it. It's just that he isn't used to children."

"Oh, there's very little problem there—not with Mr. Parrish."

"Do you really mean that? Because it's bothered me for years. I've always loved Robin, you know, and——"

"Please don't let it bother you any more. Mr. Parrish is the least of our worries."

The waitress brought them their sandwiches together with tea for Julie and coffee for Irene. Irene bit into one of the five microscopic canapés from her plate. By being especially careful, she found she could make each do for two small bites. "Oh, how delightful! Cottage cheese!"

Julie tried one which consisted of a slice of tomato topped with a few grains of chopped parsley which sent them both into a fit of laughter. "It's pretty, though, and so refined!" Julie gasped.

"Genteel, too." Irene dabbed carefully at her eyes with the corner of her handkerchief so as not to smear her mascara. "You, of all people, you introduced me to a Schrafft's tea!"

"Why me of all people? I think this is perfectly lovely."

"Aren't you supposed to be a gourmet and a marvelous cook?"

"How things do get around in our building."

Irene picked up the last sandwich and tried it. "Tuna fish," she announced, "and it's the only one that tastes."

"Don't look so disapproving. Everything is just as it should be here. This is a tearoom and it's all proper and fitting."

"And this charms you."

"It does. Reminds me of home."

"Where's that?"

"Evansville, Indiana. Fruit salad in lime aspic with Russian dressing. Lamb stew. Tapioca pudding. And tea sandwiches."

"No wonder you took to cooking."

"I've always loved to cook. Even when I was a child, they couldn't get·me out of the kitchen."

"At least that's creative work and I can understand anyone enjoying it, but, and please slap me down if I'm getting too personal, I never could understand why you don't have a maid, Julie. You can't possibly enjoy cleaning house."

"I have a maid. She comes three times a week and does the laundry and heavy cleaning. The rest is easy for me. What would I do if I didn't do most of my own work? Everybody asks me the same question and it always floors me because the answer seems so obvious. First of all, what is so disgraceful about doing housework? Why should women prefer to labor in factories rather than work in a nice home? And why, simply because one's husband makes enough money to pay for a maid, must one have one? There are so many stupid rules. At so-and-so much income per year, a proper family is expected to live in such-and-such a way; so much for rent, so much for food, so much for clothes, so much for a car and for help. Well, we prefer to spend our money as we like. Rather than have a huge apartment and a high rent and two in help and all that, I'd prefer owning a beautiful Soutine. And I must have a duty and purpose to my life. Would you rather I spent my days shopping for things I don't need and meeting ladies for a lunch I'm not hungry for?"

"But scrubbing floors and dusting and cleaning Venetian blinds, that's not even a challenge. It requires no talent, no ability, and besides it's drudgery. It's what women do because they have to, not because they want to. How can you want to? I hope you don't mind my speaking up like this, but I've always wanted to ask you about it. Perhaps it's because you make me feel guilty, I don't know."

"To tell you the truth, I don't specially like to housekeep, but it's all I'm good for." Julie grinned.

"Come now, I never heard of anything so ridiculous."

"No, really. Ty and I believe that people are put on this earth to work. People who don't work are never happy. We've checked on this and it's the truth."

"I can't argue with that, but why pick cleaning house?"

"I didn't. It picked me. I have no training and no special talents or abilities beyond the running of a home. I'm not artistic at all. I'm a good appreciator, nothing more. One has to be honest about such things. Not everyone can be born with talent. I'm just a wife and mother, period. It's the only work I can do, and don't think that it's dull either, because it isn't when you work at it like a professional. It's a much better life than most of your fancy career women have, believe me. I'm not trying to

[133]

tell you I love house cleaning, because I don't. That's why I have this little maid to take the brunt of the unpleasant part off my shoulders. I'm lucky enough to be able to afford that luxury. But even so, I still have some cleaning to do—and those damn dishes, how I hate them! But I figure we all have to do some things we don't like in life. Isn't that true?"

Irene dropped her eyes.

"Don't you do things you don't like, even though you have all the money you need, and all the help?"

"You want to know the truth?"

"Of course."

"Of how I exist?" Irene pushed the words from behind her teeth, her whole barren, hectic, loveless life thrusting itself forward like a dark and evanescent cloud, here now and soon gone without a trace. But still, of course, she smiled. "You couldn't conceive of it. I rush, rush, rush. My life is ruled by my wrist watch—here at this moment for a dull task, there in thirteen minutes for a worse one, home at precisely five thirty for Hunt. I'm always breathless, choking over my race with the clock. You think I like any part of that?"

Julie said nothing, only stared at her.

"I must say thank you, thank you, thank you all day to everyone all the time, as I said thank you to you at Barker's, I must say it to everyone I meet, even if it's for two dollars received from some tight old millionaire when I'd really like to spit in his eye. I can never say what I really think, never. Not anywhere."

Once started, the bitter words poured from her ruefully smiling lips, the truth spoken in mock jest. She also had to say thank you to every lady who graced a luncheon or bridge with her presence and then ate enough for six and refused to buy a chance at the door prizes. She had to thank every lady who attended a regular monthly meeting only once a year and then took up the entire session tearing their program apart. She had to tell them thanks for their valuable suggestions and wouldn't they serve on this committee and help to carry the suggestions out? Oh, no? Too busy? She was so sorry. Of course she understood. And thank you, thank you all the same.

"How I hate it!" Irene softened her vehemence with a low laugh. "How I hate committee meetings, luncheons, fund-raising like beggars, how I hate the women I meet!"

It was terrible to hear such words emerge from the controlled, smiling face of this beautiful woman. Julie thought how little anyone knew about anyone else in this life, how different people were inside from the beautiful covering ornaments that drew the eye. Irene Parrish was not smiles and blue velvet and pearls at all. She was something dark and tight and withered and the only promise was that she still seemed to have some fight.

They ordered more tea and coffee and sat closer together, speaking almost in whispers now. Once started, Irene couldn't stop. The round grey eyes that stared into hers seemed to grow larger, warmed with sympathy and agreement, until there was nothing before her but these eyes, that pulled bitter, truthful words from her.

She had tried everything, anything to keep busy during her time on earth. A job, a career, these were out. Naturally the wife of Mr. Hunt Parrish couldn't work. First of all, it would be beneath her dignity, and second of all, it would be unfair of her to accept a job needed by someone less fortunate. As far as doing her own housework was concerned, it had simply never occurred to her to try. It was out of the question, beyond considering. Neither her mother nor her mother's mother had ever soiled their hands with household grime. So she had tried painting, play-writing, ceramics, and she had taken random courses at Columbia. But in the end, it transpired that she was not a talented person, nor was she a student who could cloister herself within university walls. She got a C— in her playwriting course, but she went on writing at home all the same, pretending she was a professional, an unrecognized genius, until Hunt financed a play for her and it was a holocaust, a public C—, one she couldn't cover up or lie about or daydream away. So home she went, beaten, lonely, humiliated. And it was at this time that the charity organizations picked her, a ripe peach hanging ready to burst, from the tree. "I didn't look for them, Julie. They came looking for me, and they grabbed me and sucked me into their midst. *Et voilà*, I am here. Finis. 'Just help us out on this one theater benefit. We'll do most of the work. Can't you spare an hour or two out of your life for the crippled children, Mrs. Hunt Parrish?' That's how they start. Can one say no? Especially when it reflects on one's husband?"

"That's the life I made up my mind to avoid," Julie said. "My mother was a committee woman and I watched her and her friends for eighteen years, so I know what you're talking about. I made up my mind as a child that this wasn't going to be for me. Of course, with Robin and practically no help, I have a wonderful excuse."

"Not that it isn't important work, Julie," Irene said suddenly. "*Some-one* has to do it."

"Yes, that's what they say when you start to criticize the situation. 'It's important and necessary work and someone has to do it.' I agree that it has to be done, but there must be some other way. It *is* important work and a fine person like yourself shouldn't have to hate it so. The setup is all wrong, but I don't know why or where."

"I know why and where. What's wrong is that the wrong women do it for the wrong reasons, Julie. Most charitable work falls of necessity to wealthy women, most wealthy women are idle women, and most idle women are neurotic messes. A neurotic mess is the wrong kind of person for anything or anybody."

Julie laughed. "You're pretty cruel."

"Not cruel, truthful. So to begin with, you've got a bunch of neurotic messes, who go in for charitable work for a number of bad reasons. Some do it for personal aggrandizement. These are the women who have to be captain or they won't pay or play. Some do it to get business for their husbands. These are the wives of professional men, insurance men and stockbrokers, mainly. Some do it to try to climb up the social ladder and meet the right people. Sometimes you will be unfortunate enough to come across a combination of a professional man's wife who is a social climber, too, and this is a species of shrike to avoid like the plague. Then there are those who do it, like me, out of desperation and with no feeling at all, simply because they have absolutely nothing else to do. Sprinkled in with all of these, you find a rare, wonderful woman once in a while, who does it because the fate of a crippled child is really breaking her heart, but oh, how rare these women are, and how silent—how seldom do I meet one!"

Julie clasped her hands in her lap and stretched against the back of her chair. "It seems to me, if you can't be one of these rare, wonderful women, Irene, then you should get out."

"You give me a way out. Give me an alternate life at my age, and I'll grab for it. No, I'm a fish on the sand, a bird under water, and it's too late now. I should have been a wife and mother, too," she said. "I was born to be a mother!"

Julie toyed with her spoon and wondered why Irene hadn't adopted a child if she was unable to conceive, but she remained silent.

"Well, I've certainly ruined what started out to be a perfectly delightful tea," Irene said, flashing her sudden, bright smile, forcibly renewing herself.

"Oh, no, I've enjoyed it, really. I loved your description of those club-ladies."

"It's your own fault, you know. You've been such a sympathetic listener that I couldn't help taking advantage of you. But I feel so much better now. Even if you don't solve anything, it's good to get it off your chest." With a habitual motion, she glanced at her watch. "Do you know it's six thirty!"

"It couldn't be!"

"But it is. Oh, I'm terribly late."

"Good Lord, Ty and Robin must be frantic." Julie grabbed the check.

"No, let me."

"I invited you. Do you think I should phone them? No, it would take too long. I can run home just as fast. Oh, they must be so worried!"

Irene was nervously silent as she gathered together her belongings, thinking of the stern greeting that awaited her. And he'll never believe me, though he's believed me all these years, she thought. Won't that be ironic? Today he won't believe me!

Julie thrust the money through the glass archway at the cashier's desk. She gathered her change without counting it and the two of them ran out into the rain. They stamped into the lobby of Number Ten shaking their dripping umbrellas and Irene rang for the elevator.

Her heart beat fast as she tried to open the door of her apartment silently, as if slipping in unnoticed might help. He'll never believe me, she kept worrying, never. She closed the door quietly behind her and moved down the hall to her room on tiptoe. She hung her coat away and put her umbrella in the stall shower. She ran a comb through her hair, washed her hands and walked stiffly into the living room. She was certain by the silence that her husband awaited her in anger.

He was sitting in his accustomed chair with the newspaper folded in his lap. "Well!"

She put on her bright smile. "Darling, I'm sorry. You must have been worried to death. I'm terribly sorry." She kissed him.

"I was worried."

"I'm sure. And you'll never believe where I've been and why I'm late, never in a million years will you believe it."

"I won't? Then I don't suppose there's any point in your telling me, is there?"

"Oh, Hunt! And you didn't even get your cocktail! After all these years, couldn't Hilda have mixed you a drink? Poor darling!"

"She offered to. I didn't want one. No point in drinking alone. Now where were you?" Hunt's voice was stern, but his expression was strangely friendly.

Irene sat down on the couch. "Would you like a drink now?"

"I think it's a little late, don't you?"

"Well, yes. Besides I'm much too full of coffee."

"Coffee?"

"Guess where I've been."

"Don't be childish, Irene. With all the thousands of places that serve coffee in New York, how could I possibly guess which particular chef brewed your cup? That is, if the chef happened to be a professional."

"He was. I was at Schrafft's."

"Really?"

"And guess who was with me."

"Rock Hudson."

"Julie Fay."

Hunt looked blank for a moment. "Oh, yes."

"She's a darling, Hunt. So pretty and young. You'd love her."

"I'm sure."

"And I had a real woman-to-woman talk with her, the kind I haven't had since school. We both forgot the time, simply forgot all about it."

His mouth twitched and she saw the beginnings of a sarcastic smile narrow his eyes.

"But really, Hunt, that's the God's honest truth."

"I'm sure it is." Now his smile was full.

"You don't believe me."

His eyes sparkled with amusement. "Of course I don't believe you, Irene. You'll have to learn to do much better than this. Now I really think we'd better go in to dinner. Hilda is fluttering at the door over there. I understand it's a matter of a falling cheese soufflé."

Irene followed Hunt to the table. Across the long expanse his face twinkled merrily at her, bright with good humor. "It didn't fall after all," he said, tasting his soufflé.

She felt sick.

"I said it didn't fall."

"What——?"

"The soufflé, darling."

She shivered.

"I hope you didn't catch a cold running around in this rain?" He was gently solicitous, but that knowing, ironic smile lay like a gash across his face.

She looked down at her soufflé to hide the turbulence that throbbed through her body, to hide her confusion and her disbelief.

"There's nothing at all to be upset about, Irene," he said quietly, "just as long as you don't disturb my routine."

In apartment 9B, Ty and Robin had just finished giving Julie hell.

[138]

Ty had been about to call the police and the hospitals when she had come in. Now Julie, contrite and humble, was in the kitchen hurriedly throwing some kind of a meal together, and already Ty and Robin were chuckling in the living room, having made a pact to punish her properly by refusing to talk to her throughout the entire dinner. But naturally, part way through the Campbell's tomato soup (enlivened with a dash of sour cream), Robin forgot.

6 :   *Wednesday, May Sixth*

At nine thirty in the morning, Flossie Marsh was seated in her living room. Beside her on a table was a new box of candy that Walt had trudged through yesterday's downpour to get for her, but because she had already consumed almost a pound of Flora Mir chocolates, half a jar of Turkish figs, countless pecans and a package of stuffed dates, he had made her promise not to touch the new box until today. Next to the box of chocolates was the morning mail, neatly stacked. Going through this daily was a chore to Flossie because she didn't trust the mails—never had. An innocent-looking white envelope might well contain a problem that could involve one for months, like that innocuous inquiry last year from her father's lawyers concerning the whereabouts of a certain bond issue not present in his effects. A little, polite letter, but oh Lord, the fuss it had raised, for those same bonds rested in Flossie's vault, a gift from her father that the Government contended he had no right to have given her. How was she to know what he could or could not give? Yet, for a while there, she was made to feel like a traitor to her country, a conspirator to defraud the United States Treasury, and she was certain she would have to spend the next few years of her life in jail. It was all settled in the end, of course, but look what a conflagration that one little letter had produced!

In addition to possible bombshells, there were the demands of charitable organizations which flowed in daily. Greathearted Flossie was on the defensive with each request she had to turn down. It was impossible to give to all of them, no one had that kind of money these days, so to pick one meant to turn down another, and the only way she could turn down a charitable request was to convince herself that they had some nerve—some nerve to put her on the sucker list in the first place, some nerve to think if she gave to one Blind organization that meant she had to give to another, some nerve for the Presbyterians to solicit her when any reasonable check would reveal that she was Dutch Reform, some nerve for all the diseases and hospitals and sanitariums and relief organizations to separate themselves into thousands of individual groups so that she was forced to decide for Arthritis and against Heart, for MC and against MD, for Care and against UNICEF. It was ridiculous, it was unfair, and so, in a guilty rage, she would tear up requests she couldn't fulfill and repeat again to assuage her feelings, "Some nerve!"

Then there were the ads. These she longed to tear up without opening as a matter of principle since she felt it was a waste of her time, an unwarranted encroachment upon her privacy, yet even as she held the offending envelope in her hand, she would envision all that lay behind it, the amount of work that had gone into the preparation of these advertisements, the careful psychological investigations, the labor of the artists, the copy writers, the proofreaders, the printers, the anxieties of all concerned, from the boss down the line to the little girl who had addressed the envelopes, as to whether or not Mrs. Flossie Marsh would this very morning trouble to look at their message inside or throw it away unread, and so, with a murmur of vexation, she would tear the letter open and do her duty to all by glancing at its contents before throwing it away.

Even personal letters brought her little pleasure. "I'm sure you'll be sorry to hear that Aunt Emily passed away last month after a long and painful illness. . . ." "Betsey had her third miscarriage. We fear she shall never be able to bring a live baby into the world, just like you, poor Flossie, it must run in the family." "John sank practically all of his capital into this venture and now he and his family are living from hand to mouth." "We're certain Aline has cancer."

Yes, the morning mail brought anger, guilt, frustrations and sadness to Flossie often, and every once in a while, a dividend check.

She was not aware of it, but as she reached for the pile of letters this morning, she steeled herself imperceptibly for the possibility of an ordeal; her face took on a strained look as she sorted through it, placing Walt's mail to one side and making two piles of her own on her lap, the left thigh for the important-looking letters and the right for the ads and bills. It was early in the month so the right-hand pile grew high, bills from several department stores, from the meat market, from Barker's, from the cleaners, from her underwear lady, and from Mr. Rider. The ads she glanced at dutifully and tore up; the bills she handed to her maid unopened, to place in the top drawer of her desk to be paid whenever she got to them, perhaps this month or the next; it didn't matter when, her credit was always good. The personal mail she read through quickly, then added it to Walt's pile for him to see.

So it was that Mr. Rider's letter went unopened, into the drawer with all the bills. It was contained within the type envelope he used for soliciting the monthly rent and how was Flossie to remember that she had received her rent bill from him a few days before?

The mail disposed of, she turned to a more pleasant occupation, the opening of the candy box Walt had brought her yesterday. Even though it was still early in the morning, she felt she deserved one taste. After all, why live by the clock? One hour was as good as another, afternoon no better than morning. She raised the lid and inhaled the rich, heavy odor of true chocolate and knew at once that Walt had made a "find." She couldn't remember now who had told them about this little old lady on the West Side who made the best chocolates in the world, but whoever it was, she owed him her thanks. She sniffed again and then, although she was mighty guilty about disobeying her late father's strict rule that sweets were eaten only *after* lunch, she tried one, chewing it slowly with closed eyes to concentrate on the flavor. Oh, what a confection! What heavenly, delicious real chocolate! She finished it and tried another, making small sounds of amazement and pleasure. Wait until she told Walt, that sweet old guy, getting his big feet wet for a lousy box of candy for her. With half of another chocolate held in her fingers, she turned and looked out of the picture window at her garden, checking its condition, for even the new chocolates couldn't hold her attention away from it for long. She smiled because, after yesterday's cold rain, the sun was warming the foliage and even the grass looked quite dry. It was going to be a lovely, warm day. And it was time now to sit outside in the sun. She shook the little bell she always carried with her, but almost at the same time, the louder sound of the doorbell drowned it. So she finished the chocolate and with another guilty sigh, helped herself again while she waited to give the maid a chance to answer the door.

The maid came in frowning, to report that there were two men outside to see her. She spoke indignantly as if their presence besmirched this household.

"Gentlemen from where?" Flossie could barely speak. This one was a caramel.

"Some city building department. They want to see your *garden*, Mrs. Marsh."

Flossie gripped the arms of her chair and swallowed the remainder of the candy whole, choking on it. "Send—them—away!"

"But they're from the City—from the Government."

"I won't see them!"

But it was too late. One of the men came tiptoeing to the arched entrance of the living room, smiling diffidently, his right fist held up as if to knock on a door that wasn't there. He was a tall, pleasant-looking fellow, well dressed, with a friendly face, who apologized for disturbing her and requested permission to have a look at her garden. He promised it wouldn't take long.

The blood rushed to Flossie's cheeks and burned there. She had trouble catching her breath. "Why? What for?"

He explained that he was investigating a complaint of a violation——

She didn't let him finish. "There's no violation here! None!" She struggled to lift herself out of the chair.

The young man was embarrassed by her reaction and hastened to assure her that he was simply here to check and nothing more. His manner was courteous and almost timid. He hardly appeared menacing, standing there with an unhappy face, his hat in his hand, and Flossie drew in a deep breath and took hold of herself, assured that she could handle him. Craftily, she inquired, "Do you have a search warrant?"

"No, Ma'am. This is Mr. Rider's property and he sent us here."

"But this is my home!"

"You have to let us in for observation and repair. That's in your lease. How else could leaks be traced? You must understand this."

"There's nothing to repair. There's nothing wrong here. Besides, I can't let just anybody in. You must have some credentials. You could be anybody. I don't know you."

The young man's shy, friendly attitude didn't change. He brought out identification and presented it to her. He said the man with him was a special photographer and would she like to see his card, too?

She handed it back to him with trembling fingers. "No—no."

"All right to go out there now?"

"Can I say no?" Flossie drew a long, shaking breath. Inadvertently, she reached for the telephone to call Walt, then withdrew her hand. No, why should she call him? Nothing was going to happen. Nothing was wrong. They would discover that nothing was wrong and go away and it would all be water under the bridge. Just as some think to deny the existence of illness by avoiding a diagnosis, so she would deny the possibility of losing her garden by never voicing it, not even to Walt. That was the way to fight. Nothing existed unless one allowed it. The moment one allowed it, the fight was lost.

Through the picture window, Flossie watched the two men invade her garden and then suddenly, unable to bear their presence out there, unable to leave the garden alone with no one to defend it against them, she cried out for the maid to come and help her up. She wanted to hurry outside but her heavy, painful legs would only let her totter clumsily, the maid beside her with a waiting hand near her elbow.

The photographer was fussing with his camera. He was a short, merry-looking fellow with a sandy crew cut, who grinned at her and touched his hand to his temple in a salute, but he could be a menace, too, if she allowed it. The pleasant young man knelt by a flower bed and shoved something long and thin into the earth, piercing it, probing into it. He looked around at Flossie as she approached and smiled. He looked as if he felt bad about what he was doing.

"Careful there now, careful of those flowers. Watch out for their roots," she warned.

"Don't worry, I won't hurt a thing."

"You *are* hurting it."

"No, believe me, I'm careful. I know what I'm doing."

"Well, if you really do, then you must notice how beautifully it's built. Thick copper lining underneath—two layers, I think, with wonderful drainage—I can show you where some of the drains are——"

"We've got the blueprints here, Mrs. Marsh."

"You do? How did you get them?" It seemed so official, his having her blueprints, so final; much more frightening than his presence here.

"Mr. Rider had a copy of them attached to your lease."

"Oh," she said, quieting. Of course that was how he got them. Then it wasn't so bad. It was only Mr. Rider being unkind and she would handle him later. "Aren't they well planned? You can see how nothing could happen. You can see that everything is in perfect condition. After all, it's been years."

"It's magnificent, Ma'am. I never saw anything like it."

"You do the gardening?" the photographer wanted to know.

"Used to more than now"—Flossie gave a nervous laugh—"but with every extra pound, it got tougher and tougher to bend the old knees. But it *is* well built, isn't it? A man from the landscape gardener comes every other week to check and repair."

The photographer touched some orange azaleas and told her how beautiful they would be, taken in color, and the man who knelt near the flower bed praised her tulips and remarked on the number of rose bushes he saw, as he probed. They wouldn't be so nice, they wouldn't compliment her like this if anything was wrong, Flossie reasoned, letting herself heavily into a chair. "You just wait until the roses come out," she said, "if you think the spring flowers are nice. You never saw anything like them, all strong-stemmed with large heads. There was a picture of them in *House and Garden* a few years ago. They're my specialty." She spoke so fast she almost tripped over her words, watching the young man's face in profile as he bent over his work. "Maybe you'd like to come back next month and see them?" she tested him.

"I sure would," he said, standing up. He pulled the blueprint out of his pocket and examined it a moment, then moved over onto the lawn. "Green velvet," he said, giving his head an envious shake. "You should see mine. Nothing but crab grass." He bent down and poked carefully. "I'll have to open up here."

"Cut a *hole* in my lawn?"

"Don't worry, I'll slice well under the roots without hurting them and then replace it."

Suddenly Flossie pounded her fists on her lap. "Why, why does this have to happen, why?"

The young man didn't answer. His face was flushed as he bent down and sliced into her lawn.

She winced, for it was like an incision into her own flesh. "Everything all right?"

He grunted and kept working. "Just want to get a look at this drain here."

"The man from the landscape gardener checks them all the time, I told you!"

"Just routine, Mrs. Marsh. I don't like doing this any more than you enjoy watching me, believe me."

"Then why, oh why, oh why!" she whispered, covering her face.

"I don't want you to be sore at *me*, that's all. They send me out here and say 'inspect.' I have to do what I'm told."

"I know, I know."

The young man motioned to the photographer and pointed to the hole in the lawn. The photographer ran stealthily across the grass, pointed his camera downward and took a flash picture.

The sound alerted Flossie and she looked up quickly, suspicious. "What was that? What did you do?"

"Just took a picture."

"Why? What for?"

"We were told to take it, Mrs. Marsh, just following orders, that's all."

"Oh."

The photographer was finished. He came and sat next to Flossie and chattered about the prizes he'd won or was about to win, about the high expense involved in being a photographer, about how little the art was appreciated and how every Joe thought he was a professional the moment he bought himself an expensive camera, and Flossie listened only partially, her attention fastened upon the pleasant young man who kept poking into the lawn and the flower beds and making little notes on a pad.

But at last he, too, was finished. He sauntered over to where they were sitting, wiping his hands on his handkerchief. "That's that. One thing I'm glad about, we never would have seen this beautiful place if there hadn't been a complaint," he said kindly.

So it was all right! Of course it was all right. The way he dismissed the complaint and only spoke of his good fortune. . . . Flossie felt like a fool as tears flooded her eyes. The pleasant man was embarrassed and turned away to give her a chance to dab quickly with her handkerchief. She cleared her throat, but the frog remained. "How about a drink, fellers?" she asked hoarsely. "Come on, now that's over with, how about it?"

The pleasant young man was still troubled by her show of tears. He said he'd love one but there wasn't time and the photographer looked disappointed. He gathered his equipment together and stowed it away in a large black suitcase. The pleasant man thanked her for being so patient with them. She told him that wasn't hard, they were such nice young men. They grinned awkwardly and left.

Flossie crumpled into her chair with her eyes closed, feeling ill. The carefully sliced and replaced turf on her lawn was like a bandaged wound upon her own belly. She could barely reach out to ring the bell for the maid. What she needed now was more of that good rich chocolate for energy. This had been a narrow escape.

7 :   *Thursday, May Seventh*

Today would probably break all heat records for this time of year. Flossie Marsh poured sun lotion all over herself. Her tan was well under way. Suzanne d'Auriac was forced to change to her sun-repellent powder base to protect her delicate skin. Irene Parrish stepped out into the street early in the morning, walked half a block and then removed her mink stole and sent it back upstairs with Terence. Maud Harewood lay on her chaise in her nightgown drinking vodka and tonic with plenty of ice. Walt Marsh had forgotten to have his summer suits cleaned, so he worked in his office in his shirt sleeves because the air conditioning wasn't working and the hell with anybody who didn't like it. John d'Auriac, in his beautifully tailored winter worsted, suffered cheerfully and with no evident perspiration. But Hunt Parrish, Albert Harewood and Tyler Fay had learned their lesson the previous Saturday and were prepared with clean summer suits to wear downtown.

Julie Fay looked fresh and young in a pink sleeveless linen blouse and skirt and her hair tied in a pony tail with a pink bow. She felt quite comfortable sitting in her favorite chair near the living-room windows where even on the hottest day there usually was a breeze. She was embroidering another sheet-and-pillowcase set for their beds, this time palest blue on white. It was a lavish design and had taken her the better part of the winter; so long, in fact, that Ty had begun to tease her about it. "You might have it ready for Robin's wedding night." That was why she was working so hard on it, even in the heat.

At four o'clock, Robin came home with Jimmy Parker and Bobby Linkholm, all three of them streaked with sweat and grime, their faces red, their hair damp, rolled-up khakis stained with grass and earth. They each had a round bulge in their right-hand pockets where the baseball was kept and in each case, Julie noted that the pocket was ripped and wondered whether this, too, was deliberate, another fashion for the ever-conforming young "tweed." They explained that it was too hot to play in the park. Instead they thought they'd listen to records. "But no ball throwing, boys," Julie warned. "Word of honor?" She made a pitcher of lemonade and took it in to them, with fruit and cookies. They had washed in the meantime and the towels were strewn on the bathroom floor, black with all the dirt they had removed from themselves. The pitcher was empty by the time she put the dirty towels in the wash and replaced them with others, so she made grape punch this time and then left them alone.

She returned to her embroidery, determined to have the set finished within two weeks just to show Ty. Robin's wedding bedding indeed! From Robin's room, rock and roll blared. Julie listened a moment, hoping they would turn it down, hating to interrupt them, then had to put her embroidery aside and poke her head through the door. "You'll have to lower that, boys."

"Aw, Mrs. Fay," Jimmy Parker objected, "it's not that loud!"

"We have pernickety neighbors," Julie said, feeling as prissy as the word "pernickety" sounded. "I'm sorry, fellows."

Robin turned the music down and she went back into the living room. For a while, everything was quiet, but then she heard the sounds of their feet on the linoleum, measured, rhythmic sounds that told her they were trying new Lindy steps, and almost at once, the telephone rang. Julie sighed and answered it, knowing so well who it was that she said, "Yes, Mrs. Harewood," instead of "Hello," and explained patiently that Robin had company, but that she would ask them to stop dancing. Maud said she hated to spoil their fun, but——. "I'm sure you do," Julie said somewhat acidly and hung up.

An expression that was new and troubling to Julie was the deadpan look on a boy's face when he is being unfairly reprimanded. Now she saw it in triplicate before her and she stumbled on her words, trying to explain that the noise wasn't bothering her at all, but that they had a sick neighbor beneath them who had just telephoned and complained. She went back to her embroidery quickly, escaping the look on their faces, and set to work furiously, jabbing her needle like a dagger.

A few minutes later, Bobby and Jimmy left. They said good-bye and thanked her when she asked them to come again, but she could tell they wouldn't, not even because of the lemonade and punch, the fruit and cookies. Robin's face was still expressionless as he saw them out and when they had gone, he returned to his room and closed the door without a word. For a long time after that, Julie heard the low sounds of the radio playing hit tunes, and she wondered what he was doing, reading, dreaming, sulking, sleeping perhaps. Sulking, she decided, and with good reason, too. Something would have to be done about this. It couldn't go on forever.

She finished one pillowcase and folded it aside with the two completed sheets. Now all she had to do was one more. She took it out of her workbasket, fitted the embroidery rings around the central monogram to hold the cloth tight, and began to work on the J.

She wasn't aware of noise from Robin's room until the telephone rang again. It had become automatic for her to check for unwarranted sounds whenever she heard the telephone, even during the daytime when Robin was away at school. Now she could barely detect a muffled thud between the shrill rings. Impatiently she started to her feet and crossed to the foyer. Then she stopped. No, she wouldn't answer the telephone. This time, she wouldn't. This had gotten completely out of hand—an insistent cause and effect thing that was driving her insane;

one low sound of any kind and then the telephone bell. No, she'd be damned if she'd answer it. She could feel her anger as a physical manifestation, starting with an explosion in her chest that mushroomed up, a fast-beating heart and a tension at her throat, an impulse to scream. But lately, since Albert Harewood's visit, the anger was complicated by pity and consequent frustration. And the telephone continued to ring and Robin's low sounds also went on. Couldn't he hear the telephone? And didn't he know what it meant? Her anger turned upon him. How many times did she have to nag him, over and over again, keep quiet, keep quiet, keep quiet?

She approached his door and threw it open. She caught him in the center of the room in his basketball shorts. She startled him and he stood for a second, one foot raised and one hand in the air, holding a pair of rolled-up socks.

"Robin Fay, I thought you promised your father never to play basketball in your room again!"

He put his foot down and dropped his arm. He stared at her silently.

"Can't you hear the telephone? Don't you know what it means? But you deliberately place me in this position over and over again. I'm sick of having to apologize to her!"

He stared at his mother. She had never screamed at him like this before. His eyes looked frightened, his set mouth stubborn.

The telephone kept ringing.

"Why are you playing basketball when you promised your father you wouldn't?"

He didn't answer. His eyes moved away from hers.

"Answer me!"

"I'm sorry."

"What do you expect us to do with you? I never thought you were a sneak before, but it seems you are. Where did you get that baseball I saw in your pocket before?"

"Borrowed it."

"Well, you return it tomorrow, hear? And don't borrow any more. Your father is punishing you and justifiably, too. Besides, you don't need three baseballs among the three of you."

His eyes were upon hers, again, unblinking.

"You keep this up and we'll all be in trouble. Do you want us to get dispossessed?"

He looked at her, his mouth twitching, and suddenly he shouted, "Yes! Yes, I do! I hate it here! This isn't a home, it's a prison and I hate it!"

[148]

His violent answer shocked Julie into a momentary silence in which, for one small second, she felt as he did. But the telephone was still ringing and she was caught between the two. He didn't even try to cooperate, and that woman never gave up. "All you do is sneak things behind my back these days," she said petulantly. "You never did things like that before. You were always such a straightforward, honest boy. I don't know what to do with you. Shall I forbid you to close your door from now on? Dad's already had to take away your baseball and your handball, but we can't very well take away your socks, can we? What do you suggest we do?" Ashamed of her outburst, she gradually calmed and was now speaking evenly.

His stiff face showed no emotion at all as he looked straight at her and shrugged.

"Will you promise me faithfully never to play socks again?"

"Yes."

"Word of honor, now?"

"Yes."

He continued to stare at her until she could no longer bear the resentment in his eyes. She searched for something to say, some appropriate word of apology that wouldn't make her lose face, but his expression muted her. Quietly, she turned and left his room. She picked up her embroidery again, but it was no longer enjoyable and she threw it aside.

The late afternoon sun poured in obliquely through the blinds and the breeze had died down. Her cheeks burned and the room seemed to close in on her. There was no air. There was no air in the whole apartment and she felt as if she couldn't stand it here another moment. Suddenly she jumped up and ran into Robin's room. He had changed back into his khakis and was pulling a tee shirt over his head.

"Say, Rob, let's hightail it out of here and get a soda, how about it?"

His stiff face relaxed, softened, and finally broke into a grin. "You mean it? You serious?"

"Sure, come on, my treat." She took his hand and pulled him out of his room.

They left the apartment in a hurry and simultaneously, the moment they reached the street, they broke into a run, their heads back, their arms swinging, laughing because they could breathe again.

Walter Marsh brushed away something that disturbed him near his right shoulder and rolled over, burying his head in the pillow and clutching the covers close about his neck, but something continued to annoy him, fluttering fingers that tugged here and there no matter how deep he buried himself resisting them, and along with this irritation was a hissing sound which his half-sleeping comprehension at last recognized as the sibilance of a whisper. Pulling himself out of sleep, he turned his head and squinted, his eyes slowly focusing on the maid's figure bending over him. "Wha? What's it?"

She stilled him and pointed to Flossie, slumbering in the other bed. She seemed agitated. Something was wrong, something that Flossie shouldn't know about. He sat up abruptly.

"Men outside to see you," she whispered. "Hurry."

He left his bed without taking his bathrobe and moved with jerky silence, closing the door soundlessly behind him. He brushed his fingers through his stiff, upstanding hair and rubbed the sleep out of his eyes. Blearily, on naked feet, he faced the men who stood in his foyer, while the maid hovered near, clasping and unclasping her nervous hands. "Yes?" He peered about him, then addressed the one man who was not in work clothes. "What is it?"

The man said something incomprehensible about a violation on the terrace and handed Walt an order. Walt stared at the white paper that quivered in his fingers. He didn't understand.

A violation, the man explained, surely Mr. Marsh knew about it, about the corroded metal lining, about the faulty drainage that was allowing water to leak through to the apartment below.

Dumbly Walt shook his head and his eyes sought a view of the garden through the windows. If the drainage was faulty, he would certainly have it repaired. . . .

But it seemed not. Violation, Mr. Marsh. He ought to know what that meant.

Walt's eyes moved to the workmen, who stood uncomfortably in the background, and at last he thought he understood. "You don't mean you're here to tear it apart? No, couldn't be. . . ." For a moment, a disbelieving smile pulled up the corners of his mouth.

"Read the order, Mr. Marsh. I'm surprised you didn't know about this before. Your wife should have told you. She knew."

Walt twisted towards the maid, who was dabbing at her eyes with her apron, uttering miserable sounds. "Men came to look, but she—she said everything was all right after that," she confirmed, weeping.

". . . all these trees—shrubbery, the flowers?"

The man raised his palms. "Your wife had plenty of warning, sir. She should have removed them by now. I can't overlook an official order."

"I'm going to call my landlord."

"It was your landlord himself who put in the complaint to begin with, sir."

"Not Lawrence Rider. Rider? You wait here."

The dial sped around guided by angry fingers and Rider's sleepy voice answered.

"Hello, Rider? Say, what the hell is going on here? What the hell you think you're doing?"

Rider cleared the hoarseness from his voice. "I thought I'd hear from you today, Mr. Marsh. What've you been doing up to now, playing ostrich, or just plain telling me to go to hell?"

"Look, you, Rider. . . . The first I hear of this is two minutes ago. What the hell kind of way is this to treat a tenant? You knew damn well if there was a violation, all you had to do was talk to me about it. This is a low trick and I don't even know if it's legal. I didn't get any official, written warning from you—nothing."

"Oh, you didn't? What's today? The fifteenth, Friday, right? Just a minute, I've got that folder here someplace. . . . Yes, here it is. On Monday, May fourth, Mr. Gruppmann, on orders from me, visited your wife and told her she would have to remove the plants and repair the damages to the roof. I would have come myself, but my wife had just been taken to the hospital. So we started out trying to do it in a quiet, friendly way."

"But no," Walt murmured. "No, I didn't know——"

"You're kidding."

"No. I didn't know."

"I'm sorry about that, Marsh. I can't be blamed for what your wife didn't tell you, though. The apartment is in her name and all correspondence naturally goes to her. It never occurred to me she wouldn't tell you. So to continue, on Tuesday, May fifth, I sent her an official letter notifying her that the matter had been turned over to the Building Department, and still I heard not a word from either of you. That's the thanks I got after all the money I've spent repairing the results of your leaks, and the years I've waited, knowing this had to be done. I've known for two, three years, Marsh, but I've been putting it off for her sake. On Wednesday, May sixth, which was the day she must have received my letter, Mrs. Marsh was visited by Building Department Inspectors who found and photographed the violations. I certainly expected to hear from you after that! But since there was no word, I did what I had to do. This is my property and there are other people living in the building besides you, who have to be considered, too."

Walt spoke through stiff lips. "But that's—my property out there."

"I gave you plenty of time to dispose of it. It's not my fault, Marsh. Better have a talk with your wife."

"So now what?" Walt asked, after a pause. "You going to dump it all over the side?"

"Look, why don't you call those so-called expert landscape gardeners of yours and make them send men and a truck at once? Actually, I think you've a pretty good case there. I'm sure the Building Department men would wait, if offered a little something for their time."

"I have a better idea. Instead of that, why don't you call the Department and ask for a few days' grace for me, Rider?"

"Don't you think I've already done that? The report was handed in a week ago last Wednesday. They wanted to send the men over that Friday, then the following Monday. I said no, another day, another week, please. Waiting to hear from you, risking more leaks. Giving you every chance."

"Okay, Rider, damn thoughtful of you. You've given me a long, sad and saintly story. But don't think your neck is so clean. You've known us a long time. You know what this garden has meant to Mrs. Marsh and you might have figured things out, things like perhaps that she couldn't face what you were dishing out to her, so she stuck her head in the sand. You should have called me, and you know it. You should have sent me the official, written warning, or a copy of it. I won't forget this, I'll never forget it, Rider!" Walt slammed down the receiver. He lit a cigarette with difficulty, his fingers shaking. Puffing a great cloud of smoke about him, he dialed the landscape gardener. If he didn't have his truck over in half an hour, he'd haul him into court and plaster his name in the mud—he knew goddam well the whole terrace floor was corroded—he must have known it.

The gardener seemed dumbfounded, said he'd be right over himself.

"You're no goddam good to me. Send the truck and men and long ropes and pulleys to save these trees and plants, goddammit!"

The truck would be right there, if he had to drive it himself. He couldn't understand what it was all about, but the truck would be right there and so would he. What more could Mr. Marsh ask?

Walt shuffled out to the men who were still waiting in the foyer. "If you boys will wait for the gardener to get here, I'll make it worth your while. There's a fortune in plants out there I'd like to save," he said tonelessly, and nodded his thanks when they agreed. "Go out into the garden and wait. But quietly, please. We don't want to disturb Mrs. Marsh before we have to. And in the meantime, look around at what you've been called upon to destroy."

Silently they trooped out. For a moment he watched them through the picture window as they wandered up and down with sour faces, hands in pockets, inspecting the beauty around them without pleasure, shrugging now and then as if to say, "Why blame us?" Their boss, the man in the business suit, perhaps in a last minute attempt to save the garden, began probing around to assure himself the inspector had not been wrong. Walt turned away. He thought of Flossie, sleeping peacefully in her room. He looked for the time. Eight twenty. She would be awake soon. He sat down, elbows on knees, and dropped his head into his palms. How unexpectedly tragedy exploded. All of a sudden, life was being taken from Flossie—she might as well be dead. He felt numb. He knew this was no time to plan, or to try to assemble and assort the blame. Better to wait it out, endure each moment and what it brought, and do whatever he could, though, God knew, it would be pathetically little.

The gardener, Mr. Dorkas, was there before nine with three of his men. "What's it all about, Mr. Marsh, for God's sake?"

Walt waved him outside. "If you don't already know, then talk to the boss out there. And you save every goddam blade of grass or I'll sue you down to your last penny."

Dorkas swore he would, bobbing up and down in misery. He ran outside, his heavy body swaying on short, thin legs, to gesticulate with the official who handed him the metal rod to pierce away for himself. Dorkas pierced, looked up either in utter amazement or an excellent facsimile, shook his head from side to side as if in pain, and ordered one of his men to dig. The hole made, he shoved the man aside and knelt down to see for himself. His head shook again. His fist struck a section of green velvet from the side of the hole and it sailed across the lawn and landed quivering on the tiled path. He got up and walked away to the railing, looking down at his truck, his hands thrust deep into his pants pockets. He turned back, his face blotched as if hives had sprung up. He said something to his men. The official said something to Dorkas, who then interrogated the Building Department workmen. Satisfied, he gave them orders and all at once the garden became a place of wild but silent activity as two workmen installed ropes and pulleys and four others heaved and bore down on spades like blades that sliced beneath roots, then strained upwards heavy-laden, the gentle-blossomed trees wrenched slowly, painfully, their trunks held by Dorkas's calloused hands until out they shot, naked, bleeding brown blood from roots quivering like exposed nerves, wrapped quickly in brown sackcloth, tied to strong ropes to be let down in precarious ignominy over the railing to the street, eighteen stories below. All the trees first, their blossoms strewn in pink and white, shed like tears, good-bye, good-bye. . . .

Walt watched at the living-room window, stolidly, his mouth a tight inverted U, his eyes expressionless, waiting for the moments to slip by until they stood at the second of alarm when he would be needed as Flossie had never needed him before.

And then it came. . . .

. . . from the bedroom, as she awakened and looked out to see how her garden was blooming—a racking, jangled, crazy scream.

Walt ran to her.

9 :   *Saturday, May Sixteenth*

The next morning the sun poured damp heat like oven vapors, sodden rays that burned on the desolation of the terrace where garden furniture stood bleakly on rotted copper, stained with nauseous greens, reds and purples like gangrene.

Flossie would not leave her bed. Walt had made a quick trip yesterday afternoon to the little old candy lady and had returned with a five-pound box of her most delectable chocolates, but Flossie nibbled them listlessly, more from habit than desire. Although she knew that Walt was watching her anxiously for a sign of cheer, she would not attempt pretense for his sake. She was like someone on the threshold of death, whose vanquished eye gazes pitilessly into the stricken faces about her. Walt might be sick with grief over her, but it was she who was dying. She lay on her bed in a darkened room and would not speak or see anyone. She could hear the doorbell faintly from her room, but the sound of it no longer produced pleasant anticipation. Now she passed over it—a bell—someone at the door—and who cares?

Walt kept trying, a false-bright smile in place. "How about a drink, honey? Come on, kid, one of my whisky sours, do you good."

She shook her head, feeling a sudden nausea at the very idea. She even pushed the box of chocolates away.

The maid knocked at the door and Walt opened it for her. She carried their largest vase, crammed with deep red, velvety roses.

"Hey there! Did you ever see so many?" Walt helped her with the heavy vase and took the card. "Must be hundreds of them." He counted the flowers. "Three dozen, Floss. I don't have to read the card. Couldn't be anyone but d'Auriac." He opened the envelope nevertheless. "I was right. Damn thoughtful."

She looked at the roses, let out a scornful laugh. "*Happiness* Roses! How appropriate!" She turned her head away and closed her eyes over a new rush of tears.

"He sent them because they were beautiful. He couldn't have known their name." Walt flipped the card onto the table and took a few aimless steps. He sat down on his bed and looked over at her helplessly. He had been awake all night listening to her tears, trying to think of something that would comfort her. The chocolates had been a failure, but he hadn't expected them to make up for her loss. A pound of fresh caviar stood untasted in the refrigerator. *The Shock of Recognition*, edited by Edmund Wilson, a book Flossie had wanted, stood unopened beside her bed. What else could he do for her?

The doorbell rang again and he hurried to answer it, anything to keep moving, busy.

Alone in the room, Flossie reached for a Kleenex and blew her nose. It was stuffed and swollen from crying, and tender about the nostrils. She thought vaguely of nose drops to clear it, then let the thought slip away. Walt had not completely closed her door and a shaft of light lay across the carpet. She could hear shiftings and whisperings from outside and the low sounds annoyed her. She felt they should have more consideration. And Walt should have closed her door. Such a little thing to remember, to close the door. It was all she asked. Absolutely all she asked out of the millions of objects to be desired on earth—just to keep her door closed.

Footsteps, heavy, but not Walt's, forced her to look towards the door where a tall, thin shadow leaned against the frame. Flossie squinted through swollen eyes and saw the sparkle of light on flaxen hair. She raised herself on her elbows and bit her underlip. She had expressly said she would see no one, no one at all.

Her eyes accommodated and she could see Robin's face now. He was smiling in a frightened way, as if dreading what he would see, and what he did see was worse, perhaps, than he expected, for he stopped walking part way in and his smile vanished. Flossie felt his shock as if she looked at herself through his eyes. How she must look! She stretched her swollen lips into something like a smile. "Well, Robin." She attempted her old, hearty greeting, remembering suddenly that today was Saturday, but her voice was hoarse and hollow and she let herself fall back onto the pillow feeling that this was too much of a demand upon her. She had wanted to see no one, and that included Robin. She was not up to it.

"Hi—Floss." He came all the way in, moving tentatively as if each step was an effort, and he ran his tongue quickly over dry lips and swallowed a few times. His eyes traveled towards the shuttered windows that looked out onto the barren terrace and they flickered, pained. "Hi, Floss," he said again and sat down very carefully on the edge of Walt's bed. She seemed to have forgotten that it was Saturday morning. She seemed not to want him there.

"I must look a sight." She put her hand up to her hair.

"What'd you expect to look like?" He shook his head and sighed. His mouth tightened and he lowered his head.

"Oh, kid!" She took another Kleenex and blew her nose. "Help yourself."

He obeyed her, blew noisily, made a ball of the tissue and took a clean hook shot, watching it land squarely in the wastepaper basket. He dug his hands into his pants pockets and stood up, looking miserable. "I don't know, Flossie—everything's gone nuts. Everything."

She nodded.

He pulled his jacket aside and hooked his fingers under his red striped belt. "Say, you like this belt?"

She nodded.

"Matches my tie, see. You really like it?"

"Sure."

"Dad gave it to me. From Brooks. You think it's tweedy?"

She nodded.

"Jimmy Parker already wants to trade me for his orange and black."

"Don't you do it."

"No, I won't. Dad's got pretty good taste. He's a pretty tweedy dresser for a guy his age, don't you think?"

"Sure is."

He sat down again. "Now all I need is a striped shirt."

"Stripes tweedy?"

"Yep. Blue stripes with a round collar. I'm working on Mom."

"Soft touch, your mom?"

He grinned.

"Say, Rob, in the bathroom on the second shelf, a brown bottle marked 'Privine' . . ." She sniffed.

"Oh, I know them. Nose drops. We use 'em." Robin turned on the bathroom light and it poured over to Flossie's bed. She covered her eyes. "Found it," he said.

"Turn off the light."

He snapped the switch.

"Close the door, too, honey."

He did as she asked and brought the nose drops to her. She used them while he watched her critically. "You got to hold your head back much farther—way back—that's right."

She twisted the dropper back on the bottle and put it on her night table. She waited a moment, then blew her nose. "Ahh!"

"Clear?"

"Yes. Thanks."

"Welcome." He sat down on Walt's bed again, his knees apart, his hands gripping them in a determined pose. "Now, Flossie, I have something to say to you."

"You do?"

"Yes. Now—I've brought you something."

She started to object, but he held up his hand. "Now, Flossie, hear me out."

She couldn't help smiling. It was just the way Ty said it, holding up his hand.

"What I've brought you I know you're not going to like, but I happen to know that what I've brought you is good for you and you must have it."

"Well, I am mystified!"

"Look, Flossie, at a time like this, even though I'm only a kid, I really do know better. I *know* this is something you absolutely have to have."

"What is it, castor oil?"

He giggled. "I'll get it now. It's outside with Walt. But don't you say no, because it's good for you, Flossie." He went to the door. "Okay?"

"I don't know. I don't like the way you put it."

"I'm gonna get it now." He disappeared, leaving the door wide open. She shielded her eyes and waited, worrying. What in heaven's name . . . ?

His figure was a shadow again in the bright hall light as he returned carrying something in his arms, with Walt lumbering behind him. When Walt closed the door, she was able to make out what Robin carried—a wriggling brown mongrel puppy.

"Oh, no!" She stared at the little fluff with a sinking heart. The last thing in the world she wanted to bother with at this time was a puppy.

"Well. See! Isn't that nice? See!" Walt chuckled nervously behind Robin.

Robin wasn't quite as determined or sure of himself now as before. "I—I told you you wouldn't want it, Flossie, but it's good for you, really it is. I know. Don't you want her? Look how cute. Hey, Flossie, don't you want her?" Now his eyes were aghast, and he added wildly, "Because she was on sale and I can't take her back!"

"Oh, Robin, you shouldn't have done it."

"Yes I should, Flossie. Please, don't you want her?"

Flossie gave Walt a desperate look.

"Crud!" Robin said.

Flossie saw the heartbreak in his face. "Well, come on." She held out her arms. "Aren't you going to give her to me?"

Robin's face whipped into a grin.

Flossie held up the squirming puppy. "Her? Did you say her?"

"Sure, she's a—*isn't* she?"

"Her is a him, Robin. But he is awful cute. Aren't you an awful cute little puppy? You sure are. Nothing but a baby, poor little thing, wrenched from your mama. Look at him, Robin. Ouch! Your teeth are sharp, pup!"

"That's only because they're baby teeth, she'll—he'll get others," Robin said quickly.

"Who're you telling? Who taught you everything you know about dogs?"

"I forgot, it's so long. Look at those floppy ears, Flossie. I just couldn't resist her when I saw her looking out of that window at me, like she's looking now, with her head cocked. Isn't that cute? And she's so peppy. Look at this." Robin ran his fingers along the sheet and the puppy went after them with his little paws, pounced on them and chewed happily. "Isn't that cute?"

"Here, let me."

So the answer, for the time being, was a dog, Walt thought, watching them play. As simple a thing as a little dog. But not quite that simple, really, for if he had brought the dog to Flossie, she would have made him take it back. Why then would she accept it from Robin? Was it because of the comparative magnitude of his gift? For it must have cost Robin most of his savings, sale or no sale. Was it because he couldn't take the puppy back? Or was it something very much deeper? He watched them as they examined the puppy for clues as to its mixed heritage, arguing about the appearance of the ears, the tail, the nose. Forgotten was the garden for the time being. Nothing existed but this tiny, dependent creature who was now creeping up Flossie's great chest to cover her face with kisses, while she laughed and twisted away and Robin stroked the soft brown back. The change in Flossie was magical. The puppy was medicine she needed, however inadequate, and in some queer way it seemed to be medicine Robin required as well. Walt rubbed his red eyebrows and aching forehead. There was something about Robin, lately, that needed thought.

"He'll grow up to be ten pounds at most," Flossie decided.

"That's small, Flossie. Rover is seven, seven and a half."

"That's what I say. He'll be a little larger than Rover."

"A good apartment dog," Robin said. "That's another reason why I picked her."

"Robin, she's a he."

Robin grimaced. "I just don't know how I coulda made such a mistake."

Walt cackled and Robin gave him a quick grin.

"I have it," Flossie said.

"What?"

"The name."

"Yes?"

"Shezahee."

"Shez—oh, she's a he. Hey, Flossie, that's a stinking name."

"And I suppose 'Rover' is an elegant name for a female Chihuahua?"

"That was just a joke. Her real name is Baby Doll's Dulcie."

Walt grinned. "And this little feller is Fat Flossie's Shezahee!" His laughter turned on him, almost formed a sob as he heard Flossie's hearty laughter induced for the first time by something he had said.

"We'll have to outfit little Sheza—how's that, Sheza for short?" Flossie looked at Robin for approval, but he turned his thumbs down. "Well, I don't care. It's my dog," she said. "Walt, write down: leash, collar, bed, puppy biscuits, cod-liver oil, calcium powder; better let's worm him too. And a brush and comb, and"—Flossie grinned at Robin—"if you'll excuse it, Rob, some flea powder."

"Hey!" Insulted, Robin bent over and ruffled through the fur around the puppy's neck.

"Anything else I can get you?"

"I'll go down with you, Walt, I'm late for lunch."

"Okay, Rob. Anything else, Flossie?"

She shook her head. Already her eyes were becoming dull again. Already she had remembered the garden.

"I won't be long. There's a pet shop over on Lexington."

" 'Bye, Floss. Take good care of Sheza."

"Thanks so much, Robin, darling." Flossie raised a limp hand. "Don't forget to close the door."

"Back soon, honey," Walt said.

She blinked her eyes at him. The door closed and she was in darkness and silence again. She lay back and stared at the shuttered windows that blocked her view of the ravished terrace, and her eyes filled with tears again, but Sheza attacked her fingers with delight and no matter where she tried to put her hand, he followed it, thinking she was playing a game. He wouldn't let her alone, but all the same, she couldn't be angry with him because after all, he was only a tiny pup who might cry for his mother tonight if she didn't make him feel loved and secure long before darkness came—his first long, lonely night away from home.

10 :   *Monday, May Eighteenth*

Although the destruction of Flossie's garden had nothing whatever to do with Maud Harewood, Julie found herself quite irrationally blaming her for it. If Maud had not actually engineered Flossie's tragedy, her very presence in this house contributed towards it. In Julie's mind, Maud had taken on the aspect of a *mauvais genie*, a witch come to put the hex on Number Ten.

And the hex was certainly on her little family. Robin no longer came home around four o'clock from school, not even to collect his baseball equipment and leave for the park. To begin with, he had little equipment left, certainly no balls, for one by one as he had forgotten himself and idly bounced one of them, Ty had taken it away. Now Robin went directly to someone else's house from school and Julie didn't see him from early morning until dinnertime. Even Ty had defected. Twice last week he had cocktails downtown. Julie understood that he hadn't done this purposely to stay away from her. She knew it was an unconscious thing, inspired by the change in his home. The hours from five to seven had been family hours where the cocktail with Julie had been one sipped between flurries with Robin, a family time. Now the house didn't come alive until dinner, and even then, living had to be constrained.

Julie felt it most, for she was left alone with no outside activity to replace the loss of her lively home. So it was that resentment piled up in her, stronger each day, until it showed on her face in a new, discontented expression, in a pallor and in the absence of her usual smile. But unlike Ty, Julie was not one to suppress it all deep within her stomach, at least not for long.

This morning she awakened feeling angry at the world. It was going to be a bad day for her she knew, so she handed over her precious home to the cleaning girl and took Rover for a long walk in the park where she observed the spring-green trees with an unappreciative eye. She came home late for lunch and let the cleaning girl fix her a horrible old scrambled egg. She did her shopping without interest, any old thing, an old leg of lamb and some old broccoli and potatoes. She didn't care to be bothered with cooking. She stopped in at two art galleries in the neighborhood and looked unkindly upon the pictures hanging there. And home again, she prepared the roast listlessly and wandered about the rooms, hardly listening to the records she had put on the phonograph.

Ty didn't come home until twenty after six and Robin not until ten minutes later. Feeling guilty himself for his late arrival, Ty was unnecessarily severe with Robin for being late, and after Robin had retired, sullen and hurt, to his room, Julie lashed Ty with strong words for taking everything out on his son. Abashed, Ty tried to make it up to Robin, conversing with him at the bathroom door as the boy washed his hands and face, and a little later they came out to the living room together to sit and listen to Robin's collection of Glenn Miller, Armstrong and Goodman. But for the fact that Robin chose to sit on the back of the couch with his feet on the seat, there was no evidence that a thirteen-year-old boy was in the house. Coming now and then from the kitchen to peek at them, Julie made angry grunts and strode back to her old roast lamb, mumbling at the quiet dignity of the two music lovers.

But they were not naturally so, only suppressed, and after a while Ty remarked, "That's a helluva way to sit."

"We all sit this way."

"That makes it right?"

"Sure. You don't like it?"

"No."

"So what're you going to do about it, Bo?" A challenge sparkled in Robin's dark eyes, conveyed itself to Ty lounging in Julie's chair, and father and son, both aching for fun, sat only half listening to the music.

"Get off, Skeezix."

"Says who?"

"Says me!" Ty made a fist, swiped at the air.

"Make me, Bo!"

Ty considered it. Suddenly he lunged for Robin, grinning.

Startled, Robin gave a shriek and ducked. He lost his balance, grabbed for something to hold and fell crashing behind the couch, carrying the entire wall of drapery with him. The noise brought Julie running from the kitchen in time to see Robin arise from behind the couch, covered with yards of golden material like a majestic ghost, and declaim, "Batter up!"

It was too much even for Julie's depressed spirits. She had to laugh and then, of course, it had to turn into a game as Robin flayed under the yards of material, pretending to be trying to free himself. The situation was a natural. It was hilarious enough to amuse them all under normal circumstances, but added to that was their long enforced constraint and their relief at finding Robin unhurt. It offered Robin delectable opportunities to poke and pinch his father from under the cloth and then utter shrieking, exaggerated apologies, and it inspired Ty to wrap his son up tight, under the guise of awkwardly trying to help. And, as usual through all of their tussles together, Julie could only stand by and plead for the preservation of her furniture and decorations.

But then separately, one by one, they became aware of the telephone.

Julie heard it first because she was the onlooker. Its sound choked her laughter, shrieked in her ears, sent sharp nerve currents through her body. Ty heard it next and stopped playing. "Okay, come on out of there, Robin," he said. Robin giggled and flayed his arms once or twice again under the draperies, then was silent himself and crawled out on his hands and knees. "Goddam old Haretits," he muttered and suddenly was struggling with tears.

"I can't stand it any more, Ty," Julie said.

"Don't bother to answer it. She'll give up."

"That's what you think," Robin said.

"I'm going to take care of her once and for all," Julie said in a tight voice that shook.

"I'd better do it."

"No, I *need* to, don't you understand?" She darted into the foyer and snatched up the receiver. "Well, what now!" she shouted.

"Oh, Mrs. Fay, *have you no feeling at all?*" Maud Harewood wept.

Julie lowered the receiver and glared at it as it trembled in her hand. Her lips moved, but no words came. All she could do was sputter, "Why you—you——!" unable to find a proper name for Maud, unable to say one withering phrase. Instead, she hung up and stood there looking wildly about her, her fists jerking, seeking release, literally vibrating with that pitch of fury which is alleviated only by physical action. "Damn you!" she choked, looking down at an imaginary Maud through the floor. "You want something to complain about? You want some noise?" She stamped her foot. "You'll get some noise!" She stamped again and again. "Lots of noise, Madame Harewood!"

"Yes, give it to her!" Robin shouted. "Old crank, give her something to telephone about! I hate you, I hate you, I hate your guts!" He joined her, screaming with laughter, and made great noise with his feet.

Ty leaned against the wall with his hands in his pockets and watched them with an envious smile as stamping became jumping which shifted to banging chairs and even pounding the floor with their fists. He could feel them unwind as they gave way to themselves, and wished he were made of the stuff that could do this, too. Instead, his angry stomach poured forth heartburn and secretively he reached into his pocket for a Tums which he popped into his mouth.

It didn't last long. "Oh, I'm dead!" Robin threw himself into a chair. Julie gave one more stamp, then dropped into the chair next to him. Her face was pink and shining; she looked fine, now, with the strain erased. "How I've wanted to do that." She touched Robin's dripping forehead. "Look at you. I'm a fine mother, I didn't even ask you if you hurt yourself before."

"Obviously not, Ma."

"You're lucky, that's all, falling backwards like that. Oh, my poor draperies!" she moaned. She smoothed her hair, using her fingers for a comb, and replaced the clip that held her pony tail. "I'm a mess, but it was worth it. Even the draperies are worth it."

Ty's smile held a sparkle that told her he thought she was wonderful, but he said nothing. He looked at his watch. All along, he had been making note of the time.

"You don't approve of your family, do you?" Julie challenged.

"I'm with you a hundred per cent, darling."

"Then you might have helped us, instead of breeding ulcers." She went to the refrigerator for ice water.

[163]

"My turn will come." Ty helped himself to the glass she brought out for herself.

"Fine thing, I do all the work and you take the refreshment."

Ty smiled. "I need fortifying."

"*You* do?"

The doorbell rang.

Ty checked his watch. "Took him a little longer than I thought."

"Oh-oh, Harewood?"

"Honestly, Julie, weren't you expecting him?"

"I didn't even think of it. Did you, Robin?"

"No. Yeow. Now what?"

"What are you going to say, Ty?"

"Plenty. And you two stay out of it, hear? Into the kitchen with both of you." The doorbell rang again, three imperative sounds, but Ty finished the glass of water and wiped his mouth slowly before answering it.

Albert Harewood stood there in his natty tailoring, fairly quivering with rage, his fists tight at his sides. "I heard it this time!" His watery blue eyes bulged behind his thick lenses. "This time I was home to hear it! Now go ahead and try to tell me my wife is a liar! Go on and try!"

Ty had to smile. No question about it, he was in a tight spot. "Simmer down, Harewood," he said good-naturedly, "and come on in."

Automatically, Harewood obeyed while his indignant recital continued: ". . . to think that all this time I've been blaming her . . ." He noticed in time that he was entering the home of the man who had made a fool of him, and stopped in the center of the foyer, refusing to go in farther. "Well, Fay, this disgraceful display is your last. I'm taking it up with Mr. Rider in the morning, and if necessary, I'll even go to the police. Why, you could have killed us, the way that chandelier swayed over our heads!"

"For that we're sorry. But as long as it didn't fall, no harm done, right?"

Harewood admitted it hadn't fallen. "But that it didn't was a miracle," he added angrily.

"Please come in and sit down."

"That won't be necessary. I've said all I came to say. No point in further discussion between us."

Ty chuckled and put his hand on Harewood's shoulder. "All right, now that you've blown your stack, let's sit down and talk it over. There's no reason for you and me to be bloody enemies, Harewood. Nothing is ever as bad as it seems."

"There isn't anything more to talk about," Albert said. His blue eyes slid uneasily to the door, as if seeking escape. "This time I heard it and there's nothing more to say."

"But I have more, so if you won't sit in my parlor, we'll have to sit right out here." Ty brought two chairs to the center of the foyer. "Please?"

"This is no joking matter, Mr. Fay."

"And I'm not joking," Ty said quietly. "I'm trying hard to keep from losing my temper. I know what you heard, and you're going to have to hear more, sitting or standing. I didn't ask you to come up, you know."

Harewood lifted his hands, then let them drop again in exasperation. "It won't do you any good this time, but all right, no sense sitting out here like fools." He marched into the living room and sat down, but he refused Ty's offer of a drink and wouldn't accept a cigarette, either. He wasn't going to be taken in by Tyler Fay's charm a second time.

Ty lit one for himself, crossed his legs and settled back. "Now just what did you hear?"

"My God, a din like I never heard in my life——"

"But isn't it true that Mrs. Harewood telephoned us to complain before that?"

"Of course she did. There was other noise——"

"Did you hear it?"

"Of course I heard it. How could I miss it, a crash like that?"

"Weren't you alarmed? One loud crash, preceded by silence?"

"No. It was merely proof of my wife's contentions——"

"And what did you suppose Robin did to make a noise like that?"

"How should I know? Almost anything." Harewood moved uncomfortably in his chair.

"Do you suppose he could have been sitting here quietly in the living room with me listening to music, and do you think it possible that he, being perched on the back of the couch, could have lost his balance and fallen backwards? Please observe the fallen draperies."

Harewood looked, then turned back. "You're not going to talk me out of it this time, Fay," he insisted.

"I don't care if I do or not. I'm just trying to save you from further embarrassment. I'm telling you precisely what happened. Robin fell and luckily wasn't hurt. Very luckily, for had he been hurt, and had we needed a doctor, we could hardly have telephoned him since your wife was Johnny-on-the-spot, tying up our line. Ridiculous for her to call because of one loud noise, Harewood, when the house has been like a morgue for weeks. Even Robin's friends don't visit him any more. They can't stand it here. He visits them now."

Harewood sucked on his lower lip. "And that din I heard was all in my imagination, I suppose?"

"No," Ty admitted, "that was real enough. It was deliberate. If, in this deadly quiet house, your wife dared to complain about Robin's fall, we thought it fitting that she hear what real noise sounded like. For once, we decided to give her something to complain about. She deserved that little break."

Harewood made an impatient sound and leaned forward, his elbows on his knees. "Same thing all over again. She says one thing, you say another, and who am I to believe?"

"That's up to you. My job is to look out for my own family and I don't like what's happened to us since you and your wife moved in. Suddenly we speak in whispers, tiptoe around, bicker as we never did before —it's no good, Harewood. So we're going to have to call off this program of excessive co-operation with Maud Harewood. We're going to open our windows wide and I'll tussle with my son when I come home. His friends will dance and enjoy themselves in this apartment again. In other words, Harewood, from now on, we're going back to living our normal lives as we did before you came here. We're still sympathetic to your wife's problems, but she's got to learn that she can't interfere in our lives any more. That's fair enough, isn't it?"

Albert didn't know whether it was or not. He felt that it was, it sounded fair enough, but he wished he knew more about it. The last of his anger had long ago crumpled, for his stubborn defense had been only an unwillingness to admit that Maud could be in the wrong. For the second time now, this quiet, friendly young man had put him in his place, reduced him to confusion. It was more than he could take. He couldn't leave Tyler Fay's apartment fast enough, for the man's mildness cut deeper than any angry threat, a mildness that contrasted so fearfully with Maud's fever.

He chose to go down by the fire stairs and let himself into his apartment silently. Maud pounced upon him, her eyes glittering, even as she had done the first time he had visited the Fays, but he shook himself loose from her and threw himself down on his bed. "I don't want to talk about it," he said.

"They told you lies about me! And you believed them, didn't you, you coward!"

He pulled himself up on his elbows for a moment. "Look, Maud," he said, "let's forget about the Fays, huh? I'm sick and tired of hearing their name. They're just an ordinary, decent little family like any other, trying to have some fun and be happy in this world in spite of you. I don't know what you've got against them, but let them alone, will you? No more telephone calls, do you hear?"

"I should just—stand there—and let the chandelier fall on my head?"

"That was a demonstration to show you what noise can really be like. It won't happen again. But I'm warning you, if you annoy them any more, the consequences are going to be much more serious than noise and a swaying chandelier. Why don't you get out more, see people, get interested in something else instead of lying here in the dark listening for their footsteps? Either take hold of yourself from now on, or admit that you can't do it without professional help. One or the other, Maud, I mean it."

She shrank away from him, but for once the sick terror in her face didn't affect him. This time it was he who lay completely exhausted, one arm flung across his eyes.

She moved away from him until her back was against the wall. She pressed against it for support. She was completely alone in the world. And the Fays had done this to her.

11 :   *Tuesday, May Nineteenth*

Maud didn't dare stay in, for she was afraid Albert might sneak home at some unexpected moment to catch her on her chaise longue. Not that there was anything wrong with lying on a chaise longue, but Albert seemed to be making a "thing" of it, holding it up as some symptom of disease, and if he caught her there during the next few days, he would surely use it against her. It would be his excuse to abandon her under the guise that she was mentally ill, to incarcerate her in some sanitarium so he could be free. Oh, she had his number, all right! And she was more than a match for him in her own quiet way. He wanted her out in the clean, fresh air? Fine, she'd comply. . . .

She'd comply even though she knew she was in no condition to go out, for she hadn't closed her eyes all night. Albert slumbered restlessly in the bed next to hers, snoring, twisting, throwing off his covers and then clutching for them, but the sound of her sobs, which she made no effort to control, anticipating his contrite awakening, never aroused him. How could he sleep with no care for the unhappiness he had caused her? She could only take it as an added proof that she was a burden to him now that she was ill. Watching his restless but heavy slumber, she contemplated leaving him, but the thought of living alone and seeing no other face but Emma's, stolid and quietly disapproving, sent her into another spasm of tears. What a terrible choice was hers in her middle years, to be alone with Albert, or more alone without him!

And what of the Fays, who had precipitated all this? How to handle them and the problems they posed?

She considered it, tossing sleepless in her bed, cautioning herself to be as fair and dispassionate about her analysis as only a writer could be. She admitted that she had asked a great deal of the Fays, for being a naturally raucous and inconsiderate family, it could not be easy for them to have to think of others all of a sudden, and keep their rowdy spirits under control. But at the same time, she had also to consider relative values. Of the two hostile factions, which was most expendable: the little bourgeois family or the writer of exceptional gift? There could be no question of her decision in such a case. She asked a great deal of them, but they owed it to her, and in refusing to co-operate they had done her harm, deliberate and inconsiderate harm.

As the first faint grey light seeped through the blinds into the room, with eyes dry, all wept out now, the idea eventually came to Maud that she oughtn't take this lying down. She raised herself on her elbow and squinted through burning lids at the dawn behind the blinds. Yes, it could be done, and with such delicious irony! She could obey Albert to the letter, but accomplish her own purpose in the meantime. "Mix with people, make friends," he had commanded her. How easy it would be. There wasn't a woman in the building who wouldn't give her right arm to be friends with Maud Harewood.

She punished Albert by refusing to speak to him at breakfast, although he was contrite this morning. The sight of her tired face and swollen lids urged him to be even gentler with her than usual, but she turned away from him.

As soon as he had gone, calling an unanswered good-bye, she dressed herself, pulling any old thing from her closet, a black wool dress from years ago, brown Oxfords and an old black felt hat with a soiled and drooping rose. Emma was amazed to see her mistress fully dressed and ready to make a marketing list at nine forty-five.

"Stop gaping, Emma darling. I feel better, that's all."

Emma said nothing, distrustfully viewing Maud's swollen lids.

"Well, come on, let's have the list."

When Maud rang for the elevator, it was on the main floor. For once let it come directly to her, for once only, she prayed. She watched its progress on the indicator as it rose and passed her, moving all the way up to the sixteenth floor. It was positively infuriating, uncanny, this thing about herself and elevators. Never once in her entire life had any of them ever come straight to her. Just as whenever she dialed a telephone number, it was always busy. Everything had to be made extra hard for her, somehow.

Terence had missed her lately. "Up and about again at last, Mrs. Harewood."

She nodded wearily.

"You still look peaked. What'd you have, the virus?"

"I wasn't ill, only exhausted, no sleep, no peace . . ."

"You don't mean to say that trouble with Robin's still goin' on? I thought you had it all settled?"

She gave a sour laugh. "It's worse than ever. I didn't think it could be possible, but there it is."

"No!" The car settled at the main floor.

She sighed. "Every once in a while when the noise gets unbearable, I telephone them and beg them to be a little less rowdy, and do you know what they do after I hang up? You won't believe it."

"No, what?"

His old eyes had once been blue, but they were faded now to a milky grey and their eager glance appeared sightless. She couldn't bear to look into them. "They punish me," she said, looking away, "for daring to complain. They make more noise than before. They stamp on the floor, pound with hammers, bang chairs. They could have killed me last night, the foyer chandelier swayed like crazy. Mr. Harewood pulled me out from under it just in time."

"No foolin'?" Even Terence's credibility was being strained. It was true that Robin was a little brat, he averred, but Mr. and Mrs. Fay, why, he had known them for years, they were the kindest people he had ever met. He couldn't believe this of them.

"Oh, they admit doing it. They make no bones about it. Now I know what killed old Mr. Collins. He died of exhaustion, too intimidated to make a complaint. Mr. Harewood's tried to reason with them several times, but all he's gotten for his trouble has been threats. No, Mr. and Mrs. Fay are no better than their rowdy offspring. You let their handsome faces fool you, Terence."

"Oh, I don't like to hear this! Such a pleasant, smilin' couple, too. Well, there you have it. You never know about people." Terence's old head bobbed sadly.

"A pretty face and a sweet smile can cover almost anything."

"Imagine that. Well, I wouldn't take it lyin' down, Mrs. Harewood. I'd call the police, I would."

"I don't think I'll have to go that far," she said. "There must be some way to reach them. I'll figure it out."

"If there's anything I can do . . ."

"Thank you, Terence, it's kind of you. Makes me feel more secure to know I have at least one friend in this building." She gave him a grateful smile.

"You, Mrs. Harewood? You? You have many more than you know."

"I hope so. Oh, I do hope so. This whole thing has been so distressing that I . . . Well, this isn't getting the marketing done, is it?"

"Now you take it easy, your first day out."

"I will, Terence." She smiled once again over her shoulder and crept out into the spring sunshine, nodding sadly to Phil, the doorman.

Terence hobbled on rheumatic legs to the door. "Did you hear that? Did you hear what she told me?"

"Some of it." Phil coughed into his hand.

"You have only to take one look at that poor woman to see she's ready to drop dead."

"She looked the same first day she come here. Too much money, that's her trouble." Phil passed a tissue over his mouth. "Coughing, coughing, even in the spring in the sunshine," he muttered.

"Not Mrs. Harewood, she's not one of those, she's a famous woman, a woman who's done something."

Phil considered this. "It's true that Mrs. Emmerich complained of loud noise last night around dinnertime. She phoned down to Gruppmann, but it was all quiet when he got up there and no other complaints," he admitted.

"There you are, see? So it's a fact, what Mrs. Harewood says. I can't get over Mr. and Mrs. Fay, though." Terence shook his head, his face collapsed into hundreds of fine-wrinkled folds of disappointment. "Nice people like them." Still shaking his head, he went to answer a summons from upstairs.

The call was from Mrs. Lesser and Miss Forsythe on the seventh floor. Mrs. Lesser's breathing seemed more strained than ever today, but she smiled at Terence as he moved quickly to help her into the car. "Now you shouldn't be goin' out, Mrs. Lesser," he scolded.

She laughed and imitated his faint brogue, for being of Irish extraction herself, she had the right. "Now Terence Reilly, you be takin' care of your own poor health, man! There's a lovely breeze today"—she paused to catch her breath—"and it's the month of May."

"See, even Terence says you should be in bed," Miss Forsythe whined. "You're the stubbornest woman I ever met. I don't know why I bother to take care of you."

"Not stubborn at all." Mrs. Lesser's face was merry. "Just master of my own fate. Every human being has the right to choose his own end. I prefer to die with my boots on."

"What a thing to say!" Miss Forsythe gasped.

They helped Mrs. Lesser as far as a chair near the entrance and then she had to sit down for a moment to rest. It was a long and weary way for her to walk the few hundred yards into the park. "Well, Terence, what's the dirt around here today?" She grinned up at him, her cheery pink face framed with soft white hair.

Terence pursed his wrinkled lips. "Plenty, plenty."

"Well, come on, let's have it."

"Maybe *you* can do something with Robin Fay. You have influence on him."

"Oh Lord, what's that poor child done now to displease you? Honestly, Terence, for a decent Irishman, it's a shame the way you hate kids. Downright unnatural."

"I don't hate 'em when they're well behaved, but when they're brats they get no sympathy from me."

"In what way is Robin a brat?"

"He's noisy and inconsiderate."

"To you?"

"Yes. Never says please or thanks."

"You're too deaf to hear him. Does a brat spend his entire savings to buy a puppy for an unhappy woman?"

"So he's generous. He can afford to be. But that don't make up for what I know about him." Terence related Maud Harewood's story, adding a few minor embellishments of his own, which was only to be expected.

Mrs. Lesser's smile deepened until she laughed aloud. "Oh, Terence, what a fabrication! You ought to know the Fays better than that. And Robin, Lord, we've both known him since he was six days old. No one loved him better than old Mr. Collins, who died of cancer of the right kidney, which you know as well as I do. What's her name, that batty woman who's telling you all these tales?"

"Maud Harewood, Mrs. Lesser, *the* Maud Harewood, the famous writer, that's who. And they're not tales and she's a fine lady as well as famous. It's every word of it true. The Emmerichs complained about the noise last night, too."

"There must be a good explanation," Miss Forsythe reasoned. "You ought to hear their side of it."

"Maud Harewood, eh?" Mrs. Lesser chuckled. "That's right, I heard she moved in here. She must be a dilly. I'd love to meet her."

"If you stick around awhile, you will. She went marketing around the corner, and she never wastes time. Then you can see for yourself what I mean, the poor lady."

Mrs. Lesser leaned forward and Terence and Miss Forsythe helped her rise. She shuffled slowly to the entrance where Phil supported her down the step, wheezing louder than she.

"What a day!" Mrs. Lesser beamed at the world.

"It don't do me no good," Phil said sourly, coughing to prove it.

"I told you where you belong. In Arizona."

"Gotta make a living."

"I told you to talk to Mrs. Marsh. Her people come from there. She can get you some kind of job."

"She's in no condition."

For a brief moment, Mrs. Lesser's happy face clouded. "No, I guess not, poor soul."

"Here she comes!" Miss Forsythe whispered. "Isn't that Maud Harewood, Phil?"

"Yup."

Mrs. Lesser saw Maud clearly through her presbyopic eyes. "She's even got the facies of a neurotic."

"What's that?" her sister demanded.

"Features and expression," Mrs. Lesser defined patiently.

She and her twin sister had been identically raised and educated, but Miss Forsythe was the first to admit that she alone was blessed with a hole in her head through which all learning seeped out, like puffs of smoke.

Maud was coming down the street from Madison Avenue carrying two bundles of groceries. She saw Mrs. Lesser and Miss Forsythe, standing before the building entrance, looking her way. She smiled brightly as she drew near and handed her bundles to Phil to send upstairs so she could proceed to charm these ladies unencumbered.

"Shall we commence the interrogation?" Mrs. Lesser whispered and winked at her sister, who grinned with equal knavery. Mrs. Lesser returned Maud's charming smile. "Good morning, Mrs. Harewood. Lovely day."

Maud had hesitated as they whispered, but now reassured, she drew near. "Isn't it, though? I only wish I had the time to sit in the park and enjoy it."

"Well, and why not?"

"Why not? With all the work *I* have to do!"

"Oh, are you writing again? I'm so glad to hear it. I've certainly enjoyed your books and a new one would be most welcome."

For a moment, Maud hesitated, not certain as to how to proceed.

"This is my sister, Miss Forsythe. I'm Mrs. Lesser."

"Nice to meet you," Maud said, thinking hard. But she needn't have.

"All settled and happy?" Mrs. Lesser urged.

Maud clouded her face. "Settled, yes. But happy?"

"Not happy, Mrs. Harewood?"

Maud was touched by this old woman's concern. She moved closer and dropped her voice. She imparted her confidence in rapid, sometimes whispered phrases. ". . . that rowdy child . . . basketball . . . tap dancing . . . parents drink, wild parties . . . telephone to plead with them, they stamp . . . chandelier . . ."

Mrs. Lesser seemed most interested, but towards the end of Maud's tale, she grew impatient. Her small pink mouth opened and closed to interrupt and when Maud finished, she exclaimed, "Oh Mrs. Harewood, come now!"

Maud pulled herself in, elbows pressed to her sides. Anyone who wouldn't believe her was a threat, an enemy who terrified her, someone who could do her harm. "You can believe what you like, but I don't invent stories outside of my books!" Her voice quivered. "The Fays have been carrying on like this ever since I had the temerity to complain to Mr. Gruppmann about them." Her fingers dug at her purse.

Mrs. Lesser watched the convulsed hands, then raised a clinical eye to the tight, pallid face. "And you, Mrs. Harewood, are not only a very sick woman, but also a shameless liar!"

Miss Forsythe, who had been carried away by Maud's pitiful recital, was jerked back to loyal agreement by her sister's sharp words. "Yes, you are," she avowed. "You ought to be ashamed of yourself!" She took her sister's arm and they moved away towards the park, their steps too rapid in their indignation, so that they had to stop and rest almost at once for Mrs. Lesser to catch her breath. They stood apart from Maud, glaring at her and whispering, as Maud recovered sufficiently to cry out, "How dare you, how dare you say such things to *me*?"

There was a whirl of motion at the doorway and Mrs. Emmerich shot out, pulled by her exuberant boxer. In spite of the warm weather, she wore a mink coat over a gingham house dress to conceal it, but she had forgotten she was wearing house slippers. "Ooops! Oh, sorry. Baron, behave yourself, you bad dog! Did he hurt you? He's only a puppy and so full of life."

Maud dusted her dress. ". . . scared me half to death . . ."

"He only wanted to kiss you."

"You don't say?"

"Bad dog, don't you know Mrs. Harewood doesn't like to be kissed? Not by dogs, anyway, ha! Baron, *sit!*" She slapped him lightly with the leash and he cowered at her feet. "He'll behave better when he graduates. He's still going to school. I have to go with him. Imagine me a schoolgirl! And just look at the way I'm dressed." She touched the collar of her coat. "I'm dying of the heat, but I have a house dress on underneath. Couldn't find my cloth coat. No help," she whispered confidentially. "Honestly, the kind of maids you get nowadays! They don't want to work, sit all day and collect huge salaries. You're lucky if they'll dust the chair before parking their bottoms. Don't you find that true?"

Maud smiled extra-pleasantly at Mrs. Emmerich to show Mrs. Lesser and Miss Forsythe how mistaken they were about her.

"Terence was telling me you had a terrible accident last night, something about the chandelier falling? Lucky you didn't get killed. We heard all the noise and got so frightened."

"Oh, you heard it, too? I'm glad. There are some people around here who believe only what they please and the truth be damned," Maud said in a loud voice.

"What in heaven's name happened?"

Maud went on to tell Mrs. Emmerich her story, and since it was Mrs. Emmerich who claimed the chandelier had fallen, Maud made no move to correct the false impression. It wasn't her concern if Terence and Mrs. Emmerich chose to draw their own conclusions from her statements.

"You don't say!" Mrs. Emmerich clucked, interrupting her intermittently. "My, my, and I always thought they were such nice people! You see, you never know. Neighbors for years, and you just never know."

Overwhelmed by her success with Mrs. Emmerich, Maud was compelled to go further. Incidents presented themselves, came from nowhere into her mind, incidents she could clearly remember and feel with an immediate intensity. And Mrs. Emmerich was a shocked and sympathetic listener, exclaiming and clucking and shaking her head. Maud shivered gratefully under the woman's kindliness. The fact that she had planned for this reaction was now forgotten and she was aware only that she had been rudely rejected by Mrs. Lesser and her sister on the one hand, and was now so warmly accepted here.

But only a few feet away, Mrs. Lesser gave a loud, angry snort and would have hobbled away if Suzanne d'Auriac had not appeared at the entrance and caught Miss Forsythe's eye.

"Always so beautiful!" Miss Forsythe breathed, admiring the slender woman who stepped from the doorway and nodded good morning to Phil.

Only a few years older than Julie Fay, Suzanne d'Auriac was by far the most beautiful woman in the building. Like many well-to-do French-women, she paid the closest attention to her appearance from top to bottom and from outside in. She had weekly massages and pedicures; she did daily exercises to keep her figure trim and firm; she had her hair bleached, shampooed, set; her nails manicured and her eyebrows plucked every Friday afternoon; and every fourth Friday, she had her legs waxed. She brushed her teeth three times a day, used an astringent mouthwash and covered her body with lotions after her daily bath. She used various creams and unguents to dispel any incipient dryness or wrinkling of the skin. She was always deliciously perfumed. She dressed magnificently, never a wrinkle or a spot to mar her costume. She made it a point not to pay more than two hundred and fifty dollars for a dress, nor more than fifty for shoes, nor more than seventy-five for a hat. Suits and coats, of course, were another matter. It took her over an hour a day to complete her ablutions in the bathroom and another hour to apply her careful make-up and arrange her hair. Her lipstick never smudged, her nose never shone. She wore only priceless jewels, diamonds, pearls, rubies, but never gold. What was left of her day, after she had performed her toilette and shopped for her elegant clothes, she spent collecting paintings and rare books, every one of which she read.

But paradoxically, Suzanne d'Auriac was a timid and unpretentious woman, who followed the rules laid down by her fastidious Paris up-bringing as mechanically as did her American counterparts, who were forced to learn to swim, play tennis, golf, ride a horse and love purebred dogs. The expensive clothes she bought sparingly and wore for many years, and she dispelled any illusions of otherworldliness by discussing quite candidly all the functions of her body. "I feel just terr-ible! I took two enemas today and neither worked," she might complain to the Fays over a cocktail. But only her best friends really knew Suzanne. The others knew only what they saw, and what they saw was what Albert

Harewood had seen, a sophisticated beauty, coldly perfect, distant, superior and unfriendly.

Maud and Mrs. Emmerich gave Suzanne the feminine once-over, taking in all the details of her wardrobe from her dainty black calf shoes to the hat of mousseline in blues and greens like the sea that perched on her blonde coiffure where not a hair was out of place. Mrs. Emmerich looked upon her with a sneer invoked by pure envy, but Maud's face bore a scornful expression, for Suzanne was to her the epitome of all she loathed in women. She represented the pampered doll, the exquisite slavey, content to waste her days bedecking herself for the sake of her husband's vanity and very likely her own. She was everything external, an ornament that required infinite refurbishing and care. Her life was spent from the skin out, and hidden under this satin covering was a vacuum. Any woman of smart and fastidious appearance instantly repelled Maud for these reasons. She knew from experience the time that had to be consumed to achieve this end, and anyone willing to spend their days thus, deserved her scorn. So that, in better times, when she and Albert were invited everywhere, Maud would gravitate naturally to anyone, male or female, whose attire was old, ill-fitting, unbecoming and soiled, presupposing that the hours of their days were being better spent in refurbishing their hearts and souls, and presupposing, too, that beneath those ill-kempt and sour-smelling tresses there had to exist a pampered and superior brain.

Suzanne must have felt some of this scorn, for she was sensitive. She hesitated at the doorway and averted her eyes. Mrs. Lesser and Miss Forsythe called to her and she joined them, smiling diffidently. They moved a few steps away with her, talking, and Suzanne looked back at Maud for a moment, frowning now.

Maud knew they were talking about her, saying things malicious and untrue. All her life she had suffered from such looks, covert, sneering, and from the whispers that accompanied them. Even as a girl in school, she had been the one apart. She was teased for being small and physically unco-ordinated, for not being able to catch a ball, for writing fanciful poetry and for dreaming and talking about her soul. More than anything else in the world, she had wanted to be a member of the gang, but she could only dream of belonging, for its members included only those popular, healthy girls who whispered about her, giggled and sneered. Those were the girls on the basketball team, who in summertime played tennis, too, and swam swiftly, displaying their long, brown legs; who metamorphosed at nighttime into soft creatures in floating chiffon, who clung to their "dates" in the moonlight and knew love as well as laughter and sport. These were the "fits" and she the misfit, and every day they rejected her anew, so she had her revenge by writing about them. During her early career, she got even with each girl who had treated her thus, in stories and novels, sometimes going so far as to call one by name.

But their rejection was never dissipated by this revenge. New tormentors took the place of the old. She continued to stand apart whenever she met these girls and boys or their counterparts, even as she stood apart now, middle-aged, but facing the same attitude, the same whispered sneers. She heard the thud of her heart drum in her head, drowning out Mrs. Emmerich's envious chatter concerning Suzanne d'Auriac's clothes, snobbishness, foreign way of life. Maud watched the three women walk towards the park, Suzanne supporting Mrs. Lesser on the other side, and their straight backs menaced her; she could feel their dislike travel like a magnetized missile to pierce her body and send hot blood to her face and neck . . . she could scarcely breathe, she was smothering, she gasped and fanned herself . . .

"Oh, you poor thing!" Mrs. Emmerich noticed it at last and was full of concern. She gripped Maud's elbow, talking all the while. "I had a terrible time myself, when I went through the Change. Why, do you know that I . . ." She chattered on and on, beatified by the attention of this celebrity, giving Maud a complete and dramatically embossed account of her entire menopausal syndrome.

12 : *Wednesday, May Twentieth*

By the following morning, however, Maud had discovered that very few of the tenants in Number Ten were as loyal to the Fays as Mrs. Lesser, her sister and Suzanne d'Auriac. The others, for the most part, reacted in similar manner to Mrs. Emmerich, quite breathlessly delighted to be on neighborly terms with the famous writer, so delighted, in fact, that reason and judgment never entered their minds. Especially eager to listen and to believe her were the newer tenants who formed a solid block of resentment against the old guard. Mrs. Leopold, who lived in the apartment below the Marshes, added bitter complaints of her own. "These 'charter members' seem to think because they've lived here longer their money's better and they can do whatever they like without considering anyone else. We had to endure replastering and repainting for three years until Mr. Rider finally agreed to do away with Mrs. Marsh's precious garden. Take my advice, Mrs. Harewood, and don't bother complaining to him. He's on their side all the way. The next time the Fays bother you, if you want any satisfaction at all, call the police. It's the only solution."

But there were a few who were torn between their loyalty to the Fays and the axiom that where there's smoke, there's fire. In the case of Mrs. Kerakis, who also lived on the ninth floor, it was impossible to deny that she had herself heard the noise on Monday night. "I just don't know," she said to Mrs. Emmerich that morning when they met at the incinerator, "I just don't know what to think any more."

And because of her doubts, Mrs. Kerakis spent an uneasy day. Her maid didn't show up and didn't call until after twelve to mumble through blood-soaked cotton that she'd just had two teeth pulled and didn't think she'd be in until Friday. Mrs. Kerakis was filled with sympathy, having undergone her final three extractions only a few months before. "Take good care of yourself, lovey, and keep rinsing your mouth with salt water to prevent dry socket," she told her, "and don't come in until Monday if you're not completely well." But after she rang off, she looked about her dejectedly. She had already straightened her small apartment and cleaned Jimmy's box. Now the long afternoon stretched before her without the pleasant company of her maid—and tomorrow and maybe the long weekend by herself, too. As if sensing her loneliness, Jimmy jumped onto the sofa and moved coyly towards her. She stroked his back absently and returned to her vacillating loyalty, quite ashamed of her lack of faith in her neighbors, for after all, she knew how easy it was for false gossip to spread; stories that were close enough to the truth so that one couldn't protest with adequate conviction. Her eyes rested, moist and adoring, upon her husband's photograph on the table at her side, as she remembered the things they had whispered about him, about how he was a notorious Greek gangster, shot in a gang war, and how she lived off his stolen money, which was hidden in vaults all over the city. All rumors, all lies, but repeated so often and with such authority that the falsehood had nearly become the fact.

For just let her try, just try to protect Pete Kerakis's good name when the rumors were silent whispers that never came directly to her ear! Somebody told her that somebody else had heard from somebody that Pete Kerakis, etc. Go find the somebody that told the somebody that heard it from someone else!

Ironically, the only one who had ever given her half a chance was Robin Fay, who, possessed of that innocent sense of fair play which is common in children, had asked her directly if the story was true. He had been a little fellow then, not much more than seven or eight. She could always tell when he was out in the hall from the sound of his restless feet as he hopped or ran about until the elevator came. She opened her door only a crack to peek out and watch him, for it comforted her to see people around, and no harm to it, either, since no one ever knew she was observing them: she was most careful to see to that. But this one time, she must have been remiss, for Robin discovered her.

"That you, Mrs. Kerakis?" He squinted fearfully at her eyeball through the crack in the door.

So she opened the door wider and smiled to reassure him. "Hello, Robin, out for a stroll?"

"Gonna ride my bike. Why're you peekin' at me?"

"I wasn't peeking! I just came to the door to—go to the incinerator."

Just then Jimmy (the first Jimmy) rubbed along her ankles guilefully and in a second darted free into the hall. Robin caught him for her.

"Naughty cat! Would you mind bringing him in, Robin?" She could have taken Jimmy herself, but Robin was company.

He came into her apartment still holding Jimmy. His round eyes took in everything with a curious, rolling glance as if he were searching for something particular. He put Jimmy down and walked over to her husband's picture. "This Mr. Kerakis?" He studied it a long while. Then, "Would you be insulted if I asked you something?"

"I don't think I would."

"Was Mr. Kerakis really a gangster?"

"He certainly was not! He was a hero, who fought the gangsters when they came to take over his trucking business. He was a brave, honest man, a real hero who wouldn't be pushed around."

She proceeded to tell him the whole story. It was the first time anyone in the building had given her the opportunity and she held Robin there, fascinated, as the words surged from her. But the ending of the story horrified him. His eyes stared blackly when she told him how Pete's body was found in the woods near Philadelphia with a neat hole in the back of his head; nevertheless, he made her repeat the story over again. For a long time afterwards, he made it his business to visit her, ostensibly to play with Jimmy, but actually to hear her tell it once more. "Only this time make Pete kill the gangsters. Okay?"

Mrs. Kerakis took a cigarette from a flattened pack on the table, but the lighter had gone dry and she was too lazy to go into the kitchen for a match. She put her feet up on the couch and settled back. Strange how being alone made one sleepy. She smiled, remembering how the story she told Robin about Pete Kerakis had grown and twisted over the years, deviating even in point of origin, so that once he was a cowboy defending his cattle and another time a direct descendant of Alexander the Great, preserving his heritage of a fabulous jeweled sword. But after a while, Robin grew up and didn't want to hear her stories any more. Mrs. Kerakis sighed. She had become poor competition for the television set. She wriggled her shoulders and closed her eyes. Yes, Robin had grown up . . . so big now. . . .

In another moment, she was asleep.

When she awakened, it was four o'clock and her stomach was crying for nourishment. Confusedly, she thought back over her eventless day and reached the conclusion that she hadn't eaten since breakfast. She prepared herself a light meal of canned pea soup, eggs and canned asparagus with mayonnaise and refreshed herself afterwards with three cups of strong coffee and a cigarette. Then she fed Jimmy and, remembering the dry table lighter, searched in the kitchen and bathroom for fluid. She found the can in the medicine chest, but it was empty.

So now she had an errand to do.

"I'll be back soon, Jimmy. You behave while I'm gone," she told the cat while she carefully applied make-up to her wrinkled face and fitted a black straw hat upon her head. She selected black kid gloves from the drawer, pinned a blue silk scarf in place with a diamond crescent Pete had given her for their third anniversary and threw her mink scarf around her skinny shoulders. Now she was ready to go downstairs to buy a can of lighter fluid.

Mr. Levy's stationery store was crowded at this hour with men wanting evening papers and perhaps some commercial sweets to munch on while reading them, and the women picking up last-minute, nearly forgotten items such as Scotch tape, wrapping paper, greeting cards, ink, or like Mrs. Kerakis, lighter fluid. She stood beside Mr. d'Auriac, who was poring over the candy counter, and with shocked eyes, she watched a small boy sneak a Hershey bar into his pocket and dart away scot-free.

"Did you see that boy, Mr. d'Auriac?"

He was so deeply engrossed in studying the chewing gum that he started. He turned to her, flashed her a warm smile and bowed deeply. "Good evening, Madame."

His greeting made a lady feel that he was entranced by her presence, and if Mrs. Kerakis hadn't seen him deliver it with the same elation to everyone he met, she would have been flattered. "Didn't you see that child next to you?" she repeated.

"I don' think so."

[180]

"He stole a Hershey bar right under my eyes!"

"No! Why, the little devil!" Mr. d'Auriac threw back his head and laughed heartily, then returned with a quick duck to his perusal of the candy counter. "What kin' of chewing gum do you prefer?"

"I don't chew." She heard the prudish overtones and added hastily, snickering, "Mouth full of bridges, you know."

"But gum is good for any kin' of teeth. Very cleanly. Here." He picked up two large handfuls and dropped them on the counter before Mr. Levy.

Mr. Levy counted them, unperturbed. "Thirty-four packs. A dollar seventy."

"Make it two dollar even." Mr. d'Auriac added six more. "You sure you won't try some, Madame? Delicious."

"No, thank you. But, oh, you've got so much there, it'll all go stale on you." Her Scotch soul was offended at his extravagance.

"So? Maybe." He shrugged. "But then, they might stay fresh for a whole year, too, an' then I don't have to buy them again so soon." He waved his arm. "Nothing is certain in this world!" Every motion John d'Auriac made was large, his smile broad, his stride long and his spending wild. He took his package and bowed to her. "Good night, Madame."

Mrs. Kerakis nodded to him, somewhat hurt because he hadn't remembered her name. But it was always that way. She knew everyone's name and nobody seemed to know hers.

Over at the newspaper counter stood three ladies from Number Ten, and from the excited sounds they were making, something special was obviously going on. Mrs. Kerakis edged past crowding customers from other buildings and reached them. Maud Harewood was there, hidden by the other three, the center of attention, addressing herself to them with sad confusion.

Her great, liquid-coated eyes were like those of a muddled child, outlandish in her pale, aging face, and her soft brown hair, cut short, added to the illusion of youth. An old child, she was, dependent and clinging to the women before her, and to each in turn she addressed the full force of her frailty, lashing them into an ecstatic indignation, for each one would have followed her to hell and back for a chance that she might one day grace their dinner table. What a prize to show off to their envious friends!

"But don't they realize what they're doing?" the first lady exclaimed.

". . . to prevent *Maud Harewood* from writing!" cried the second.

"If you don't complain to Mr. Rider, Mrs. Harewood, *I* will!" stated the third. "With the chandelier falling on your head and all."

"Well, not exactly on my head," Mrs. Harewood said. She looked very sweet when she smiled and, underneath the smile, Mrs. Kerakis had to admit that her face looked tired and sad.

"Your chandelier fell? I didn't hear about that," said the second woman.

Mrs. Harewood gave her a soft, liquid stare. "It's all over and done with now, dear."

"Her husband pulled her away just in time——"

"She could have been killed!"

"You mean to say the Fays created such a commotion that . . ."

The three voices joined, interrupted and interlocked and Mrs. Kerakis peered over their heads to see deep into Maud Harewood's soul, to see beyond the soft sadness she exhibited, searching for a sign of falsehood or a confirmation of the truth. But she was all meekness and humility, such a frail little thing that one wanted to take her in tow. Even Mrs. Kerakis found herself thinking, "Why, the poor thing," and felt a surge of pity.

Then Mr. Parrish came into the store. Mrs. Kerakis didn't notice him at first. What she did notice, however, was a sudden change in Maud Harewood that killed any feeling of pity she had experienced. It was a wandering away, a withdrawal that had in it something of pride and something of superiority. She no longer seemed to listen to the ladies; in fact, she no longer seemed to be there with them at all. Her great eyes stared past them to another part of the store, and Mrs. Kerakis turned to follow their direction and noticed Mr. Parrish paying Mr. Levy for a ream of typewriter paper. Maud Harewood waited until the package was in Parrish's hand, and as he turned to leave the store, she raised her arm so he could find her and called, "Hunt darling!" Even the timbre of her voice had changed. Now it was deep, lilting with sophistication.

His intelligent eyes found her and he broke into a delighted smile. The three ladies, almost as awed by him as they were by Maud, parted and let him through. He murmured something to her, and then, as inevitably as if it had been planned, Maud moved away from the ladies who had been paying her court. She moved away regally, without a backward glance, hanging on to his arm, and the two of them passed out of the stationery store together.

The ladies chattered excitedly. Not one of them was offended by Maud's withdrawal. Rather were they impressed by the fitness of the situation, for it was only right that Maud Harewood and Hunt Parrish should have become friends. "Water seeks its own level," the first lady pronounced.

Clutching her little package, which she had almost forgotten to buy, Mrs. Kerakis returned home thoughtfully, wondering why Mrs. Harewood, who had been so relentless in her denunciation of the Fays ever since she moved in, would hesitate for one moment to complain to the landlord. And she wondered, too, about that chandelier. If it fell, some repair must have been necessary. Mr. Gruppmann would have to know about it, and everything Mr. Gruppmann knew, Mr. Rider knew, too. So then Mr. Rider must know all about it, anyway. Why hadn't Maud Harewood told this to the ladies?

She wavered this way and that, one moment pitying Maud or admiring her, and hating her for a blackhearted liar the next. And still she could not possibly conceive of why a great writer like Maud Harewood, who was a friend of Mr. Hunt Parrish, would want to lie about plain people like the Fays. So that actually, although she didn't admit it to herself, she believed Maud Harewood a little bit more than she believed in the Fays. But only a very little bit.

Downstairs on the eighth floor, Maud wandered into her dark north bedroom and looked longingly at the chaise longue. Perhaps it was the sight of the chaise that did it, but her sour expression returned and momentarily she lapsed back into miserable reality. As usual, Albert was late and she was exhausted from her day of unaccustomed activity. Besides, she'd had a terrible time in that stationery store. God, it was awful the way those housewives embellished honest stories and twisted them into falsehood, and disgusting the way they fawned upon her simply because she'd written a book, without knowing or caring what kind of a human being she was. But she had carried everything off quite nicely, she thought.

Oh, for an hour's rest! She'd even passed up cocktails with Hunt, she was so tired. But it would erase everything she had accomplished today if Albert were to come home and find her on the chaise longue. He'd never believe she'd left it. So instead of that . . . Her expression changed. Her mouth curled into a smile and her eyes glittered. She darted into the kitchen and shoved Emma aside, joking. With her own two hands, she mixed Scotch sours, impulsively making an extra drink for Emma, presenting it to her in an old jelly glass with much fanfare, but no orange slice or cherry.

When Albert came home at seven minutes after six, he was moved to the point of having, secretly, to wipe his eyes, to find Maud waiting for him in the living room, fully dressed, with a plate of cheese and crackers and his favorite cocktails in the icy shaker instead of those eternal Bloody Marys. It was almost like the old days, and now he knew that he had been right to scold her as he had, for it was obvious that his forcefulness had turned the trick and that she was now safely on the mend.

Maud was animated and her pretty smile returned in its former brilliance as she told him of her day's activity and her new-found friends. She grew increasingly animated and her eyes no longer seemed coated with liquid. The heat behind them had burned it away. Her cheeks had good color and she laughed often and Albert laughed along with her and pressed her hot hand. Although she told him about her new friends, she didn't mention how she had acquired them. However, in all fairness to her, it was at this point that she forgot, that she lost herself in her role and, like an actress of the Stanislavsky school, she became the character she played. She moved through the minutes, following without question impulses which came upon her. She had passed from the stage where she wondered or worried, where she asked herself why or how. She only knew for certain that the Fays had treated her foully and that everyone agreed with her that they had. She only knew for certain that her own dear friends, of which she had many, were not going to let this pass.

13 :   *Wednesday, May Twentieth*

"Stop!" Irene Parrish whispered to herself. "Stop right here." The hand that held the lipstick shook so hard that she smeared her mouth. She wiped it clean and dropped her trembling hand into her lap. "Relax," she commanded herself. She let her shoulders sag, exhaled, closed her eyes in imitation of rest, but merely succeeded in freeing her attention to concentrate on the nervous buzzing of her body. She could relieve this buzzing if only she could scream. There ought to be a screaming room in every home, she thought. If she could lock herself somewhere in a soundproof closet and let loose, it would be like massage to an aching body.

"Now what's your hurry?" she asked herself, meeting her tired eyes in the mirror. So what if she wasn't ready and waiting for Hunt? Really, so what? So what if she hadn't changed into a fresh dress and washed and put on new make-up, new jewels? Really, so what? Why did she bother to look nice for him instead of bathing in hot scented water and taking herself off to bed?

She'd torn through Manhattan like a wildcat all day and barely managed to beat him home. Then, almost in a single motion, she'd pulled out of one dress and into another, kicked off one pair of shoes and toed into a second, and run to the toilet table to lift a shaking hand to her lips. All this so she would be lovely, fresh and sweet-smelling for her husband's return. And what would he do with this soft, scented woman who was his wife? Who was she enticing? For what?

She should have known better. Now that she looked back on it, all the warnings were there from the very start, but she had refused to heed them. See no evil, hear none, admit none; she had been all three monkeys rolled into one. Even before she went to the dinner party that marked their first meeting, she knew enough about Hunt Parrish to tell herself to beware. He was only a fringe member of their crowd. She'd never met him, but once in a while someone would speak of him, so the name became familiar in the sense that she would pause to think where had she heard it before, and then would be reminded: Oh, you know, he's that overbearing genius of a Georgia-cracker fellow who put himself through Columbia working at Damsfield Paints. Oh, yes, then she would remember; Damsfield Paints had become Parrish Paints when he was still in his early twenties, and he had built it up into one of the largest organizations in the East. "Why don't *I* ever meet him?" she asked several times. "He sounds fascinating."

But they were not anxious for her to meet Parrish. For one thing, it would be a waste of her time; he cared very little for women, no matter how beautiful. As a matter of fact, he cared very little for anyone; he had no close friends, no one really liked him, only respected him for what he had accomplished; just a barefoot boy from the South, who was building one of America's fortunes; it was interesting to watch, but nothing more. Already he had installed blocks of experimental laboratories with grants from the Navy together with private money from Great Britain and France. Anyone could tell what that meant. But he was a complete bastard, she was told; you don't want to meet him. He's pompous and vain and thinks the world begins and ends with himself. You can marry any one of a dozen fine young men who come from your own background.

For someone wiser and older, perhaps, this would have been warning enough, but for young Irene, it was a challenge. "I must meet him, he sounds fascinating," she repeated. "Who said anything about marriage?" And finally someone consented to see that she did.

In those days he was somewhat quieter than now, but bore himself with the same arrogance. Irene, radiantly beautiful, was not accustomed to the indifference with which he accepted her presence by his side at dinner. When she spoke, he turned to her with a small, amused smile like the smile adults bestow upon charming children. He wasn't more than five or six years older than she, but he acted like a tolerant father. Only once or twice during the course of the dinner did the conversation seem to interest him enough for him to contribute to it. Then everyone listened. He had a soft voice, a self-cultivated voice with only the faintest remaining trace of a Southern accent. He phrased his sentences so clearly and carefully that what he said could have been printed without changing a word. And the substance of what he said seemed to Irene to be frankly above the heads of the company present, frivolous college men, pleasure-loving but hardly intellectual. They discussed the newest novel in terms of plot, but he lifted the conversation into the realm of comparative literature. They praised the latest play; he demolished it with clear-cut references from the world's drama, ice-blue points that no one present could discuss, much less disprove. They mentioned the world situation in terms of present events. He tied it up with history and philosophy, with mathematics, sociology and anthropology from the beginning of man so that everyone else was reduced to the status of pupils not eager to learn, who listened, bored, but respectful of his knowledge.

Except for Irene who gazed at him with love-smitten eyes. His indifference challenged her. His cold strength and assurance frightened her and sent thrills running over her body. He was a man of steel, overpowering, who could crush her in a savage, ecstatic embrace, who could hurt her, perhaps—drive her wild with sweet pain.

She knew she had nothing to say that would interest a man who was so different, so vastly superior to any other man she had ever met. So she contented herself with playing the part he forced upon her. She was gay, laughing, flirtatious, childlike, and she succeeded in amusing him. She discovered that if nothing else, she could make him laugh, and she could make him like to look at her.

So eventually she won him. She succeeded where other women failed.

They were married in April and sailed the same day for Europe. He engaged the bridal suite on the ship and filled it with roses for her. There was champagne and caviar for the friends who saw them off, and later there was a special tête-à-tête dinner served in the privacy of their sitting room. But as the evening passed, Irene observed a phenomenon. The man of steel slowly dissolved. He became less assured, his face softened into boyish innocence and there was confusion and even fear in the little nervous chuckle that she heard then for the first time. Subtly, their positions reversed. Now he was the child and she the parent. And he didn't know what to do.

Irene drew her arms close to her body and closed her eyes tight, remembering the torturous, disappointing wedding night, the fumbles of a somehow guilty man, the fumbles of two virgins with his strange guilt between them. What was this guilt? She didn't know, never knew, but knew only that what should have been sweet was made loathsome by it, a sneaky, sinful, crawling thing. In the months that followed, he was the strong parent by day and they were comparatively happy in foreign lands, but at night she became a resented mother whose will must be gratified. In her innocence, she was convinced the fault was hers. They never discussed it, pretended it didn't exist, but she knew that Hunt blamed her. His impatience was always because of her. She was doing something wrong. She grieved in silence and wept in silence. She thought she detected disgust in him, felt she offended him in some way and became increasingly fastidious with her personal habits. Every inch of her she scrubbed and scented. She never let him see her naked or disheveled. She never wore anything even faintly soiled; everything she put on her body was silky, pleats and ribbons and lace, alluring and feminine, a totally lovely creature by day or by night.

But there was no change. Each night was the same. Even with his hands upon her in a touch that was too furtive and light, she still could not control her passion, though it seemed that the more passionate she became the colder he became and eventually she approached the bed with distaste and reluctance, so that when they moved into this apartment after a few years, into separate rooms, it was more of a relief to her than a defeat.

Their near-celibate marriage was a secret both kept to themselves. Over all the years, she had not once dared to complain directly, had not once demanded to know the truth. She was afraid to ask him. Something about his nervous chuckle warned her against it. Often she considered leaving him, but either she was a transparent soul or else he had a direct wire to her brain, for he would suddenly become so charming, so attentive and so delightfully in need of her, that she would have to change her mind. He would entertain her by clowning, shadow-boxing in a circle around her and landing kisses on her face instead of blows. Or he would all at once be unable to make his own selection of suit, necktie or socks. He would bring her presents, not a diamond she had to go out and select for herself (although he gave her many of these), but the thoughtful little gifts that he had to go out of his way to remember, like an avocado pear, perfectly ripened, or a pocketful of Hershey almond bars. At such times, even when he lied about his age (for he always made himself two or three years younger), or claimed to be six feet tall (he was five-ten-and-a-half), he would give her the credit of knowing the truth by means of a covert, conspiratorial smile.

Added to this was the fact that she was a luxury-loving female with very little money of her own and Hunt was unduly generous with her. As if to make up for what he wouldn't supply, there was nothing material she couldn't have for the asking. And he was so very successful now, having expanded from paints into lead, zinc, uranium and oil. He was called to Washington for consultation, his name appeared often in the papers, and *Fortune, Life,* and *Time* had done lead articles on him. A good part of this glory was reflected upon herself. As Mrs. Hunt Parrish, she held a leading position in the world of Society, she providing the background he lacked, and when it came right down to brass tacks, only a fool would give up all of this merely for the chance of finding some man who was good in bed.

For Irene did discover finally that the fault lay with Hunt and not herself when, a year after moving into Number Ten, she fearfully consented to enter into an affair with one of Hunt's business associates. "I don't know anything about this sort of thing . . . you'll have to do everything . . . all the arrangements . . . I don't know how . . ." she whispered wildly that night as they danced at El Morocco under Hunt's bored eye. The young man pressed her closer. "I'll take care of everything, darling," he whispered. And he proved to be an experienced and careful philanderer. He rarely called her, but the few times he did, he made sure to ask for Hunt first, fully aware that he wasn't home, and as an afterthought, had Irene come to the telephone. His apartment was on the ground floor of a converted brownstone so there were no doormen or elevator men to recognize her. Each time they met, they arranged the hour and place of their next meeting. And for the first time, Irene knew what it was like to be loved by an erotic man. But after a year, he grew tired of her; and to tell the truth, she grew tired of him, too. There had never developed between them any emotion other than passion, which had to fade. She found him a bore. He found her too serious and intense, and so it was over.

Her sadness returned and her hysterical need to rush here and there. Since then, there had been two little affairs which didn't amount to much, and she hardly counted them. But she never entered into another serious liaison (although she could have), for it was all too difficult

—the sneaking, the planning ahead which took most of the joy out of it, the dodging, the constant fear of detection, notoriety and divorce.

But maybe, Irene thought, with a quick drumming of her heart, maybe she shouldn't have been so fearful?

No, she wouldn't think of this, she couldn't think of it; it was too horrible, the waste, the waste of everything . . . if she shouldn't have been so fearful . . .

The best thing was not to think at all. She was safest this way, for it was best not to admit certain things: how much she loved him in spite of everything he was or was not, or how much she admired him, not so much for his intellectuality (for she had begun to suspect that he was not the philosophical genius, not the high-brow he claimed), but for his strength of purpose, his fantastic memory and his vision in the field of chemistry. Best not to admit how much she worshiped and adored him, so that any gentle word or heedless caress was often enough to bring tears to her eyes. . . .

"Now stop it!" she told herself again.

Thank goodness, Hunt was late tonight. Lucky for her. She picked up her lipstick again and resolutely painted her mouth, her hand firm and controlled. She heard the doorbell. Quickly she patted her hair smooth, sprayed herself with fresh perfume, took one more look at herself in the mirror and practiced her brightest smile. Then she rose and went out to greet her husband.

14 :   *Thursday, May Twenty-first*

At noon, Albert Harewood sent his secretary to lunch, locked the door of his office and went to the telephone. He used his private wire. "Hello there, Dr. Ettinger," he greeted jauntily, puffing on a cigarette.

"Things seem to be picking up. You sound positively cheery."

"You bet I am! She's been out all day for two days in a row making friends. When I came home last night, she had whisky sours and cheese waiting, especially for me. I can't believe it, doctor, it's like a miracle the way she's pulled out of this thing."

"Maud Harewood making friends!"

"Yes, with all her neighbors. She's been having a fine time."

"Is she writing at all?"

"No, but I wouldn't be surprised if that came next. Really, doctor, she's like she used to be before you knew her. I scolded her the other night. She'd been nagging about some boy in the building who occasionally makes noise, using him as an excuse for not writing. I gave it to her straight for the first time. I told her to behave like a normal woman and get out and talk to people, or else admit she needed your help. I had no idea it would work like it did. She's a changed woman."

"Mmm. Eyes bright?"

"Snapping."

"Laughs a lot, moves quickly?"

"Like a ten-year-old."

"Talks fast?"

"And incessantly, as if she were trying to make up for the years of silence. She's like a bubbly kid, doctor."

"Mmm!"

"What's the matter?"

"I'm wary of these sudden changes."

"Oh?" Albert sank back in his chair, deflated.

"I hate to put a damper on your good spirits. You may be right about her, of course, but I have to warn you——"

"Yes?"

"She may very well sink back into depression again."

"Oh. . . ."

"No one can predict when. But be prepared for it. Or her elation might increase—uncomfortably."

"I see." Albert ground out his cigarette like his crumpled hope.

"There's nothing more I can do unless I see her. What you tell me now only makes the need for treatment seem more imperative."

"What can I do? She tells me if she's treated by a psychiatrist, she'll lose her ability to write entirely. She quotes me from Jung——"

"You can't do anything but wait. So far, she's done nothing to enable us to force therapy on her. As for her losing her ability to write under my care, I don't see her writing extensively without it, do you?"

"Oh, I don't believe all that hogwash, doctor. It's her excuse, not mine. You don't think she can become dangerous, do you?"

"It's hard to say. There is a possibility, but very slim. From all you tell me, I would venture to say no——"

"Even with this—new thing?"

"Now you're putting me on the spot. How can I make a diagnosis without examining the patient? I have to rely on what you tell me, and in all fairness, you're hardly a trained observer."

"I realize that. I realize your position and you're very kind to bother talking to me at all. If you could only help me to get her to see you——"

"She has to come of her own will. Or something must happen."

"You keep saying that. It scares the daylights out of me."

"I don't mean to alarm you, only to alert you."

"Thank you, doctor. I won't keep you any longer. I'll watch her and keep trying, that's all."

"It's all you can do. Chin up. Once we get hold of her, we'll fix her up for you."

"You sound so sure."

"Menopausal psychoses are almost always treated with a certain measure of success, Mr. Harewood."

"What a statement! You boys get me. 'Almost always with a certain measure . . .' How careful can you get? And what the hell does it mean, anyway? Not a damn thing."

Dr. Ettinger laughed.

"I'm sorry. Pretty soon I'll be lying on your couch."

"Any time."

"Thanks."

"Call me whenever you feel like it."

"Yes. And doctor, how's—the boy?"

"Same."

"Yes. But is he eating better?"

"Only sweets, steak or roast beef. Same diet every day. But he's doing better since we've been putting those new vitamins in his chocolate malteds."

"He enjoys those, doesn't he? I mean, he gets pleasure from them, doesn't he, real pleasure as we know it?"

"Of course he does. His face brightens perceptibly when the orderly brings it to him."

"And you're making them with ice cream now, as I asked? They taste much better with ice cream."

"The whole works, everything straight from Schrafft's. Chocolate ice cream, chocolate syrup, double portion of malted milk, sweet fresh milk and vitamins into the Waring blendor, beaten to a rich froth and served with sweetened whipped cream on top. What more could you ask?"

"A cherry. I'll bet he'd love it."

"Who wouldn't? All right, I'll tell them to add the cherry."

"Thank you, doctor. I've kept you long enough."

"You're quite welcome. And don't forget, feel free to call me any time."

Albert Harewood replaced the receiver slowly, staring ahead at a smudge on the walnut-paneled wall. Suddenly he dropped his head into his hands and began to sob, the choking dry sobs of a man who is ashamed to have to cry.

15 :   *Thursday, May Twenty-first*

By now the lady tenants throughout the building had been deliciously brainwashed with false and malicious tidings carried by everyone to everyone else: not nearly so titillating, perhaps, as physical assault, abortion, murder or divorce, but one had to make the best of what was available. Each time Julie left her apartment to do her errands, she was exposed to slurs and resentful looks, to groups of whispering women turning her way to stare curiously as if she had some corrupting disease and then dive back into their busy little huddles. There was nothing she could do about it. Perhaps someone cleverer than she might have handled the situation, but Julie was a straight-thinking young woman, who could only move in an undeviating line. She was timidly truthful and, unfortunately for her, there was an element of truth in the story that was being whispered around. She couldn't say they hadn't stamped on the floor on Monday night. She couldn't say Robin didn't play a form of basketball, however harmless, in his room. And she couldn't deny that they were a high-spirited family, who "hacked around," as Robin put it. Had she been someone else, the result might have been different. Had she been able to say, clear-eyed and smiling, that there wasn't a particle of truth to the entire story, and—pointing meaningfully to her head— that Mrs. Harewood was "a serious case of you-know-what—it's in the family, their own son and all that, just refer to her last book if you want proof," the tide of opinion might very well have turned in her direction in spite of the fact that she was one of the old guard, snooty and privileged. Variety being the spice of life, the ladies might have enjoyed a reversal in alliance.

Julie realized all this but unfortunately had neither the heart nor the turn of mind to manage it. The mean little advices given her by various tenants never seemed to afford her a proper starting point for her own defense and she was always at a disadvantage, always protesting instead of being able to assume the attack. For instance: "Better tone down that boy of yours, Mrs. Fay." This from Mrs. Leopold.

"There's nothing wrong with Robin; he's a perfectly normal—"

A wise smile from Mrs. Leopold. "Just the same, better tone him down. In all *decency*, Mrs. Fay!"

"This whole thing is so unfair—he's done absolutely nothing wrong."

"Only banged so hard he loosened the chandelier!"

"What?"

"Look, I know how high-spirited young boys can be. I've had boys of my own, although I must say they never——"

"Mrs. Leopold, what's this story about a chandelier?"

"It's none of *my* affair. I was only giving you a friendly piece of advice. Please don't get *me* involved in this. I've had enough trouble in this building already." And off Mrs. Leopold click-clacked on tiny Italian heels.

Even from Mrs. Kerakis in the butcher shop, a quick whisper as she was leaving: "Better tell Robin to quiet down, Mrs. Fay, just a little you know," accompanied by a confidential wink to indicate that she was in Julie's corner.

"But . . ."

But Mrs. Kerakis had fled.

Or a loud statement by one of the newer tenants, ostensibly delivered to a huddle of ladies, but actually for Julie's benefit as she passed: "If one of *us* carried on like that, Mr. Rider would have us out on our ears!"

Even Terence had the nerve to inform Julie that Robin "needs a good whaling, if you ask me."

"I didn't ask you!" Julie exploded. "Take me up to the penthouse, please."

She was close to tears.

Flossie, rocking back and forth in the living room, sourly examined a set of plans for a new garden that complied with every Building Department ordinance. The draperies were drawn to hide the view of the terrace, but they couldn't drown the sounds of the workmen who were outside repaving. Sheza sat on Flossie's broad lap, happily chewing the sash of her housecoat to shreds. Flossie was too downhearted herself to be of much help to Julie. "Who the hell cares what they think or say? They're all a bunch of goddammed bastards; the whole lot of them can go to hell, Julie, for all you and I care," she said listlessly. But then, observing that Julie was more upset than she had supposed, she put aside the plans, remarking that they were "hideous, anyway," and applied herself to comforting Julie. Having herself suffered such a hard blow so recently, however, Flossie could not take Julie's problem as seriously as Julie did. "So what if someone whispers lies behind your back? 'Sticks and stones,' Julie, nothing but 'sticks and stones.' You have the true happiness that counts in life: your husband, your boy, your home and your good friends and not a hundred Maud Harewoods could take any of these from you. So let her shoot off her big mouth and to hell with her, I say, to hell with them all."

Unconvinced, Julie left Flossie to whisper further obscenities at Mr. Dorkas's sketches and draw thick blue lines through each of them in turn.

Even Robin—who had come home from school in good spirits earlier and stayed long enough to grab his bat and glove and down a Coke before he was gone for baseball practice in the park—returned at five o'clock in a rage, his black eyes shooting indignation. "What's goin' on around this joint anyhow, Ma?"

Julie stuffed the Rock Cornish hens she was preparing for the d'Auriacs that evening. "Now what?"

"I was coming home. Stopped by Dennis's to pick up something to eat. I had fifteen cents left. Mr. Dennis takes me back where he's got a ten-pound can of fresh caviar and he gives me a whole spoonful for nothing, me and his cat; he feeds Cleo caviar, how do you like that?"

"What's so terrible about that? She earns her keep."

"No, not about that. So I'm eating it and I got my baseball bat tucked between my legs, when Mrs. Emmerich comes in. She says to me, smiling in a mean way, do I use my bat often to pound on the floor to torture poor Mrs. Harewood, or do I prefer using my feet? So I said——" Robin broke off, whispered, "Damn!", and looked miserable. "You just don't know what to say, you don't know where to begin when they put things to you like that."

"I know what you mean. So what did you say?"

"I said I never used the bat. How dumb can you get? Just like admitting I always stamped with my feet! So she said I ought to try the bat because it would make much more noise than my feet, and she thought that was such a belly laugh. How she roared! I felt like bashing her head in. So I finished the caviar and left like a dope."

"I don't know what else you could have done. I'd forget it, if I were you. It isn't important, Robin, only annoying," Julie said dishonestly, promising herself to get back at Mrs. Emmerich for this. The noisiest family in the building . . . what right did she have to make cracks?

"The thing I don't understand, the thing I don't get is, people used to like me, mostly. I know they used to, but they don't any more. Suddenly they don't like me at all. Not just Mr. Parrish and Terence, but none of them. Why, do you think? I don't get it. I haven't done anything." His mouth pulled downwards and twitched once or twice.

"That's nonsense. Of course people like you, Robin; they always have."

He shook his head, pressed his lips tight and went into his room to bathe before dinner. Julie couldn't follow him, for she was late as it was and would have to rush to be ready to greet her guests on time.

Ty came home in a foul humor, slammed the newspaper on the table and reported he'd gotten either the cold shoulder or the heehaw from nearly everyone in Levy's and a few biting words of advice from Jesus Christ himself, Mr. Hunt Parrish. Muttering, Ty went to work on the drinks while Julie changed her clothes.

The house was cheerless and divided. They were all separate. Ty fumed in the kitchen, Robin brooded in his tub, and Julie worked hard to control the tears that burned behind her eyelids. She looked at her face in the mirror, downcast and almost disagreeable. She didn't know herself or her husband or son. "Who are we?" she asked herself and moved quickly away from her image.

Were they nothing at all in themselves, nothing more than the reflection of the opinion of strangers? In the sum of their three lives, separately or together as a family, they had heretofore elicited only smiles from others. Now it was the reverse. Had these smiles disappeared because something within the Fays themselves was gone, some inner radiance that used to reflect upon others and bounce back to them? Or was it really possible that a few malicious whispers could overnight reverse the attitude of their neighbors? Were people so eager to hate that they would grasp at any nonsense and let it flourish inside them? For when she got right down to it, the whole situation was nonsensical. Precisely what was their crime? Noise. They were accused of making noise, of being boisterous, perhaps even rowdy. No, she couldn't believe anyone would hate a whole family for such an offense. For example, did anyone hate the Emmerichs? Of course not. Then what was it? What was the difference between the Emmerichs and themselves? If Maud Harewood had complained about the Emmerichs instead of the Fays, would the tenants have been equally aroused? Or to go further back than that, would Maud Harewood have complained about the Emmerichs at all? It was very confusing and the more she thought of it, the more her mind teetered on the edge of a dangerous crevice. Rather than fall into it, it was simpler to blame herself, to blame all three of them, to believe they had lost something that had attracted people to them before.

She approached the mirror again and tentatively practiced a smile. Perhaps she hadn't been smiling enough lately. A smile usually elicited a smile. She shook her head and tried the smile again, but the second was no brighter than the first. It was true, then, what she had first suspected. Something attractive had died within all three of them. Just because of Maud . . . No, not only Maud, for she couldn't have done this alone. It was because of all the other people, who wanted to listen to her. That they *wanted* to. No use trying to kid herself. They did want to listen to Maud. Sadly, she turned away.

She had intended wearing her new navy blue, but suddenly she needed color, needed brightness to brighten her, so instead she slipped into a festive melon cashmere ensemble and applied more rouge to her cheeks. She wore her pearls to brighten her throat and pushed the sleeves of her sweater to her elbows for a jaunty effect. It was a beautiful ensemble, but it didn't reflect her mood tonight. She didn't have time to change into the navy, but it would have been more appropriate.

The d'Auriacs' arrival, precisely at six thirty, was no more boisterous than before, for they always came in bursting with delighted surprise as if they hadn't seen the Fays in years and hadn't expected to find them home tonight, either, but their noise worried Julie, whose ears were now attuned to silence, and she found herself quieting them nervously with little phrases about "the neighbors, you know," and closed the door quickly behind them. Every sound coming from the Fay apartment would now be noted and enlarged upon, reported and repeated, exaggerated and intensified not only by Maud, but by everyone else in the building. And the d'Auriacs, subdued, nearly tiptoed into the living room with tight faces, hoping they hadn't done any harm.

"Everyone want Martinis?" Ty asked unnecessarily, for everyone always wanted Martinis before dinner, just as they always wanted them before lunch when they went out together on Saturdays. While he mixed the drinks, Suzanne, as usual, admired the tray of hors d'oeuvres and then dived in, tasting hungrily, chewing, wiping her finger tips on the napkin, murmuring how good they were. She looked as if she couldn't eat a thing, but had the appetite of a laboring man. And as usual, the initial conversation between Ty and John centered briefly about their work, for Ty handled John's advertising account. Between mouthfuls, Suzanne tried to make light conversation and Julie tried to listen to her, to Ty and John and to enjoy the Martini. But she had said "Shh!" as the d'Auriacs arrived and everything had been stiff and changed from then on. Even the powerful cocktails couldn't replace what was lost.

For a while there was a complete silence as Ty brooded, Suzanne ate, Julie tried to think of something cheerful to say and John gulped the drink he usually sipped and tapped the arm of his chair. Suddenly he unfolded and sprang to his feet like a jack-in-the-box. "I can't stand it!" he cried. "I can't take this one more second. It's got to be stopped, Suzanne!"

Ty and Julie stared at him.

"You tell them!" he shouted, waving an angry arm.

"Tell us what?"

"That beetch downstair. Have you an idea the lies she's telling?"

Julie and Ty gave each other sour looks.

"She says Monday night you made such a noise with the feet and bats and sticks that her chandelier fell down, almost keeling her! Which is a black lie. That you do this every time she calls, begging you to be quiet; that you give wild parties and kick the feet on purpose and that you get your friends to help you. She tells this all over, in the elevator, in the lobby, in the street and in all the stores of the neighborhood. She is one crazy beetch and she must be stopped."

"Just what we figured," Ty said morosely. "Imagine her claiming the chandelier fell!"

"I saw her myself," Suzanne said, "gathering groups together to listen to her lies and the bad part is, so many do believe her, particularly the new tenants, who don't know you so well."

"It's a disgrace." John refilled his glass and took an excited, noisy sip. "I tell you what we must do. A militant counter-campaign! We enlist all our friends."

"And we tell everyone what a liar she is," Suzanne agreed. "How about that?"

Robin, shining with cleanliness, neat and handsome in his dark slacks and blue cotton jacket, with his pale hair trapped by thick hairdressing, came into the room bringing with him a wave of sickening perfume. Rover trotted at his heels and greeted the d'Auriacs behind her master. "What's all the shouting about?" Robin wanted to know, piling three smoked oysters on one Melba round and stuffing it into his mouth.

"We're going to give it to that horrible woman downstairs, Robin, who is spreading lies," John said. "First we must institute our campaign of attack."

"Now you're cookin'!"

"What's that you stank of?" Suzanne wanted to know.

"New hair goo. Like it?"

"It's lovely," Suzanne pinched her nose. "Just lovely."

Robin giggled.

"Now how about what I sujested, Ty?"

"It's right loyal of you, John, but I'm afraid it isn't as simple as that. If we were dealing with an ordinary malicious gossip, it would be another thing, but we've got a much more serious problem here."

"Just because she's a writer?"

"Hey, Dad, don't chicken out on us!"

"I'm not chicken, Robin, just realistic. You all say do something about her. What will we do? Talk to her? Threaten her? We've tried that before and it didn't work. There's only one sure way to stop Maud Harewood now. We can call Mr. Rider and tell him the whole story. He will be sympathetic, indignant, but he will advise us that there's very little he can do, that we should take it up with the police. So the next step would have to be a formal complaint to the effect that Maud Harewood, *Maud Harewood*, remember, is so touched in the head that she has interfered unreasonably with the normal course of our lives and resisted all our attempts at co-operation, and therefore we wish her to be restrained. Can you just see the headlines? Can you imagine the fun the newspapers will have with such a juicy bit? And don't think, even if she was found to be mad as a loon and put away because of our complaint, that our names won't be mud anyway. So we'll have peace, if you can call it that. Who's going to be the one to do this? You, Robin? You, Julie? And don't forget Mr. Harewood. Who's going to be the one to do this to him?"

"She's going to have to be put away anyhow. She's really crazy, Ty," John said.

"Okay, does anyone here want to be the one to lodge the complaint that will do it?" Ty challenged again. "It would settle this thing for good. If people hate us now, they'll hate us twice as much for it, but we'd be rid of Maud Harewood."

John sat down, deflated. "But she has it coming to her all the same."

"You know what I think?" Julie said suddenly. "I think we're taking this too seriously and we're letting it get us down. It isn't that important, really. Let her tell all the lies she likes, if it gives her that much satisfaction. We know what she is, our good friends know it, and that's all that counts. Funny, Flossie told me this today, but it took all this time to sink in. She's right. We don't care about Mrs. Leopold and Mrs. Emmerich or even poor old Mrs. Kerakis for that matter. If we can only learn to disregard Madame Harewood completely, we'll have won the fight. She isn't going to change—she might even get worse—but we mustn't let her change us. That's the important thing, we mustn't let her do that!"

"Well, honey, this from you!"

"But I'm right."

"Of course you are. We all take that crazy *artiste* too seriously. And you people, you go around like unhappy—*qu'est-ce-que c'est orphelins, Suzanne?*"

"Orphings."

"Yes, orphings. We all love you and to hell with Mrs. Harewood!"

"Just the same, she should be stopped," Suzanne said somberly.

"Darn right," Robin said.

"She will be. Life, Liberty and the Pursuit of Happiness. . . . Ever hear of that, Rob? Time will take care of her." Ty stood up. "Dance, Julie?"

"Are you crazy? Without music?"

"Music, Robin, please."

"I get you. Something soft and low, comin' up." He giggled and made for the machine.

"And more Martini. Don't fall down on your own job." John held the empty pitcher upside down and caught the last drops in his glass. "Fine host!"

Rock and roll pulsed through the room. Suzanne slithered around the couch and attempted a jerky version of the Lindy while Robin called corrections to her and demonstrated them, finally taking her hand. Ty stirred the new drinks in tune with the music, singing hoarsely in a Southern accent. John waltzed over to Julie and gravely led her through the steps of the tango. Suzanne interrupted her Lindy lesson long enough to look about her with satisfaction and proclaim, "This is more like eet!" She flung her arms in the air and bumped three times. Ty and Robin let out wolf whistles and clamored for more. Rover snapped at the dancers' shoes and growled. "For 'eaven's sakes, give us some air!" John called.

Downstairs in 8B, Maud Harewood heard the sudden laughter and the music as Ty opened the window. She darted behind the drapery and hid herself there, listening. She closed her eyes and imagined herself with them. Her feet tapped to the music and she swayed while tears coursed down her dry-skinned cheeks. "Oh Lord," she whispered. "They're having a party!"

PART THREE

As a general rule, Cartwright Academy closed earlier and opened later than the public or parochial schools in the city and today was the last day of school for Robin. Only Mr. Ewing in Algebra was churlish enough to try to conduct a proper class. In English, Mr. Samson gave out almond bars and composed limericks on the blackboard, bewailing the miserable vacation months that lay ahead for all. In History, Mr. Wilson spent the entire period recounting a much-embellished tale of fire in his Vermont summer cottage the year before. In French, Mr. Jones had great plans for a song fest, but a few "hackers" in the back of the room messed it all up by booming the dirty verses from "Mademoiselle from Armentières." After lunch there was a farewell assembly, following which the boys raced for their lockers. For a moment, it seemed that the school might be empty sooner than the faculty had dared hope, but no such luck. Now that it was really over, the boys didn't care to leave the building in such a hurry, but perversely sparred in the halls and chased each other from room to room throwing chalk and erasers. They emptied their gym lockers, finding indescribably filthy tee shirts, shorts, socks and handkerchiefs they had forgotten they owned; and, of course, nothing could be greater fun than to throw a smelly old sweat shirt into a good friend's face; therefore it wasn't long before the locker room was transformed into a blizzard of soiled clothing. Only stern Mr. Ewing was able to control them, bellowing threats of punishment to be carried over to the following September. "I'm taking down your names right now!" he shouted, and started to write in his little black book. Silence was immediate since infractions were punished by extra study assignments, but it took time after that to sort and gather together whatever was still intact, and then there were bags to pack, summer addresses to exchange and finally the Coke machine to empty, with a hack on the head, a ripped shirt and torn pocket for the boy who got the last bottle. So that, although the day ended officially at two, the boys were fortunate to get home by four thirty or five with their clothes all in one piece. But this was always the case on the last day of school. It was only to be expected, so in the privacy of his office, Mr. Ewing threw away his list of names and the janitors went to work to clean up the mess.

With his heavy book bag full of soiled clothes dragging at his arm,

Robin strode into Number Ten whistling. Old Terence was at the house phone in the lobby.

"Last day of school!" Robin cried, swinging his laundry in an exuberant arc over his head.

"Watch out with that thing!" Terence snapped. He returned to the telephone. "Look, I have a full car waiting down here, lady," he shouted. "What's it with the toilet? I can't hear you."

"Oh, shame!" Robin mocked.

"Shut up. . . . Talk louder, lady."

But Terence couldn't dampen Robin's spirits today. Grinning, he listened as Terence's voice grew shriller, spurred by the fact that Mrs. Lesser and Miss Forsythe were waiting for him in the elevator. He didn't seem to hear Mrs. Lesser's repeated protestations that she was in no hurry, that he should calm down and take his time.

"Last day of school," Robin called to them and swung his laundry for their benefit, too.

"And what a great day that is! Don't I remember!" Mrs. Lesser said.

Hunt Parrish walked in. His eyes passed over Robin with a look of dislike and he entered the elevator, removed his hat and nodded stiffly to the waiting ladies. "Where's the doorman? Eating again?"

Miss Forsythe said she believed he was.

Mr. Parrish clucked, annoyed, and said something about the house staff being too limited.

"Keeps flushing, you say? Look, I'm alone down here!" Terence screamed.

Robin watched Terence writhing with impatience at the telephone and suddenly he had an idea. It was a wild and beautiful thought, perfectly suited to the day and the circumstance. He made for the elevator. "Keep cool, Terence, I'll take them up."

"Don't you dare!"

But Robin was too quick for the old man. He sped to the car, flung his bag into the corner and pressed the button just as Walter Marsh came running into the building, calling, "Wait for me, Robin!" But it was too late, the doors closed on Marsh's puffing red face and on Terence, pale with fury.

"You'll pay for this!" Terence screamed, his voice fading as the car moved upwards.

"Why I never, why never in my life——" Parrish fumed.

"Don't worry about Robin; he's the best elevator man in the building," Mrs. Lesser said.

"Yes, he is," her sister confirmed.

[204]

Robin slapped his knee. "Say, did you get a load of Terence's face? So mad he could've killed me. Boy, was that rich!"

"Serves him right," Mrs. Lesser said. "He's always so cranky with you."

Only Hunt Parrish was outraged. "This is absolutely—never have I . . ."

But Robin's fun didn't last long. Now he watched the instrument panel anxiously. He had pressed seven for Mrs. Lesser and Miss Forsythe, but the elevator was only inching up, barely at the third floor now, and the gravity pull in the car seemed wrong, as if it might be stopping but was taking too long to stop. A streak of fear passed through his chest. The elevator had never behaved this way before.

"Something wrong, Robin?" Mrs. Lesser's voice sounded breathless and frightened.

He turned and shook his head, smiling to comfort her because above all, he knew she should not be allowed to worry. For a long and terrifying moment the elevator seemed suspended in mid-air, seemed not to move up or down but to sway there with that strange pull of motion within. They should have been at the seventh floor long ago.

"What's the matter? This isn't the time or the place for jokes, Robin," Hunt Parrish scolded.

"I know, I know, sir," Robin said, eying the emergency-stop button. They were only inching past the third floor and something had obviously gone wrong with the machinery. He pressed the button. The car jolted, then came to a halt. "It's okay now. Whew!" Robin's voice issued windy with relief. "Something——"

A tearing sound shrieked from above. The car jerked, quivered— then plunged.

Miss Forsythe screamed.

Robin was catapulted backwards over his book bag, headfirst.

Hunt Parrish gripped tight on the handrails and shut his eyes.

The fall lasted only a moment. Then the car crashed to the basement with a shattering sound of cracking wood and twisting steel. Hunt was tossed like a limp puppet into a heap in the corner and then was held fast to the bottom of the car by the pull of gravity as they bounded upwards, sent by the four huge safety springs beneath. Down they crashed again, and up they bounded, down and then up, the walls cracking and splintering ominously. Hunt's hands reached to clutch at anything, his head bent under for protection. He was grimly terrified, breathlessly silent, sick with the crazy bouncing. His stomach churned and revolted, his fingers dug at his own flesh, until at last, with a creaking rock that felt ludicrously like the sweet motion of a ship at sea, the car settled to rest on the great coiled springs that had saved them.

Dazedly, Hunt moved away to sprawl exhausted on the floor, breathing heavily with closed eyes, too shaken and shocked to move. After a few moments, he pulled himself with care to his knees, hearing a buzzing signal from the instrument panel. He moved his joints warily, but he seemed all right except for a shoulder that ached. The signal came again and again. Slowly he drew himself to his feet and tried the jammed door that now bore great, jagged cracks in the wood. Seeing that it wouldn't open, he shuffled to the panel and gravely rang the emergency bell. He did all this unconsciously. Then, his duty done, he crouched down again in another corner alone, holding his bad arm by the elbow with a hand that shook, winking as the buzzing signals increased in urgency.

"Ah-h-h!" Miss Forsythe whined.

That new sound cut through the fog in Hunt's mind. He shivered, his teeth chattered and he clenched them together. Until just now, he had forgotten about the others in the car. "You—all right?"

"Bella?" she said. "Bella?"

Hunt stared at where Mrs. Lesser lay queerly, with one leg twisted under her and her hat pulled down over her face, revealing only her sagging mouth.

"Ahhhh God!" Miss Forsythe screamed. "Bella!"

"Lord . . ." Hunt whispered, sliding over. He took one limp white hand in his shiny moving fingers and searched in vain for a pulse.

"No, Bella . . . no, Bella!"

He found Mrs. Lesser's handbag on the floor. He took out the mirror and held it shaking before her open mouth. "No breath," he whispered.

But Miss Forsythe didn't have to be told. She moaned and sank down with her head against her sister's shoulder, weeping, calling her name.

Nauseated, Hunt pulled himself up by one hand on the rail. He touched his left shoulder, tried to raise it, gasped and let it dangle. "I think it's broken," he said aloud, dazedly looking about him. Then he saw Robin crouched in the corner under the instrument panel. The boy sat with his legs extended and his hands at his sides. His eyes were wide and fixed and there was a foolish smile on his face. Now Hunt remembered, and he looked with fury upon the grinning boy. "See what you've done? My shoulder is broken and Mrs. Lesser is dead. I hope you're satisfied now."

Robin only stared and kept smiling.

"You think it's funny, do you? You can smile? You, the one who did it?" He stepped closer to Robin. "Stop smiling! Stop it at once!" he commanded, his voice hoarse with rage. But the boy persisted in grinning at him with his loose, foolish mouth. Hunt bent towards him. "You killed Mrs. Lesser, do you hear? *You killed her!* You vile, loathsome, grinning fool!"

He struck Robin full and hard across the face.

As if he had struck a rag doll, Robin crumpled with the blow. He collapsed at the waist and slumped into a curled mound in the corner, his eyes closed, but still smiling, his bony hands limp, palms upward, grimy from play, and at that moment the buzzer sounded loud and without interruption, on and on this time, filling the car with a crazy grating noise from which there was no relief.

Parrish spun away and leaped to the door. He pounded. "Get us out of here! Somebody, get us out of here! Get us out!" He leaned against the door panting and his eyes slid unwillingly back to Robin. He passed his hand over his dry mouth. He dropped to his knees and took the boy's hand, shuddering. He could barely feel the pulse beating in the smudged wrist. He tapped the firm cheeks, one striped from the force of his blow. "Robin . . . Robin . . . ," but the boy remained unconscious. He laid him straight on the floor of the car and put his head to rest on his book bag. His hands came away stained with blood. He snapped up and backed away until the wall of the elevator stopped him. "I didn't do that, I had nothing to do with that . . ." He glanced covertly towards Miss Forsythe, but she was prostrate over her sister's body, too grief-stricken to notice anything. A cold perspiration broke out over Hunt's body and he wiped his forehead with his hand. Panic seized him again and he leaped forward to the door and pounded and screamed to whoever was still ringing that damn bell.

This time, over the sound of Hunt's shouts and Miss Forsythe's weeping, Klaus Gruppmann's voice was heard from outside: "Ho, there!"

"Here! Hurry—get a doctor—ambulance!" Parrish screamed. "Hurry, for God's sake!"

"They're coming in a minute—and we gonna get you out in a minute. Anybody hurt?"

"Hurt, my God, Mrs. Lesser's dead and Robin's unconscious, bleeding from the head—get a doctor quick—what took you so long? Who the hell is ringing that bell? Disgraceful . . . oh my God!"

For a moment there was silence out there. Then the sound of excited voices, all talking at once, distilled into one strange voice that called, "Parrish, you say Robin's unconscious?"

"Yes, get a doctor, damn it!"

"Christ! Get them out, Klaus——"

"Everybody else okay?" Klaus called hoarsely.

"I guess so—I don't know . . . Stop talking, man, and do something."

"We're trying. It's only been ten minutes, Mr. Parrish, only ten minutes since you fell. Please try to keep calm. . . . You, too, Mr. Marsh."

Hunt sank down against the far wall and dropped his head into his hands. Only ten minutes since the crash? Only ten minutes. He could hear them working at the door now, fumbling and getting nowhere. Perhaps his sense of time was still askew, but it seemed a half hour or more until someone yelled something about calling for a blowtorch, to which Hunt muttered, "Idiots, now they think of it!" But then Klaus bellowed, "There we got it!" and a point of metal appeared at the top of the jammed door. With a grating sound, it gave way and crowbars were inserted to force it open.

The car had fallen into a subbasement and the floor of the basement appeared at the top third of the elevator doorway. Faces looked down at him, foremost that of Klaus Gruppmann, greenish and sweating. "Joe, get me that ladder down. Everything gonna be all right, folks."

He climbed down backwards and turned first to Mrs. Lesser. "Please, Miss Forsythe." She let him move her, weeping silently. Klaus put his ear to Mrs. Lesser's chest. He felt for her pulse. There was a commotion at the top. Someone said, "Here's the ambulance doctor now," and a man in a white uniform climbed down.

"Please look out for the boy," Hunt said dully. He saw Walter Marsh's worried face at the top of the ladder trying to get a glimpse of Robin.

The doctor looked briefly at Mrs. Lesser, touched Miss Forsythe's hand and whispered, "Sorry . . ." and turned to Robin. Klaus was kneeling next to him, supporting him in his arms, whispering something in German. The doctor took only a moment. "Okay, bring that stretcher down here. His mother around?"

Walter Marsh crouched near the top of the ladder. "Is he all right?"

"Head injury, can't tell yet."

"His mother must be upstairs. I'll get her."

"Bring her out to the ambulance."

They bound Robin's limp body to the litter so he wouldn't tumble out and lifted him up. Hunt watched them, retching, his hand clamped across his mouth.

The doctor paused at the ladder. "Better get the others out first," he said to Klaus. "No hurry with the old lady, I'm sorry to say. Are you all right, Mister?"

"Just my shoulder, I think—I'll get my own doctor."

"Better let me take a look."

"No, you get out to the boy. I'm all right."

"And you, Ma'am?"

Miss Forsythe stared at the doctor without understanding.

"You all right?"

She stared, then nodded tearfully.

"She wouldn't know," the doctor said; "she should be looked at later."

"I see to it," Klaus said.

The doctor climbed up the ladder.

Klaus took Miss Forsythe by the arm. "Come on, dear lady."

"No . . ." She swayed towards her sister.

"Please, Miss Forsythe."

"No, I want to stay."

"Only up the ladder, you can wait there."

So she let him help her, let him push her up from behind, while Joe and Phil hauled her from above. Parrish made it next, crying peevishly, "Watch out for my shoulder!" Wheezing, Phil hurried him through the basement hall, past Miss Forsythe, who leaned against the wall sobbing as she waited for her sister's body to be brought up. A policeman comforted her. He left her when he saw Parrish. "No, not now, not now," Hunt snapped. The policeman raised his hand in understanding and turned back to Miss Forsythe.

A small crowd of whispering tenants had already sneaked down the fire stairs to see what was going on in spite of the efforts of Carney, the porter, to keep them away. The doctor, who had been stopped a moment by the officer, hurried past Hunt to follow Robin's litter to the ambulance.

"You all right, Mr. Parrish?" one of the tenants called to him. Wooden-faced, Hunt muttered, "For Christ's sake, get me upstairs." Phil led him into the back elevator where Carney was standing guard to see that no one used it right now except for those involved in the accident.

Julie was waiting for Robin. She anticipated his bringing several boys home with him to celebrate the end of school as he had done the year before, so she was prepared with a double batch of rich chocolate brownies fresh from the oven and a large pitcher of her special fruit punch waiting in the refrigerator. But it was eighteen minutes past five and no sign of him yet. She opened the record cabinet and selected "La Bohème." She adjusted the tone on the record-player and moved to the window, parting the slats of the blinds to look out into the street, still sun-drenched. She hummed with the first beautiful strains of the opera and closed her eyes to hear it better.

Standing there at the window with the sweet music all about her, she heard the first crash of the elevator like an explosion from downstairs. At first she was not particularly alarmed. Curiously, she walked into the foyer and heard another explosive sound and then a third and a fourth, each fainter than the last. She went out into the hallway, leaving the door open behind her. Mrs. Emmerich was already there, standing before the elevator door, wrinkling her apron with worrying hands. "You hear that?"

"Yes, sounded like an explosion. Maybe the boiler."

"You think so?"

"I don't know. Everything seems quiet now."

"If it was anything—bad—I mean, would it be so quiet now? I mean, wouldn't there be screams?"

Julie had to laugh. "Listen to the two of us—explosions, screams. Joe probably dropped a garbage can or something equally devastating."

Rover came slinking out of the open door. She paused and looked up at Julie with great, worried eyes, fearful lest she be chased back home. Mrs. Emmerich's boxer, though safely locked in the bedroom, sensed Rover's nearness and whined and barked. Rover wagged her tail and trotted to the Emmerichs' door, cocking her head from side to side as she listened to her swain. Julie picked her up. "You know I don't allow you to associate with boxers."

Mrs. Emmerich said, "Shh! Hear that?" There were muffled shouts from downstairs now, but it was impossible to make out what was being said. The music of "La Bohème" came clearer into the hallway than did the voices from below.

"I just know something dreadful's happened," Mrs. Emmerich whined, rubbing her hands together, "I just know it—and I feel so helpless."

"Should I ring? The elevator doesn't seem to be moving." Julie didn't know why she hesitated, but while she stood there, someone else rang from another floor and their courage was a go-ahead signal for others who must have been standing, wondering, in their own hallways, and now the two women could hear the sound of buzzers from everywhere. But still the elevator remained where it was. "Either it's stuck or something exploded on the third floor."

"Remember the time that drunken Southern woman opened the gas jets in her kitchen?" Mrs. Emmerich squinted unhappily. "I remember because Mr. Emmerich was so upset. He said she could have blown us all to kingdom come. If she wanted to do away with herself, that was her business, but it was downright selfish to endanger the lives of hundreds of others."

Julie made no comment. She went to the back hallway and listened at the elevator there. "Just voices. Can't understand a word."

"Oh, I'm *so worried!*"

"Wait a minute—yes, the back elevator's coming up." Julie hugged Rover close and shivered. She couldn't explain why she felt so queer, unraveled, as if the mission of that moving elevator had to be destined for herself. She rubbed her cheek against Rover's satin fur and the little dog grunted happily. But when the car did stop there, with a metallic clap and some creaks, Julie leaped back to the wall, already terrified that her premonition had come true. The door opened and Walt Marsh hurried out. Not expecting to find her facing him, he turned right, stopped with his hand on the door that led to the main hallway and turned back slowly.

She was motionless, her eyes stretched wide.

"Now it's all right—it's going to be all right, Julie. It's Robin—he's got a bang on the head. The elevator fell—but only three floors. He's all right."

"Oh my God!" Mrs. Emmerich cried.

Julie's cheeks blanched. She thrust Rover into Mrs. Emmerich's arms. "Would you take care of her, please?"

"Of course, for as long as you want. Don't worry, my dear." Mrs. Emmerich's eyes were streaming as she clutched Rover to her breast.

"Don't you want to get your purse?" Walt suggested.

"No—come on, let's go down."

They rushed through the crowded lobby to the ambulance. Walt watched Julie climb in, white-faced, biting on her underlip, and bend towards Robin, motionless on the white berth. The ambulance doctor followed, closed the door, and they pulled away, the siren starting.

Walt went back to the basement where they needed him for questioning.

Ty came into the lobby whistling, with the evening paper under his arm. A crowd of tenants pressed around the fire-stairs door to the left of the elevator, which led to the basement. "What's up?" He peered over their heads. One by one, they turned to him with such queer eyes that he knew at once something had happened to Julie or Robin. Moving in a rigid, white calm, he pushed through the crowd. Someone caught his arm and murmured something about an elevator accident and at the stairway two policemen stopped him, but voices called out that this was the boy's father. So it was Robin, it was Robin who was hurt. They let him through and he ran down the stairs where Klaus met him, sweating, trying to explain in words sputtered so fast that they ran together. From the center of the hallway, two attendants carried towards him a litter holding a covered body. He heard a woman weeping. It wasn't death Ty had been expecting, not death, and the blood left his head, he swayed and Klaus grabbed him, pressed his arms. "Robin's okay, Mr. Fay, okay. That's poor Mrs. Lesser."

From the rear of the basement, Walt Marsh broke away from a group of men and hurried down the hall to Ty, partly recovered now and wiping his streaming face. "He's going to be all right, old boy. Don't be frightened. He's got a nasty bump on the head, that's all. You grab yourself a cab and get on over to Roosevelt Hospital. I'll take care of everything here and be over later."

"Everything here?" There was such a buzzing in Ty's head, he wasn't sure of what Walt was saying. "Anything I should be—attending to?"

"You? Hell, no. You get over to Robin and Julie. I'll see you later on. And, Ty, he's really okay." Walt gave him an encouraging wink and a slap on the shoulder, but his face sagged as he turned away.

"I get you a cab," Klaus muttered and preceded Ty up the stairs to the lobby. "Out of the way, Cheesis Gr-rist, move away, will you?" he shouted to the tenants. "Go on upstairs. You can use the back elevator now. Go on to your own apartments already!" Arming his way through the crowd like an angry bear, he made a pathway for Ty. Out in the street, he whistled so loud and waved his arms so forcefully that three taxicabs stopped, their brakes screeching.

3 :   *Friday, June Fifth*

There was turmoil in the basement despite the withdrawal of Robin to the hospital, Hunt Parrish to his apartment, and Miss Forsythe to follow the remains of her sister to the Bellevue morgue. The white-washed brick hallway was crowded with police, elevator mechanics and officials, newspaper reporters, curious tenants who refused to leave, and the oppressed house staff trying to keep order and execute their duties all at once. Most harassed of all was Klaus Gruppmann, thrashing back and forth, streaming with sweat in the airless, overcrowded hall, bellowing orders, answering questions and trying unsuccessfully to reach Mr. Rider, who had picked this day of all days to drive up to Westchester on a real-estate deal.

Terence, shaking and inarticulate, was being questioned at one side of the hall. Walt Marsh, grim and eying his wrist watch constantly, stood at the other. A young detective had been sent over from headquarters and it was to him that Walt Marsh gave his account of the accident after Terence had garbled up time and circumstance until the only intelligible information that came from him had to do with his personal opinion of Robin Fay. At the same time, a petty official from the elevator company, who had been questioning anyone who happened to be present in the basement, approached Walt for his version, so he was able to give it to both of them at once and save himself a little time. Actually, there wasn't much to tell. He and Terence had stood before the elevator door wondering why the car had stopped just above the third floor (they could watch its progress on the indicator), and then there issued a wracking noise from above—yes, above, not below—and the car had fallen. It had bounced three or four times, Walt judged. He and Terence had run down the fire stairs to the basement. Mr. Gruppmann was already on the job. He had sent Joe, Phil and Carney to gather rescue equipment and had telephoned the elevator emergency crew and the police department for a stand-by ambulance. After that, Gruppmann had made contact with Parrish through the jammed elevator door. Walt had stood around until they began to pry open the door and escape hatch, both of which were jammed. Then he had given a hand until the emergency crew arrived. The whole thing took only a matter of minutes, maybe twenty, twenty-five; he hadn't looked at his watch. In his opinion everyone behaved efficiently and well, especially Klaus Gruppmann, and the only one he could criticize was himself for not making immediate contact with Parrish while Gruppmann was busy on the telephone. It was foolish, inconsiderate—but he was afraid to. He didn't know why, but he just didn't.

"You never know how you'll act in an emergency," the detective said. "Look at Gruppmann, he orders an ambulance before he knows if anyone is hurt. But I suppose, from his point of view, that was efficient. Maybe he was right."

"I disagree," said the elevator official whose name was Purdy. "He should have found out if anybody was hurt before bothering the police."

"A stand-by ambulance, in the case of an accident like this one, isn't a bad idea," the detective said.

"In this case, Mr. Purdy, we all knew. About Mrs. Lesser, that is," Walt said; "we knew she couldn't stand such a shock."

"What about the boy, Robin Fay?" Mr. Purdy asked. "Beats me, wild kid or not, I still don't know how he could have done it." He wiped his forehead with a yellowish handkerchief.

"Are you kidding?"

"Why would I be kidding, Mr. Marsh?"

"You can't seriously infer that Robin had anything to do with this accident? Why, that boy can run the elevator as well as any man in the building. There's no great skill involved."

"That may be true, but this time it fell, sir, while he was running it. And it's impossible for an elevator to fall, absolutely impossible."

"Yeah," the detective drawled, "impossible." He snorted.

"That's the point—how the kid managed it, I'll——"

"Jesus Christ, so help me—!" Walt pounded his palm with his fist.

"Look here, Purdy," the detective said, "what would be the worst the boy could have done—push every button on the panel at the same time for the hell of it?"

"Maybe—I don't know what he could——"

"Say he did, what would happen then?"

"That's what I mean when I say I don't understand what he could've done. If he pushed them all at once, all that would happen would be a jam; the car might get stuck, but it wouldn't fall. I'm not accusing the kid, mind you, I'm just saying how could he have done it?" Purdy closed his notebook and slid his pencil into his breast pocket.

"You figure maybe he climbed up to the ceiling of the car and out the escape hatch, sawed away the cable with his teeth and nails, then climbed down again and started the car just so it would fall and kill a sick old lady he was crazy about while the rest of them waited patiently in the car? You figure that's the way it was?"

"There's no point discussing it if you're going to act like a clown."

"I'm not clowning. You've made a dangerous accusation, Purdy. Why don't you back it up?"

"Well, so maybe he didn't have anything to do with it."

"Damn right he didn't. He couldn't. So let's get this straight right now. If this accident is anybody's fault, it's not the boy's. This is the same type of elevator that's installed in all self-service buildings with the only difference that a paid operator runs it instead of the tenants themselves. Any small child can operate it safely and kids a lot younger than Robin Fay are running these same elevators by the tens of thousands all over the country. So lay off the kid, huh Purdy? It won't work."

Purdy spread his hands and looked put upon. "Look, Lieutenant, I don't know that kid from Adam. What I said was what they all told me upstairs. I'm only repeating what I heard. The whole building's shooting their mouths off about that kid, and I always figure, where there's smoke there's fire." Offended, he turned away.

"Oh, great!" Walt said.

The detective gave his head an angry shake. "I don't know why people do it, Mr. Marsh, but any time anything happens and there's a kid involved, no matter how farfetched, no matter how impossible, they always try to blame the youngster. Only last week I made a call at an apartment building over on Park Avenue where a six-year-old child was seriously hurt. The bathroom sink broke away from the wall as he was washing his hands and fell on top of him. It was a Sunday and there wasn't one man in the building who knew where the water shut-off valves were located, so for three, four floors below, apartments were flooded and everything ruined. And what do you think they tried to claim? That this little kid, no bigger than a minute, climbed up on the sink and jumped on it until it fell! Everybody was ready to sue the kid's father and no one gave a damn that the kid was in the hospital on the critical list. To tell you the truth, no one even asked if the kid was hurt."

"And what really happened?"

"Negligence. The family had been complaining for two years that the sink was loose, but no licensed plumber was sent for. It beats me what people will try to pin on a kid, what people will believe when a kid's involved! Seems as though they want to. Seems to me there's a kind of natural hatred exists in some people for kids, just any kid, it don't matter whose. And you take a little gentleman like the Fay kid, trained to say 'Yes, Sir' and give up his seat in the bus and hold the door for everybody else in the world, why a kid like that hasn't got the chance of a snowball in hell against his elders because he's trained not to fight back. Oh, don't tell me—I've got kids of my own, I see it all the time."

"But Purdy knew he couldn't pull it off. Did you watch his face? Why did he try when he knew it wouldn't work?"

"They try, Mr. Marsh. It's the first thing comes to their minds. If a kid's around, he did it. Man, I'm glad I'm not a kid any more!"

The crowd in the basement had thinned out considerably by now. Klaus was still trying to contact Mr. Rider. Terence had been given permission to go home, but obstinately remained on the job, ferrying people up and down in the back elevator. He gave his shattered nerves only one concession, a good snort of Klaus's Scotch. A single policeman remained, watching the work of the elevator crew, and the house staff made sure that at least one of them would be standing there as a witness when the cause of the accident was discovered. A city inspector and two assistants had arrived by now, and were supervising the crew. Most of the time, Klaus remained on the spot himself, but he was only one man, valiantly looking out for his building, his tenants, and his absent boss, so that when he was needed elsewhere, Joe, Carney or Phil took his place. Most of the tenants had gone back to their apartments, but now and then someone could be seen sneaking down the back stairs to view the wreckage with horror. One of these was Mrs. Kerakis, who, upon learning where they had taken Mrs. Lesser's body, exclaimed, "Why, Miss Forsythe is *down there* all alone? The poor dear, I'll go to her at once." Only too well, she knew what it was like to wait at the Medical Examiner's office in solitude. So she went upstairs, donned her mink scarf and black straw hat and taxied down to keep Miss Forsythe company.

There was nothing more for Walt to do. He had repeated his story to every official and reporter. Now he was anxious to get over to the hospital. He asked Joe to go up to Flossie and carefully, without revealing enough to alarm her, tell her what had happened; that he was leaving for the hospital now and would be in touch with her as soon as possible. Joe made an O in the air with his thumb and forefinger and rang for the back elevator.

Walt climbed the fire stairs to the lobby where a handful of tenants were still buzzing. He heard what they were saying before they saw him emerge and his beefy cheeks blazed. As he stepped out, they surrounded him and poured forth a torrent of questions, archetypes variably worded, that all boiled down to a concerted denunciation of Robin Fay with a courteous question mark at the end. Walt stood in their midst for a moment, glaring at them through burning eyes, too enraged to speak. Then he charged through them into the street, pushing aside anyone who happened to be in his way.

4 :   *Friday, June Fifth*

As Hunt Parrish stepped out of the back elevator at the eleventh floor, he was mobbed by neighbors, some of whom had climbed several flights to confront him. They pushed to get to him with frightened questions and he pressed his hands to his ears to drown out their voices while Phil wheezed, "Let him through (heugh!), please, ladies, let Mr. (heugh!) Parrish through." To make it worse, Irene darted out of the apartment in her bathrobe crying, "Darling!"—which made him wince, for his position lacked dignity enough as it was. He refused to answer any of the questions put to him but stalked angrily through his front door, nursing his right shoulder, with a small thought of wonder as he remembered that he had been able to move it quite without pain when he had put his hands to his ears a moment before. The door closing behind him stilled the voices from outside, but a clamor throbbed within his head, tuned to each pulse, to each beat of his heart, and he let Irene lead him to a chair in the living room where he collapsed, feeling stabs of pain everywhere. For once he was glad of a soft armchair that enfolded him comfortingly, but along with it, he had to accept Irene's eternal fussing, the only part of which he appreciated was the brandy she brought him. This he swallowed gratefully, noting that his hand shook as he held the glass, and no wonder! He had never expected to escape alive; it was a nightmare that he'd been through.

Irene knelt on the floor at his feet and for a while he wasn't aware of her there, but then he felt her stroking his hand. Her touch was warm and meant to soothe, but it irritated him to the extreme and a sob broke in his throat, a shameful sound which he controlled almost at once, but which accomplished nothing, for she continued to stroke his hand, believing she was helping him, and he finally had to pull it away.

The brandy brought warmth to his chilled body and as he rested there and felt somewhat better, his indignation returned and gathered.

He moved his shoulder again to test it and enjoyed the fact that it hurt. Now for the first time, he let his eyes travel to Irene's face, upturned and patient. Why, she couldn't know much about what had happened, she had obviously been taking a bath at the time. It had been the neighbors' noise as Phil brought him to the eleventh floor that had brought her, still damp from the tub, to the door. He looked at her, wondering at her self-control. "You don't know about it, do you?" She shook her head and bit at the skin of her underlip, a nervous habit he deplored. So he told her in a low, tight voice. He told her up to the point where he had pronounced Mrs. Lesser dead and then, quite suddenly, something clamped tight inside of him and would not relax, but gripped and twisted so that he wanted to pound the arms of the chair. Instead he loosed all of this upon the image of Robin and epithets poured from his damp lips while his fingers writhed, pulling at the material of his trousers.

She listened to him, her breast rising and falling rapidly. At first she expressed her horror with small gasps and sighs and shakes of her head until he reviled the boy and then she looked away and he no longer felt her alliance. This, without his telling her what he had done to Robin, or what he had said, but only what he personally thought of the boy. She went away from him although she remained where she was. He could not allow such disloyalty. She must condone him, she must! "You always take his part against me," he said bitterly, letting his head drop back against the soft cushion of the chair with his eyes closed.

"That's not true. You ought to know I wouldn't do that," she denied to placate him.

"You always have. Even after this, even after he's been responsible for killing another human being——"

"You can't believe that! It was an accident. How can you——"

"Accident? Accident?" he said wildly.

But her eyes made him shrink and he began to shiver, for she was not all-loving, all-embracing, all-agreeing as she pretended. Seeing his distress, she softened. She brought him another brandy. She tried to get him to go to bed, but he wouldn't move. She wanted to call the doctor, but he said he was all right. If he could only rest here and be left alone. That was all he ever required of her. Hilda came in and out on tiptoe to ask about dinner, her face drooping in awesome sympathy, but unable to hide the gleam of excitement in her eyes, fed by secret trips to the incinerator where she met and whispered with the other servants and then sped back to the kitchen to impart all she had learned to the cook. But Hunt's stomach lurched at the very mention of food, so Irene played with a piece of French toast and a cup of tea, which she took on a tray beside him.

But they didn't let him rest for long. A Mr. Purdy from the elevator company arrived to question him and although Irene tried to put the man off, Hunt insisted it was his duty to co-operate no matter how he felt. He answered Purdy's questions in a whisper, with his eyes closed. No, he hadn't called the doctor because he didn't feel up to an examination yet, but he would in a while. No, the boy had not pressed all the buttons on the panel. He had watched him very closely because he had been nervous right from the start. What the boy did was inexcusable—inexcusable to take over the running of the car when others were in it—but Robin Fay had exhibited a consistent, brazen lack of respect from the time he was born . . . allowed to run uncurbed. No, he had pressed seven and eleven. Not at once. First seven, then eleven. Yes, after the door had closed, not before. No, he hadn't touched the panel again until they had all become worried because the elevator wasn't moving as it should. Only inching up. Then he had pressed some button and that was what did it. Whatever button the boy pressed then, did it. Yes, it was a separate red button at the top, obviously the wrong button which any trained operator would know better than to touch. No, he had nothing else to tell. That was all that had happened.

And almost immediately after the inspector left, a young detective arrived. "You can't see anyone else, Hunt, you're ill," Irene objected, but Hunt held up his hand to silence her.

"These men are here to help. An accident like this is unheard of, unheard of. They should be given every opportunity to get to the bottom of it. We can't have this happen again, you know."

He told the same story to the detective in the same whispered tone.

"That was the emergency-stop button the boy pressed," the detective observed.

"Whatever, whatever, officer, we were all right until then, whatever."

"Thanks," the detective said tersely. He jammed his hat on his head and left quickly, slamming the door before Irene could cross the foyer to see him out.

She came back into the living room to reproach him for what he had said to the detective. Always the boy was right and he was wrong, always she would take the part of fools. So he pretended not to know she was there. He pretended to rest, forcing his eyelids to meet, although they quivered. He pressed himself into the chair, every muscle taut, and pretended to sleep, hoping she would not disturb him in that case.

But he didn't fool her; she knew he wasn't asleep and her voice came across the room, thin, wailing, like a flabby missile. "Oh, Hunt, how could you say what you did about Robin? He's only a baby: he meant no harm!"

Sickness clutched at his belly and he doubled over in the chair. As from a great distance he could hear Irene's voice, now alarmed and penitent, and feel her hands upon him again. He shook them away and uttered angry noises, shocked sounds, but they were only something he did to make her leave him alone so she wouldn't discover that with his head pressed against the arm of the chair and with his eyes closed, he saw crimson stripes on the boy's white cheek and the sudden slump as consciousness left him. He heard sounds, too, the sharp crack of his palm against firm skin, the rustle of a clothed body crumpling. . . . Suddenly his stomach revolted and he leaned over the arm of the chair and heaved.

He lay back, wet with a cold sweat, and whispered humiliated apologies while Irene and Hilda cleaned up the mess at the foot of the chair. "Now I insist you get to bed at once," Irene worried. "I'm going to call the doctor. I should have done it long ago instead of listening to you, but I didn't know how sick you were."

He let her help him into his bed and let her fuss around him. He suffered her ministrations if only because they helped to dim the vision of those black, staring eyes that had irretrievably attached themselves to his own burning face, and innocently Irene deducted that any sounds he made were grunts of pain and reported this to the doctor when he arrived.

But all the doctor found were bruises, minor abrasions and a mild shoulder sprain. He allowed that Hunt might be in shock and some considerable pain, so he was able to take advantage of this to give vent to his anguish all through the night. He moaned and occasionally cried out while Irene comforted him, but still the boy tormented him and repeatedly, until dawn, he saw the stare, the silly smile, heard the crack of his hand, and watched the boy drop.

5 :   *Friday, June Fifth*

Although order was being restored gradually throughout the building, Joe had to wait a considerable time for the back elevator. One of the complicating factors was that the accident had occurred at the hour when most of the tenants returned from downtown, so that, in spite of those who chose to take the stairs, a crowd gathered in the lobby, and once the back elevator was freed for general use, it required many trips to get them all upstairs. In addition to the tenants, the regular back elevator traffic continued, and to make it more difficult, it was a weekend night and several dinner parties were in progress in the building.

But Joe made it to the penthouse in due time. He found Mrs. Marsh in the living room, engrossed in reading a book called *The Idiot*.

Nowadays, all Flossie did was read. Tucked away in the corner of the living room with her feet on a stool and Sheza sleeping on her lap, she read by lamplight and still kept the curtains drawn even though the terrace had been neatly repaved with gay, coppery tiles. Her sun tan had faded, for she could not be prevailed upon to step outside no matter how pleasant the weather. Clean and barren the terrace was now, without so much as a bridge chair, for she refused to compromise in any way. "Potted plants and trees!" she scoffed at Walt's timid suggestion. "Are you kidding? You might as well ask me to buy wax fruit for the bowl and artificial flowers. Oh, yes, and one of those horrible mechanical singing canaries." No, she would have none of it, and she would go on tearing up Dorkas's blueprints until he came up with a totally acceptable garden. Meanwhile, she'd sit indoors and read and it was all Walt could do to keep her supplied, for Flossie was not fond of light literature and only once in a while, when the criticisms were unanimously favorable, would she consent to scan a new novel. Right now she was rereading all of Dostoyevsky much against Walt's wishes, for he had suggested that the subject matter was too gloomy for her present state of mind. He tried to steer her towards Dickens. "You and your damned psychology," she mocked, and stubbornly went through *Crime and Punishment* and *Ten Years in a Dead House*.

Flossie looked up at Joe over her glasses, marked her page and closed the book. "What's up? That hot out?" She indicated his damp clothes and perspiring face.

Joe shifted from foot to foot, grinned and clasped his hands behind his back.

"Nothing wrong, is there?" She frowned at him. "It's late and Mr. Marsh——"

"He's okay. Matter of fact, he sent me up with a message. You see . . ." Cautiously, Joe began. She listened quietly to the edited version he gave her and took Mrs. Lesser's death in stride.

"That's the way she wanted to go, poor soul, quickly, without doctors and medicines and hospital beds," she said. "Who else was in the car? Spill it, Joe. Mr. Marsh doesn't give up his cocktail hour for nothing."

So Joe ventured further and mentioned a little something about Robin's participation, but he might have known that one couldn't hedge or tell half a story to Mrs. Marsh when it concerned someone she loved. She removed her glasses, looked suddenly shrewd and suspicious and darted question after question at him, so in the end he had to give in and tell her everything he knew: what the ambulance doctor said word for word, what hospital they'd taken Robin to, what Terence said, what the elevator inspector said and what the tenants were saying.

She sat quite still in her chair and seemed to digest it all without a sign of emotion. "You know, Joe, I heard that noise all the way up here," she said dreamily, "and it didn't mean a thing to me. I sat here reading and heard the noise and knew, subconsciously, that something serious might have happened to someone, but it was only a gleam of a thought and then I went back to Prince Myshkin here"—she tapped the book—"without giving another good goddam. And all the while, it was Robin." She looked wonderingly at Joe. "All the while it was Robin!"

"But you couldn't be expected——"

"Couldn't I? It was Robin!" she cried. "And I went on reading. Reading!" She slapped the arms of the chair and suddenly pulled herself up, unaided. "All right, Joe," she puffed. "Thanks for taking all this time with me."

He couldn't help staring, for he'd never seen her get up without help.

"Okay, Joe, I'm fine."

"Yeah!" he said, breaking into a golden grin. "You need me, Mis' Marsh, I'll be in the basement like always."

"Thanks." She hobbled into the bedroom. She tore off the soiled cotton wrapper she had worn ever since the loss of her garden and, muttering to herself, pulled out her best flowered print dress and shook herself into it. Painfully, she stuffed her swollen feet into flat black pumps. She combed her hair and streaked a line of lipstick across her mouth.

Dumbly her maid watched her waddle into the foyer. She found her voice only as Flossie reached the front door. "Mrs. Marsh!" she screamed. "What's got into you? Where you goin'?"

"To the hospital. You think I'm going to sit here in the living room like an invalid and get *reports*?" She stalked out and slammed the door behind her.

She waited for the back elevator, hearing it groan and creak up and down, overburdened, ignoring her call. She fumed out there in the tiny, hot hall and rang repeatedly. Finally, in a rage, she pounded on the door and that brought old Terence up to the penthouse, all right! He gaped at this mountain of a woman, resplendent in red and black silk, who shoved angrily into the elevator, causing it to sink four inches under her weight.

"Main floor!" she barked.

Terence nodded and closed the door with difficulty. The back elevator was manually operated and the door was heavy. It was hard work at best for an old man, and coming on top of everything else, was almost too much for him this evening. If there hadn't been so much excitement downstairs, with everything at sixes and sevens, he would have gone home. But even fatigue couldn't nullify Terence's curiosity. He had to know everything that went on. He glanced at Flossie from the corner of his eye. Aware of her attachment to Robin, he wondered how she felt about him *now*. "You goin' to the hospital, Mrs. Marsh?"

"I am."

"Then you know all about Robin?" He was feeling her out to ascertain the direction of her anger.

"Just what do you mean?"

"I mean about the accident. That he took the elevator without my permission, do you know that?"

"So?"

"So now look what happened."

"I see. It was his fault."

"Well, I'm not saying——"

"No, you're not saying, Terence; you never say, do you? You only accuse. Damned old fool, too stupid to realize that Robin probably saved your life. What if he hadn't taken that elevator from you? Where do you think you'd be now? Down at the morgue on a slab next to Mrs. Lesser, that's where you'd be. You ought to kneel right down here in this car and thank the good Lord that Robin did what he did. Ever think of that?" Flossie waved her fists dangerously close to his face.

Terence recoiled, for he thought she was going to strike him. His faded blue eyes blinked fearfully and he fumbled at the door latch, sudden tears blurring his vision. He was tired and what she said had frightened him.

"Well, did you think of that?"

His lips moved. It was a new and terrifying thought.

"All right, all right, open the door," she said testily, noticing his tears.

He managed to open it and she struggled out. The elevator rose four inches, relieved. Her heavy footsteps shook the walls as she hobbled through the lobby, majestic in her rage, and demanded that Phil get her a cab at once, a checker cab, not one of those miserable little stock cars that nobody could get in or out of.

6 :   *Friday, June Fifth*

The long corridor, because it was lit by night lights near the floor, had a weird, upside-down look, and the nurses walked silently on rubber-soled shoes, their faces in the shadows, their white legs gleaming. From the nurses' station near the elevators, their low voices could be heard clearly in the waiting room at the other end of the hall. In there it was dim. Only two small lamps stood in diagonally opposite corners leaving the opposing corners dark, and the lack of light in itself induced the visitors to speak in whispers. Every sound from the corridor was important and had to be investigated by Ty, too restless to stay long in one place or position. But there were plenty of chairs for him to range among, for all visitors had long since left the hospital with the exception of the six of them—the Marshes, the d'Auriacs, Julie and himself—waiting for Robin to regain consciousness. Everything that could be done, was being done for him by strangers. All that Ty could do was to wait, to sit and whisper in the waiting room and pretend that everything was going fine, to talk of thousands of inconsequential things and not hear what the others were saying or know what he was answering. And then, after a length of time that seemed endless, to stand up and excuse himself idly and tiptoe down the hall to sneak again into Robin's room; to stand by the bed and nod meekly as the nurse put her finger to her mouth demanding silence from force of habit only, since Robin would not hear it if Ty were to shout; to hold his son's warm, limp hand and note with a pang that this was the first time in years that it was absolutely clean; to look with sickened eyes upon his immobile face and hear strange breathing that differentiated his state from that of sleep. Then back to the waiting room once more, having helped no one in any way at all, to be greeted by a silence of disappointment, since they clearly prayed each time for him to return with a smile and good news. But the heavy silence that ensued would be broken consistently by resourceful John d'Auriac who could be counted upon to summon forth still another joke from his endless repertoire.

These were warm and exceptional friends and their presence helped immeasurably. Ty scrutinized their shadowed faces, smiles superimposed

[224]

over strain, and wondered how each of them had known to come here and to stay. There had to be a sixth sense to deep friendship, and it was only in time of trouble that one had the opportunity to perceive the rarity of what was being offered.

He heard new footsteps approaching, heavier than those of the nurses, and he rose again, thinking it might be the doctor returning. But it was a stout figure that hurried towards the waiting room, a round-shouldered man, who held a coat over his arm. Lawrence Rider. He grasped Ty's hand. "How is he?"

"Still unconscious."

Rider's face looked haggard in the dim light. He dropped his coat over a chair and smiled briefly at the others. "Believe it or not, it was chilly when I left the house this morning."

"It was?" Julie felt she had to say something, but even two short words were an effort. She sat on the couch, devitalized, as if her life had been suspended, and let the others do the talking.

Rider nodded and murmured something. Flossie, glaring unforgivingly at him from across the room, made him uncomfortable. He wet his lips, preparatory to speaking. His voice issued too loud and he dropped it abruptly to a whisper. "Just how—bad is it, Ty?"

Ty ranged nervously from the corner table where he extinguished his cigarette butt to the doorway where Rider stood. "His skull isn't fractured and that's encouraging. The doctors feel he'll come around soon." With a sudden movement, he folded his big frame into a chair at Rider's side.

"Of course he will. Of course he will." Rider tapped the arm of Ty's chair. "Knock wood." He looked around, trying to think of what else he could say. "I might have known I'd find all of you here." He gave a self-conscious laugh. "Now we just have to get that young fellow up and about and everything'll be squared away."

"Yes, please God," Julie whispered.

"He'll be out of here in no time flat," Rider assured her.

She closed her eyes a moment and then gave him a weak smile.

Rider had been up since six thirty that morning and had come back from Westchester to face the shock of the accident. He was exhausted. It was close in the waiting room and the dim light made his eyes want to close. He could barely stay awake, but he had never learned how to terminate a visit gracefully. It was always a chore for him. He tried hard to suppress a yawn, but the more he tried, the stronger grew the desire, so he bent down to tie a perfectly tied shoelace and gratified his urge in secret. His eyes watered and he wiped them with his handkerchief. Then he made an elaborate search for his coat, although it was right there before him, and, for some reason, this seemed to afford him the proper excuse to look at his watch. "Oh-oh, I've got to get home! Just dropped by to see how Robin was. I haven't seen my wife since last night. She must be going out of her mind with worry by now. It's always so hard to stay at home and wait for news." He buttoned his jacket over his fat stomach.

"Nice of you to come around, Rider," Ty said. "We appreciate it."

"Oh, it's nothing." Rider waved his hand awkwardly.

"I'll walk you to the elevator," John said.

"Don't bother, thanks. I can find my way."

"I'll walk you all the same."

Their feet made echoing sounds in the silent hallway. John didn't speak until they reached the nurses' station and then he whispered, remembering how sounds carried. "Do you know what they're all saying about Robin, those kin', gentle tenants of yours?"

"No, what?"

"That the accident was his fault."

"That's ridiculous."

"But it's what they're saying."

"Don't tell me this worries you?"

"Of course it worries me. How do you think Robin is going to feel when he gets home and hears what they 'ave to say about him?"

"Forget it. Robin's one boy who can take care of himself."

"Even when he hears he's killed Mrs. Lesser?"

Rider looked skeptical. "Aren't you dramatizing this a little, Mr. d'Auriac? I doubt even *my* nutty tenants would go that far. And if they did, who cares what irresponsible people say? As long as the important people know the truth, what's the difference? Don't make a mountain out of a molehill. Tenants always gossip and they always complain, but who listens to a bunch of muckrakers?"

"Gawn down," a sleepy elevator man mumbled.

Rider stepped in. "Don't worry about the little things," he advised John.

The door closed. John thrust his hands into his pockets thoughtfully and returned to the waiting room.

At eleven thirty the doctor stopped by to check on Robin and ordered the Marshes and the d'Auriacs home. A cot was set in Robin's room for Julie, and Ty spread out on a chair and ottoman. But neither of them slept. They lay in the darkness, listening to Robin's breathing, jumping up hopefully at every low sound he made, only to be crushed by the nurse's regretful headshake. Now and then Ty would sneak out for a cigarette, thinking that Julie was asleep at last, but always she came running after him, needing his physical closeness to sustain her. So the night dragged on, incredibly long, and Robin remained unconscious.

7 :   *Saturday, June Sixth*

In the hot back hallway, waiting for the elevator, Rider mopped his face. Mechanically he pulled out a pencil, erased a four-letter word written on the wall by some damn delivery boy and returned the pencil to his pocket. He could feel perspiration running down his ribs from his armpits. Today was another scorcher and so early in the morning, too. This was the hottest, rottenest spring he could remember.

Terence slid open the elevator door.

"Good morning, Terence. Eleven, please. Feel okay after yesterday?"

"Sure, I'm fine."

"Lucky thing you weren't in that car."

Terence swallowed. "Guess so."

"Damn lucky. I've just been around to see Robin again." Terence's back was to him, a skinny, bent old back which seemed to shrivel at the mention of the boy's name. "He's still unconscious. I can't tell you how worried I am."

Terence stopped the car at the eleventh floor with a jerk and opened the door.

"I've been looking over the reports and speaking to Mr. Gruppmann. Why did you say what you did about Robin to everybody yesterday?"

Terence averted his face. "I was all excited. . . . I liked Mrs. Lesser; she was a fine lady."

"So did Robin like her. He wouldn't hurt her."

"Well . . . thought he did something to the car."

"You know better than that."

"I didn't think, Mr. Rider. I felt too bad. I just didn't think."

"That was no reason to take it out on him. He's a tenant in this building."

Terence said nothing.

"He's to be treated with courtesy, the same as any other tenant."

[227]

Terence nodded, tight-lipped.

"What have you against him anyway?"

"He's a spoiled brat," Terence muttered. "I'm sorry he's so sick, but he's still a spoiled brat. And I'm not the only one who thinks so."

"Well, you can think what you please about him, but keep your mouth shut from now on."

"Yes, sir," Terence mumbled.

Rider found Hunt Parrish in his room, sitting in a leather chair by the window, reading the morning papers. He looked ill. His heavy lids were red from lack of sleep and his normally pink skin was a sallow color.

"How's the shoulder?"

"Rotten. Painful. I didn't sleep a wink last night. Sit down." Hunt folded the paper and put it aside with his good arm.

"I can't stay too long." Rider sat down. "You had the doctor, I hope."

"Yes. He said it was a bad sprain."

"Aren't you going to have an X ray?"

"He didn't think it necessary."

"Of course, you know we're covered for this. I don't know yet where the responsibility lies, but you'll be compensated."

Hunt raised his eyebrows. "You don't know where the responsibility lies? Then I can tell you. It lies with Robin Fay. That boy's very presence in this building constitutes a danger to your tenants."

"Robin?"

"Yes, Robin. Isn't yesterday's affair enough for you, Mr. Rider?"

"But Robin's a victim of that accident, too. He's a very sick boy. He hasn't regained consciousness yet, Mr. Parrish."

Hunt grew pale. Little tendrils of pain shot over his right palm and left it stinging, as if he'd just delivered the blow. Weakly he said, "He took over the controls——"

"Yes, but he's an experienced elevator boy. This had nothing to do with him. The mechanism of the elevator was faulty and it would have fallen no matter who ran it at the time. I'm surprised you weren't told this."

Parrish heard Rider unwillingly, incredulously even, and still he persisted, driven by some illogical force. "But I saw him press a button that shouldn't be pressed."

"I read your statement. That was the emergency-stop button. There's always the possibility that Robin did you a good turn by stopping the elevator before it went higher. No saying what would have happened to all of you if you had fallen from, say the seventh floor. No, Robin did the sensible thing. That's what the button is there for."

Hunt didn't want to hear this. He wanted no part of what he was being forced to hear, even though he was aware that his incredulity was only surface. Deep within him, there was no surprise, no disbelief, as if he had known this all the time and deliberately kept it suppressed.

"What have you against that boy?"

"Pardon?"

Rider repeated his question.

"Against? You make it sound personal and it isn't. Robin happens to be an objectionable child and it's difficult for me to believe, when such an accident occurs, that he wasn't the cause of it, he's that destructive."

"He really is?"

"Have you talked to anyone else about him? Mrs. Harewood, for example?"

"No. It's strange, so many people seem to dislike him all of a sudden. A few months ago, he was everybody's darling."

"No he wasn't!" Hunt gave a dry laugh.

"I always liked him. I thought he was a bright, fine boy."

"That's because you didn't know him well enough. Perhaps he was on his good behavior with his landlord."

"Must be so. One complaint or two, all right, but when they come from every side . . . Nevertheless, we have to be fair with him. Like him or not, he had nothing to do with the accident."

"If you say so, then it must be true. I stand corrected."

Mr. Rider chuckled suddenly. "We seem to have spent the whole time discussing Robin when, actually, I came because I was concerned about you."

"Thank you. Very considerate. As you can see, it's not serious. I'll live."

"Good. Well." Rider wanted to leave, so he looked at his watch as if it suddenly occurred to him that it was late. "Oh-oh, I've got to be going!" He stood up, took two steps towards the door, then paused. "Damn it, I still can't get it through my thick skull—that boy looks like an angel!"

Hunt leaned his head against the back of his chair and closed his eyes, but he only saw Robin clearer that way. And the boy's face accused him. But he hadn't done anything except deliver an opinion. Certainly there was nothing wrong in that. He was entitled to feel any way he wanted to about Robin, and entitled to express it, as well.

"I'm sorry. You're in pain. I'll go."

Hunt tried to smile. He put his hand to his shoulder and winced, wishing it hurt him more.

8 :   *Saturday, June Sixth*

It was approaching noon and out in the streets the heat was intense. Cement sidewalks underfoot and brick and stone buildings on either side formed an oven that absorbed and radiated the sun's rays, only faintly dimmed by a shimmer of humidity in the sky. The tar was melting, bespeckled with sharp indentations from the ladies' heels, and tire marks were beginning to show. There was no movement in the heavy air. But the uncomfortable weather did not keep the tenants of Number Ten from gathering in frenzied groups this morning. Up and down Madison Avenue, in and out of the stores, in front of the building itself, they dotted the streets while Maud's small figure moved from circle to circle, weaving her triumphant web. With her eyes shining and her blue silk dress glued in wet wrinkles to her back, she recalled for the tenants' attention all of Robin's behavior of the past, to add to the general indignation. Like a boy scout, she blew on the smoking sticks to make the campfire burn bright, and its sparks ignited eager eyes, most luminous of all those of Mrs. Leopold, who attached herself as Maud's lieutenant, an unexpected advance.

Mr. Rider's tenants were eager for any little piece of information. No detail was too small, no exaggeration too gross. And since it was impossible to learn anything from the house staff, they had to rely upon each other and upon Maud Harewood, whose creativity today seemed to know no bounds. Terence had suddenly become tight-lipped and silent as a mummy, Klaus was too busy to be found anywhere, Joe had never been a good source of information, Phil had taken to wheezing and coughing when approached for a tidbit or two, Carney rarely opened his mouth at best, and Mr. Rider's haggard and forbidding face was only seen briefly as he rushed about the building.

But they were richly informed nevertheless. They were reminded of Robin's atrocious behavior of the past; of the chandelier that nearly killed Maud and Albert, of hammering on bare floors, stamping, bouncing balls, blaring music after midnight, drunken brawls. And, whispered

Mrs. Leopold viciously, she wouldn't be a bit surprised if there wasn't something even worse, orgies conducted by all of them, "the unholy six," consisting of the Marshes ("That woman is absolutely *depraved,* have you ever *seen* the size of her?"), the d'Auriacs ("What can you expect from the French, after all?"), and the Fays ("Television people, do I have to say more?"). "Yes," she muttered through thin, moist lips around which her melting lipstick spread, "it isn't normal the way they stick together, the so-called aristocracy of Number Ten." She snorted. "They'll be raided yet, you wait and see." Still rankling over Mr. Rider's lack of consideration for her over the past three years, and his obvious partiality towards the Marshes, and further incensed by the fact that, although it was not in any way her fault, the "old guard" and some of the building staff, too, seemed to blame her for the loss of Flossie's garden, Mrs. Leopold today let loose all her stored-up rancor and allowed it to fall wherever it might. It must be said to their credit that most of the tenants found her opinions rather difficult to swallow; therefore they straddled the fence, open-minded and perfectly willing to be convinced otherwise if given positive proof, but the conglomerate story of the accident and its consequences was questioned by no one.

There could be no doubt that Mrs. Lesser had lost her life, that Mr. Parrish had broken his shoulder, or that Robin, who had been running the elevator without permission, had pressed the wrong button deliberately, in macabre celebration of his last day of school. It was also an established fact that Tyler Fay was being sued for all he was worth by Miss Forsythe, Mr. Parrish and Mr. Rider, and that there was going to be a rip-roaring court battle in the near future, bringing notoriety and ill repute to the building as a whole.

Had the accident occurred without previous incident, the results might have been different, but only a fool would withhold judgment after such a history as this. More intense than the heat ran their indignation. Mrs. Leopold suggested, and it was generally agreed, that this dangerous boy and his family should be removed from Number Ten, and the result of this was that, under Mrs. Leopold's direction, a petition was drawn up on the counter of Levy's stationery store and passed around the street for signatures. It requested Mr. Rider to dispossess the Fays for the safety of all. The entire block from Madison to Fifth Avenue buzzed and shook with misinformation generously supplied first by Maud, then by Mrs. Leopold, chewed and regurgitated in intensified form by the worthy tenants of the building.

And now, since it was almost lunchtime, they gathered closer to the building itself, chattering on their way home with bundles of groceries in their arms. A good portion of the men in Number Ten worked on Saturday mornings, taking advantage of the quiet of their empty offices to catch up on back work, for the Boss knows nothing of a forty-hour week. Some of these gentlemen now straggled over from Madison Avenue, mopping their wet foreheads, so that the circles of women were augmented by an increasing number of dark-suited, masculine figures, who placed their signatures readily upon the petition in firm, bold hands and added to the soprano chorus some much-needed touches of tenor and bass.

Amid this confusion, two skinny, fragile figures in black crept slowly towards Number Ten from Madison Avenue, one moving painfully with bowed head, supported by the other. It was Miss Forsythe returning for lunch from the funeral parlor in the company of Mrs. Kerakis. The chorus hushed to an occasional whisper as they drew back to let her pass, not knowing whether to speak to her or not, for any bereaved person, even timid little Miss Forsythe, could seem formidable in grief. They noted with pity that she moved with difficulty and seemed to limp, favoring her left leg. She, too, must have been injured in the accident, but her sad loss apparently overshadowed physical pain.

Only Maud Harewood was not afraid to approach her. Grief never intimidated her; to the contrary, all forms of misfortune instilled her with love. These were emotions she could understand, having experienced them so poignantly herself. She touched the bony shoulder and her voice choked a little over the onrush of her tenderness. "I can't tell you how grieved and shocked I am at the circumstances of your sister's death, Miss Forsythe. A terrible, terrible thing."

Miss Forsythe raised tear-reddened eyes to Maud and murmured her thanks.

"When I think of what an experience that must have been for you, I get all—my heart goes out to you."

Miss Forsythe was gratified by Maud's evident sympathy. "Thank you so much. . . ."

"That vicious boy," Maud said.

Miss Forsythe looked blank.

"She means Robin," Mrs. Kerakis whispered; "she's back on him again."

"Robin?"

"Don't tell me you didn't know the accident was his fault, Miss Forsythe?"

"Don't believe her," Mrs. Kerakis whispered uncertainly.

"Robin's fault?"

"He pushed the wrong button."

"You're sure?"

"Everybody knows it but you, it seems."

"Oh, no!" Miss Forsythe fumbled for her handkerchief. "Oh no, don't tell me that!"

"I thought you knew."

"We didn't know," Mrs. Kerakis said, still distrustful.

"Oh, that poor boy, it isn't bad enough he's so seriously hurt! Oh, poor Robin, he'll never forgive himself. I know him; he'll never forgive himself! Oh, I wish you hadn't told me!" Fresh tears gathered in Miss Forsythe's weary eyes and she bent over, pressing her handkerchief to her face.

"I'm sorry—I thought——"

"Poor child, he loved Bella—poor child." Miss Forsythe wept.

Maud's head whirled. She felt dizzy and she shivered. She stood there rubbing her bare arms, noting with a tightening of her throat the supplicating manner in which Mrs. Kerakis, whispering words of comfort, supported her new friend to the back elevator. Gone was the triumph of Maud's morning and her elation. The unexpectedness of Miss Forsythe's reaction and the pathetic coupling of the two old women had touched off a terrible loneliness within her. She felt she was standing on a great, vacant plain of stubble, stretching empty for miles, with a grey sky overhead and no one, no one else wherever she turned.

"What was she so upset about? What did she say?" Mrs. Leopold prodded.

Maud looked at her with great, gelid eyes. Who was this old biddy with the familiar air? And what was she, Maud Harewood, doing out here with these gossiping housewives, these old *bavardes*? She belonged better to that plain of burnt grass, belonged more to the silence of its miles of uninhabited land upon which she alone wandered, calling for someone to answer.

"What did she say, Maud?"

Maud's head was throbbing; tight, tight it felt. "None of your damn business!" she muttered and ran into the building. She left the street and the gossiping tenants that crowded it and went back to her apartment, back to her room where she lay—drinking bourbon, trembling with chills in the intense heat—and listened to the terrible silence that poured down from the apartment above, while Albert toiled innocently in the other room, busy with his monthly accounts, unaware that she was back on her chaise longue.

It was a dull, grey day, intolerably dreary in the city where cement, stone and asphalt abound. On such a day even the air seems colored grey and there is no relief from drabness anywhere, not even in the sky where the blue is veiled by threatening clouds. The absence of the sun brings no relief for humidity saturates the skin and one breathes in water-sogged air.

On a day such as this, only the most devout show up at church and only fiends play golf. Air conditioners fill the street with an eternal buzz, for everyone is living indoors. It is hardly the kind of day on which to take a walk.

All this is what Maud informed Albert when he came into her room, wearing the smile of strained cheer he had acquired of late and rubbing his palms together to demonstrate to her the pleasantness of his suggestion as one rubs one's belly after a mouthful of medicine to prove how delicious it tastes, and although she protested, he would not budge from his intention. He had convinced himself that she had to get out, even on a day like this and even if only for a few minutes. He was certain the walk would do her good. The proof was, look at her since she had left her apartment and mixed with her neighbors! She was a different person. No, to allow her to sit around in a nightgown, even for a day, was perilous and he couldn't take such a chance. The out of doors was medicine for her.

She knew he was distressed because he had discovered her on her chaise longue yesterday afternoon and, although she couldn't care less about Albert's opinions, still he remained a danger to her. At any moment, he was liable to carry out his threat of a few weeks ago and call the doctor. So she had no choice but to obey him. She dressed herself in silent fury and paraded with him up and down the block, from Fifth to Madison, refusing to enter the park. He attempted conversation, but that wasn't part of their bargain and she strangled each effort with a derisive remark until he, too, subsided into silence.

"Had enough?" she asked, after a while.

"Yes, I've had it." He quickened his pace as they turned around at the corner of Fifth Avenue.

A taxi passed and stopped in front of Number Ten. Maud saw a foot emerge as the door opened. "Biggest foot I ever saw," she thought to herself and repressed a giggle so Albert wouldn't think her mood had taken a turn for the better. The owner of the foot was attempting to squeeze his large frame out of the tiny door backwards. He was folded in half; his rump followed the foot, then two elbows as he grasped the doorframe. He eased his shoulders through and his head cracked against the top of the cab.

"Ouch!" Maud said aloud and couldn't resist a short laugh. The man, holding his hand on the tender spot at the back of his head, turned slowly. His light hair fell over his forehead in untidy spikes. His eyes, puffed and haggard, seemed sightless although they were pointed in her direction. He was unshaved and his shirt was open at the neck. One end of his tie dripped from the right pocket of his wrinkled cotton jacket. Slowly he turned back to the cab and held out his hands. "Watch it," he said dully. To protect her, he placed one hand on her head and half lifted her out of the cab by the waist. While he paid the driver, she stood exactly where he deposited her, without bothering to straighten her twisted skirt. Her arms dangled forlornly at her sides and her head drooped. Hair escaped in many small wisps from the rubber band that held together a disjointed pony tail.

Maud clutched her bag to her chest and stared at them. Her legs felt unreliable, foreign to her. "The boy must be dead; he's dead," she whimpered soundlessly, for there was no laughter in them now, only hopelessness. Tears of sympathy sprang to her eyes and she felt the warmth of love spread in her breast. She could love them now, oh, how she could love them now, love pallid cheeks and dark-circled eyes, love the man unshaven and in wrinkled clothes, love the woman no longer rosy and fresh. These were her kind of people now, tortured, nearly supine. She could love them as strongly in their grief as she had hated them in happiness.

Ty put his arm about Julie's shoulders. "Come," he murmured. Close together, they moved into the building.

"What——? Do you suppose——?" Albert sounded frightened.

"I feel sick." She leaned against him and closed her eyes.

"Let me take you in."

"No!"

"You won't meet them. They must have gone up already. Come."

"In a minute. . . ."

He stared at her. "Why, Maud, I really believe you care!"

She put her hand to her throat. She was breathless, she was choking, for a moment she couldn't speak. "Oh—what do you think I am?

[235]

What do you think I am?" she screamed, and flung herself ahead, legs moving awkwardly, arms flying, shoulders dipping in a clumsy flight into the building, with Albert fast behind her, terrified at her reaction. She shook violently in the elevator and as Albert opened the door, she ran past him into her room. Sick with horror, she flung herself onto her chaise longue. "Leave me alone!" she shrieked at him. He ducked quickly out of the room. He ran for the telephone, picked up the receiver, but couldn't summon the courage to dial. Twice he tried, then slammed the receiver down and sank into a chair, impotently fingering the telephone cord.

In the sanctuary of her chaise, Maud pressed her hands to her head and turned from side to side. She sobbed; wracked, painful sobs that came from her bowels and tore upwards. She sobbed and gasped and pulled at her clothing. She didn't know what to do with herself because of what Albert had said, without malice or bitterness, simply a statement uttered in incredulity. He couldn't believe it of her. He thought her a woman so vacant of love, so lacking in warmth that she couldn't care if a child died, or if part of two young parents died along with him. But this was not so. Oh, she did care, she cared immeasurably; that was the source of everything that made her what she was today, because she cared too much! Didn't he know that? She was moved to tears at the sight of their limp misery and the thought that Robin might be dead had torn through her like a flame. She had felt actual pain. She did care. How could he have made such a statement? What was there in her that made Albert doubt she could care about the life or death of a child?

Oh, she must think! If only she could think again, as she used to! Thinking and Reason were still in her; she knew it because she could feel them there in her head, she could almost grasp at them by pressing herself together, by tightening her body into a ball there on the chaise, by rolling up and doubling together and then concentrating with all her powers to get down there to that Reason which was covered over by a mesh of confusion. Oh, claw at it; tear it away! But each time she tried like this, tightening her legs against her chest, her arms around them, her head meeting her knees, eyes shut tight (There, I've almost got it . . . almost got it . . . yes, careful now; hold tight . . .), it would slip away again, back beneath the layers of haze and fuzz, leaving her gasping, sobbing in frustration. "Albert! Albert!"

He upset the telephone as he jumped to his feet. He left it where it fell and ran in.

"Do I care, Albert? Oh, do I care? Tell me," she wept.

He could hear the frightened beating of his own heart as he held her close. "Shh, shh, darling . . ."

"No, I mean it, do I care? Do I care about life and death? Don't I cry if a child dies? Don't I cry?"

"Of course you cry. God, Maud, I'm sorry. I didn't mean to hurt you like this."

"I know you weren't being unkind. You meant what you said. What has happened to me? Who am I? This isn't me any more if you could say what you did. And yet, of all people you know best what I'm really like."

"I know, I know. I'm sorry. It was thoughtless. I'm sorry," he soothed, rocking her, caressing her.

As always with these hysterical attacks, she calmed eventually in his arms and even seemed to enjoy his attentions, enjoyed it when he wiped her face with a wet cloth and brought her a sedative and a bourbon highball and plumped the cushion behind her head. Suddenly it was all over, as if it had never occurred. She rested quietly on her chaise longue and gulped her drink. It seemed that she had forgotten all about Robin now.

But Albert hadn't. He left her for a moment and went out. He rang for the back elevator, knowing Terence could surely tell him the condition of the boy.

10 :   *Sunday, June Seventh*

Coming down the street from the drugstore on Madison Avenue where she had bought a tube of Baum Bengué for Hunt's shoulder, Irene Parrish saw the Fays' arrival and Maud's abrupt flight into the building. The front elevator was still out of commission, so she had to wait in the stuffy back elevator hall while Terence took the car to the basement and left it there to relieve himself. Years ago, when he first came to work here, he used to be fidgety at such times and, while trying to hurry, would whisper obscenities at the tenants who persistently rang, but then one day it occurred to him with indignation that they damn well ought to know and have respect for what he was doing down there; that he was a human being just like them, and ever since he had taken his time and ignored the impatient sounds from the car.

Irene was not one to keep her finger on the bell, although today she was tempted. She did, however, ring once again timidly, to denote a certain amount of haste and was sorry she had, for she heard the door close immediately afterward; her second summons had been unnecessary. She apologized to Terence for her impatience and explained that it was prompted by the anxiety she felt after seeing the arrival of the Fays.

"Felt it myself," Terence said. "Such a shock. I thought for a moment I was gonna pass out."

"Well?"

Terence frowned. He hadn't heard her monosyllabic question and hated to admit it.

"How is Robin?"

He shook his head and made a worried sound with his teeth. "Still unconscious, Mrs. Parrish. Imagine, since Friday evening."

"Oh, dear. That's bad enough, but I *am* relieved. I thought for a moment—to see Mr. Fay *unshaven*—I can't explain what it did to me."

"They haven't been home or slept a wink since the accident, poor things . . . could hardly talk to me. They wouldn't have left him even now, but the doctor forced them to come home and get some rest. He promised, word of honor, to phone them the minute there was any change."

"Oh, I hope they hear from him soon. What a terrible thing to live through!"

Once again Terence missed what she said, but he didn't ask her to repeat herself. He was satisfied to give her a wise frown.

Hunt was sitting with his arm on a pillow. He had tried to read the Sunday *Times* but his eyes traveled over the same sentence and instead of printed words, he saw Robin's black eyes staring back at him from the page, so with an angry cry, he had thrust the paper from him just before Irene came in.

"Did you get it?" he asked her wearily.

"Yes."

"What's the matter?"

"I feel sick. I just saw Robin Fay's parents downstairs in the street."

Hunt's heart plunged. "Yes?"

"They looked as if they were drugged, as if they couldn't see or hear, their clothes were unpressed, their faces grey, he was unshaven——"

Hunt closed his eyes. "Get to the point, Irene."

"I got such a fright, Hunt, I'm still trembling from it. But it wasn't what I thought. He's still unconscious and the Fays were sent home to rest awhile. Imagine, that boy is still unconscious! I'm so worried about him. That's an awfully long time—since Friday . . . today's Sunday——"

"All right, all right, that's enough!"

She looked at him, surprised.

"I'd like to rest."

"I didn't think it would upset you. I'm sorry."

"It doesn't upset me at all. He's a strong boy. He'll be all right. It happens I'm in pain. Just leave me alone, please, Irene?"

"But don't you want me to rub this——?"

"I'll do it, thanks. Now Irene, please . . ."

"All right, then!" Hurt, she tossed the ointment on his desk. "You know, it's a joke, this thing we call a marriage, this companionable life of ours!" She slammed out of his room and went to her own room where she sat at her vanity and fretted over this strangely disturbed man, who sat alone, obviously tortured by something infinitely more serious than the aching shoulder he claimed. Could it have something to do with Robin? It didn't seem possible, and yet . . . No, of course it couldn't be.

Alone again, Hunt dropped his head into his hands. Why, why couldn't he get that boy out of his mind? He was aware that ever since the accident, he had sought a lonely refuge where he could give vent to his suffering without loss of dignity. It had been a phase brought on by shock, something he had to go through, but it had solved nothing, changed nothing. Now it was high time he pulled himself together. He had to answer the questions that tortured him.

First of all, he had to admit that he would have suffered quite a shock just now had Irene told him the boy was dead. And yet, he had no use for Robin, so why would he care?

Only because he had given him that blow, and perhaps the blow had some . . . No, this was trivia, he was off on a tangent, he had to get down to fundamentals, think in a straight line no matter how it hurt.

How could he, a civilized, controlled human being, stoop to strike a child in the face so hard that . . . ?

No, Hunt reasoned, it couldn't have been the blow. Robin must have suffered a delayed reaction to his injury. He had heard about such things. Chances were that the glazed eyes and silly grin had been indications that he was not quite conscious before the blow. So that he should have no feeling of guilt on that account, but only because he had struck the boy at all (although the blow *could* have contributed toward the injury). *No*, now he was being melodramatic again and he would have to struggle back to the point, which was, which was . . . yes . . .

What was it that made him *want* to hit Robin in the face, he who had never been a physical person, who had never lifted a hand against anyone else in his life? A quick answer could be that the boy was a perfect example of that smug, unthinking middle-class society he so scorned, but that wasn't the answer, either, for what he had experienced had been much more intense than scorn. He had lashed out viciously at Robin in a moment of deepest hate. He might even have killed the boy had he held a lethal . . . In all fairness, neither Robin nor his parents had ever done anything to him to incur such hatred.

Then what was it?

He forced himself to think of Robin, of how he looked and how he behaved, that idiotic expression of delight on his face as he careened before Joe in the lobby, sparring with quick, catlike motions . . . God! . . . as though all there was to life was his own strong musculature . . . and after all, what more was there for a boy like him or a man like his father, blessed with size and athletic prowess and such stupid good nature that everybody, everybody swarmed to them, charmed by nothing more than a vacant grin? Sure they were happy, happy as animals are happy, unaware of their mortality.

So he hated Robin because he was a fool. That made sense, but it was hardly a new discovery.

Most infuriating to him was a certain look. There was a way Robin looked at him when he was being scolded, for instance, with his face immobile and scornful, jeering eyes, pretending respect. Yes, that was it, too. He could feel his anger rise, it was that look that never failed to drive him wild, like the look on the face of Willie Lamar. . . .

Willie Lamar! How interesting that he should think of Robin in connection with him when there didn't seem to be the remotest resemblance between the two, coming from such different worlds. But there were similarities, all right. Yes, now that he thought of it, they were similar in build and had the same tow heads; they were the same insensitive, physical types. Like Willie, Robin represented the damn fools who had all the fun and who invariably jeered at him for having none. Oh, what joy Robin and his father must take in mocking Hunt Parrish behind his back! Just like Willie. So, of course, he hated Robin; and, of course, he hated Tyler Fay; and the face he struck at in the elevator might as well have been the face of Willie Lamar because they were one and the same.

Now he had traced it. Oh, that Willie, if he could only get back at that Willie for what he had done, for his unforgivable cruelty!

Hunt leaned over his desk with both fists clenched on its bright mahogany surface.

His father's cottage was frame which had once been painted white but had peeled and stained over the years. Where there were cracks and separations in the outer boards, his father had tacked black tar-paper patches. The roof, which had once been a uniform green, was now a checkerboard of various shapes and colors made up of any loose shingles his father was able to filch from the junk piles on the edge of town. To the east of his cottage stretched a row of similar houses, hardly more substantial than the shacks in nigra town, a block away. The land to the west of Hunt's father's house was a tangle of weeds and dying trees from which dripped the ghostly Spanish Moss, forming an eerie, unhealthy forest and dump-lot for the neighborhood. This land extended for two hundred feet and terminated abruptly at the clean, tall hedges of a red brick house, isolated, standing on a well-kept lawn. This was the town whorehouse.

Hunt and his friends used to pass it slowly, peering through the hedges, hoping to catch sight of hell-raising going on. But Hunt was not sure what it was these women did. He knew it was bad, because his father told him he'd beat the livin' daylights outa him if he ever caught him near that place. His friend, Willie Lamar, who was eleven, once offered him the information that you could do anything you pleased with them for a buck or so, but Hunt had been too ashamed to ask him what he meant.

One particular evening, the boys, along with Sam Johnson, their nigra friend, met as usual around six thirty. They never made appointments, but showed up near the end of the dirt road where the fields began, wandering together as if they didn't expect to meet. A drunken tramp staggered towards them down the road and they stopped tossing their ball to watch him. "Man, he's buzzed!" Willie said, grinning. The drunk veered a few feet from them, lurched to the left and staggered through the little white gate that divided the hedges of the whorehouse. The boys crept up to the gate and crouched there peering through the freshly painted lattice. The tramp stood on the porch, swaying. The door opened and a huge, powerful, redheaded woman cried, "Well, Sandy McNeil, you here again?" She stepped up to him, put her palms against his shoulders and gave a great shove. He sailed backwards across the porch and down the steps to the path where he lay without moving. The redhead laughed and slammed the door.

"He ain't movin'," Hunt whispered.

"Think he's daid?"

"Naw, he's jus' sleepin' it off." Willie, the authority, spoke. Then he snapped his fingers. "I got an idea! We could sneak in an' if they ketch us, we could say we was only helpin' that pore old man."

Willie's eyes were sparkling strangely and Hunt's heart beat faster. "Whut you mean to do in there?"

"They's low windows in the rear. We could take turns heisting each other up."

Goose bumps raised themselves over Hunt's scrawny arms.

Sam whispered, "C'mon."

Hunt went first to the drunk who lay on the path. Close up, he saw that the man was breathing, so he crept after his friends.

Not too far above them was a row of three small windows, all of them wide open to let in the air. They tossed a coin and Hunt won. He was to go first. He climbed up on their shoulders, his heart beating fast, and peered in.

A moment later, he was running down the road to his house, retching, with his hand clapped over his mouth.

Hunt couldn't remember going home or going to bed. He partly remembered a succession of days after that when he seemed only half conscious, vomiting and sleepless. His mother kept him in the house and dosed him with salts, thinking he had caught a fever, but she had to care for his four younger brothers and sisters and his father was a night watchman at the new power plant and had to sleep during the day. So Hunt was mostly alone. He was nauseous all of the time and when his mother questioned him, he blanked out all hearing because he couldn't bear what men were, what women were, what filth covered everyone. After two days, his mother sent him out of the house to play and he heard her voice as from a distance and obeyed. He sat down under a tree in the back yard and felt somewhat better. Far off, in the fields beyond the whorehouse, Willie and Sam were playing ball, but he wouldn't join them, although they whistled and waved. Finally they came to him. Willie sat down on the sparse crab grass near Hunt and so did Sam.

"Hunt Parrish, whut's got into you?" Willie asked. "Why you run off like that the other night?"

Hunt didn't answer. He was feeling sick again. Willie's expression challenged him and he saw that scorn was gathering in his friend's eyes.

"Maybe he's jus' too young," Sam suggested. "He ain't even ten."

Willie stared at Hunt. "No, he's queer." Scorn burned from Willie's eyes. "Puny and scairt and queer."

"No, I ain't!" Hunt screamed and covered his face.

"You boys quit teasin' Hunt; he ain't well." His mother called from the kitchen window. "You quit it now, heah?"

"Mother's baby," Willie said. "Come on, Sam, he's no friend for us."

All of the children teased Hunt cruelly from that time on and Willie's brand, "Downright queer, a regular sissy Momma's boy," stuck to him until he left town. As a substitute for friends, Hunt delved into studies. He discovered that books could be like narcotics. They made trouble seem far away. He discovered, too, that he could get attention and admiration from his teachers, at least . . .

A knock at the door startled him and he sat back in his chair so quickly that he almost fell backwards. "Yes?" he called irritably, "what is it now?"

Hilda opened the door a crack.

"I don't want anything to eat and I don't want to be disturbed!" he cried.

She closed the door soundlessly.

He banged the desk with his fist. Why couldn't they leave him alone? Here his thoughts had been interrupted just as he had been coming to a conclusion, and he would have to reach back into his mind, gather them together again, sort them out . . .

Well, at any rate, that was about all there was to it. So much for Willie Lamar, who had been his closest friend one day and a scornful tormentor the next, who called Hunt names until the day he left home forever to take up a scholarship at Columbia College, because he was young, sensitive, intelligent, out of the reach of Willie's understanding.

And since he had already established the fact that Robin, Tyler Fay and Willie Lamar were alike, it followed logically that as Willie had tormented and irretrievably hurt him, Robin must have done the same to some other bright, sensitive youngster like himself, therefore Robin justly deserved the blow and he should feel no guilt at having delivered it.

Hunt expelled his breath and relaxed. The importance of "thinking time" could not be overemphasized. Every intelligent man should make it his business to put aside an hour or so daily, if possible, to think through each problem dispassionately, and readjust erroneous judgments and values. Thus, complexities unravel as motives are examined and explained. He smiled and stretched, feeling only a slight ache in his shoulder. That was that, and he was hungry. He would reconsider Hilda's offer of lunch.

The bulb in the hallway was out and Ty had difficulty finding the keyhole in the dark. From the Emmerichs' apartment they heard Rover barking.

"She doesn't even know it's us," Julie said sadly, accepting it as another sign of hopelessness.

"Just as well. Too tired to take her wild greeting right now. She's better off where she is." Ty opened the door and switched on the light. The cleaning girl had shuttered all the windows the day before.

"As if she never expected us home again," Julie whispered.

"God, it's hot in here!" he said.

She bent wearily to pick up an envelope that had been slipped under the door. "Mr. and Mrs. Fay" was scrawled over its face and darkly underlined.

"Another request for charity. Got to be a millionaire. Forget it."

Julie sighed. "It's such a dark day." She twisted the envelope in her fingers.

He put his arm around her shoulders. "Come on, honey, into bed with you."

"I couldn't possibly sleep, Ty."

"You promised you'd try."

They went into the bedroom, averting their eyes as they passed Robin's room.

"I don't feel right being away from the hospital," she said. "I know the doctor meant well, but sometimes people should leave other people alone."

"He promised he'd telephone us at once, so what's the difference if we're here or there?"

"You know."

He took off the bedspreads and laid them over a chair. "Come on, Julie, don't make me angry now; get undressed."

She put the envelope on her night table and removed her skirt, blouse and shoes with the languid movements of a sleepwalker. She lay down on the bed in her slip and sighed as her tired body reclined at last.

"Close your eyes," Ty said.

But there was a limit to her obedience. "Enough is enough, Ty. I'm lying down, I'm resting. Now let me alone," she said irritably.

Wisely, he said nothing. He stretched out on his own bed in his underwear and lay motionless.

Still irritated, Julie snatched the envelope from her night table and opened it. She spread the single folded sheet. It was written hastily in ink with one illegible word crossed out and corrected. There was no salutation, only a short message: "After all the misery and tragedy and trouble you people have caused in this building, the decent thing for you to do would be to get out before us tenants take legal action. Amy C. Leopold."

"Oh, no," Julie whimpered.

Ty took the note from her. "Bitch!" he muttered and threw it to the floor. "Damned bitch!"

In her exhaustion, all Julie could feel was a feeble despair. "I told you," she said. "I told you what it was like living here—how they all hate us."

"It isn't important now. Nothing is important now except for you to go to sleep. Please, Julie, try." He reached over and stroked her arm. "We can't afford to worry about how Mrs. Leopold feels. There are so many other things . . ."

She nodded and closed her eyes over the coating of tears his gesture of affection had produced. She tried to summon sleep, tried to loosen muscles she had held taut for days, but she couldn't dispel the frightened thoughts that occupied her mind. "If Robin should die, if he should die . . ." The words rolled about in her head like a record that never stopped playing and she opened her eyes hoping the familiar objects in the room would distract her, but they only brought Robin's presence closer. There, the marks on the side of the dresser, where as a baby he had gnawed with budding teeth, carefully filled in and refinished but distinguishable still. There, the Staffordshire basket of tulips he could never resist touching— "Put it down, Robin; you'll drop it!" The boudoir chair, over which Ty had dropped the bedspreads, where Robin invariably sat when he came into their room to talk things over. (Wasn't it funny how people had favorite chairs?) "If he should die . . . ," Julie thought, wrapping her arms tightly across her breast. But she never finished the sentence.

Ty was already asleep. She listened to his regular breathing with tenderness and envy. Lucky man, he wasn't thinking of anything now. He wasn't even dreaming, for his face was peaceful. He wasn't worrying about Robin, or Mrs. Leopold's hateful letter. He was in a state of blissful nothingness. Thinking of his sleep, her own eyes closed and she dozed lightly, waking every time Ty turned in his bed. Once she dreamed and awakened, sitting up in her bed, terrified from her nightmare. But she couldn't have screamed aloud, for Ty remained undisturbed. She lay back, her lips moving soundlessly, and once again she dozed.

At three forty-five the telephone rang. Ty raised his head and looked about him with muddled eyes.

"The phone, Ty!"

It rang again. Julie made a sound of impatience, slid off the bed and darted towards Ty's night table, but he already had the receiver in his hand. "Yes?" he whispered, cleared his throat and repeated, "Yes? Hello." He held the receiver at right angles to his ear so she could listen in as the doctor reported joyfully that Robin was coming out of his coma and if they hurried over, they could be by his side when he became aware of his surroundings.

"We'll be right there!" Ty shouted. He dropped the receiver and pulled Julie to him. He held her so tight that she gasped. "He's coming out of it, honey; he's going to be all right!"

She let out a sob.

What he had intended as a chuckle of fond, male condescension emerged suspiciously like the sound she had made and his voice was husky as he said, "This is no time for tears, baby, we've got to hurry."

"I've been—so—worried."

"Of course you have, darling. But now you can cheer up. We don't want any sour faces for Robin to see. Snap to it, baby." He turned her around and slapped her behind.

"That hurt," she sobbed, rubbing her buttock on her way to the closet. She pulled out the first dress she touched.

"I only tapped you."

"You—hurt me . . ." she sobbed, pulling the dress over her head.

"Sissy," he said and turned away to blow his nose.

In five minutes they were ready. True, Julie wore no make-up, but she had taken a moment to run a comb through her hair. Ty was still unshaved, but he remembered to grab a handkerchief to lend her in the cab.

Robin was drowsy and his head hurt. He was still too disoriented to wonder how he had come to this strange place, but since his parents were there with him, he seemed satisfied. He slept most of the time, waking intermittently for only a minute or two, each time somewhat clearer in his mind. At ten after seven, as the nurse was trying to convince Julie and Ty to go out for a bite to eat, he woke up again.

[246]

"F'r chrissakes, Dad, why'nt you get y'rself a shave!" he muttered
disgustedly.

12 :   *Monday, June Eighth*

Hunt slept solidly for eleven hours and awoke feeling cheerful. His
shoulder was healed and his bruises, great colorful patches though they
were, no longer bothered him. He decided to go to the office. Irene parted
her lips to object, then clamped them shut again without uttering a
sound. He observed her carefully across the breakfast table and decided
she was sulking from his rebuff of yesterday. Therefore, on his way out,
he stopped by her chair, gave her a loud kiss on the cheek, assured her
she was the only woman in the world who looked lovely in the morning,
asked her wistfully if she'd mind having sidecars waiting for him at five
thirty, and left the house humming.

The sun was shining and already it was too hot. His regular taxi
driver was ill and had sent a friend, who drove one of the small cars
Hunt loathed. He lost his hat climbing in and, once settled, there was
no place to put his feet. Hot and uncomfortable, the ride downtown
seemed endless and he was not so cheerful when he greeted Mrs. Lawrence. She fidgeted around him with so many questions about the accident that he had to silence her and then, of course, she retired offended.
"Neurotic old maid," he muttered, disregarding the wide gold band on
the third finger of her left hand.

The mail irritated him; one annoying detail after another. He thrust
it from him, told Mrs. Lawrence to take it down the hall to Albert
Roach's office. What in hell was he First Vice-President for if he couldn't
take some of this drivel off his hands? And while she gathered it sulkily
to her bosom, he changed into his lab coat and told her he wasn't to be
disturbed.

The lab was just as he had left it last Friday, the unfinished experiment neatly tabulated before him. He picked up his notebook and
scanned through it, but could not concentrate on what he was doing.
Something else was demanding his attention. He tried to ignore it, tried
to read through his notes once again, but it was useless. He put the book
down.

It was obvious he had come back to work too soon and that his
earlier cheerfulness had been euphoric. He couldn't have tied off every

loose end yesterday because he was beset by a sense of uneasiness, a most unreasonable feeling of guilt that persisted in spite of how carefully he believed he had thought the matter through. No, he was far from being free of this thing; he wasn't clear of it yet, and he was sick and tired of this damnable new sensation of not being able to admire himself.

Yesterday he had arrived at the conclusion that Robin deserved the blow and therefore he should feel no guilt at having delivered it. Why then did he persist in feeling this guilt? Could he have indulged in evasive thinking? If so, what was it he should have faced and didn't?

Squirming on the laboratory stool, he saw himself deliver the blow again and saw the boy drop. He recalled the violence of his fear when he thought Irene was about to tell him the boy was dead. He reviewed the process of his thoughts that followed and was forced to admit that his evasions were now apparent.

There was no question but that he had to accept the responsibility of having perhaps endangered Robin's life by the blow. There existed a distinct possibility that he had committed criminal assault—he, Hunt Parrish. His shining fingers twisted about each other, for it was agony for him to bring forth this admission. It would be so much simpler to let it slide back into his subconscious, but a man like Hunt Parrish could not go on living unless he regained his self-respect, and he couldn't do that without first admitting that it was lost. Well, he admitted it. Now he had to tackle the problem of earning it back. How does one throw off such a burden? The act could not be undone. The wrong existed perpetually, even though known only to himself, and could never be made right.

But this was not altogether true, either. For wrongs were righted daily in the courts of law. Men committed crimes and paid for them.

Then what was it he had to do?

Confess, obviously, to start with.

But confess to whom? The police? That would be foolhardy, for, if Robin recovered, which he had every chance of doing, Hunt would be left in the idiotic position of having publicly confessed to a crime that was not conclusive and of which he had never been accused. Actually, if one analyzed it further, his complicity in Robin's "accident" was highly questionable. All he had done was to strike a boy who had already seriously injured his head. It was a question more of personal ethics than of public crime or guilt, and were he not the completely honest and righteous man he was, he would have forgotten the whole matter long ago and gone his merry way. Therefore, since it involved a matter of personal integrity rather than out-and-out crime, obviously this matter had to be between himself and Tyler Fay.

Hunt grimaced. The very thought of confronting a big, dumb athlete like Tyler Fay with the story of how he had struck his son, was enough to make him want to turn tail. Was there no other way? Could he confess it to Irene, for instance, or easier still, although he was not a particularly religious man, to his minister? But no, the guilt would still be upon him, for if there was any religion in him at all, it was the worship of Truth. Another man might not require its release, but he lived by Truth and Right undiluted and uncorrupted. So it followed that he had no choice but to face Tyler Fay.

It would be a frightful ordeal. He would ask to speak to him alone. Fay, barely polite, would lead him into the bedroom where Hunt would tell him what he had done to Robin. Oh, Lord, to have to relate such a story to a man like Tyler Fay, to that great, brawny, American Male, to that Madison Avenue Boy in a sports jacket, to that back-slapping, living-with-the-Joneses, conforming, conservative, unthinking braggart! Hunt's fingers whitened with the force of their writhing as he faced what Tyler Fay would do then.

Hunt was a physical coward, mortally afraid of pain. And there was no question in his mind but that Tyler Fay would snap out but one incredulous question—*"What did you say you did to Robin?"*—and then swing out at him with all the force behind his great, powerful body. Maybe he wouldn't be satisfied with only one blow . . . but no, Fay was not the brawling type. For all of his physical strength, he was a man of background. He would hit him only once. The blow would strike Hunt in the face, of course, the eye or the nose or the mouth—whatever, it would be a painful blow, a staggering blow, and Hunt would be thrown to the ground. Fay would stand over him, contemptuous, and wait for him to pull himself together. Then he would say, "Now get out!" And Hunt would stumble from the Fay apartment, possibly with a broken nose, possibly with the loss of a few teeth or serious damage to an eye.

He knew that this was what he was letting himself in for.

Would it be worth it?

Although physically he shivered at the prospect, he realized its inevitability. He had to look upon it as an emergency surgical operation upon his soul, and even now, thinking of the torturous hour that lay ahead for him, he was aware of a sense of relief. It was not the physical blow itself that would deliver to him this relief (for he was no self-flagellating fanatic), but rather the laying of the truth, no matter how damaging, at Tyler Fay's feet. This would be the act of a worthy man, honest enough to admit error and be willing to pay for it.

Hunt wiped his streaming face and rested. At last he had made peace with his conscience. His decision was a careful, judicious one. This time he had not evaded Truth. It was undeniable that, by facing Tyler Fay, by this act and this act alone, could he bring about the final assertion of his own superior integrity.

13 :   *Wednesday, June Tenth*

The morning newspapers predicted a storm that was likely to break the heat wave, but at midday the sun broke through the clouds and the temperature and humidity met in the nineties. Every once in a while, however, a few hopeful rumblings came from behind the sunshine.

Hunt worked well at the office. He had such remarkable success with the new compound that he packed up his test tubes and took them out to the experimental plant in New Jersey where they were set up for more extensive tests. It was past four by the time he finished explaining his notes to the chemical engineers, so rather than return to his office, he drove straight home.

It was early and Irene was still out. Dinner wouldn't be for another two hours at least and it occurred to him that this was the perfect time for his talk with Tyler Fay. There was no point in putting it off any longer. Two days had passed since he had made his decision and he had not changed his mind. So, quite calmly, he sat down at his desk and dialed the Fays' number. There was no answer. Possibly they were at the hospital visiting Robin. Well, he wouldn't waste time waiting. He would use it for precious thought. He leaned back in his chair, crossed his legs and closed his eyes. Almost immediately, ideas, like newborn cobras, raised themselves from the bed of his mind and an essay took form, based on the experience he was about to undergo. It could be a fantastic piece of work, original certainly, depicting the superhuman powers of a highly developed mind in the process of turning wrong into victory. What a tour de force! It might well be the finest essay he had ever attempted; far better, even, than the piece on Maud Harewood's books. Ideas soared and tumbled in his head and he pulled out a piece of paper and proceeded to write them down.

He heard Irene come in, heard her frantic steps rushing through the hall to her bedroom, and a while later, she knocked on his door and came in, beautifully gowned, newly perfumed, with her hair gleaming.

Although Hunt was far from nervous about the interview with Tyler Fay, still it was going to be a physical ordeal. He considered himself well prepared for it and yet he was certainly in no mood for Irene's brand of small talk. But as usual, she did not understand. Her fresh smile turned upside down into a look of angry martyrdom as he explained that he had to ask her indulgence once more, he had to be left alone, that there was something important he had to do this evening and after it was accomplished, they could return at last to their normal routine. She questioned him, but he cut her short. In spite of himself, his voice registered impatience and once again she left his room in a rage.

At five forty he called the Fays, but there was still no answer. Nor were they home when he called at six thirty or at seven. His dinner hour came and passed and there was no knock on his door. Although he had asked to be left alone, he realized now that he would have appreciated Irene's company. If only she were wise enough to know the value of judicial silence in the presence of a man who had something on his mind! But she wasn't. Her method was always a direct attack upon the source of the trouble in the mistaken belief that there was no problem she could not solve personally, simply by talking it over.

So she ate in the dining room alone and punished him by obeying him to the letter, and he sat in his room alone, hungry, and punished her by refusing to beg for his meal.

It was not until nine thirty that Tyler Fay answered the telephone. Robin was much better, thanks, he said, and would be coming home soon. He would be glad to speak to Hunt at any time, but right now he was quite tired and couldn't they make it another day? Reluctantly he agreed only when Hunt insisted, and Hunt insisted only because he himself was tired, hungry, sick of the whole business and anxious to get it over with once and for all.

The front elevator was back in service at last, the final O.K. having been signed only a few hours before. Hunt hesitated before stepping in, then clutched at the railings and held his breath as they descended to the ninth floor. He wondered if he would ever be able to enter this elevator again without a moment of fear. Standing before the Fays' door, he drew himself erect, smoothed his lapels, pulled his jacket down in back and pressed firmly upon the bell.

Tyler Fay opened the door. His white shirt was open at the neck revealing his great chest covered with fine blond hair. His sleeves were rolled up, disclosing strong arms. He wore flannel slacks belted with cordovan. His waist was narrow, his belly flat and muscled as a boy's and he stood almost half a foot above Hunt. His features, too even for Hunt's taste, were controlled, but his eyes looked down upon him with an expression of annoyance at this intrusion, accompanied by a faint dislike.

Although Hunt had never considered himself a short man, he felt minuscule, standing so close to this giant whose body fairly glowed with animal virility. One hardly thought of him as possessing a head at all, Hunt reflected with a small smile. He noted, for later employment in his essay, the dramatic contrast between brute and brains, the great blond hulk in shirt sleeves, standing aside to allow the neat, black-suited egghead to enter his home. Smiling confidently, Hunt stepped in.

The foyer glowed golden and white, a soft background to the paintings that made lush spots of color on the walls. The room enfolded him with an insistent tenderness that sent a sudden shock of instability through him. Mrs. Fay was there in a white chiffon negligee, with her pale hair streaming down her back, and in spite of the heat, the touch of her fingers was cool as he shook her hand. She made polite inquiry concerning his shoulder, Irene's health, and was leading him straight into a golden living room when Hunt shook himself out of the trance the surroundings had imposed upon him and, with great embarrassment, asked to speak to Ty alone.

Mrs. Fay pretended there was nothing unusual about his request and said in that case, she would say good night and retire. She sent her regards to Irene and went into the bedroom.

Once she was gone, a part of Hunt's disturbed equilibrium returned. Still, the rooms continued to upset him. "Is there anywhere else we can go?"

"There's Robin's room, if you prefer it," Fay said.

Of course, how fitting that they should go into Robin's room, into that mess of athletic equipment and banners and stolen street signs, all the paraphernalia collected by the sons of men like Tyler Fay! Hunt followed Ty, rubbing his dry palms together.

He saw the gleam of polished primavera, encasing more than a thousand books, a small piano, two couches that served as beds. Soft beiges and browns predominated with touches of autumn red, and the unscarred surfaces of wood, the unstained upholstery bespoke it the room of one who respected its beauty. *"Robin's* room?"

"Yes." Fay gave him a curious look.

Hunt wanted to turn and run. The situation, that had seemed so imperative to him before, now appeared ridiculous. The instability he had felt in the foyer had become more pronounced in here. What was he doing, about to blurt out some triviality that had occurred in a moment of emotional shock, something that nobody knew about or ever had to know? Why was he placing himself in this subordinate position? Yes, it was ridiculous. It was ludicrous, purposeless.

"Like to sit down?" Ty stood before him, his stance wide, his hands clasped behind him. His great chest bulged.

Hunt couldn't think. He couldn't remember why all of this had seemed so important to him before. He walked away from Ty, towards the piano and tapped out a note or two, searching furiously in his mind. Oh, yes, it was for truth's sake, yes, for right and for truth, that was why he had to speak. And now that he had gone this far, it was too late to reconsider anyhow. He had to trust his decision which had certainly not been lightly made. The impulse to run away was only to be expected and ignored. He cleared his throat twice. "This isn't going to be easy for me."

Ty was silent. Hunt turned away from the piano and faced him. "I'm—a man who worships the truth," he began. His heart skipped a beat, which gave him a momentary sensation of faintness and he took a deep breath. Ty faced him expressionlessly, offering no help. "The truth has been to me what religion is to others." That was a good beginning. From that statement, he could plunge ahead. "As others pray, I search myself constantly for falsehood and when I find it, I cannot live with myself until I turn it to right." It was going to be easier than he anticipated. He was able to make these initial statements with pride. He no longer felt quite so humble, no longer subordinate, for he had managed to place his confession on the high plane where it belonged. He stood straighter. "Ever since the elevator accident, I have been tormented by a sense of wrong, and having wrestled with myself for days and nights, I have decided to come here and face you." In spite of his perfect start, his heart raced and blood pounded in his temples. It was stifling in here and his clothing clung to his body. Tyler Fay stood before him, tall and impassive, with eyes that continued to reflect a cold dislike. Hunt thrust his hands in his pockets and continued: "What I have to tell you is something no one else knows about or ever would know if I chose to remain silent. But instead, I have decided to speak up because, for a man like myself, who has lived his whole life in truth, the smallest falsehood must be intolerable. It would stain everything I am or hope to become." Hunt thought he detected mockery in Ty's cold eyes and could not resist a small smile himself, thinking of how quickly that mockery would be erased. Quite calmly now, he concluded: "It happened after the elevator fell, while we were waiting to be released. Miss Forsythe didn't see it, for she was

[253]

crying over the body of her sister, and Robin doesn't remember it, I'm sure, for he was nearly unconscious, although I didn't know this at the time, mind you. I struck him. I struck him a—hard blow with my open palm straight across the face because I believed he had caused the accident."

He thought Ty would spring at him then, for his body snapped into tension and his knees flexed. All color drained from his face as he said in a tight, outraged voice, *"You did what?"*

"I struck your boy." Hunt pulled his elbows close to his body and blinked, holding himself tight, preparing himself for the blow. With his eyes closed, he stood there rigidly, waiting. He heard sudden thunder from the skies and his body shook. The thunder passed and there was silence. Still he waited, feeling Ty's infuriated presence as a blind man feels, with his pores. He wanted to cry out, "Come on, hit me, get it over with," but he dug his teeth into his lower lip and forced himself to go on waiting, knowing that this was to be a part of his suffering.

"Why you goddammed son of a bitch!"

Hunt quivered. It was coming now—now. From the corner of his eye, he could see the fist. It was poised in mid-air, and it clenched and loosened, clenched and loosened again. "Hurry, hurry," he begged silently.

But the fist never descended. Instead, it crashed into Tyler Fay's left palm with a sound that made Hunt leap away and, when he opened his eyes to look, he saw that both fists were now pressed so tightly against Ty's thighs that the knuckles showed white and, with an agony so real that a pain streaked through his chest, he realized that Tyler Fay was struggling for control.

"Go on, hit me!" he screamed, throwing his arms into the air.

But it didn't do any good. Instead of propelling Ty into action, Hunt's high, tight cry only betrayed him, and Ty's fists slowly unclenched. He looked up and met Hunt's wild gaze head on, full force, his eyes now frigid with conquered fury and contempt. "I wouldn't stoop," he said, "to touch you, not even with my fist."

Hunt swayed. All of his remaining strength seemed to leave his body and he collapsed on the piano bench.

He heard Ty laugh, a short, familiar laugh that tugged sickeningly at his memory. "You hit a kid that was down. Trim it up all you want, Parrish, go ahead and use words like Truth and Right, but they don't mean a damn thing because—face it—all we have here is an ugly case of physical assault. How much damage had already been done before you hit him or how much further damage you inflicted, is also not the question. You hit him, goddam you, and he fell. That's the truth, the only truth."

"But I didn't have to tell you," Hunt whispered. "Don't you see, the point is, I didn't have to face you with it. No one saw me, no one knew."

"Oh, aren't you the saint, though! Aren't you the great one! And you'd love me to smash you in the face and make a martyr out of you to boot, wouldn't you? Well, not on your miserable little life, bud, would I deliver to you the blow that would purge you, free you from your rotten little sense of guilt and allow you to go on scot free and washed clean."

"That's not it . . . you don't understand. I hoped you would, but you don't understand——"

"Understand? Who gives a damn about understanding you? Who the hell are you? Just someone I want out of here. Go home and live with *this*, Parrish, that you're nothing but a sniveling little shit-heel who hits kids when they're down. Now get the hell out of here, and on the double because this is my home and being in the same room with you makes me want to puke. Get going, I said!"

Hunt listened to him, heard every punishing word that successively drained him until he felt empty and near senseless, but from somewhere he found the strength to pull himself together and leave, blindly reaching the elevator, weakly ringing his own doorbell. He stumbled past Hilda into his room. "Quickly . . . call Mrs. Parrish . . ."

14 :   *Wednesday, June Tenth*

In her own quiet way, and totally unperceived by her husband, Irene had been going through a siege of soul-searching herself. Hunt's behavior since the accident had precipitated that sediment of unhappiness which, although always present within her, had been emulsified heretofore, tiny droplets of discontent permeating each hour of each day. But her aloneness, her complete uselessness to her husband, had become shockingly apparent. That he suffered, she had no doubt. That he needed help was also obvious. That he might not come to her at once, she allowed. But that he should separate himself so totally from her at a time of trouble, took from her the last reasonable excuse she might have to remain with him, the excuse that in some important way, she was necessary to him. Now at last she knew that she served only as a housekeeper, and as official hostess on the few occasions when they entertained.

So night after night, while Hunt tortured himself in his room alone, Irene, behind her own closed door, reflected upon her past and future. She had loved him maternally, this love fed by his quick changes of mood, sullenness followed by incredible charm; and fed, too, by the occasional moments when he gave her that shy, strange chuckle which told her how unsure he was inside. At best, it had been an undernourished little love, which he had allowed to starve to death. That she was Mrs. Hunt Parrish was still important to her, but not important enough for what he required of her now. To come home at night to a husband who hid behind a locked door, to be forced to maintain complete silence, to absent herself from him totally and yet live in the same home, was too much to be endured. If she had to live alone, at least she could allow herself the freedom that aloneness grants, to dress as she pleased, to choose her own friends, to come and go as she liked.

But could she, after so many difficult years, decide to leave him at a time when he was so disturbed? This was the question that kept Irene from any final decision. She continued to hope he would break down and admit he needed her, but day succeeded day and still he locked himself away.

When a person wavers, it is often a seemingly unimportant incident that precipitates the decision. All Hunt had done was to beg her indulgence for one more night and to promise that tomorrow they would return to their normal existence. Taken alone, this statement should not have provoked the rage Irene experienced, but dropped casually upon her overburdened spirit, it acted like the proverbial "last straw" and she slammed out of his room in a final, cold anger. He had fought through some great battle with himself, come to a decision and was about to carry it through, all without a word to her. And tomorrow he would expect to find her waiting for him at cocktail time, bathed, manicured and perfumed, to chat idly and never ask a question. Well, let him hire someone else for that. She had stooped admittedly low to remain Mrs. Hunt Parrish, but she would not stoop as low as that. She was worth more, far more than that. She didn't fool herself about her future, she knew she was no longer young. It would be entirely possible that she might have to live out the remainder of her life completely alone. But with self-respect. With freedom.

While Hunt was with Tyler Fay, Irene went so far as to start to pack her bag, but then she thought better of it and put the bag away. She would take no chances. She had lived an arid life with Hunt and deserved to be properly recompensed for its lack of sex or love, for the friends she no longer saw, for the children she'd never had. Yes, she would do this in orderly fashion. First thing in the morning, she would see her lawyer. Her mind was made up at last.

She propped a pillow behind her head, lit a cigarette and made her plans. The first thing she would do would be to resign from every damned club and organization. Then perhaps she'd travel. Yes, she'd go to Europe on a long vacation. Oh, how she needed a vacation! It had been years since she'd gone anywhere. Of course, there'd be a problem about money, though. Hunt was too proud to fight a divorce, but he'd make her suffer in his own way by seeing to it that she had the least the court would allow. So perhaps she wouldn't be able to travel. Well, she'd live in her own little apartment, something small but gracious: a hotel would be convenient. Agnes Beer lived in a hotel—but she paid eight hundred a month for her two rooms and kitchenette. Well, she wouldn't have to live in such a grand establishment. She could choose a more modest hotel. Modest! Face it, it would have to be a dingy little place with small, dark rooms and she'd cook her own meals over an electric burner alone. No more lovely clothes, no more beautiful surroundings, no servants, fine food, no more prestige. Yes, Hunt would see to that. Even if she wanted to continue with her club activities, she wouldn't have the money to do it. She would no longer be Lady Bountiful. She'd be nothing and have nothing. He would see to that. So what would she gain?

She wiped away a tear before it slid into the dark curls in front of her ear. It was always like this whenever she thought she'd made up her mind. She couldn't stay, but she couldn't leave. Maybe she had very little now, but what she had was munificent compared to what she'd have if she left him. Oh, for the wasted years when she could have gone, and the hell with the money, she'd find another man soon enough! Oh, for the barren days ahead: nothing to look back on, nothing to look forward to except the daily collapse of her beautiful body as it aged and drooped towards the grave. So let the tears sink into her hair and spoil her finger wave! What did it matter whether she cried or not, if her eyes got swollen and her hair hung straight?

She heard the doorbell ring. That had to be Hunt, returning from his mysterious errand. She mopped her eyes hurriedly and smoothed her hair. Not that he would come in, of course, but there was always that chance. . . .

Hilda knocked on her door. She looked frightened. "It's Mr. Parrish, Ma'am, he wants you quickly."

"He wants *me*?"

"Yes, in his room."

"What in heaven's name?" She slipped into her dressing gown.

[257]

His appearance shocked her. His thick white hair was disarranged, his collar was open and his tie pulled down and askew. His jacket was on the floor where he'd dropped it. He leaned over his desk, breathing heavily.

He's having a heart attack, she thought. "Let me get you into bed. . . ."

He shook his head.

"I'll call the doctor. Don't be frightened. You'll be all right."

"No. No, I'm not sick."

"Then what is it? Have you had a shock of some sort?"

He nodded.

"Anything happen to—anyone?"

"No, no, nothing like that." He passed his hand over his face. "Would you—sit down?"

She obeyed, eying him warily.

Suddenly he dropped his head into his hands. "I need—a little help." The drawl of Georgia emerged in his speech and she detected the heaviness of tears along with it. He was like a broken child sitting there and without thinking, she ran to him and put her arms around him. He responded at once, buried his head against her breast.

"What happened?" she whispered.

He lifted his head a moment. His eyes were wet. "I don't know—where I stand. . . ."

She tightened her arms about him to help support the collapse of the armor he had built around himself. He dropped his head again and gasped out his story in the accents of his youth which came strangely to her ears. She could not believe what she was hearing, nor that it was happening at all. What he told her, although devastating, was unimportant. She could not believe that it was the austere, egotistical Hunt Parrish who clung to her and wept. She could not believe that he had come to her at last, contradicting all the conclusions she had drawn earlier, giving purpose once more to the arid life she'd agreed to live with him, justifying her belief that he needed her. This was the naked man beneath the protective layers of years that she held in her arms, the real man, unbearably unhappy, confused, timid, uncertain, and she had been right all along, believing that strange little chuckle of his to be a giveaway.

"I went to him—I didn't have to go," he moaned, "but he wouldn't give me credit even for that."

"He was wrong," she said unhesitatingly, "he was intolerably cruel to you."

Hunt looked up at her, surprised. "You mean that?"

"Of course I do. Come with me." She led him to the bed and sat down next to him. She took his hands. "You're a great man, Hunt, a brilliant man, and he was wrong. The whole world recognizes how great you are; your discoveries have benefited mankind both in peace and in war. So who's wrong, the world or Tyler Fay? And as for living a lie, darling, you've never stopped searching for the truth and you won't until the day you die. I live with you and I ought to know." Like a mother assuring her child that his hairy mole is a beauty spot, she comforted him, agreed with him, complimented him, fed him back his life's blood.

Then she watched him revive. He grew calmer, stronger, and as he did, he moved away from her. She let him. She watched him arise, finally, pick up his jacket and drape it carefully around the back of the chair, a sure sign of recovery. Then he paused in the middle of the room. "What I don't understand is, why didn't he hit me? A big, dumb athlete like——"

"He did worse than hit you," she said.

Hunt thought about it, then nodded.

There was something she wanted to say, but she was afraid. All at once she sat up straighter and dared. "The only fallacy, darling, in your thinking, was to call Tyler Fay dumb."

"I don't agree with you at all, no, I don't . . . Well"—he leaned against the desk and passed his fingers through his hair—"well, perhaps that was—a fallacy," he admitted grudgingly.

"That was why the interview went wrong," she ventured.

He looked off into the corner, his eyes veiled by his heavy lids, red from the tears neither of them would ever mention. "Yes," he said, "now that you point it out to me, that's where I went off in my thinking. You're right, Irene. For once, you're right." He pushed away from the desk and went into his bathroom to wash his hands. He spoke above the sound of the tap water. His Georgia drawl had disappeared. "That's probably why he was so vindictive, too. He simply lost his temper because I had underestimated his intelligence. Then he had to get back at me somehow, and being smarter than I gave him credit for, he hit me below the belt."

Irene, sitting on the bed where he couldn't see her, hung her head and smiled wanly.

"Right, Irene?" he called.

She closed her eyes and sighed.

He came out, rolling down his sleeves. He had also washed his face and combed his hair neatly. He was almost himself again. "Right?" he repeated.

She nodded.

He gave his little, shy chuckle. "I don't blame him, Irene. No man likes to be called stupid when he—obviously isn't."

"So you'd better cut out the fallacies." She pointed at him sternly.

He grabbed her finger, smiling. "Even the Master sometimes fails."

"This is so nice, Hunt. I wonder how long it will last?" she sighed.

"What?"

"This—friendly feeling between us."

"Why, Irene, except for an occasional bout or two, we've always been friends."

"Another fallacy."

"You say it's not true that we've been friends? All right. What is a friend, Irene?"

She smiled strangely and stood up. "I think it's time we both got some sleep."

"No, Irene, answer me now. What is a friend?"

She turned on the air conditioner. "It's stifling in here. When will it ever rain?"

"Irene, I asked you a question."

"Oh, shut up." She kissed his cheek. "You look exhausted. Take a shower and I'll fix you a light snack. You must be starving." She left the room before he could say another word.

In spite of himself, he had to smile. He undressed slowly and stepped into a cooling shower. As he scrubbed himself with strong soap and a brush, he thought that although he had been through hell in the past few days, it seemed as if it was Irene who had changed the most. He had collapsed before her; he had even wept; he had fallen from his pedestal and this had somehow given her strength. But was this a good thing? After all, whether she wanted to admit it or not, a good seventy-five per cent of her attachment to him was based upon admiration. And who admires a fallen idol?

He stepped out of the shower and toweled himself dry, feeling unaccountably refreshed, purged, freer than he had felt in all his life. Now it occurred to him that whatever had changed had to be to the good, otherwise why would he feel like this after all he'd gone through tonight? If there was danger ahead, wouldn't he sense it? Perhaps this was another case of a fallacy. As he slipped into his pajamas, he lined up the direction of his thoughts, replaced them in neat order and pulled out the original premise: that he was a fallen idol.

She came back with his tray. She had prepared it quickly and yet had remembered to make it look attractive, too, from the lace doily and fine china down to a bright pink rose in a bud vase. And she insisted it gave her pleasure to sit and watch him while he ate, even though there were dark circles of weariness beneath her own eyes.

Yes, it was entirely possible, he thought, that he wasn't a fallen idol at all. It was an interesting new idea, that the poor, broken spectacle of a man that he had presented to her before, might be part of something she admired. Certainly he felt her close to him tonight. He wasn't lonely any more. He didn't feel that he had to search the surface of the earth for someone to talk to.

15 :   *Wednesday, June Tenth*

A series of sharp pains contracted in the region of his stomach and Ty doubled over and sank onto Robin's bed, thinking angrily of the incipient ulcer he was breeding with his self-control. All of a sudden, he turned sideways and beat the mattress with his fists. Gradually the contractions relaxed and the pain disappeared, but when at last he stopped, winded and spent, he saw Julie watching him from the door.

"Well?" she said. "Now what?"

"Oh, nothing . . ." He gave her a foolish smile.

"Come on, Ty, let me have it." She walked slowly to the bed and sat down.

He cursed himself silently, for if she had not seen him pound the bed, he could have spared her from this and she badly needed sparing. He had never seen her mouth so straight and thin. "He came to tell me some—little thing he did. And I lost my temper, that's all there was to it."

"*You* lost your temper?"

He shrugged, threw out his arms, and went into the bathroom to gain time.

"What little thing, Ty?"

"Be right out. Just want to wash my face."

But she was waiting with the same expression as before, when he came out. He sat down next to her and made another attempt. "Listen, honey, must you know everything? It's all over and done with. It wasn't important in any case. Can't you leave it at that?"

"Unimportant, you say. Something that made *you* lose your temper?"

"Well, it was maddening, all right, but trivial."

"All right, get me mad, too. I'm ready."

"That's the point. You're too ready. Besides, it was between Parrish and myself and we settled it. There's nothing more you can do."

"Quit hedging. I saw you pound the mattress. It's got to be something very bad and you're going to have to tell me about it, or I'll imagine worse things."

"So unnecessary! Damn it, so unnecessary, if only you hadn't come in here when you did. . . . All right, you insist, so here it is. Parrish came to confess to me, in a very lofty manner (reminding me what a great guy he was for taking the trouble), that in the elevator, while they were waiting for help, he hit Robin because he thought Robin had caused the accident. . . . Now it's not so awful, Julie, don't look like that——"

She gripped the edge of the mattress. "He hit an unconscious boy?"

"Not exactly. That's what upset him most. He—uh—he hit him and then——"

"I'll kill him," she whispered. "I'll kill him!"

"You don't have to. I almost did."

"Did you beat him until he was senseless, Ty, bleeding, screaming, begging for mercy? Or did you beat the mattress instead?"

"I beat him with my tongue until he almost passed out. He expected and wanted a physical beating, but what I did was worse. I called him every name in the deck."

"Name! What name could be bad enough? What's the matter with you? He might have killed Robin, and all you do is give him hell and then feel sorry for that!"

"He didn't have to tell me, Julie. Nobody saw him do it and Robin doesn't remember anything about it. It takes a special kind of man to come out with a thing like that, even if he did try to twist the truth. Look at it from his point of view——"

"The hell with his point of view! The hell with anybody's point of view from now on! People stink, they positively stink! We're getting it from all sides. We're being stoned. Get us out of here, Ty, you've got to get us out of here!"

"Honey, take hold of yourself."

She took a deep breath, then dropped her head into her hands. Her voice was hollow, muffled by her palms. "When I think of bringing Robin back to this building with all these hateful people, when I think of submitting him to their vile tongues and miserable little minds, a gentle boy like him, I could die. I suppose we've got to bring him back here,

[262]

we have no choice, but only until camp starts. After that, I don't care if we have to live in a cold-water flat, but I won't bring him back here again. You write Mr. Rider this minute, Ty, and tell him we're moving out of here July first. We can put our things in storage and go up to the Cape. After Labor Day, we can take a hotel apartment until we find another place. But I won't stay here. We can't stay here after all this."

Ty looked gloomily around the beautiful room.

"Robin once called it a prison and he was right. When he comes home next Monday, I'll have to guard him like a watchdog to keep him away from everybody until it's time for him to go to camp, so that no one will be able to hurt him any more. And by God, if anyone so much as dares to open his filthy mouth, I'll smash my fists straight into it and knock out all his teeth!"

"Ah, sweetie——"

"Don't you ah-sweetie me! Boy, have I grown up all of a sudden! Have I learned what people are made of! I'd tell you, but I'm too much of a lady to use a four-letter word."

Ty regarded her sadly. "You don't sound much like a lady right now. Know what you sound like? Like Hunt Parrish, rationalizing your bitterness by calling it maturity, looking down from your high perch to call everyone else hateful and stupid."

"That's not fair. I suppose it isn't stupidity to believe any old malicious rumor one hears?"

"No, Julie, it's human nature. Where in hell would I be in advertising if people didn't believe a repeated statement? We're all too preoccupied these days. Who has the time or energy to personally test every soap powder on the market, and who has the time or energy to check on each repeated rumor? You hear it over and over again and you believe it because it's convenient and you're careless, but not necessarily because you're stupid."

"That's a lot of talk," she said, "all just talk. It means nothing to me. All I know is that everybody loathes us and we haven't done a thing, not a single thing to deserve it. All I know is that one man loathes Robin enough to have come near killing him. And that we can't go on living here."

"Have you forgotten we've got some pretty good friends in the building, too?"

"They'll always be our friends. We don't have to live in the same house with them."

"All right, Julie, if you're sure that's the way you want it, I'll write to Rider tonight."

Still she brooded, with narrowed eyes.

"Now what's bothering you? I said I'd write him."

"I'm killing Mr. Parrish in my mind. I'm punching that smug face until the blood spurts, I'm scrounging out his horrible fisheyes, I'm——"

"Julie, stop it!"

She folded her hands in her lap.

"His blow didn't harm Robin. The serious injury was at the back of the head."

"How do you know he didn't get that when he fell? After fisheyes hit him?"

"Because if that was the case, Parrish would have told me."

"Oh, you think he's a *great* guy, don't you?"

"I think he's a man who tries to be honest, but who's not as bright as he thinks he is; lonesome, bitter——"

She made an exasperated sound and stood up.

"Maybe *you'd* better try pounding the mattress, honey."

"I don't want to. I want to stay mad."

"What good will that do you?"

"I'll tell you what good. People stink and I don't ever want to forget it. If you start out knowing this, you'll get along. If I hadn't been such a damned simpleton in the beginning, I could have nipped this whole thing in the bud so easily, simply by telling everyone in the building everything Albert Harewood told us about his wife. But I was too nice, too sympathetic, too sweet to do a mean thing like that to poor Maud. You think that one over awhile."

Ty leaned back and massaged his ribs where the muscles ached from his long, rigid stance. "Go to bed, Julie," he said wearily. "Let's not talk about this any more. I'll write the letter and then I'll be in."

"You mad at me?"

"Disappointed is a better word. I don't mind your throwing a fit, but afterwards, I expect you to revert back to your own sweet, reasonable self."

For a moment, he thought she was going to cry, but she didn't. "Sorry to be a disappointment," she said in a stiff, small voice.

16 : *Wednesday, June Seventeenth*

Early in the morning, every tenant of Number Ten received a communication from Mr. Rider. In it, he (1) refused to accept the petition to dispossess the Fays and stated that he had filed it in his wastepaper basket, (2) refused to release the Fays from their lease as they had requested, (3) made clear, in detail, all the true facts concerning the elevator accident, (4) added that anyone who didn't like it could get out, and (5), in a noteworthy postscript, remarked that no chandelier had ever fallen in any room of any apartment in the entire building.

It was delivered as early as 7:30 A.M. by Joe, who slid it under each door with a grin that revealed all of his gold-capped teeth.

17 :   *Wednesday, June Seventeenth*

Mr. Rider's letter had the desired effect of silencing most of the tenants of Number Ten. The men reacted in proper masculine fashion by disclaiming any part in the matter, other than having been the recipients of misinformation from their wives. "It served me right for listening to women's gossip," was pronounced in various ways behind closed doors all through the building that morning. In many cases, the letter constituted the curtain raiser to an all-out family argument terminating in feminine tears, always an efficacious solution. Mrs. Leopold blamed it all on Terence. The old tenants blamed it on the new and vice versa. "I only repeated what was told to me," the ladies protested unanimously.

But in the end, most of the ire, both masculine and feminine, descended upon the head of Maud Harewood and by noon, little groups of whispering tenants dotted the streets and the park paths once more, this time whispering about her. The general consensus of opinion was that she was a vicious, malicious creature, who had deliberately gone about the business of creating this falsehood because she was jealous of the Fays' fine young son, and every lady in the building confided to every other lady that she, herself, had never personally been taken in by that mad writer. "They're all of them nuts—belong down in the Village with the rest of the queers, not up here with decent people."

And, having first disclaimed any part in the matter, the ladies then proceeded to obey their husbands and keep to themselves thereafter, so that by late afternoon, all gossip groups disappeared from the neighborhood and the tenants went about their business separately, offering each other only nods and cool smiles when they met.

Joe had the decency not to provoke old Terence about the letter.

Klaus Gruppmann roared long and loud over it, toasting his employer with an appropriately large schnapps. Flossie and Walt Marsh read it several times with relish. Flossie immediately forgave Mr. Rider for all his former sins and filed the letter away as a keepsake, pronouncing it a masterpiece of American Literature. Then she returned to her list of last-minute changes on Mr. Dorkas's drawings for the new terrace garden which was under construction at that very moment. The d'Auriacs shrieked over it, hugged each other, and John crammed his Homburg on his head and rushed downstairs to send three dozen long-stemmed roses to Mr. Rider. Mrs. Kerakis and Miss Forsythe read it together, and Mrs. Kerakis shed a few tears as she confessed to her new friend that she had been momentarily taken in by Maud. Mrs. Emmerich, still without a proper maid, sat in her nightgown with an apron tied around it, resting awhile before washing the breakfast dishes. The boxer lay at her feet, sleeping. She roused him and showed him the letter. "See, darling, now nobody will say any more nasty things about your sweetheart's family." The boxer sniffed the paper ("Just as if he was reading it, the clever boy," Mrs. Emmerich thought admiringly) and then pressed his head against her shoe and went back to sleep with a sigh. She put the letter aside without the faintest twinge of guilt. Hadn't she taken care of Rover from the time of the accident until Robin's return on Monday? Everyone knew she had. She was a good neighbor and disclaimed all memory of ever having, even for a moment, strayed from the winning camp.

Ty found the letter when he shuffled sleepily to the door to pick up the morning newspapers. Fortunately, Robin was still asleep and need never know the extent of the uproar that had centered about him. Ty sneaked the letter into the bedroom, awakened Julie by tickling her neck with it, and when she'd finished groaning and yawning and finally sat up in bed, he handed it to her, saying, "So people stink, do they?"

The letter was brought to Hunt's bedroom by Hilda, along with the newspaper and his morning hot-water-and-lemon-juice. At first reading, it angered him. Of all the dogmatic, imperious attitudes he had ever conceived of, this was the pinnacle! No longer satisfied to remain merely a landlord, Lawrence Rider had now become the little Czar of Number Ten. Think his way or get out. It amounted to just that. Most infuriating of all was the manner in which he reduced not only the incidents of the past month or two, but the accident itself to a mere fribble, a pinprick, a trifle, forget it, boys, nothing happened at all. Lawrence Rider has spoken.

Hunt wasn't eager to show the letter to Irene, but he knew if he didn't, she would hear of it from someone else, so after breakfast he pulled it from his breast pocket and tossed it across the table with some little remark about how it might amuse her. Then he watched her face as she read it.

"Well, it's about time!" she said.

"About time what?"

"About time someone put a stop to this farce." She folded her napkin and rose.

"An elevator accident in which a woman is killed, a boy is seriously injured and your own husband hurt, you classify as a farce?"

She turned slowly to face him with an expression of calm good humor in her navy blue eyes. "It's no use, darling, I'm never going to answer your questions again. Besides, I'm in a hurry. Lady Bountiful has got to get moving."

Hunt pursed his lips and tapped on the table with his shiny fingers. Then he nodded, a smile lifting the corners of his thin mouth. Good for her! He pulled out Rider's letter and read it again. Admittedly imperious, still, on second perusal, he was forced to admire how worthily it accomplished its purpose. It allowed for no further discussion. It discredited poor Maud completely without once mentioning her name. With seeming innocence, it also put him in a bad light by sandwiching his minimal injuries between Mrs. Lesser's death and Robin's serious accident, and yet there was no misstatement there, nothing tangible for him to object to.

The more Hunt thought about it, the more he had to agree that the letter was a masterpiece. He couldn't argue with anything it contained; therefore, it had to follow that it stated the simple truth, and if this was so, then Hunt was in a bad position. If, for instance, all of Maud Harewood's complaints and accusations were complete falsehood as implied in this letter, then why hadn't he seen through her, especially since he admitted how sick she was? If he was actually as superior a person as he considered himself, why had he reacted like the flock and believed a liar because she bore a celebrated name? If this young Fay family was truly as lovable as Rider stated, then why was Hunt Parrish among those who disliked them? Yes, if this were truth, then Hunt Parrish had to be a liar, he thought, remembering the cruel words of Tyler Fay, and if it followed that truth was right and falsehood wrong, then Hunt Parrish had to be wrong as well, and how was it possible for a superior man to be a liar and wrong?

Conceding that this line of logic seemed to lead clearly to an irrefutable conclusion, still Hunt only thought about it as a sort of mental exercise. Actually, logic, like statistics, could be controlled, and had he the time, he could start all over again, with the letter in hand, and come to a completely opposite, equally irrefutable conclusion.

Thus convinced, he forgot about Rider's letter by the time he reached his office. He was involved in the creation of a new compound and went through his desk work in less than an hour, anxious to lock himself away in the privacy of his laboratory. Perched once again on his tall stool, the blissful feeling of being where he belonged reflected itself upon his relaxed features as he ran through his notes, oriented himself, and proceeded with the experiment.

But he hadn't worked an hour when the laboratory telephone buzzed. Mrs. Lawrence never disturbed him unless it was important. With an impatient grunt, he picked up the receiver.

"It's a Mr. Albert Harewood on the telephone, sir. He put it this way—you would never forgive me if I didn't buzz this call through to you. Is he right?"

"Yes he is. Put him on." Hunt was overcome by a feeling of dread. The possibility of Maud's suicide flashed through his mind.

Harewood was apologetic. He would never have bothered Parrish at his office had he not been desperate, but Maud had gotten hold of Rider's letter and was in a state of complete collapse, threatening to kill herself by refusing to eat. It was urgent that the doctor be called, but Maud had promised to throw herself out of the window if Albert did this. In any case, she was suicidal. Parrish had so much in common with her. She respected him more than anyone else she knew. Did he think he could convince her to accept treatment? Would he at least try before Albert took the final, drastic step of having to commit her forcibly? Because he could no longer delay. It was horrible to see her like this, horrible.

Hunt pushed his notes aside. "I'll be right over." He couldn't walk out on Maud Harewood; it would be like walking out on himself.

"I can't thank you enough."

"Save your thanks. Let's see what I can do with her, first."

Hunt could only see the back of Maud's head denting the cushion of the chaise longue which was turned towards the window. He tiptoed to her. She lay motionless, her nightgown twisted about her, her left hand resting flaccid on her thigh, her right hand encircling a half-empty highball glass on the table next to her. He was shocked by the change in her since he had seen her last. She had lost considerable weight. Her hair was oily and matted and she exuded an unwashed odor. Hunt brought a chair to her side. Although her appearance was repellent to him, his pity overcame it. The author of *The Gesture,* he thought.

She had glanced at him once when he entered, through her great, crazy eyes, but she had not uttered a word. For a while he sat there silently, thinking over what he would say, how he would best begin.

"Things are pretty bad, aren't they, darling?" he said at last.

He had meant to touch her and succeeded. She gave a trembling sigh and her lower lip quivered.

He took her left hand, which lay passive on her thigh. "It's all too much to face, too much to fight," he said.

"Licked," she whispered.

"Of course you are. Why shouldn't you be?"

"Only you—understand." Tears gathered, shelved by her lower lids, then spilled over and rolled down her cheeks.

Hunt relaxed with a deep breath. She had given him the clue he needed. Now he knew in what direction to proceed. He would not worry about the evasion of truth, the deliberate employment of the lie, for in this case, the lie and only the lie would accomplish his most righteous purpose. "I do understand," he said, "because we're so much alike. We've each had to face something intolerable in our lives."

"Intolerable!" she whispered, and her fingers tightened around his hand.

"But in view of the circumstances, and in view of the kind of people we are, we both did a pretty good job of handling ourselves."

Now her eyes moved to his, holding an expression of mixed mockery and confusion, as if to say: *I* did a good job? *I?*

"By that I mean that we both escaped from what we considered unbearable situations by withdrawing into our work. Wasn't that true of you, Maud? Didn't you substitute your own unhappy situation by writing, by entering into the lives of the characters you created, by living their lives instead of your own which you hated?"

Her eyes grew wild and more tears flowed from them. "I used to!"

"You could stand almost anything then, couldn't you? That's the way it's been with me. I know I am nothing as a human being, as a person living in society. I am only my work," he lied. "Doesn't this ring a bell with you? When you were writing, wasn't that really the only time you lived? Wasn't everything else a painful performance? Even your relationship with your husband?"

She let go of the highball glass and passed her hand perplexedly across her forehead. "I—can't think. It's so hard——"

"Don't be upset. I'm going to think for you. Just listen to me and follow what I say. I'm going to take it slowly, step by step, so you won't have to think it out yourself."

Her eyes pressed upon his trustingly.

"I don't want to go back too far in your life, but I'll start with the time that something intolerable happened to you. Whatever it was, you were able to bear it somehow, weren't you?"

"I guess so . . . ," she whispered.

"Because you could escape from it when you wrote. You never stopped writing in those days, did you?"

"Only wrote at night—sometimes all night."

"And the real thing was the book you were writing, and the real people were those you wrote about. Your characters were your friends."

"Yes."

"And then something happened so that you were free to write all the time. I know this because you became suddenly quite prolific."

"All day."

"And at night, even if you went to a party and mixed with others, it was not as plain Mrs. Albert Harewood, but as The Author of *The Gesture*. In other words, even though you weren't writing at the moment, you never left it."

"Never," she whispered. Her eyes were fastened upon his desperately now, devouring his every word, concentrating on what he said with a supreme effort as if aware that this was a life belt he was throwing her.

"And then suddenly, you couldn't write. Your real sustenance, the one thing that kept you going, was taken away from you, and so you collapsed. Of course you did. You existed only in your writing and when that was gone, there was nothing left of you. Isn't that the truth, Maud dear? Isn't it?"

"Nothing left," she wept, "nothing."

"Well, then. As I see it, you have only two alternatives. Either you get that writing ability back again, or you might as well die."

"I'll die, then. I have no other choice . . . the end of my rope."

"If you had a choice of being able to write again or of dying, which would you choose?"

". . . but I can't. It's gone."

"It never goes. It's only temporarily lost."

She shook her head.

"Do you want to write again, Maud?"

". . . stupid of you! Of course I do!"

"What would you give to be able to write again? Would you give one eye?"

"Yes, yes."

"Would you give one leg?"

"Yes, I would."

"You're sure?"

She raised herself on one elbow and spoke wildly: "I'd give one eye and one leg and an ear and all my hair and teeth, both breasts, all of that if I could only write again the way I used to, if I could write a book like *Gesture* again, or face the possibility of writing one even better than that. I swear I'd give all that for the chance!"

"Then you really don't want to die at all. You want to write."

The answer was patent in her eyes.

"Of course, we both know that to cut away an eye, an ear, your leg, your breasts, would not help you to write, but if they would, you'd gladly undergo it."

"Yes."

His point properly prepared, Hunt narrowed his eyes and pounced upon her. "You'd undergo pain and disfigurement, Maud Harewood, but you wouldn't think of spending a few months on a beautiful estate in the country where a highly intelligent, compassionate doctor is ready and willing to knock himself out to help you get back to writing!"

She pulled her hand away and sat up, glaring at him through dangerous eyes. "You're trying to tell me I'm crazy?"

"I never said that and I don't for one moment believe it. You're sick and that's different. We're both sick in the same way except that I'm lucky in that I don't have the additional burden of menopause. I would be as sick as you, if not sicker, if my work were taken away from me. Look, Maud, it boils down to this. The way you are now, you can't write and you're preparing yourself to die because you can't."

She lay back, both hands pressed tight over her face.

"If you continue like this, you're sure to die. But you have one chance left to write again, only one chance to live again, and that's to let the doctor help you. Nothing else matters. What else in the whole world matters to you right now except to be able to write again?"

"Nothing, nothing," she sobbed.

"And what other chance have you, except to go with the doctor?"

"But he won't help me."

"Let's say he doesn't. What have you lost? At least you've tried. It's like a safety play in bridge, there's only one way to make the contract. If you don't take that finesse, you're lost anyway. The doctor is your safety play."

She seemed to be excited by his vehemence, to be going along with him for a moment, but then she drooped and her hands fell heavily into her lap. "Then Albert will say it was my fault, that I was the crazy one. He'll blame it all on me."

"Blame what on you?"

Her face contorted and bright scarlet spots appeared suddenly on her neck. "My son, my son!" she screamed. "Don't you know he was out of his mind from the day he was born, a born schizophrenic, an animal living in an asylum right now? They'll say it was me, my fault, if I go, too! Everyone will say it! And they'll be right! They'll be right!"

Hunt's skin crawled and sudden perspiration soaked his shirt. He could barely keep himself from shivering. So that was it! Good God! But there was no time for him to dwell upon this horror. She needed even stronger words now, and quickly. He forced his emotion aside and spoke indignantly, "What are you trying to do, Maud, punish yourself for something you couldn't help, something that had nothing to do with you, something that is past and done for? Are you a writer, or are you not? Are you dedicated to your art, or not? Will you do anything in the world to get your ability back, or won't you? That's the only issue in this case. Everything else is extraneous. Everything else is hysteria. Everything else is unimportant and beneath you. There's nothing in the entire world that you can change but your own condition of the moment, no one you can help but yourself. As for me, there's only one thing I require of you and that is to write me another great book, and another and another. I demand this of you. Are you going to fulfill yourself and do it for me, or aren't you?" he shouted, raising himself from the chair to glare down upon her. "Answer me!"

She stared at him, her fingers trembling at her lips.

"Will you write me another book?" he asked more gently.

"You—believe I could?"

"I know it. That's what infuriates me. All you have to do is take a few months' treatment. For God's sake, Maud, it's little enough to do. You can't toss away your talent on female hysteria. You can't let a goddam menopause lick you. I won't let you!"

"I can't think . . . more confused than ever . . . ," she whimpered.

"I'm doing the thinking for you."

She closed her eyes.

"You trust me?"

"Only you."

"Then you'll go with the doctor for my sake?"

She raised one hand, then let it drop in weary acceptance. "But it won't do any good."

"Yes, it will. You have my promise." He bent down and kissed her damp cheek. "I'll make you eat those words, darling."

Weakly, she began to cry.

"I'll see you soon. I'll visit you."

She wouldn't answer him.

He was shaking when he went outside. Albert was perched nervously on the edge of a chair in the foyer and jumped to his feet when Hunt appeared. "I haven't convinced her of a thing except that she has no alternative other than to go. Hurry and call before she changes her mind again."

Albert's lips moved soundlessly for a moment. "How did you ever do it?"

Hunt gave a short, ironic laugh. "With lies, Mr. Harewood. For the first time in my life, I deliberately employed the use of the lie, and it had the twisted consequence of accomplishing good."

"Then perhaps it wasn't a lie."

"Are you doubting my ability to——"

"God, no! I'm sorry, Mr. Parrish, please forgive me, I don't know what I'm saying."

Hunt scowled. "Well, you'd better stop wasting precious time and get on that telephone."

"I don't know how to thank you."

"Don't. People like Maud and I have to stick together. Maybe one day I'll need her."

"There was a time she used to help many writers who couldn't sell, lots of them."

But Albert had said the wrong thing again. Hunt resumed his scowl and moved towards the door. Albert murmured another thanks and let him go.

For a moment he stood in the foyer, trying to pull himself together. He had Dr. Ettinger's office number in a little book he carried in his pocket. He dialed, then heard the doctor's voice answering. "You can come over and take care of her now," he told him dully, and repeated a few details of her recent condition and the circumstances of Parrish's visit. His fingers felt numb and the receiver nearly fell from them when he replaced it. He shuffled into Maud's room. He stood behind her and patted her greying, matted hair. "Anything I can get you, darling?"

Her voice was thin, almost a whisper, full of despair. "Only another bourbon."

For Albert Harewood, Dr. Ettinger's arrival late that afternoon was a great trial. Now that the long weeks of anxious planning had become the reality, now that the moment of parting was at hand, he was filled with unhappy memories of another such parting long ago, and he suffered a sense of finality. It seemed like only yesterday that he had first shaken the large, comfortable hand and met the steady gaze of this man to whom he had then entrusted his child. And now, more than twenty years later, here it was again, the same large hand, though less firm of flesh, and the same gaze through eyes that had grown tired over the years, but that still held their steadiness. It was a sickening moment for Albert and he choked over his greeting. First his son and now his wife. For him this was the end. He had no one else to give away.

He had been too fearful of Maud's reaction (in spite of her submission to Parrish) to tell her he had called the doctor. This he confessed to Ettinger in a short, whispered conference in the foyer, and it was decided that he must announce the doctor to Maud, to temper the shock his presence might bring her. So he approached her chaise longue feeling like her executioner.

But she took it quietly. "I'm surprised," she whispered, while the tears spilled out from under her closed lids, "that it could be done so quickly."

Dr. Ettinger came in and motioned Albert out of the room with a nod of his head. Albert returned to the foyer chair where he had always felt most secure, possibly because of its proximity to the front door and escape. When Albert was called back into the room, the doctor was smiling. "I've just told Mrs. Harewood that she isn't nearly as sick as she thinks she is. As a matter of fact, I'm pleasantly surprised at her condition. I expected to find her much worse. She won't believe me right now, but she isn't going to be hospitalized for as long as she thinks, and I'm sure she'll write again." He turned back to Maud. "I want you to understand that, although I used the word hospital, it isn't really a hospital in the usual sense of the word. You're going to a sanitarium in the country where you'll have a program of exercise, fresh air, entertainment and rest as well as treatment and when the time comes for you to leave, you aren't going to be so anxious to go. You're going to have a good time there, Mrs. Harewood."

"I know, I know," she sighed. "Don't you think I know where I'm going? Like mother, like son. You got yourself some bargain, Albert, when you married me. Your wife and son under the same roof at last. Together again! What a joke!"

"No, no, darling . . ."

"You weren't listening to me, Mrs. Harewood. You're not going to be with your son. You're going to a place where they never accept a desperately sick patient. The men and women you'll meet there will be only mildly ill. You won't even be able to tell there's anything wrong with most of them."

"Yes, yes, I'll bet," she whispered.

"You'll see when you get there."

"Well, get me there! Get me there and get it over with! Lock me up and let me die there, only stop this talking and take me where I belong, where I can't hurt anybody any more!" she screamed, and pounded the arms of her chaise. Then she dropped back and closed her eyes.

"You'd like to go tonight?"

"Yes, yes, get it over with."

"All right. Nothing to it."

Dr. Ettinger called the sanitarium and arranged to have a limousine pick her up in a few hours. She was not to be afraid of where she was going. She would have a large, beautifully furnished room and bath with every comfort and luxury. There was even a beauty parlor on the premises and a golf course and swimming pool. All this Maud accepted with grim irony. "Sure, sure." Her lips formed the words, but when Dr. Ettinger said good-bye to her, she sat up suddenly and stretched out her arms. "Help me, please, you promised to help me write again!"

He held her hands tight and assured her he would help her, he repeated he was certain he would help her, he hadn't any doubt of it at all.

But still she would not believe him and fell back into apathy, dry-eyed and motionless on her chaise longue while Albert saw the doctor to the door.

"Did you mean what you said to her? She really isn't as sick as you thought?"

"Well, she's admittedly depressed, but whereas in the past I don't believe she was able to distinguish clearly between right and wrong, she's beginning to now. You heard her say she wanted to be taken where

[275]

she couldn't hurt anyone any more. She'll be all right, Mr. Harewood. I have every confidence in her complete recovery. Pack a few things in a valise for her and you can bring the rest of her clothes tomorrow. You'll have to get up mighty early in the morning if you want to pack and arrive up there in time to catch me."

"I don't mind."

"And don't be depressed about this. You should be relieved and confident now that she's going to receive treatment. In the meantime, why don't you take a vacation? You've been through a bad siege. Take a trip somewhere—fly over to Europe, why don't you, and bum around for a while?"

"How can I do a thing like that, with her up there? How could I?"

"That's up to you, but I'd hate to send Mrs. Harewood back to a sick husband she'd have to nurse. That wouldn't be fair to her, would it?"

"I'm fine. Nothing wrong with me."

"You think it over anyway."

"Yes, well, we'll see. Do I go up in the car with her?"

"No, it's better that you don't. There'll be a nurse and a driver. You come up in the morning. I'll meet you there around nine."

After the doctor left, Albert went back into Maud's room. In silence, he packed her suitcase and helped her to dress. When she was ready, she returned to the chaise longue to wait. He watched her lying there, detached and hopeless. He thought of how little anyone really knew about her. There was no one to see her now, no one to pity her, therefore, but himself. No one would ever understand why she did what she did, nor would they ever forgive her for it. They would never know what she had been through all her life. They would know nothing of the years of courage and devotion that preceded her illness. They would only know about these last few months and all those brave years would go for nothing. Any explanation from him would be accepted as a poor excuse for her deliberate malice. She was through here. To bring her back among these people again would be to plunge her once more into hopelessness. "There goes the lunatic," they would whisper behind her back.

He looked about him at the dim room and saw the top of her head silhouetted against the open window. In a short while, her chaise would be empty. The apartment would be silent and he would hear strange creakings in the night. For the first time in a quarter of a century, he would be alone.

He shuddered. No, he wouldn't spend this night here. As soon as she was gone, he would take refuge at his club. He would get up early and come back and pack her clothes. And then he would send everything to storage, give up this apartment that had brought them so much grief. He would find another home for her later. They would start over again.

The doorbell rang. "That must be the car, darling." He tried to make his voice sound cheerful.

Silently she rose from the chaise longue. She picked up her purse as she moved to the door. He draped her short coat over his arm and took her suitcase into the foyer. He opened the door. The nurse was a young woman in a cheerful, print dress. Thank God, she wasn't wearing white.

"You're from the sanitarium?"

"Yes, I'm Miss McCaffrey."

Albert shook hands with her and Maud nodded stiffly.

"She's all ready."

"Well, that was quick. Sure you have everything?"

"Enough for tonight. I'll bring the rest tomorrow."

"Fine. Well then, if you're ready, Mrs. Harewood, we'd better get started. We have a long drive ahead of us."

There were tears in Maud's eyes as she turned to Albert and touched his cheek with her fingers. "Poor Albert, you never deserved this."

"Now, now, what a thing to say when you'll be home before we know it."

She gave him a sad smile through her tears. "Good-bye."

"It's not good-bye. I'm going to see you around nine tomorrow morning. I'll be seeing lots of you."

"Yes, from behind bars."

"Oh my, we are gloomy, aren't we? There are no bars at the sanitarium. Goodness me, wait until you see the place, Mrs. Harewood. Bars, indeedy!" Miss McCaffrey laughed. "She'll be much more cheerful by morning, sir. We'll see you then."

Albert nodded.

The nurse took the suitcase and the coat and Maud moved heavily and sadly through the door to the elevator, her purse drooping from her fingers. The nurse rang.

"You'll be fine," Albert said.

"Sure."

"I'll bring your clothes tomorrow."

"Yes. All of them."

"No, darling, just the summer clothes."

"You'll only have to make another trip."

[277]

"Dear, dear, we're gloomy!" The nurse winked at Albert as the elevator doors closed behind them.

19 :   *Thursday, June Eighteenth*

Ever since Monday, when Ty had so carefully told Robin about Mrs. Lesser's death, the boy had been depressed. When his friends called, he refused to speak to them. If Julie suggested a walk, he growled "No," and looked outraged at the mere thought of such levity. No matter how often Julie and Ty reassured him, he still believed that in one way or another, he must have been responsible. He could give them no reasons. He could only argue blindly, "Maybe if I hadn't run the elevator—how do you know?—she *might* be alive; she *might!*"

In every other way, however, he was well. During his visit yesterday afternoon, the doctor had given him permission to toss a ball and to pinch-hit in a game, but to go easy on running for the next week. Robin hadn't been interested. "But you must go out in the fresh air," the doctor insisted. "Promise me if it's a nice day tomorrow, you'll go?" Unwillingly, Robin promised.

So after lunch, Julie took him to the park. They sat in the sun near the ball field. Julie had brought the newspaper. Robin took the sports page from her and began to read. A little while later, Jimmy Parker and Bobby Linkholm, looking like Mutt and Jeff, passed by carrying their baseball equipment.

"Hey, Fay, I thought you were still sick in bed," Jimmy said.

"Yeah, Fay, what's with you? Thought you weren't allowed out yet."

Robin pretended to be engrossed in his sports page. "This is my first day."

"Where'd you get hurt? I can't see any scars. You're a fake."

"Yeah, there's nothing wrong with you."

Robin looked up and smiled sarcastically. "I just was unconscious in the hospital for three days, that's all. How's this for a scar?" He showed them the back of his head, the jagged red line clearly discernible beneath two weeks' growth of pale hair.

"Yeow!"

"You can say that again. I almost kicked the bucket." Robin turned back to his sports page complacently.

Bobby said, "Our team's been losing steadily."

"I've been striking out your men one after the other," Jimmy bragged. "They can hardly get a run offa me."

"Couldn't you just pinch-hit? We only have a week before camp to make up our losses." Bobby pleaded.

"Sorry, but I can't. I've been damn sick, I tell you."

"Okay, just thought I'd ask."

The boys moved off, whispering to each other and looking back at Robin. They joined the others who were warming up on the baseball diamond and a noisy game began with Jimmy Parker inquiring of the other team, "Give up, fellers?" Robin watched them off and on without real interest even though his side was losing again, until three young girls came by, gay in bright cotton dresses over starched petticoats. Their arrival very nearly broke up the game and there was much hacking around, much hair-pulling and grass-throwing, screams and laughter as one chased the other, then paused for no reason while another chased another in a seemingly meaningless rigmarole, which Julie watched with a feeling of regret for the boy who sat next to her and wouldn't join in. But suddenly she heard Robin chuckle and turned to see him poised on the edge of the bench. "Did you see Sally bop Parker on the head? Boy, she's got guts, that girl!"

"She's very cute." Julie pretended to read again. The game resumed, but this time a different type of game, a game that abounded in heroic plays and grandiose spills, a game designed to impress the girls, who sat on the grass and watched, calling out wise remarks to the players.

Eventually, Robin got bored sitting on the bench with Julie and he wandered around behind her on the grass, toeing pebbles. He bent and picked up a stone and threw it at a tree. He thrust his hands into his pockets and watched the game from a distance.

And then, kicking at things real or imaginary beneath his feet, he edged towards the ball field until he stood directly behind Sally, pushing his fists hard in his pockets. "Hi," he said to no one in particular.

The girls looked around.

"Gee, Robin, good to see you!"

"How are you? You look fine."

Sally only smiled at him.

"Change your mind, Fay? Your team is two runs behind already," Jimmy taunted.

"Naw, I don't think so."

Jimmy wound up vigorously and sent the ball spinning over the plate.

[279]

"Good pitch, Jimmy!" Sally cried, applauding. "Strike three! What a pitcher that Parker is!"

That did it. Robin took off his jacket, gave it to Sally to hold and ran out onto the field. "Okay, I'm pinch-hitting. Enough is enough."

Bobby Linkholm ran around in a frenzy. "*Now* you bums are gonna get it! Watch out *now*, Parker!"

Professionally, Robin picked up three bats, swung them, selected one and ambled to the plate.

Julie hid herself behind the newspaper and wiped furtively at her eyes. She had become such a tearful fool of late. But she couldn't help it, for each little act of her son's that she had taken so for granted before, was something precious now and not to be taken for granted ever again.

20 :   *Thursday, June Eighteenth*

Terence, who was too old to change in spite of his promises to Mr. Rider, was the one to tell Ty when he came home at six o'clock that the Harewoods had moved out. He had reserved this information for the ears of the head of the family and imparted it confidentially, man to man. "She went out last night with a nurse to some nuthouse, they say." His faded eyes held a delicious, internal glow. "And he left after her, wouldn't even spend the night here. This morning early, he packed more of her things and took out and this afternoon, Mr. Gruppmann says their apartment is up for sublet. So that's that." He sighed contentedly. "I guess it's for the best. Maybe things'll come back to normal now."

It was only with the greatest effort that Ty was able to control the pure joy that rose within him at Terence's information. "It's for the best all around, Terence," he managed to say with proper solemnity.

As he stepped up to his door, the fragrance of Julie's cooking perfumed the dank air of the hall. He recognized the odor; something she called "Cheekin-een-ee-wahn-sowse" when she imitated the accent of the French Chef who had given her the recipe. Rover was waiting for him, scrambling dangerously close to his feet, uttering such hysterical cries that he took time only to throw his hat into the closet before he picked her up. Julie was smiling, her face flushed from the heat of the kitchen, and as he kissed her, still holding Rover in his arms, Robin strolled out from his room, stringy, gawky, still a little pale and not too clean. "Hi, Dad."

So he'd been out and played with his friends, from the looks of him. "Hi, Skeezix." He rumpled Robin's hair, careful not to touch the back of his head. "What have you been up to, rolling in the mud?"

"Baseball. We beat the pants offa them. You shoulda seen Jimmy Parker! Was he sore!" Robin smiled pleasurably. "I pinch-hit, got two homers and a double, bringing in four."

"Well, good for you!" Ty found it increasingly difficult to behave calmly when his impulse was to caper about, to shout for the sheer delight of all that waited for him here at home once more—for the little dog that wept at his return; for the smell of fine cookery, for the pretty wife, who smiled as he entered; and for the healthy son black with dirt from the playing field. Ordinary aspects of a man's home-coming? Oh, no, far from ordinary! He had learned to know how precious this was, so precious that every second had to be savored, digested slowly like hundred-year-old brandy, and not one minuscule portion of it should ever be forgotten or accepted as routine again.

"You're not angry because I'm late?" he asked.

"I expected it, with all that work you've got piled up."

"See, that's the kind of wife to have, Robin, completely unpredictable and unreasonable. It's the very spice of life not to know when your wife stands there smiling, whether she's got the rolling-pin hidden behind her back. . . . How would you like a gin and tonic tonight, honey? It's hot enough."

"Love one, thanks," Robin said.

"I'll get them," Julie said. "You look tired. Go relax in the living room with your filthy son."

"I feel like a guest. See what I mean? Unpredictable, Rob. How about some music?"

"Benny Goodman concert?"

"Fine."

While Ty waited for Julie to bring the drinks, he considered how he would present them with the news of the Harewoods' departure. Undue solemnity was to be avoided, and yet to celebrate would be barbaric in view of the circumstances of their removal, he told himself. Still he was itching to celebrate. The long day of work had not nearly nullified the new-found energy in his system which continued to be enhanced, in spite of himself, by the thought of the quiet, empty apartment downstairs. He ought to be ashamed of himself. He would have to be careful.

In the meanwhile, Robin had a small argument with Julie over why she had brought him a Coke instead of a gin and tonic. Julie agreed to allow him a gin and tonic if he would promise to finish the entire drink, like it or not. Robin considered this and promptly changed his mind, remembering only too vividly the time she had forced him to smoke a whole cigarette.

Then Ty ventured to give them the news, trying to tell it with the proper touch of sympathy for the unfortunate couple who had brought them so much grief, but in his guilt at feeling no sorrow whatsoever, he apparently laid it on too thick. Julie looked confused and Robin turned suddenly too sober. "There's not a damn thing to be sorry about, you two, let's face it," Ty hastened to add. "That's the trouble with us, we're too busy being sorry for everyone except ourselves."

"Oh-ho, and who thought of that first?" Julie wanted to know.

"You did, dear, but in somewhat stronger terms, if I remember. What I want to point out to you, Robin, is that there is a boundary to sympathy and fair play, understand?"

"You mean we shouldn't go too far."

"Right. And we're all of us guilty of going too far. When I think of the crazy concessions we made in order to placate Mrs. Harewood, I could cut my throat, because what good did it do in the end?"

"I know I shouldn't feel this bad about her, but I do," Robin insisted. "And worst of all, him, Mr. Harewood, he wasn't a bad guy."

"Robin, it's the best thing that could have happened to both of them. It's no big deal, her going away. All it boils down to is that a sick woman is going to get the treatment that will cure her. She'll be well soon; she'll start writing again and everyone will benefit from her cure, because there's no denying it, she was a great writer once. And her cure will bring happiness to him. It's all for the best, Robin, and there's no earthly reason why we should feel the least bit sad, nor be fool enough at this very moment to ignore the delicious reality, kid, that—just think of it, picture it: *there is no one downstairs!*"

Robin frowned.

"No one downstairs, Skeezix!" Ty put his glass on the table and lunged for him.

Robin said, "Don't, Dad," and tried to continue looking sad.

Ty went for him again and tickled his ribs.

"Quit it," Robin giggled, breaking away. Ty caught him and pinioned both arms behind his back. "Say 'Uncle.'"

"I will like hell! This is war!" Robin shouted. He broke Ty's hold and they were off. Rover barked and leaped around them, snapping at their shoes. Julie cried, "Watch out for his head—he's supposed to take it easy. . . . Watch out for the steps . . . watch out, oh, my table—the lamp, Ty, catch it! Stop it, you two, or I'll call the doctor. Stop it or I'll beat you both to a pulp. Stop it I say!"

All at once, as if prearranged, the two of them turned upon her and blew hard in her face, chasing her screaming into the kitchen where she belonged, if they were ever to get anything to eat that evening.

21 : *Saturday, June Twentieth*

Robin was leaving for camp the following Friday night and this would be his last Saturday with Flossie until the fall.

It was true that the garden was far from finished. Even Dorkas's wizardry could not coax flowers and plants to grow at a faster rate, nor could the foundry do the impossible, so that the new fence which was to surround the entire terrace and one day was to be covered with various flowering vines, was not yet delivered and many of the huge, planted boxes contained only a fraction of the color and variety they would one day reveal. Sheza barked and came running to sniff at Robin's trousers and made such a fuss, scratching at his socks with his sharp claws when he recognized him, that Robin had to pick him up. He wandered slowly towards the spot where Flossie sat, examining the trees, flowers and shrubbery, recognizing here and there many old friends. Flossie's prize roses, the only flowers in the garden right now, were in excellent condition considering what they'd been through, blooming in masses of white, pink, red and yellow. It was amazing what punishment these delicate trees and bushes could take and still continue to flourish. Mr. Dorkas must have given them very special care.

"Well, say something already!" Flossie cried.

Robin smiled. He put Sheza on Flossie's lap and helped himself to some dates from the assortment of sweets on the table beside her. He sat down, popped one in his mouth and jiggled the rest in his palm. "Of course, it's not as nice as the other garden," he admitted, "but it's still the prettiest penthouse in the world."

Flossie sighed. "They didn't get the fences in and there's nothing but roses this year."

"You shouldn't complain. Brother, what they did in no time at all!"

He stretched out on the reclining chair and put his hands behind his head. "Boy, this is great, Floss. This is great."

"Yes, I guess it is." Flossie's voice was low and lazy now. "Even though there's only roses today, we'll have a fine fall garden for you when you get back from camp."

"You know, Floss——"

"What, dear?"

"This is kind of a—more ordinary garden," he said slowly, thinking hard, "but in some ways—well—for instance, it'll be more private."

"How do you figure that?"

"You're way off up here, set apart, I mean, especially when the fences are in and the vines grow on them. You know what I mean?"

"I think so."

"You never had vine-covered fences before. It'll be gorgeous."

"Yes, it will."

"Bad things don't last. When they're happening, you think it's for good, but it isn't. Things work out."

"I know."

"And, gee, Flossie, even though there's no lawn underneath us and even though it isn't exactly real like the other was, it's still the best penthouse in the world!"

Flossie sighed. He didn't have to try to cheer her. She knew she was lucky to have a garden at all. One must settle for less and less as one grows older, she reflected, and maybe one day this garden, too, would have to go. Little by little, everything ends. At first she had the whole of the Arizona countryside to ride through, with the wind in her hair, breathing that light, pure air. She thought she would never be happy away from there, but then she had come here and built her garden. It wasn't Arizona by a long shot, but she accepted it, she settled for it and was happy in it. Now here she sat alongside an oversized flower box, looking across to another and another, and to potted trees; a long cry from her garden of before, but wonderful in its own way, she supposed. See, already she was making excuses for it, already she was trying to present it with a special flavor to make up for all the things it wasn't. And she would be happy in this garden, too. All the grandiose hopes of youth boil lower and lower with time, she philosophized, but it's only the vapor that flies away; the essence is still there, increasingly rich and more savory for the absence of all that steam.

"Of course, when the fence is put in, we'll be more closed in and the garden will be more unified," Robin said. "The whole thing'll be more in proportion."

"That was the idea." How busy he was, growing up before her eyes, settling for this new garden with her!

Robin sighed. "I feel so good. Seems like years since we were out here together."

"Doesn't it, though?" Flossie smiled down at his peaceful face. Yes, it wasn't a bad garden at all, she thought, stroking the puppy who dozed in her lap. Robin was content with it and so was she. It was serving its purpose, after all. What more could she ask?

22 : *Saturday, June Twentieth*

Irene came into Hunt's room, interrupting his reading. She opened the draperies and let the sunlight in. "Come on, bookworm, let's take a walk. It's such a beautiful day, I'm sure no one in the entire building plans to stay indoors. They'd be fools if they did."

But Irene was wrong.

Upstairs in the penthouse, Robin had terminated his Saturday visit and the Marshes had finished their lunch. Although the sun was shining and a soft, cooling breeze rustled the leaves in the garden, they were, for the time being at least, occupied in the bedroom. They had locked Sheza out and he scratched at the door, cocked his head, listened and scratched again. He tried yelping and whining, tactics which, up to now, had always brought immediate attention. Finally, furious over his rebuff, the little brown puppy reached adolescence in a tumult and surprised himself by lifting his left hind leg for the first time against the door that locked him out. Delighted, he tried it again, this time from the right. Then he trotted off, satisfied, the defiant gleam in his dark eyes voicing clearly his sentiment of the moment: "So there, take that and see how you like it!"

In the street, Hunt and Irene walked arm in arm. Hunt was quiet, occupied with a new dilemma; the question of Irene's increasing strength. He was trying to understand how it came about that she dared to interrupt his reading to take him for a walk, and more surprising, how it was that he came to allow it—yes, and even be pleased by it. The truth of the matter was that he almost enjoyed her company lately since she had gained so much in insight and sensitivity that she no longer resented his limitations but rather accepted them, and what was more, with a deep affection. He might even dare to call it love. He patted her hand and smiled shyly at her.

She returned his smile, covered his hand and pressed it. There was something quite different about him. It was an absence of a degree of hate, she thought: there were holes in his armor now, and she wondered if he knew this.

A moving van pulled up to the entrance of Number Ten. Hunt tugged on Irene's arm and they crossed the street again and stood under the canopy, watching. "The Harewoods," he muttered. "There they go."

Klaus Gruppmann charged out of the doorway, shouting directions to the moving men. He was only telling them to take the back elevator to the eighth floor, but it sounded for all the world as if he was cursing them out, and there ensued a battle of violent language from which Klaus emerged, his feelings hurt, perspiring, but victorious.

As the moving men, mollified, followed Klaus down the service entrance to the basement, the Fays and the d'Auriacs stepped out on their way to lunch. Suzanne looked cool and elegant in grey printed silk and Julie, positive that she was sexually alluring today because she had twisted her hair into a sophisticated French knot, gave the impression instead of a delicate sea nymph in her striped sheath of violet, blue and green. They were laughing over a joke John had whispered to them in the elevator, but they sobered abruptly when they confronted the Parrishes. They looked ashamed, as they gathered themselves together with sudden dignity, not knowing whether to greet Hunt or pass him by. Hunt looked downward, veiling his eyes with his heavy lids. "Let's go," he whispered to Irene. But her linked arm tightened and held him there. She smiled at her neighbors. "Deserting Robin for the day?" She spoke quickly and there was a shade of anxiety in her effort.

Her approach baffled all except Julie, who, after a moment of silence, answered her perhaps a little too brightly, "Heavens, no! *He's* deserting *us*. He has a lunch date with a young lady by the name of Sally."

Thus the two women set the precedent for their future relationship in a swift moment of thrust and receptivity. It was to be Good Manners, which had been basic training for each of them, and no matter what brewed inside, their surface behavior had always to conform to the rules their mothers had taught them.

But for Hunt there was no such heredity. His instinct told him this was the civilized approach and he felt forced to make his own contribution to the new relationship, but the only word he could summon was "Oh?", for in addition to being placed in a difficult social position, it was also difficult for him to imagine a child like Robin being consumed

[286]

by any sexual interest that wouldn't appear vile and offensive to his own mother. It put still another chasm between himself and the Fays.

"Yes sir, great ladies' man, Robin—like his father," Ty said.

Hunt gave his shy chuckle, feeling hopelessly inadequate, certain that he was the only one discomfited by this encounter.

The familiar sound of Klaus Gruppmann's bellows issued from the service entrance as two of the moving men emerged with the first of the Harewood furniture. There was a sudden silence as the three couples watched uneasily.

"Well," Hunt said, "guess we'll be moving along."

His shy dismissal released them; they cried good-byes and went their way, chattering carelessly again, with many jokes and small exclamations as they tried to flag down a taxi at the corner of Fifth Avenue.

Hunt and Irene strolled slowly into the park. Hunt felt old and incomplete. "They don't think about anything at all," he said perplexedly. "All that furniture coming out and they're off to lunch, laughing and goofing like children, as if nothing had ever been wrong. . . ."

Irene gave him an inward, secretive smile. "Forget them. They're not in the same league with you, dear, but they do make the world go round."

He put his hand over the small gloved hand that rested on his arm. It was a pleasure to have her on his side, infinitely warming to hear her loyal words, even if they didn't ring absolutely true.

Now the street in front of Number Ten was empty. Klaus leaned out of the eighth-floor window and waited for the moving men to emerge from the service entrance with another load of the Harewood furnishings. "Leave them on the street and high-tail it back up here!" he shouted. "And I mean high-tail it!"

One of the men shook his fist upwards. "Who're you to give us orders, big mout'?"

"I gotta clear this apartment quick!" Klaus roared. "New tenants coming by at four o'clock to look, so you men get up here quick before I bat your ears in!"

The men huddled together and whispered. Then they separated, shrugging and gesturing, and vanished into the service entrance again.

Robin came out of the building all spruced up for his date. He wore charcoal flannels newly pressed, black loafers brightly shined, a blue and white pin-stripe cotton jacket and a black knit tie. He looked real cool, at least sixteen, and he knew it. He had shaved the first bit of white fuzz from his upper lip with his father's razor and applied styptic pencil to the wounds. He had splashed his face until it smarted with his father's lotion. He had brushed his teeth and washed his mouth with Lavoris. He had used his mother's cream deodorant under his armpits. Even his neck was clean.

Maud Harewood's chaise longue stood forlornly on the sidewalk. Robin passed it, whistling, and idly slapped the perspiration-stained cushion as he went by without a thought to its ownership, for he was having lunch with Sally and on Friday he was going to camp and the long, wonderful summer days lay ahead of him, every single one of them a joy that was yet to come.